Luminous

Silvia Park

MAGPIE
BOOKS

A Magpie Book

First published in the United Kingdom, Republic of Ireland and Australia
by Magpie, an imprint of Oneworld Publications Ltd, 2025

Copyright © Silvia Park, 2025

The moral right of Silvia Park to be identified as the Author of
this work has been asserted by them in accordance with the Copyright,
Designs, and Patents Act 1988

All rights reserved
Copyright under Berne Convention
A CIP record for this title is available from the British Library

ISBN 978-0-86154-641-1 (hardback)
ISBN 978-1-83643-046-9 (trade paperback)
eISBN 978-0-86154-642-8

Interior design by Paul Dippolito
Printed and bound in Great Britain by Clays Ltd, Elcograf S.p.A

This book is a work of fiction. Names, characters, businesses, organisations, places and events are either the product of the author's imagination or are used fictitiously. Any resemblance to actual persons, living or dead, events or locales is entirely coincidental. No part of this publication may be reproduced, stored in a retrieval system, or transmitted, in any form or by any means, electronic, mechanical, photocopying, recording or otherwise, without the prior permission of the publishers.

Excerpt from *Novacene* by James Lovelock, copyright © 2019 by James Lovelock (introduction by Bryan Appleyard). Used by permission of Allen Lane, an imprint of Penguin Press, a division of Penguin Random House LLC.

The authorised representative in the EEA is eucomply OÜ,
Pärnu mnt 139b–14, 11317 Tallinn, Estonia
(email: hello@eucompliancepartner.com / phone: +33757690241)

Oneworld Publications Ltd
10 Bloomsbury Street
London WC1B 3SR
England

Stay up to date with the latest books,
special offers, and exclusive content from
Oneworld with our newsletter

Sign up on our website
oneworld-publications.com

Advance praise for *Luminous*

'Wildly and, yes, luminously emotional.'
                    Matt Haig, author of *The Midnight Library*

'A spectacular debut, taking place in a thoroughly imagined, vividly written future. Harrowing but full of heart, a work of enormous ambition and brilliance with an ending that fully justifies the title and brought me to tears.'
   Karen Joy Fowler, author of *We Are All Completely Beside Ourselves*

'Searching and masterful, Park's *Luminous* engrossed me completely. Each broken robot, child, and warrior takes the elusive promise of family to a whole new level. I was honestly blown away.'
                              Sierra Greer, author of *Annie Bot*

'*Luminous* is warm, expansive, and particular. Park renders the intersection between family and technology with wit and philosophical depth, but ultimately this is just incredibly exciting to read. It's utterly beautiful.'
                              Raven Leilani, author of *Luster*

'Inventive, rollicking, and poetic, *Luminous* is a future classic novel about robots that reveals itself to be profoundly, beautifully human.'
                         Juhea Kim, author of *City of Night Birds*

'*Luminous* is full of complex characters, damaged and broken and beautiful. It's a novel full of pleasures, big and small, gorgeous sentences from which Park weaves a rich, layered story of family and work, of history and speculation, of Korea, past, present and future.'
                       Charles Yu, author of *Interior Chinatown*

'It's a cold stunner of a novel. Park masterfully balances complex characters in a very creative world. The family dynamics in this future-tinged novel are brilliantly written.'
                                                          Debutiful

'A well-crafted take on the vagaries of memory and what it means to be human, with a satisfying investigative backbone.'
                                                           Booklist

For my parents

Luminous

We may be their parents but they will not be our children.

—Bryan Appleyard, *Novacene*, Preface

Prologue

THAT SUMMER WAS IMMORTAL. JULY WAS ESPECIALLY savage with sixty-two heat deaths in Seoul, punctuated by the spectacular fizzing breakdown of a GS-100 security android when it crumpled knees-first outside a United Korea Bank. A cleaner broomed away the remains. The head was left grinning on the pavement, chirping at passersby to warn them of today's heat.

Then the monsoons came. Undeterred, hundreds of Red Devil fans flooded the World Cup Stadium, waving flags of their reunified nation. Their dreams vaporized after the first round. Mexico: 7, United Republic of Korea: 0. The very next day, the sky cleared. A white sun buttered a salvage yard with rust while an old bomb-disposal unit, the Grumman A-1, moved in a figure eight. It cleared the path for a young girl named Ruijie, who was dragging the body of a woman by the ankles, naked arms thrown back as if shouting hooray.

The woman might have been beautiful once. Lips pink and plush, and long blond hair, the kind that shone with each brush. She was falling apart. Her face had been shredded into confetti, held together by one bleary blue eye, while her torso was a smooth bioplastic vest, translucent as a milk carton. Ruijie had tried pressing the power button located on the nape of the woman's neck. She'd gotten a twitch of the ankles, a froggy jolt, but nothing. The robot was dead.

Still, what exquisite legs. Ruijie planned to take them home.

She paused to check the battery level of her robowear. Two hours to go. Affixed to her legs were battery-powered titanium braces; the latest model, customized circuitry to aid her ability to walk. For she was beloved.

Close to the edge the salvage yard bloomed into silvergrass. Tufty reeds stirred from the breeze while broken war machines slept like ancient dinosaurs, abandoned from the unification war. Ahead of them lay what could be the second-deadliest robot in the yard, the SADARM-1000. When it was still active and nimble, it was a house of horrors from whose impenetrable womb wave after wave of bladed robots would emerge, whipping through the air, keen to slice and beep and blow.

Decades later, now retired, the SADARM reclined on its side like the Buddha of Miamsa, indolent in the shade. The belly had been decimated by a stray blast on a bridge, then pried open and plundered for wires, chips, anything glinty. Ruijie backed up against it, pulling the woman by the feet, but the woman's head knocked against a piece of buried metal, and her blue eye popped out. Cursing, Ruijie chased it through the grass—the one eye!—until it slowed to a crawl at the base of the SADARM's belly and kissed the pregnant curve.

Ruijie took a minute to crouch and a second to reach for the eye, then froze. A hornet had landed on it with a flick. It unfolded wings of black glass. Another skittered down the slope of the SADARM's belly. More crawled out of the smelted head. Maybe under the visor, she'd find a gold blanket trembling inside the SADARM's skull. They could be drones, the kind that slipped into your ear and slid a long thin needle into your brain, or maybe they were just yellow jackets, sedate until they weren't. Which was more deadly, real or not real?

The real knew no restraint.

She decided to be perfect and still. Like a robot. Except a robot wouldn't need mechanic braces to walk. A robot would be thrown away for needing anything at all.

Back away, back away.

Then a hum stirred from deep inside the SADARM. With a tilt of their wings, the hornets buzzed back, a righteous swell of anger, but the singular hum drowned them out. Low and peaceable, it lifted and dipped, from treble to bass, land to sea, the tide rising and pounding against time, the shudder of a temple bell, the *ohmmmmmm* in the vibrations that snaked up her robowear and scraped the hairs on her arms.

The hornets fell silent.

Someone's inside. Even her thought was a whisper. And it must be a magical someone to hum a nest of hornets to sleep.

RUIJIE WAS THE ONLY GRANDCHILD from both sides of her family. Her relatives in Fuzhou called her Rui-Rui and Mingzhu, and her father especially thought of her as a precious pearl.

Her symptoms first appeared in the fourth grade when her father was regaling them at dinner with Ruijie's science fair project, "The Great Silence and Why I Think We're Not Listening," which took the grand prize, and her mother joked about how the table could benefit from their own great silence. Ruijie snorted shacha sauce up her nose and she reached for a glass of water. Then dropped it.

Later that week she dropped her chopsticks. They clattered to the floor, dragging the slippery noodles by the hair. Her father remarked on her clumsiness. Ruijie remembered feeling sheepish, maybe defiant, but not scared. Not yet.

The tremors grew. Her fingers refused to fist. She took advantage and flipped off the annoying kids in front of the teacher. But she couldn't hold a pen, or type; then she couldn't stand without wobbling. Then came the tests, between endless waits in endless hospital lobbies, the glow-in-the-dark scans, the shots drilling deeper and deeper into her spine. The doctors lobbed acronyms, like ALS, PMA, and MMA, which regrettably was not the martial arts. There were nights she couldn't sleep because her body clutched her awake in a squeezing iron fist. These nights she'd pretend to breathe softly when her parents sneaked into her room and knelt beside her bed so they could wrap her hand in sandalwood beads and pray.

She was measured for her first set of robowear. Ivory oblong disks, serving as both sensors and motors, rested on her hips to usher her gait, like a gentle push on the swings. For the first time in weeks, Ruijie stood on her own feet. Her father said she looked "super." Her mother took a picture and touched it with two fingers, as if the Ruijie frozen in time were more precious and real.

Prepare your hearts, the doctors told her parents, instead of her.

But Ruijie, three-time winner of the science fair, believed in the miracle of science. She believed in the trillions of tenuous threads tying the self to the rest. 物我一體. Matter and I are One. The grace of union so the swimmer flowed with the ocean, so the archer flew in the arrow, so the calligrapher bled from the brush. With this belief, she would wake, walk, and breathe with cosmic synergy, full of darkness and spinning lights, and her body, which broke down day by day, remained a solar system where all the stars would burst and burn, but until then, every quantum speck quivered bright with integrity.

RUIJIE SAW A HAND stretch out of the SADARM's belly and pluck the eye from the dirt. When the fingers opened, slow as a lotus flower, the eye pointed toward the sky, resting on the crease of the lifeline, like the world in the palm of your hand.

A boy peeked out. He had staticky hair, wide, crusted eyes. He looked a little bit homeless.

"Is this your eye?" he said, with what little Korean she understood.

When he continued speaking, she shook her head and reached for the eye. He pulled away with a smile. This time he said in English, "Do you have something to eat?"

She rummaged her backpack and found an old ginger candy. "It's a little spicy, but I eat it whenever I'm dizzy."

His fingers worked fruitlessly at the wrapper. She offered to try, expecting him to shake her off, throw some of that boy bluster. He handed it over without pause. His smile grew private as she struggled. Growling, she threw it back to him. He ripped it in one go.

"Well," he said, grinning now, "you did all the work."

The ginger candy had melted into jelly. He popped it into his mouth and chewed on one side. "Liu Ruijie?" he said, from her name embroidered on her backpack, a clever guess pulled from the gold-threaded strokes. He placed the eye on her palm. "My name is Yoyo."

"Is that in English?"

In one movement, he pulled himself out of the robot's belly and landed on the dirt with a clunk. He was her height but felt smaller, listing to the right where his leg ended at the ankle. The shin was covered in shredded skyn, like the hem of his pants had gotten caught in an angry chewy machine, exposing a calf full of wires in red and blue. His stump was so white it felt fragile, more ceramic than bone.

She was staring until he took her hand. Pressing his index on her lifeline, he wrote out his name. Soft circle, then two little strokes, a cut long and swift. Repeat. In hangul, then English.

"Does it hurt?"

"My leg?" He glanced at it. "Not very."

She peeked at his wrist, his skinny elbow. "How bionic are you?"

"One hundred percent."

"That's impossible," she said, and he laughed.

He slipped past her. A leg like his should wring his muscles, each thump sending shocks up the spine. Yet Yoyo moved like he was free.

Her parents flinched at the risk of bionic surgery, but Ruijie had found the idea of it inevitable. Converting herself from oxygen, hydrogen, nitrogen, and carbon into a different chemical blend of wires, titanium, and nanofiber made the purest sense to her. She collected success stories and relayed them to her mother: the bedridden-turned-bionic woman who climbed Mount Everest; the burn victim in Germany who survived a 67 percent transition;

even the sixteen-year-old boy, paralyzed from the neck down, who received a spinal implant that was only a tiny bit invasive and look at him now, point guard on the varsity basketball team.

Bionic. Transhuman. Posthuman. The world made a promise to her: death is a problem that can be solved.

YOYO DIDN'T SWEAT. Together they dodged the sun between pockets of shade. They found little cover, just the thinning shadows cast from the towers of stacked cars, their metal husks veined a crackling orange especially around the fenders.

She led Yoyo to one of the shallow piles in the yard where trucks would swirl in on Dump Day and tilt containers full of jumbled fizzy robots. She was collecting specimens for research, she told him. Today she'd scored big, with a fully intact robotic body, but any limb would do. Mecha or organic, hirsute or hairless, for the fated day a pair of long sturdy robot legs would be hers. "I pull them apart and put them back together," she said. "Even though I won't be in charge of my own surgery, I want to know how my body will work."

They dug around scrap at knee level, and she could feel gravity and heat draw the swarthy flush to her cheeks, the ripening of her armpits. For the first time she was embarrassed to sweat in front of a boy. Yoyo was bionic and almost perfect, while she oozed like a slug.

She gulped water and offered Yoyo her bottle, but he shook his head, distracted. He seemed to possess a preternatural sense for danger. He'd freeze, long before she could spot the bright orange uniforms of the scrappers who worked here, who dallied during lunch breaks and emerged late in the afternoon, angling their hard-shelled construction hats to smack chalky sunblock on their reddish napes, willing to scavenge only after the sun had started to droop. These scrappers, who knew her by sight, cursed her in Mandarin or Korean that sang like Mandarin, and she'd curse them back.

The scrappers were foul tempered but harmless, she thought. Yet she could feel Yoyo tremble against her shoulder. "It's okay," she said. "They won't hurt you."

"If they catch me, they'll destroy me," Yoyo said.

Which was a tad dramatic. But they made a point to hide.

They found three more legs that day. One leg was too long, one for mechas, and when she picked up the last leg, it slumped like pantyhose. Yesterday's rain had left puddles. Yoyo found a worm drowning. The worm panicked and squirted weakly on his palm, but he watched it twist around his fingers in awe, as if it were a jewel.

"You're like my cat," Ruijie said when Yoyo crouched to smile at a frog that was even smaller than a cricket. "Smaug would catch everything. Frogs, mice, birds." Her cat had the lovely habit of bringing sparrows into the house. Feathers ruffled but alive, if humiliated.

Smaug had passed away at the start of this year. On their last day together, her mother took a picture of Smaug, the black tufted head resting on Ruijie's shoulder, then her father carried her cat into the vet's office, and Smaug opened her eyes and looked at her.

Ruijie was still feeling her way around this darkness. Sometimes it felt like a game of hide-and-seek, and all she had to do was search very hard and find Smaug, pumpkin-eyed behind the couch.

When she looked down, she saw Yoyo had placed on her knee the ginger candy wrapper, tied into a ribbon. Comfort often budded from the inexplicable.

"When do you go home?" Yoyo said.

"My mom's going to pick me up." Summer school ended at three and it was already nearly five. "She thinks I'm at the school library. What about you?"

"I'll be here."

"Where do you live?" An inkling grew, itchy and uncomfortable. "Do you have a home? A family?"

He went still, so still, you'd think he froze.

She saw another orange shape closing in from a distance, still twenty meters away. The scrapper was whistling, a spring in his step, a lurching sway.

She tried to move but couldn't. Her robowear had gone rigid. A light on her belt blinked red. "My battery's dead." She twisted her waist, took a deep breath, and tried to sound composed instead of the careless, helpless creature she was. "Yoyo, can you go get my backpack? I need my charger."

He knelt in the mud and reached for the flap on her belt.

"What are you doing?"

He looked at her, but not in a way a child or adult would. His eyes asked for permission. When she granted it, he reached behind his neck to pull out a wire, glinting silver, as if he'd torn his own essence from his spine. He plugged the wire into her robowear; she shivered. She'd felt the shock.

The whistling drew closer. Yoyo sat down and crossed his legs so the stump rested on his knee. Her robowear charged quietly, blinking blue. A light appeared over his head. Like a firefly, it spun in a lethargic circle.

She studied the whorl on his head. His hair curled wet around his ears from the humidity, and she tried to imagine the inside of his skull. If there were gears buzzing like a hornet's nest, or if, beneath his staticky hair and thick layer of skyn, his mind was a river that wound silent and silver.

As the whistling grew faint, Yoyo hummed along. He caught her stare and grinned.

"Wish I could whistle," he said.

Can you charge anywhere? she asked and he said yes.

Are you powered by the sun? she asked and he said yes.

Her battery was fully charged, but she didn't want to go home. She wanted to lie beside Yoyo in the silvergrass and search for the stars that shine no matter how shy. She'd tell him how her parents had met during a month of study abroad and kissed in front of Amsterdam's floating houses, how she used to be an ice-skater and swimmer and placed first in butterfly, the most difficult of the forms. When she erred on the side of self-pity, she talked about her future, how she was going to study astrology and graduate summa cum laude from her mother's alma mater and become the first bionic astronaut who wouldn't even have to breathe in space. She was willing to wait for Yoyo to open up to her, like the lotus that rose from the mud. They could whisper secrets that flowed only when the sky was watching you.

"Will you live forever?"

He said, "Yes."

PART I

1. Lost Soul

DETECTIVE CHO JUN OF ROBOT CRIMES ANSWERED THE PHONE with a sly, proud emphasis on *detective*. The caller said it was an emergency: last night her child never came home.

"Sorry," Jun said, "just to clarify—child? Or robot?"

He leaned on his elbow and cranked up his hearing. The people in his office were shouting at each other. Someone had been stealing lunches from the break room. It was the ferocious first of August and the AC was dead. Over the weekend, someone else had grabbed a ladder and vandalized one of the flags—South Korea and United Korea left beautiful and whole, only the North Korean flag torn down the middle.

Jun searched for his tablet, but his desk was collateral damage, so he grabbed a pen and scribbled on his palm the description of the missing robot child, name and address, all the while leaking sympathetic noises for the caller.

"Another lost soul?" said Sgt. Son, who was wearing a puffy neck pillow, poised for his power nap.

"Very lost." Jun looped his tie around his neck and tried to remember the direction of the knot. "Can I go pay the owner a sincerity visit?"

"You're not leaving me here."

Earlier that morning, Jun had parked their patrol car in the slim shade of a tree that had skirted capriciously to the left, leaving it white-hot, the insides smothered in leather. He tossed his jacket in the back seat, cranked up the fan, and *ahh*ed at the blast of AC.

"You don't even sweat," Sgt. Son said.

"Still pretty fucking bliss, Sergeant."

Driving through Itaewon from their precinct in Yongsan was

slow but smooth if only Jun left the car on autopilot. Which he didn't. He could feel the locked-jaw anxiety from Sgt. Son, as Jun shouldered the car into the tightest, twistiest road to avoid the main traffic. Every corner bulged with storefronts and every crossroad was a potential jump scare from a motorcycle. In the last two decades since the Unification War, twenty or so years ago, Itaewon, with its hanok-styled bars and subterranean clubs, had become an area run by robots. At the end of the road, a plasticky PS-19 whistled and waved for traffic control, stoppering the flow of cars. "That was still green," Sgt. Son groused at the red light. "Why fire the whole department if all these mechas do is the macarena?"

"I was going to apply for Traffic," Jun said.

Two years ago, he'd quit riot police after he knocked down a seventy-year-old North Korean protester. He put in his application for Traffic, feeling resigned enough to don the blinding neon vest and shrill at drivers too rageful to let their cars drive themselves. Then the roaring whisper—Traffic was doomed, automating itself so quickly that cops were handing their vests to the brand-spanking-new PS-19 androids, like stripping your clothes to cover up the nakedness of a store mannequin.

Robot Crimes wasn't Jun's second or third choice, but it promised to be low commitment. He'd get to work from Yongsan, close to Itaewon, which had good food and great vibes, and by virtue of proximity, he'd also have a real shot at applying for Major Crimes, where detectives solved the big, weighty cases headlined by North Korean gangs.

Not that Jun cared one lick about joining Major Crimes. His lack of ambition was his favorite trait.

Past Itaewon, the traffic punctured open. As they slid into the Hannam neighborhood, the genteel, prim older sister to Itaewon, the type of robot shifted from mecha and controlling to placid and humanoid, pushing strollers, walking lavender designer dogs. Jun put the car on autopilot and tried to decrypt the smear on his palm; he'd forgotten how easily ink rolled off his skyn.

Their missing robot was a companion model, designed to look ten years old. The child version of the Sakura, the popular "girl next door" from Imagine Friends. "Her name's Eli," Jun said. "For Elisha."

"Fancy English name."

Jun admitted he'd seen her a couple weeks ago at the police station.

"What'd she do?"

"Robbed a store. Kidding. She got lost, of course."

Jun had found her alone on the bench outside the office. A baseball cap was pulled low over her sweet, forgettable face, which her owner hadn't bothered to customize. "A thirty-nine-year-old man dropped me off," she told Jun. "I'm glad I was not stolen."

Jun had ransacked his desk for a compatible charger and eventually found one in the evidence room, an eroded skein of wire. Eli plugged herself in with a little squeal and it fairly broke his heart. Her battery had to hit 30 percent before she could remember her address.

"Already janky," Sgt. Son said.

"Just old. She's a second-gen Sakura. I bet they're not even sold online anymore. They were never popular."

"Isn't the Sakura the face," Sgt. Son said, gesturing at his own, "you know, for the company?"

"This version was too clumsy. Imagine Friends tried to spin it as cute."

"'Cute?'"

"Like a real kid. Tripping, bumping into furniture, then they were breaking plates, making a mess. Owners got sick of it."

They took the leisurely drive around the well-wooded park of the apartment complex where Eli's owner lived. "Fancy Hannam apartment," Sgt. Son said.

The aesthetic mimicked traditional Korean, a nostalgic mock-up of Joseon architecture. Pine waterwheel attached to an artfully sun-bleached pavilion. Jeju statues of artificial volcanic rock, so porous they looked like foam. Jun could hear the shrill of cicadas through the sealed car window. Ridiculously cheerful. Feast for magpies.

He and Eli had strolled through this park the last time he took her home. He got judgy looks from women for being in plain clothes, holding hands with a girl-child robot—the Sakura face, too much of a giveaway—and his vibe hadn't screamed "fatherly" as much as "embarrassing uncle." When he tried to shake off Eli's hand, her fingers tightened, like a steel trap. The grip loosened only when they reached the apartment building where her owner lived. The thirteenth floor, ominous now, but the older apartments were likelier to strike off the number four as unlucky. Jun had watched Eli prance up; as the wind lifted, her shirt billowed, a gauzy white curtain, and he'd seen the tremendous scarring on her back.

Once Jun had strategically parked under a tree with a generous shadow, Sgt. Son asked the question that must have been troubling him all along.

"Is the owner a man?"

The last owner to call them had reported a burglary and tried to file an insurance claim for his robot, who was deemed damaged beyond repair. She was murdered, he said. He was misinformed. Ink washed off biosilicon skyn with a brisk hand-wring, but the texture often preserved fingerprints like yeasty dough, and the ones wrapped around his robot's throat had matched his own.

But Jun had never met Eli's owner. He didn't even go inside the building. He could have, but what could he do if the owner had turned out to be another sicko? Call Child Protective Services? For robots? That would route him to his own number. Why risk entering this beautifully tended apartment, one of the most expensive properties in not only Hannam but the greater Gangbuk area, all of Seoul, and South Korea, and might as well include the North, and risk running into his younger sister, whom he had been avoiding for the last five years?

Like most things, Jun put off answering this and went inside.

ELI'S OWNER WAS AN imperious woman with a cotton cloud of hair who hid long and sinewy limbs under a dress of handwoven hemp. "We spoke over the phone?" Jun said, but her gaze slipped past his face, like rain off the windshield, landing instead on Sgt. Son in his grim-dark jacket, the ironed trousers that bared his sandaled feet. Prone to sweat rash, Sgt. Son avoided socks in the summer.

She asked if they were truly police in a tone that suggested she'd rather send this dish back to the kitchen. Sgt. Son assured her that they were from Robot Crimes and, fanning his face, he suggested they talk inside. His face scrunched delicately when they entered. No AC. In the living room, a small electric fan was aimed at a wooden Virgin Mary who prayed from the coffee table. The TV flickered mutely.

Jun heard the clink of glass, Kim Sunduk in the kitchen. Some minor signs of chaos: the bathrobe puddled on the floor, the pair of umbrellas lying crumpled like drowned crows. The rest was an immaculate home. Calligraphy draped the walls, rippling in holographic paints and gems. Behind the dining table was a wall-sized canvas of a jade and ice mountain, and in the corner he recognized the hanja for Kim Sunduk's name, her austere, elegant signature. Of course Eli's owner would be an artist. A collector would never buy a failed android model, but an artist would. An artist would try to make it their own.

"She's North Korean," Sgt. Son said, plucking from the wall a framed news article. In the cropped picture, Kim Sunduk smiled thinly beside a snow-haired man.

Jun shrugged; North Koreans could be rich and famous too. "The man beside her, that's Kanemoto Masaaki. Founder of Imagine Friends."

Kanemoto, the article said, had diligently collected the artist Kim Sunduk's *White Tiger* series on Mount Baekdu—North

Korea's most mystical mountain, and deadliest—once exhibited in the likes of the Guggenheim and the White Cube. Now the entire series was being displayed in Imagine Friends' Seoul headquarters, after Kanemoto's passing.

Sgt. Son placed the framed article back on the wall, leaving it slightly crooked. "If she's friends with a tech billionaire, why keep a janky old robot?"

They quieted down when Kim Sunduk returned from the kitchen empty-handed. She turned off the TV and they sat around the coffee table. Jun felt tempted to pick up the Virgin Mary and feel around the folds of her robes, in case she was a covert lighter.

"It helps to walk us through the day," Sgt. Son said, pulling out a handkerchief to dab around his neck.

Eli had disappeared last night on Tuesday, July 31. She was wearing an oversized tee of Einstein (with the tongue) and jean shorts, muddy tennis shoes. A black baseball cap with the slogan TOO COOL FOR SCHOOL.

"You sent your robot out around seven?" Sgt. Son said.

"Seven thirty."

"For cigarettes?"

"For cigarettes. I called the 7-Eleven last night. They didn't see her come in."

"Convenience stores let kiddie robots buy cigarettes?" Sgt. Son said, turning to Jun, but Kim Sunduk continued in her toneless affect:

"This 7-Eleven is attached to our apartment complex. Eli knows the robots who work there and they know her. They know me."

"What's her last GPS signal? Did you try Find My Robot?"

"Her GPS doesn't work. I took her to the Imagine Friends store, but their updates no longer apply to her. They said"—here she laughed, quiet and mocking—"they said I should take advantage of the trade-in program."

Heaving a sigh, Sgt. Son slumped into the sofa. He asked her to consider this: The heat was brutal, the worst in years. They had to push back the World Cup semifinals. What about the poor bank robot that broke down last week? What if, maybe, Eli collapsed in the middle of the street and it was garbage that picked her up?

The silence stretched long enough for Jun to eye the kitchen, the bathroom, escape.

"I said I don't want a new robot," Kim Sunduk said.

"You'll learn to love the next one," Sgt. Son said, not unkindly.

"I don't think you understand," she said slowly. "Do you think I took Eli in because I wanted a child? I have a child. An ungrateful son who'd sooner leave me in the mountains if the nursing homes were full. Eli isn't a replacement. Eli is—"

She looked at Jun, suddenly lost. "Eli is special."

Jun asked if he could use the bathroom, which Sgt. Son would take as permission to snoop. He had to be efficient. Sgt. Son was willing to invest on a missing robot no more than forty-eight hours (thirty-six with the heat). They had been burned one too many times. While Jun searched the kitchen, Sgt. Son would now be cajoling Kim Sunduk, trying to dim her expectations. It's not like we're *bad* at our job, Jun thought as he opened the cabinets, finding plastic cups of pastel elephants and giraffes. Within the year, Officer Kim had quit to take over his father's sauna business, and Detective Kim, the only woman on their floor, was headhunted by Sex Crimes, and now they were a two-man show.

Jun heard Sgt. Son ask, "Do you have any water?" and he slipped out of the kitchen. He spotted something lying flat and secretive on the dining table, covered with the kind of cloth that ought to be folded into a swan. He pulled away the cloth.

Chrysanthemums spilled red instead of funeral white across shoulder blades, garlanding the horns of a devil-faced dokkaebi. The spindly petals faded into pink around the violent, marred grin. Half the dokkaebi's face was scarred. Cigarette burns puckered down the spine.

A hand reached for the cloth. Kim Sunduk drew it over the canvas, like a sheet to cover a body in the morgue. "This is unfinished."

"I recognize it," Jun said. Eli skipping in front of him. The wind lifting her shirt. Tremendous scars. "Isn't this the tattoo on her back?"

"She had it when I bought her."

"The burns on the canvas, you used an actual cigarette?"

"I purchased a bolt of skyn in her coloring and stapled it to the canvas. It burns like human skin. But you can smell the preservatives. Like chicken nuggets."

"Why didn't you replace the skyn on her back?"

"Couldn't you have replaced the flesh on your face?"

He ducked his head. "Okay, good point."

"Is it a war injury?"

"It was a robot, carrying an IED until she dropped it. Homemade bomb."

She stared at him, wide burning eyes. "How you must despise them."

"I used to work with robots, actually," Jun said, with a light laugh. "On the field, as their operator. My military buddies called me the robot whisperer, but really I was a babysitter."

She touched the edge of the painting, adjusted the cloth. "Eli said you were kind to her."

"Yeah, well, I felt sorry for her."

Kim Sunduk nodded. "She felt sorry for you too."

SEVEN YEARS AGO, Jun had woken from his induced coma. The doctor said he'd flatlined twice during surgery, which was a mild way of putting it, as if he'd tripped and fallen on his face.

Apparently, his father had visited him in the ICU. The doctor said his father took one look at him and forbade anyone else in the family from seeing him.

"That sounds like my dad," Jun said.

"The thing is you looked barely human," the doctor said.

Another week slunk by before Jun could sit up without wanting to kill himself. The doctor said the reconstruction of his body had flipped his organs, his stomach and spleen shoved where his uterus used to be. His liver was swapped for a tinier freight train. His bladder was bigger. Urination would be infrequent, once or twice a week, which was a nice perk, but expect a stream of darkly concentrated yellow. If it smelled pungent, it meant it was working. Jun tuned out the doctor somewhere between the liver and missing uterus, fancifully imagining his organs as colorful *Tetris* blocks in doomed teetering piles. The IED damaged 78 percent of his body beyond recovery. It was a miracle he was alive. No, it was Science. They repaired him by attaching not the bionic to his body but his body to the bionic.

Jun had burst out laughing then, imagining himself as a Humvee with pink fleshy ears for side-view mirrors.

After three weeks of tender and wincing sponge baths, with the help of a pretty robot nurse who smiled through the worst of Jun's spectacular temper, he finally took a shower.

He washed everything in worship and terror. After maneuvering himself out of the stall, he faced the fogged mirror over the sink. An opaque oval, soft as the moon. He opened the door a crack and waited for the fog to lift. He could be patient. He'd waited all his life for this.

Before the IED blast, he had been on testosterone since his sophomore year of high school. His voice had cracked, slipped, plummeting in free fall, reckless and delightful. Hair had grown in strange, strange places. He'd come out in the Army to the less shitty half of his squad during boot and earned some pats, one vigorous, baffling noogie. He'd scheduled top surgery and fantasized so precisely, it became sharp and real and he could taste it, like the scald of blood in his mouth before the IED decimated his body.

The mirror cleared. He had to reach for it to ascertain it was him. He looked different. Different from what he'd imagined. No incision marks. No grafted nipples. No nipples at all. *Where the hell are my nipples?* and it sounded shrill even in his head. Later, he'd chuckle at that. Later, he'd buy his nipples. But the mirror gave him everything else, this gorgeous, hurt thing. His chest, which he could stroke in awe, the greening archipelago where the flesh was still tender and alive, then it smoothed into blank arctic skyn stretched over his ribs where he traced a long scar shaped in a white lightning bolt on his hip. The coy seam of a teddy bear.

He could feel his heart pounding. Muffled, as if packaged then misplaced. The mirror proved this was him. His existence, his resolve, threaded into every nanostitch, for he was alive, but at what cost? Self-obliteration. He'd prepared for this—had he not? Relinquishing his old body so he could live, so he could face his blurring reflection and whisper, *This is everything you ever wanted.*

Then he heard a knock. The door opened, his sister, Morgan, fresh from a semester of her could-be Ivy League, bug-eyed with shock. Are you *crying*?

The old Jun would have cracked a joke, called her a perv, but he was so furious he could barely breathe. Get the fuck out, he had shouted, because she didn't get it and she never would.

JUN MOVED THROUGH the apartment complex with Sgt. Son, knocking on doors. Door-to-door canvassing was their least favorite part of the job. People were nosy and mean, neighborliness on a steep decline. The war had ended with a burst of "jeong" to celebrate the quivering, disbelieving joy in the unification of North and South. This led to an uptick in communal-based housing that mimicked the supposed rustic closeness of North Korean communities, sharing parks, playgrounds, and shopping centers, like this building. But affection dried up quick with every bump of the reunification tax.

Most neighbors reacted with shock over Eli's disappearance. A lost child! The horror, so swiftly to wither into scorn when it became evident Eli was just a Sakura, a mere imitation.

"Have some water." An old woman handed them two bottles. "Suffering like dogs in this heat over a robot."

"Ice-cold!" Sgt. Son said, flushed and pleased.

Jun pressed his bottle against the back of Sgt. Son's neck. He got swatted.

Every time he rang a doorbell, his spine stiffened and he plastered on a smile. Morgan could be behind any one of these doors. Probability wasn't on his side. He wondered if she still had that dyed hair, the frosted tips.

They covered the whole floor, circling back to Kim Sunduk's home, which left just the unit next door. He knocked. No answer. He raised his hand again, paused.

"We're with Robot Crimes. We won't take long. Promise."

Like a pendulum, the door swung open. Then it decided to close. Jun, moving not on autopilot but on frightening compulsion, as if the past had reached out and gripped him by the lapels, seized the edge of the door before it could shut.

2. Middle Child Syndrome

MORGAN WAS LATE FOR WORK AND SHE BLAMED EVERYONE else. She was normally punctual, as the rare night owl who could code bright-eyed and alert until dawn and still wake up at six from nature's most reliable alarm—her nervy bladder. But the morning had gotten away from her. While brushing her teeth, she'd opened an email from Joe, her VP, and panicked, swallowing toothpaste, which she hacked up and spat, and watched spiral down the drain. She sat on the toilet for a long time.

Now she was shimmying into a pair of nude tights. At the knock on her door, she shouted, "Just leave it outside," expecting a delivery.

Tights were not her usual workwear, but today was T minus thirty-one days until the worldwide release of Imagine Friends' Boy X. And Joe's email declared that the prerelease reviews had come in, the equivalent of the gladiatorial thumbs-down or thumbs-up.

From the kitchen, Stephen asked if she'd like onions in her omelet.

No onions, but, also, *No lunch*. All these meetings came with a table of artfully clumped hummus and lox, carrot and celery sticks and beet jellies for those who wanted to maximize their nutrients colorfully, and cereal dispensers of Fast Feast pills for those who couldn't bother. However, Stephen was on a bento box kick. It kept him nicely occupied, so she put up with it.

He greeted her with a cup of French-pressed and a warm, worshipful smile. Her bento lunch sat on the dining table, wrapped in a Hello Kitty tenugui, the silken ends tied into a handle for convenience. If she were still living in New York, it would look chic. Here, she'd get the stink eye for carrying something so Japanese.

"I used the rest of the ingredients to make fried rice," Stephen said. He was wearing a heart-shaped apron that said, I CODE THEREFORE I AM.

"Great. Did you put in onion?"

He leaned in for a kiss. She expected it, still cringed. He drew back, his smile rueful, but she had to be reading too much into it. Stephen wasn't made to feel the sting of rejection, only the urge to respond to the action of it with tact.

Feeling sorry for him, she tried to peck his chin. But he was too tall. By the time he bent down, she was late for work.

"Morgan, you received another message from your mother this morning. That leaves you with six unread messages. Would you like me to read these messages?"

"Keep up the filter." She gave him a thumbs-up and blew on her coffee. "Give her, like, a neutral reply."

"She wants to know if you will have a room ready for your father when he visits Korea. Would you like to respond with a neutral yes or a neutral no?"

"*Here?* I told her I don't have space—"

More knocking, this time with the flat of the fist. Whoever it was shouted, "We're with Robot Crimes. Won't take long. Promise."

She went to the peephole with her coffee, took a resentful sip. Two men, both in suits, supposedly police. Authority figures terrified her. But then again, her brother was a cop and he had barely been functional his whole life, so. The cops, heads down, were made further insignificant by the fish-eye lens. Oh, the thrill of surveillance. I can see you, but you can't see me. As if one had heard her thoughts, he lifted his gaze, and she opened the door before she could grasp the weight of that scarred smile.

"Minjun?" she said.

Jun let go of the door with a grimace. It was so weird to see him in a tie.

His cop partner, slouched somewhere in his fifties, introduced himself as Detective Sergeant Son. "We're looking for a robot girl who went missing last night." He sounded truly apologetic, like he couldn't imagine a bigger time suck.

In her defense, Monday night was overtime at Imagine Friends. All hands on deck. Every year Imagine Friends hosted a lusty worldwide launch between Seoul, Tokyo, and San Francisco that swept everyone up in a frenzy, but this year was even more special. It was their tenth anniversary, so they'd grudgingly included New York. Their CEO, a New Yorker with too much to prove since the death of their vaunted founder, had staggered ambitious releases throughout the year.

The Future X Children launch was on September 1, and their Boy X was positioned to be the star. Joe, in his email, had delivered a freak-fit, but the rousing kind. The hype is real, he said. No matter what anyone says, our Boy is going to change the world.

The grandness of this moment—what could be the zenith, or just the beginning, of her career—was distilled into: "I was at work."

Morgan tried to elaborate. "Until one. These days I come home late." Her Korean swirled thick and awkward, a mouthful of medicine she could never quite swallow. "I work for Imagine Friends," she added, with the shy pleasure of confessing, *I went to college in Boston.*

Usually this spurred people to shed their disinterest and, with a sycophantic glint in their eye, attempt to befriend her. But Sgt. Son didn't look too impressed. "What do you do there?" he said, like he expected her to be a receptionist.

She was a personality programmer, a job title that sounded twee but required a master's in neurorobotics, five years at one of the Big Three, and a little code puzzle you were supposed to crack on the spot.

She tried her best to describe their upcoming release, the latest child robots. "Boy and girl. The girl is going to be a new Sakura."

She heard a snort. A furious upward glance failed to catch Jun in the act. His face looked so serious as he was taking notes, she wondered, Is this really him? Doppelgänger? Hard stop. No. She had put that damn scar on his lip when they had yanked hairs over the new VR controller and she shoved him into a celadon vase, which shattered. You cut off my tongue, Jun had cried out, and she started crying and he started laughing, ghoulishly, blood streaming down his chin. It was their older brother who dabbed Jun's mouth with a towel and said, so sad but sure, That's going to scar.

The memory must have turned her somber, because Sgt. Son told her not to worry. "We don't think it's a serious threat; it's another missing Sakura."

"This seems like a lot of work for just one Sakura," she said.

"Her name's Eli," Jun said.

Which was what, an insinuation *she* didn't care about robots? But that name. *Eli.* Her neighbor's robot. Surly old lady who would ignore her in the elevator. *Eli* carrying three Bibles. *Eli* holding the elevator door open for Morgan. Her hurried *Thanks* had prompted Eli to say, *You're welcome, ajumma*, which had drawn an indignant gasp.

"Ohh. The Sakura from next door."

Morgan blushed. The Sakura·2C was a travesty, the sophomore slump to the iconic original. It physically hurt her to see someone own a 2C, although her neighbor fell squarely into their target market: 65+ years; 68 percent female, 27 percent male, 5 percent other; single or divorced. Lonely Losers.

"I thought something would happen to her," Morgan said, slipping into her pool of confidence, voice aloof and steady. "I should let you know her model had problems."

"It was too cute," Sgt. Son said.

"It was shit—I mean, bad code. She was inflexible. Non-learning." Perfect little eyesores. The Sakura·2Cs could read their owners' moods but they'd insist on selecting the tactless response, as if they were aiming to collect every Bad Ending in a game. "It was practically"—Morgan fumbled for the Korean word for *relic* or *redundant*—"trash."

She glanced again at Jun, who was still typing notes. His

disinterest heated the pit of her stomach, stoking every slight she'd collected since the genesis of her memory. She *ahem*ed, ready to say, *Hi, does Mom know you're still alive?* when suddenly he looked up and gave her such a friendly and polite smile, a miraculous combination of *fuck* and *you*.

"Sergeant, could you give us a moment?" Jun said.

Sgt. Son tapped the face of his watch. "We have to be back in Yongsan for"—here, her Korean collapsed, since she wasn't wearing her Delfi to autotranslate.

Jun gestured toward the neighbor's door, channeling *I'll be done soon* and *I'll join you later* with a pat of Sgt. Son's shoulder. Jun was the touchy-feely type who'd bump fists with teachers and strangers and put a hand on your shoulder because he was laughing so hard. Then, when he abruptly withdrew his affection, which was only a matter of when, it felt all the more like a punishment.

As soon as Sgt. Son left, Jun's service smile slid right off.

Morgan switched to English. "You barely look like a cop."

"Too hot for the force," Jun agreed. "Can I come in?"

He shouldered past her before she could find her bearings, seared by the panic of *Where is Stephen?* Jun was already in her kitchen eyeing a breakfast omelet deflating in the fry pan. He looped around the living room, opened a door at random, and whistled. "I can't believe you have a walk-in closet."

"Are you snooping?"

"I told my boss I need to talk to an important witness."

Morgan slammed the door to her bedroom. Stephen should be inside, sitting by her vanity table, charging himself from the outlet where he'd have to unplug her air purifier. "Well, tell him I didn't see anything."

Jun picked up the fry pan with the omelet—"Are you going to eat this?"—and sat down before she could deny him.

"There's no time to eat. I have a big meeting," she said, grabbing her bento lunch. The meeting wasn't until later in the afternoon, but Morgan needed the morning to brace herself. Joe always picked a random (fun!) time on the dot, like 8:07 and 13:24, to keep them playfully on their toes, a tragic symptom of his Western horizontal leadership. "You have to go, now."

Jun fed straight off the pan. "But I want to meet your robot," he said, mouth full.

How? Her throat clutched. How did he sense Stephen?

"Are you that embarrassed by him?"

"How do you even know it's a him?"

"Ha! Knew it."

The calories must have loosened him up because he became less jittery, more chatty, and he asked how was life, how was work. As if he even cared. Rather cruelly, she asked if he was still living in their parents' old house, which he was.

"Rent-free, how nice," she said.

"It's great. I love my job," he told her. "Lots of missing robots, some dead ones. What sucks is the office politics. Major Crimes wants us so badly to sink. I can already hear the violins whining." He scraped the pan; she winced at the screech. "How are the parents?"

"They just moved to Boston."

"I thought Mom hated Boston."

"They can't afford Oakland anymore, which you'd know if you called. Plus, Dad got a better offer from MIT, so now they're renting a one-bedroom near that café, Tatte."

"They're pretending to be grad students again, how sweet."

She sat, passed Jun the pepper shaker. "We do virtual dinner, like, once a month. Well, it's breakfast for them."

"Dad's eating?" Jun laughed, a sharp, warm sound. "How'd Mom pull that off?"

"He's a lot better now. MIT wants him back and he also pulled millions from the NIR grant for his extinct animals. He's flying in early September to do an exhibit at the robot museum here."

It was a disgrace. Her father used to be for neurorobotics what Karl Schwarzschild was for quantum physics. The architect behind the Hopper Network, the elegantly impenetrable solution to Sharon Hopper's theory on the layers of artificial consciousness. Then, at the peak of his career, he made the astounding decision to pivot from neurorobotics to zoobotics. As a Stanford ex-colleague said in an interview, *It was like watching a famed brain surgeon put down his scalpel to become a horse doctor.*

"I think he made a whale?" Morgan said.

"Oh God, Kobo the whale. Isn't it swimming somewhere around Antarctica?"

"It's actually the Arctic."

"I was on a call with Dad once, and he played whale acoustic songs."

"When was the last time you talked?"

He shrugged.

"Could you pick him up from the airport? He's arriving at some awkward time, and I don't think I'll be able to get out of work."

"You think I have free time? Book a cab."

"You know Dad doesn't do autocabs or auto-anything. And his driver's license expired a gazillion years ago."

Jun stood up, taking the fry pan with him, and she called after him, "He should be allowed to stay in his own house."

"Why don't you host him? Your walk-in closet could fit a North Korean family." Jun dumped the pan in the bowl of frothy sink water and reached for the rubber gloves.

"Just leave it in the sink. You live in *their* house. How can you mooch off our parents and act like they're a complete inconvenience?"

Jun lifted a bemused eyebrow, and pulled on the rubber gloves with an emphatic snap, but she refused to budge from her seat. For how long was he going to act like a bruised teenager, blaming their father for literally everything? Jun had been trying to shed their family since he was in high school. And it had nothing to do with his gender; their mother threw a nauseating party for him with everything frosted blue.

Morgan had tried to be supportive from a distance. She didn't have to serve as a direct witness to the changes Jun was going through, and maybe in her head, she'd preserved him as the Jun from high school, devil-eyed and loose-gendered, which was now an effigy collecting dust. Every time she saw him, he'd have changed so fundamentally, it was a shock to the system. But the power balance between them had shifted ages ago after he dropped out of college and eloped with the Army and ruined his life, leaving her to pick up the slack.

Jun scrubbed the crackly layer off the pan with a sponge. "You just don't want to show Dad your robot. I still can't believe you own one."

"I don't *own* him, I made him."

"You sound like Dad." He lifted his chin and suddenly his voice pitched much friendlier. "Oh, hello there."

Morgan turned around. Stephen stood in the doorway, still wearing the apron I CODE THEREFORE I AM.

"Morgan, you left your Delfi in the bathroom," he said, holding out her glasses. "I finished cleaning the bathroom. I also lit a scented candle."

"Nice apron," Jun said, sliding off the soaked gloves. "I'm Jun. Morgan's brother."

"My name is Stephen. I'm Morgan's lover." Stephen's eyelid twitched, a giveaway that he was looking something up; she'd meant to fix it. "In the family registry, you're recorded as—"

"Male," Jun said. "Older brother. Middle child. Whatever you want to call it."

"Middle child? Aren't you the oldest?"

Jun, marvelously, managed to smile. "Right." He ducked his head with a small laugh. "I guess I am."

"Stephen, can you go inside my bedroom," she said, "and clean something?"

And yet, Stephen decided he needed cleaning supplies. Jun scooched aside so Stephen could kneel in front of the cabinet under the sink, and cocked his head, and she could tell he was checking Stephen out, the scoundrel.

"So, Stephen, how old are you?"

"I'll be one soon," Stephen said, pulling out too many sponges, gathering them all in a bucket.

"Happy birthday. Have you been here the whole year? How well do you know your neighbors?"

"I know our neighbors well. Kim Sunduk is kind to me. Eli is my friend."

Friends? Since when did Stephen have friends? Morgan felt the confused pang of a mother who had just discovered that her teenage daughter was sneaking out the window every night.

"You talk often with Eli? When was the last you spoke?"

"We spoke yesterday at five minutes past seven."

Jun pursed his lips. "You might've been the last person to see her before she left for the 7-Eleven."

"Eli didn't go to the 7-Eleven. She went to the MiniMart."

"What MiniMart?"

Morgan made a show of checking the time because she was late for work. "I'm late for work," she told them.

"Relax," Jun said. "I'm here on police business. Am I bothering you, Stephen?"

Stephen shook his head.

"You're bothering me," Morgan said, but Jun ignored her.

He was watching Stephen with a glint in his eyes. "Are you modeled off of someone?"

"He's a prototype," Morgan said desperately, trying to snag his gaze. "I took the baseline personality of a Tristan model—"

"In high school, Morgan had a huge crush on this actor. Completely vanilla, but he'd always go for these psycho roles. What did he star in?" Jun rattled off movie titles. *The Devil Knocks. Sad Candy. The Dispossessed. River Melancholy. Foxy Detective.* Unerringly in chronological order.

Stephen straightened up, spray and sponge at the ready. "My physical appearance, adaptive personality, and speech patterns are modeled after the actor Ko Yohan."

"You look just like him," Jun said, gleeful. "She must have 3D-printed your face."

Like it was that easy. Before them was a year's work, the robot she'd built practically by hand. Meaning she took a Tristan·VI shell and gutted it. Everything she'd customized, from his Black Olive eyes to his profound appreciation of the tortured musculature in a Rodin and the Christian despair of Kierkegaard. One hundred ninety-two centimeters tall, according to Ko Yohan's probably exaggerated celebrity profile. His limbs lean and proportionate, his hands surprisingly calloused. His hair, perpetually blow-dried. His mind, sweet and quick.

She made him, unmade him, named him Yohan, renamed him Stephen, and he had been hers ever since.

He was a masterpiece. But one glance at Jun, and Morgan saw in him their return to childhood equilibrium, a look of utter peace on his face.

3. Finders Keepers

EVERY BREAKFAST, RUIJIE'S MEDICINE CAME IN THREE CRYStal glasses of varying shades of brown: Korean herbal hanyak. Watery black-goat extract. And a tall pillared glass of I'm Real Cocoa Milk to wash down the bitterness. Her mother left a silly straw in each glass, which Ruijie knocked aside with an imperious hand. She could still grip things.

Ruijie counted her pills, eleven in total, including a giant ruby capsule she liked to imagine as a blood pill, and she a morally disciplined vampire.

Her father joined her with his plate of burnt-scraped toast by the time she swallowed pills number four, five, and six. Her mother was still pacing in the living room on the phone with the hospital, murmuring, "I just don't believe you're a person. I'd like to speak to a real representative . . . ," and while Ruijie would rather wait for her mother, she knew her father was most pliable before breakfast in his sluggish state. This was hardly a small request, what she had in mind. It was a birthday and Christmas and graduation present rolled into one.

"Baba, can I have a robot?"

"We have a robot," her father yawned, gaze flicking up as Sichun, their housekeeper, brought a pot of coffee. "Sichun is family."

"Not that kind of robot. I want a real robot, something that looks like us."

Her parents were weak to her, a power imbalance she tried not to abuse. Be not one of those kids who whined and tantrumed for things, things, things. Rather, be sly and hoard requests, dole them out with great pomp, so her parents would know that when she did ask, it was worthy.

Her father was chewing slowly, which meant he was thinking, because he had grown up with four brothers and he usually inhaled his food. "You know how I feel about those robots."

"Amelia from my school has an android."

"Isn't Amelia that bot-wired kid?" He turned in supplication to Ruijie's mother, who strode into the kitchen, still on hold. "I don't want you depending too much on them."

"I'll do all my chores and homework. I won't use them like that."

"No social skills whatsoever," her father told her mother. "Amelia's the one who couldn't go anywhere without a nanny, right? The robot was supposed to do all the talking for her."

"That girl couldn't speak any English," her mother said.

"No, there's another girl, an American."

"Amelia's Canadian," Ruijie said. She shoved back her chair, her robowear scraping against the wood, and grabbed her dishes for Sichun, who was waiting by the sink. Sichun was an old model who had followed them across three continents. Her father swore only a Chinese-brand robot could make proper Szechuan food.

Ruijie noticed a dent on one of Sichun's silver fingers, water running over it, as she washed each plate. "Did you hurt your finger?"

"It's okay," Sichun told her in Mandarin. "It doesn't hurt."

When her cat, Smaug, had died, Ruijie had been furious with Sichun, who felt, to her, no different from the mosquito Ruijie had slapped and left as a smear on the wall, another reminder of an unjust world where a mosquito or an old robot would get to live and Smaug would die.

But Sichun was slowing down and would break down one day. And when she did, she'd leave this tiny teal kitchen to end up as scrap in the salvage yard.

"Mei, you're going to be late for school," her mother called out. "Did you charge up?"

Upstairs, Ruijie plugged in her robowear. Stuck to the charging station, she stretched out one hand for her closet and grabbed bags and scarves, and pulled out a cat. A little black cat, rigid but still so warm in her lap. Ruijie remembered the hopeful look on her father's face, bright as a sunflower, when he sang softly, We have a surprise for you, and he unzipped the cat carrier. She'd heard the mewl and for a moment she was deceived. *Smaug,* she thought. Smaug fell sick but now she's better, and Ma and Ba waited for the right moment to bring her home.

But it wasn't Smaug. Ruijie stroked the cat, scratching behind the tufted ears, and could not bring herself to turn it on. The cat was designed to look like Smaug and act like her, affectionate and frightened and a little needy. A pretender.

Still, Ruijie hugged the cat, a long squeeze, then put it back in the closet.

"WHAT TIME SHOULD I pick you up from school?" her mother asked as she adjusted the strap on Ruijie's backpack, the belt of the robowear.

"Five," Ruijie said.

"Why always so late?"

"I told you, we're working on our history project. Second Korean War."

"Oh, I think this country is going to need more time to figure out how to tell that story." Her mother leaned over to open the car door and hugged Ruijie one-armed. "Text me, okay?"

Ruijie passed a familiar commotion in the parking lot. Her classmate Mars, full name Martin Koo, tumbled out of a car, shouting, "One day I'm going to become rich and famous and you'll regret this," and his mother shouted back, "Put on your socks!" flinging a ball of socks in his face.

Mars stuffed the socks in his pocket and growled "What?" to Amelia Delacroix, who was holding hands with a slim woman in a suit. With a roll of her eyes, Amelia whispered to her robot, who bent her knees to tilt an ear, and they parted in laughter of tinkling girlish collusion. The robot looked Korean. She had a classic

Imagine Friends shine in her blue-black hair and rosebud lips that she pressed to the top of Amelia's head. "Have a great day at school. You'll win them all."

Summer school was like normal school, but worse because it ruined the summer. It finished at three o'clock. All the classes were advanced, like Intermediate Coding, but also indulgent, like Korean History, which had neatly compressed North Korean history into a chapter. Ruijie spent class gazing out the window toward the steel fence that ran between the school and the silvergrass field, where she could see, hidden behind the rust-furred statue of Dolly, the first Shweep, a secret entrance to the salvage yard.

At quarter past three, she tossed her backpack to the dirt and army-crawled through the hole in the fence, straining her robowear at every joint. She waded through the thick, fluffy field. A mysterious pleasure, stumbling upon the abandoned. Robots sleeping like long-necked dinosaurs. Robots in sleek jeweled tones. Robots with magnetic hooks hanging from their mouths like a pair of shoes by their laces.

She found the SADARM closer to the edge of the field. The womb was empty.

"Yoyo?"

She called out his name in a shout-whisper in case any scrappers were nearby. The battery of her robowear was full. Leaving the safety of the silvergrass, she wandered out into the open, and after ten minutes of aimless sweating, she came across the nose of an abandoned bullet train, still attached to four carriages. It cut neatly through the middle of the salvage yard. Kids from her school called the train the DMZ, although most high schoolers used it for making out. Beyond the train was no-man's-land, where discarded robots, increasingly humanoid, whimpered for their owners. Waves of electromagnetic life flickered from crushed innards as their limbs twitched, their eyes juddered. Scrappers, wearing the lurid orange uniforms, picked at their bones.

There were rumors of still-active killer robots locked away in warehouses. Of a seventeen-year-old scrapper who had taken a misstep and been crushed into a cube, his death written off as a workplace accident.

Ruijie ducked into the shadow of the train and drank some water. She peeked through one of the cracked windows to see if Yoyo might be there.

"Hello?"

A voice repeated this in English. Then in Korean, "Excuse me?"

Ruijie shoved her water bottle back into her backpack and circled the train, but the voice wasn't coming from inside. She went west, following the patient cries of "Excuse me?" to a pyramid of cars. Most were old white cabs, which had been overtaken by the blue autocabs. In one, the doors were missing and a passenger sat in the back.

"Hello." The woman smiled at Ruijie. Her face was super familiar. "What is your name? Where is your mother?"

"She's at work. She works from home."

"Are you lost?"

"I'm all right."

"Would you like me to sing a lullaby?"

Ruijie squinted. "Oh, you're a Yuna. Are you an older model?"

The Yuna's head twitched. "I'm sorry, I don't understand your question. It's so noisy in here."

The beauty of her face was striking, and it clashed with the horrid shade of her hair, a red so blunt it must have been squeezed out of a bottle. Something was also wrong with her legs. She was sitting upright as she talked to Ruijie; she'd steer her head, her torso, but her knees stayed locked together.

"Wait here, I'll go get my friend. He's a robot, too, so he'll be able to help you."

Ruijie cranked up the speed of her robowear to loop back to the SADARM, in case Yoyo had returned. Where could he have gone? Whenever she called his name, he'd show up, intuitive as a stray cat.

Reluctantly, she returned to the taxi.

A boy was already there, but it wasn't Yoyo. He was bespectacled and whip thin, holding a bucket and a crowbar slung over a hard shoulder as he studied the Yuna robot in silence.

It was Taewon Kim, the tallest kid in her grade. Which wasn't that impressive, since he was supposed to be twelve going on thirteen. He was one of the North Korean scholarship kids, so that could have been why he was held back a year. He hadn't signed up for summer school, but she knew he worked here part-time, and every time she'd spotted him in the yard, she'd turned in the opposite direction.

Like now: Ruijie hid behind a construction bot and watched. Her Delfi could zoom in to count the freckles on Taewon's nose, but she had to rely on her ears to hear what they were saying.

"Your bucket looks heavy," the Yuna said. "Would you like me to carry it for you?"

She reached for the handle, but Taewon took a wide step back and she fell to the dirt. He dropped the bucket and hauled her out by the arm, yanking the rest of her body from the car.

"Stay down," Taewon said, and Yuna dutifully laid her head on the dirt. "My uncle's looking for you."

"Did you find your mother?" Yuna said.

Taewon crouched and Ruijie thought, Maybe he's found a switch that will loosen the lock on Yuna's legs and he'll help her up. Instead, he lifted her arm and unhooked a rose-gold bracelet from her wrist, which he then pocketed.

WHEN RUIJIE RETURNED to the SADARM, she found a chittering pile of gold bees on the ground. The gold on their bodies was a thick metallic paste instead of fur, the stripes silver. They faced her in one cold movement, eyes glossy and tame. She stepped closer, and they rose in a mythic cloud, leaving behind Yoyo, who was lying with his hands folded, eyes shut. Tranquil.

"Are you dead?" Ruijie said.

"Not yet," he replied. "They were helping me charge."

"You have to get up. We have to hide you now."

Yoyo sat up. His leisureliness both frustrated and relieved her. It had taken her about a week to notice how Yoyo would often accommodate but not exactly obey her.

Could he run? His leg was damaged, a stump that could skew and skid. And Taewon, he wasn't just the tallest boy in their grade. He was stronger and faster than anyone she'd ever met.

"We need to fix your leg," Ruijie said.

The bees agreed, crawling up and down Yoyo's leg fretfully. The skyn below his knee was scraped clean. An archeological dig of his shin, the translucent mesh wrapped around muscle and bone, the wires tangled purple. Chunks of precious gold embedded in the bone. His ankle ended in a stump where another pair of bees clung, quivering.

"Hey, you." Yoyo plucked one of the bees. Solid gold. It squirmed, legs scrabbling. "What are you still doing here?" The queen perched on his finger. "Go home," he said, and the queen launched into the open sky.

"If they find you," Ruijie said, "promise you'll act like you're not a robot."

"Okay."

Then he said, "What does it mean to act like a robot?"

She thought of her housekeeper, Sichun, who was slowing down, of Amelia's nanny kissing the crown of that coppery head, of the cat she hid in her closet. All the robots trying to be something they were not.

She told him, "Just be yourself."

4. That's All, Folks

A PAIR OF ROBOTS BOWED IN UNISON, WITH THE FLUORES-cent cry "Welcome to the MiniMart!" They looked like watermelon prisoners in their uniforms, striped white and green.

This was the closest MiniMart to Eli's apartment, fifteen minutes away in Itaewon. The ratings weren't even that great. "Rude manager" and "junk cashier." But Stephen had pointed out it was the only store to stock I'm Real Strawberry Juice. Strawberries were Kim Sunduk's favorite fruit. A rarity in Pyongyang.

Jun hummed as he looked for the juice. He loved convenience stores, their orderly, sumptuous chaos. Shrimp-flavored chips and peanut butter bombs. A whole verdant shelf devoted to matcha, from the tea to the crepes. Rice milk and persimmon makgeolli from North Korea. Under fresh foods, North Korean tofu rice and kimbap in different flavors, like bulgogi, tuna kimchi, spicy pork, and wasabi mayo fried chicken. Refrigerated aisles of lamb burgers, red curry, blood sausage, meat on sticks, and bento boxes, with eleven different banchan, from seasoned spinach to quail eggs stewed in soy sauce. A venerable castle of ramen. Beside it, the hot water dispenser had a blue speech bubble that read OW! HOT!

Then, his right ear gave a brusque ring and he tapped with his pointer finger. "Hi, Sergeant. Yeah, I'm at the MiniMart. Not yet. Yeah, CCTV, but I don't see the manager anywhere. AWOL for sure." Jun weighed a bag of roasted pistachios in his palm. "Do I have time to swing by the apartment after? I have to talk to the robot from next door. Stephen. I know, fancy English name."

Jun gave the rundown on Stephen, who was a "friend" of their missing robot ("Are they having sleepovers?" Sgt. Son said) and had been the last to see Eli before she disappeared. When Sgt. Son asked if Jun had obtained the owner's permission to further question Stephen, Jun cut in, "Yeah, not going to happen."

"You know her," Sgt. Son said, a smidge too shrewd. "Who is she? An ex?"

The horror! "My younger sister."

"You told me you were an only child."

"I know, I'm just really ashamed of my family."

"Your sister's a roboticist?"

"My father too," Jun said. "Explains a lot, doesn't it?"

Sgt. Son sighed eloquently. As soon as the call ended, Jun found what he was looking for. Strawberry juice, certified fresh, though the brand screaming *I'm Real* made it rather suspect.

"Is that all for your owner?" the cashier said.

Jun gave a sharp laugh and flashed his badge, which prompted an apology. It wasn't the first time he'd been mistaken for a robot, but the reckonings felt gentler these days. A shy beep when a text message arrived in his head. The subtle pings to indicate the precise fullness of his bladder. Kindly reminders that just 22 percent of his body was him.

"You've seen this robot before?" Jun said, holding up a picture of Eli.

The cashier studied Eli's cheery, common face. "This customer visited on July thirty-first our Itaewon branch MiniMart. Everyone's favorite and friendliest convenience store."

Questioning a robot was usually refreshing. No motive to lie. Eager to be of service. Impeccable memory. He asked if he could check the security cameras and was told he'd need permission.

"Fair enough. Can I talk to the manager?"

Manager was obviously a trigger, because the cashier bowed in a series of quick, painful snaps. "I'm sorry, customer! I'm sorry, customer! I'm sorry—"

A very tall, thin man groaned through the employee door. "Sorry, sorry. Just leave it. Lemme—" He grabbed the cashier's chin, which felt more violent than smacking her.

She quieted.

"What do you need?" The manager squinted at Jun's badge. "CCTV? We wipe everything at the end of the day."

"Well, that's convenient. Can I sync up with her?"

"Sync who?"

Jun reached for the back of his neck. Wireless exchange was cleaner, but he didn't want to risk interrupting the download and starting over. With his thumbnail he flicked open a skyn-covered lid and pulled the wire feeding directly from his brain stem. The friction of the wire against his skyn pinged a ragged shudder up his spine.

"Sick!" the manager said, delighted. "Are you some kind of new silicon?"

"Cutting-edge," Jun said.

While he never enjoyed it when robots mistook him for their own—it came with a slight pressure for reciprocity and commiseration—he indulged the occasional power trip in tricking people. He got to feel like a magician, a master of misdirection, his partial robotness a shiny distraction to cement how, in fact, he was indisputably, irrevocably male. In the past, every time he was misgendered, he'd felt it, sharp and cool, like an ice pick between his ribs. But this? This was just a tickle in the throat, of amusement or a viral cold.

"Where do I stick this?" Jun said, holding up the tip of the wire.

The manager yanked up the cashier's shirt. "I dunno, somewhere here?"

"I'll do it, handsy." Jun snatched the hem, lifting the shirt enough to air the side panel in the cashier's ribs. He eyed the name tag above her shirt pocket. BONGSUN. A folksy country-girl name. "This'll hurt," he told her.

The cashier smiled beatifically as he jabbed the wire into her flesh.

Like an injection from a needle, the memory bloomed from a tender, itching pinprick. It surged up the pole of Jun's spine, wrapped around his shoulders and neck until he could feel his

Adam's apple throb. He closed his eyes. Watching the cashier's memory overlay his vision in crackling panes stuffed up his head, and his lone bionic eye burned within the socket. He wanted to touch it, gingerly, but resisted. The memory was a camera-eye, a crystalline view of what had happened without the blur of subjectivity. He couldn't control it. Pause, fast-forward, rewind, none of that. Time rolled. Numbers blinked green in the corner.

Eli's elfin face came into focus. TOO COOL FOR SCHOOL.

Hey, Eli, Jun thought, and he almost smiled.

She placed the bottle of I'm Real Strawberry Juice on the counter, some salty snacks. Jun, possessing the cashier, rang it up, his lips in a rictus of friendliness. Eli asked for cigarettes, "Arctic Fire Mary, please," which struck him as rather hip for a woman in her eighties. To pay with her owner's account, Eli lifted her wrist, and Jun aimed his barcode scanner over her pulse point. She was shockingly lifelike for "shit code." As the cashier bagged everything, Eli drummed her palms on the counter, singing the mountain bunny song, except she'd tweaked the lyrics, swapping *bunny* for *strawberry*:

"Mountain strawberry, mountain strawberry, where are you going? Hop hop hopping into my mouth. There you go."

A man behind Eli laughed, a gusty chuckle, more air than mirth.

"Will that be all for your owner?" the cashier said, the shape of this phrase familiar to her mouth, and now, his.

The LED behind Eli's ear lit up. "That's all, folks!" and she laughed, pleased with herself. Then she walked off the frame, quite literally. Jun tried to follow her, but he remained rooted behind the counter.

Next customer. A reed of a man, even taller and thinner than the manager, held out two soju bottles one-handed, long fingers wrapped around their necks. Jun couldn't see his face, but the skin on the hand was dark and cracked, a laborer, maybe a foreigner. Hard to tell with sun-wrecked skin. A bright orange windbreaker hung loose over his shoulders while the left arm ended above the elbow in a knotted sleeve, which the man had tucked into his front pocket.

Jun heard the door jingle as it opened—Eli, about to leave—when the man hollered, "Hey, Sakura!"

A polite pause, as if Eli had stopped and turned to look at the man. He slouched by the counter with a greasy air of confidence, almost flirtatious. "Come over here."

Obediently Eli skipped up to him. Jun again tried to look at the man's face. But the cashier's attention was fixed to the flat teal surface of the counter. Not once had she looked a customer in the eye.

Laughter and music, both deranged in volume. The man handed Eli one of the soju bottles. She cradled it against her chest. Now they had a point of contact. Jun willed the cashier to *look up* and *look* at the suspect, but her gaze remained meek, so all he could do was commit the man's hand to memory. The tremor of his knuckles, the bluish hue of his fingernails, a voice in Jun's head murmuring, *VR addict*.

5. Imagine Friends

BELIEVE IN YOURSELF GREETED MORGAN AT THE ENTRY TO Imagine Friends' headquarters, the heart of the golden vein in Gwanghwamun Square where the resurrected stream of Cheonggyecheon, sprawling longer after reconstruction, flowed past their manicured lobby.

This was the highlight of her day: prancing past the revolving doors, the cool veil of air-conditioning draping over her face like a benediction, dominoes of holographic walls coming to life, whispering, *Good morning, Morgan* and *Are you ready to change the world, Morgan?*

The lobby was enshrined within the lifelike Arashiyama Bamboo Forest, where the air was mysterious and moist without the disruptive taint of tourists. She stammered hello at the security guard who grunted back, and skittered through the gate, clutching her jasmine bubble tea, just relieved she wasn't ignored.

Someone shouted "Wait up!" and Cristina ("Hi, I'm Cristina without the *h*!") spun through the door, waving effusively.

Morgan wished she could shut the elevator doors to save her life. Dutifully she held them open. Then Cristina greeted the guard, handing him coffee from Bitter Monday, and asked about his daughters, his back pain, and meanwhile Morgan was still holding the elevator like an imbecile when the guard told Cristina "Go right in" and opened the gate for her.

"Sorry, sorry," Cristina said, and the elevator finally took off. "Morgan, how are you? Oh, we're both so late. Did you get any sleep last night? I was up until two finalizing the talking points, and then I couldn't just lie down on my bed, so I went for a run in the rain! Best feeling ever."

"That sounds so healthy," Morgan said.

Cristina was their project manager, which meant an MBA and a month of coding boot camp. A tragically pretty thirtysomething who had ruined her cheekbones with excessive biohacking, she had eyes that dazzled violet from installed Delfi lenses. Her piercings, studding her brow, nose, and ears, were infant satellites. Her bionic ratio was definitely lighter than Jun's, but after seeing him this morning, Morgan found it sobering to realize Cristina looked more like a freak.

They chatted emptily about their project, Boy X, which would be available in stores from September 1. It had already been a few weeks since Boy X was delivered to celebrities and critics for the unboxing reviews. So far, they'd only gleaned reactions for the female counterpart, the Sakura·X. Predictably positive. Just a few caveats, like the slightly slow response system, which Marketing would spin as Sakura's "dreamy" persona. But today they had been promised their first major review.

TEN YEARS AGO, the first Sakura had debuted at the World Robot Expo. Kanemoto Masaaki had lifted the Sakura's arm, a referee anointing his champion boxer. Since that dizzying standing ovation, Imagine Friends had hijacked what was a middling companion market littered with cutesy dogs that could rap and R2-D2 rip-offs, changing the face of robotics by molding it firmly in their own image—that of man.

Last year, at the same World Robot Expo, Christian Po, former venture capitalist and now their CEO, had announced the Future X Project. For their tenth anniversary, they would roll out special-edition X models throughout the year, tiered for each season.

CHILDREN IN THE SPRING
GIRLFRIEND IN THE SUMMER
BOYFRIEND IN THE FALL
CARETAKER IN THE WINTER

"This," Christian Po had said at the expo, "is our Future."

Everyone sneered at the Children's team. Coding children was tricky, but most developers, fresh out of college, thought of them as simpering, lisping dolls to wind up and release. This had resulted in generations of shitty children, incestuously compiled from stale repositories and a tainted genome, the personality equivalent of the Habsburg jaw.

In her senior year at MIT, Morgan had applied to Imagine Friends for the Women's department. The most lucrative. Maybe slightly misnomered. They soft-rejected her by referring her to Children's, supposedly a better fit. In hindsight, she was relieved. When she was still working on Sixth Avenue, she'd look out the window and spot the Women's department on the basketball court shouting stuff like *offside* and *backcourt*, terms she had to look up, while some of the grungier, gothier members of the team had heckled from the sidelines.

"Ready for today's meeting?" Cristina said. "The review has to be great, right? It needs to be good."

Everyone from the Boy X project had been invited to the meeting, from the dev team to design, forcing Morgan to grab a chair in the back. Better than being a tardy who'd have to stand against the wall as their feet swelled.

The conference desk was a slab of soft pale wood, as if they had taken the blondest tree they could find and sacrificed it. Little David, their lead programmer, sat near the head, showing off his new Delfi to a gaggle of design girls. He'd finished registering his fingerprints and now he was manipulating a screen midair, gloating about how intuitive it was, the way it could stretch instantly like taffy to cover the walls and ceiling and warp into an immersive theater.

Big David, sitting in front of Morgan, was watching a soppy Platinum Age film with Zhang Zizhen, a reclusive actress who had retired years ago. Two or three from the Sakura·X team flitted around the buffet, ladling hummus onto their paper plates, which were prone to drooping. No doubt here to gloat if the reviews for Boy X flopped.

The meeting began with Cristina warming them up, ticking off the three Ts (Today's Tangible Tasks), before segueing into Marketing's efforts to hype up the Future X Children.

Morgan stress-ate strawberry jellies. They were organic, which meant they tasted like rubber, and sat awful and heavy in her stomach. Everyone in the office called them strawberry bellies. She messaged Stephen, who was always online, This is nerve-racking.

His reply: The wait must be awful. Would you like to read an article about your father instead?

She muted him. Stephen's predictive response pattern had become too predictable.

A bang on the table. Cristina must have punched it. Every meeting, Cristina tried to sell action against robot abuse as a top priority, citing "abused Sakura" this and "murdered Yuna" that.

"We should think of a stronger safety valve in our first update for Boy X, so they can defend themselves."

"Wait, what?" Big David said. "Isn't that dangerous?"

Imagine Friends companions stored twice the strength of humans in half the muscle mass. Say someone broke into their home: Stephen could conceivably protect Morgan in the name of self-defense. She liked to imagine he'd whip out some Taekwondo moves like Ko Yohan, who played a double agent in *The Dispossessed*, but obviously deadlier. Still, once in a while, people tried to kick up a legal kerfuffle, claiming they'd been attacked by an IF. Most famous was the Jiho-5 who broke a man's arm in an elevator, but the leaked security footage turned the public's opinion overnight. *Robot beats up would-be rapist* had trended for a week.

Self-defense meant the owner's defense. If companions began defending themselves, that'd be the premise of every terrible bot flick and, more importantly, a huge problem.

"What I mean is, we could program stronger aversive stimuli. More flight over freeze." Cristina's voice quivered, not with fear, but worse, with passion. "I've submitted a proposal. After Boy X, I want a team of hand-selected warriors to focus on our most ambitious update yet so we can protect our children and our future."

Cristina was like an eco-flush toilet, well-intentioned and ineffective.

"La Capitana makes a fantastic point on safety valves." Joe pointed at Cristina with finger guns. "I'll make sure to add it in the next Cup o' Joe."

The Cup o' Joe was their daily morning email, which sounded more annoying than it was. Unlike Cristina, Joe was an engineer. The rare unicorn, an MBA and a doctorate in neurorobotics, and under his belt was the lauded study he had led at Stanford's infant research center on the sociomoral development from human-robot interaction. A few weeks into her Korea transfer, Morgan had the glowing pleasure of Joe taking her aside and quietly telling her how her father's theory on artificial empathy had caused a "significant paradigm shift" in his approach to robots. "Always was a fan," he said, with a wink. Then she had fretted for a week anticipating accusations of nepotism.

Joe hopped to his feet. "It took us years to earn our customers' trust. All it takes is one faulty robot to lose it."

In late February, the Boy X prototype had been a disaster. The girl was never going to be the issue. The Sakura·X was assured to be the lovable, if exhausted, face of the company. After rolling out a tauter, smarter Sakura child, the Children's team tried to cast an equally magnetic costar. Blond and gray-eyed, shy and bookish, a charming contrast with the bubbly Sakura, the Toby·X.

They were touching up the Toby·X for a run with focus groups when Joe herded them onto the roof on a windy Sunday morning. He yelled over the howling Shakespearean squall:

Dan Carson, twenty years writing tech for *The New Yorker*, also founder of the magazine *Singularity*, had published his opinion piece on the just-released Toby·IX.

After highlighting the flaws of Toby the Ninth, Dan Carson had eviscerated the entire children's line from Imagine Friends. He called them at best "saccharine" and at worst "coyly sexualized," like the "pouting, powdered contestants of a child beauty pageant." Most criminal was the Toby's non-corrective habit of watching his owners sleep because it made him feel "safe," which Morgan herself had pointed out as a potential issue, only to be dismissed.

We have two options, Joe shouted into their shivering huddle. Revamp Toby, or start from chicken scratch. Actually, they had only one option. But with six months to launch, the former was just barely feasible.

Joe negotiated a switcheroo for the release dates. The Yuna was still set for summer. Her prototype, filmed volleyballing in a sheer bikini made from jellyfish skin, had already broken preorder records. But the Boyfriend was now rescheduled for spring, targeting careerwomen with credit and anxiety to buff on White Day. By waving his magic wand, Joe was able to push Children X to September 1, no later.

Then he quarantined all forty-four members of the dev team in a conference room stocked with enough energy drinks and Fast Feast pills to last them until the end of the world. They were the crisis triage team for the brand-new Boy X.

Little David suggested digging up a child version of the sporty, cheery Jiho, dusting it off for a spin. He had fixated on just one of Dan Carson's criticisms—that Imagine Friends had elevated flaxen-haired whiteness as a shorthand for childhood innocence—and he said they should put out an Asian model. Just not another Japanese one.

What a moron, Morgan thought, then sneezed.

Twenty-six hours after Joe locked them up, Morgan raised her hand. She proposed her own prototype, which she'd designed in her spare time. She showed them simulations. Possible Boy X would be 140 centimeters tall, which was short for his preset age (twelve) but tall for the age they'd release (ten). Bowl haircut. Round face, wide, puckish eyes. A smile that needed braces.

"He's perfect," Joe said.

BEFORE REVEALING THE REVIEW, Joe gave them an eleven-minute bathroom break to clear their minds and unclog their chi.

Morgan slunk past Cristina, who was loudly reassuring the smug Sakura team that Boy X wouldn't become another Toby, which was fast fated to become a word for failure.

Morgan stepped out into the hallway, masticating strawberry jellies. Covering the walls was a sampling of Kanemoto Masaaki's art collection. The paintings of Mount Baekdu, each a different angle of the mountain. A tiny white tiger hid in every version among the evergreens and it took a quick and lazy Internet search to be able to Waldo all the tiger sightings. At the end of the series, Morgan encountered a freshly erected bronzed bust of Kanemoto. Brow crumpled, lips pursed, as if racked by Sartrean agonies.

He would have hated the bust. Not for immortalizing him but for the triteness of it, using such a dull, common replica. Kanemoto had his infamous *In Thy Image* series, where he'd made a robot of himself once every four years, since he was forty, an Olympics lit from the torch of his own ego. In his later years, when he seemed to have succumbed to Grothendieck's curse, wandering out onto the road barefoot and spitting—which was spun as *eccentric*, a nonsensical word that could apply only to a certain subset—the rumor was Imagine Friends had sent out his robotic replicas to present onstage at tech expos.

One of Kanemoto's replicas spoke at his own funeral. At least one journalist noted the replica was Kanemoto at fifty-two, which was his age when the first Sakura debuted. Morgan had a feeling her father had been invited to the funeral, but he definitely didn't go. The two had met at Princeton as roommates, starting out as psychology and mathematics majors, before their paths merged into neurorobotics. History now rather unfairly designated Kanemoto as the more dominant of the pair, but Morgan, growing up in the house, had overheard fights between her father and Kanemoto when they worked together on Project Jeju. At the end of every spat, it was Kanemoto who marched out, but Kanemoto who came crawling back. Until the day he didn't.

Project Jeju then crumbled, and within two years Kanemoto had established Imagine Friends, and her father began building his first animal, a green sea turtle, while sending his family pictures of baby bats from the window in his lab. She despaired for him. Her father was now obscure in the way younger roboticists would consider it hip to revere him. He had been wallowing in zoobotics since Kanemoto's passing. He needed a jolt. And this was why Boy X was partly his. The personality matrix was a design from Morgan's SB thesis, but the foundation belonged to her father, and every success she garnered would give him the credit he was rightfully due. Any failure would be her desecration of his life's work.

AFTER THE BREAK, Joe announced that the review would be published seventy-two hours before Launch Day, when Christian Po presented the Future X Children from New York. The name of their robot would remain secret, as stipulated for all the prerelease reviews.

Then Joe looked straight at Morgan with those unnerving blue eyes. She swallowed a strawberry jelly.

"Do you want the good news or bad news?" Joe said.

Morgan wheezed quietly. Dear God, she was choking on a strawberry jelly.

Little David drumrolled on the blond table, but was silenced by a glare from Cristina. Morgan coughed. She slunk to the water dispenser in the back and tried to fill a glass, but this was fruit infused and the overabundance of slices had colorfully dammed up the exit to the spout, so all it yielded was a pitiful dribble. She slunk back to her chair.

Her fingers raced to message Stephen. I'm choking on a straw-berry belly

Stephen sent a lurid chart of the self–Heimlich maneuver, but Morgan could not bring herself to stand in the middle of this meeting and line her stomach up against the back of her chair, so she pounded her chest instead, trying to dislodge the jelly, which Joe seemed to take as a sign of excitement.

He pulled up the review, lighting the whole wall.

BOY X IS REVOLUTIONARY

"Holy SHIT." Cristina bolted up, sending her chair careening into Morgan, who rammed against the edge of the table. A glutinous strawberry jelly bounced off the table, hit the floor. A Shweep promptly slurped it up.

"This is the good revolution, right?" Big David said. "This isn't, like, evil robot revolution, right?"

Little David lit virtual fireworks. Cristina hugged Morgan; repulsed but stunned, Morgan let her. Joe shouted but people were shouting over him. Cristina was crying messily without tears. Morgan tried to scream too, "Ahh!" "Ahhh!" quietly, testing if she was ready to be happy.

"Wait, what's the bad news?" Cristina said, finally calming down.

"Dan Carson emailed saying he wants to profile the team behind Boy X," Joe said.

"Isn't that *great* news?"

"He wants to talk to the 'main' personality programmer. I told him, 'Dan, we're a team, this is a team effort,' but he wouldn't budge. We'll have to discuss who's going to be our rep."

"It's got to be the lead," Little David said, even though he did fuck-shit.

Her glasses dinged with an emergency message from Stephen. **Morgan, are you all right? I've called the ambulance.**

ABORT!!

Paramedics burst into the room, shouting about a choking incident; Cristina yelled, "Joe, there's an ambulance outside"; and in a surreal turn, the lead paramedic was one of their own, the Jiho·5, whose sales for first responders had skyrocketed after the elevator wannabe-rapist incident.

"Is someone having a heart attack?" Joe said, alarmed.

Morgan studied a goop of hummus on the floor as the paramedics swooped on Little David, whose heart rate was judged as most at risk, even though he shrieked, "Wrong David!"

The rest of Dan Carson's review appeared in their most triumphant Cup o' Joe email yet:

> *Of the Big Three, Imagine Friends is the magician. The master of sleight of hand and illusions. The status light on the X models is a redesigned cherry blossom, tastefully hidden behind the left ear. Since the Sakura·5, they've switched to TongueNCheek skyn, purported to turn white if pressure is applied, just like the real thing.*
>
> *Previous child models from Imagine Friends have been criticized for being <u>unnatural</u>, <u>needy</u>, and—most egregious—<u>creepy</u>. The uncanny factor may be impossible to overcome. Boy X is fluent in more than 150 languages, including Gaelic. He will ask for his own stool in the kitchen, but he's too marvelous of a cook. For the World Cup finals, I invited friends who had the chance to enjoy a full-course Korean meal, inspired by the Royal Joseon Court.*
>
> *This time, Imagine Friends may have outdone themselves, and I'm not certain they're even aware of it. Once you select a base personality for Boy X, there's no fiddling with parameters, an option available for older models and the likes of those from Talos. In essence, you're ceding control, as if you're raising a real child.*
>
> *The reason is that Boy X uses a different kind of memory palace to digest his experiences, called the Hopper Network, conceived by lesser-known virtuoso <u>Yosep Cho</u>, the Steve Wozniak to Imagine Friends founder Kanemoto's Steve Jobs. Resetting Boy X's personality would be tantamount to killing him.*
>
> *Our first night, I took the boy with me to the grocery store because my wife needed eggs. I brought with me only one umbrella, and when it began to rain, he held the umbrella, which was a little awkward since I'm in a wheelchair.*

Briefly, I wondered how he'd react if I forced him to walk in the rain. When a robot skirts the line, I've noticed a cruel urge in myself, at least, to test the limits.

A car drove past, hitting a puddle. He jumped in front of me. He was drenched from head to toe. But he wore an impish smile, as if he had conquered a puddle, instead of following a tyrannical directive to shield me from the splash. It's details like this that moved and terrified me. He may have pretended to need me, but over the course of one week he persuaded me to need him. During this strange, feverish week, I struggled with two opposing impulses: to hug Boy X and never let go, or to open him up and see if he just might be human.

6. Magpie Boy

THE MOST VALUABLE PART OF ANY ROBOT WAS THE HEAD. Taewon cradled one in his lap, sitting on the roof on the old bullet train, with a pile behind him of mostly skulls and grins. He started digging out the eyes with the good spoon he'd swiped from the cafeteria. Uncle Wonsuk had promised to help during his lunch break, but here he was smoking through his pack, complaining about his supervisor, who'd accused Wonsuk of misappropriating equipment from the factory warehouses, which he had, but this supervisor was obviously a prick who expected a dog's death of all North Koreans. Wonsuk flicked his cigarette at a darting dragonfly but missed. The dragonflies slapped their tails on the steel roof, mistaking the lustrous surface for water, laying their eggs to melt.

Taewon crossed his legs, tingling from the heated steel, but he liked the height, the feeling of looking down on the rest of the world's trash.

"There she goes," Wonsuk laughed.

They had the vantage eye of the silvergrass field as Liu Ruijie made her pilgrimage to the junkyard, three times a week. Her robowear was too bright, shiny as an airplane. She did not belong here.

Wonsuk tossed his dead cigarette to the ground. "What's wrong with her legs?"

He asked this every time he saw Ruijie.

"Nothing's wrong with her," Taewon said.

"She must have some high-end parents," Wonsuk said, another cigarette between his teeth, leaning into his lighter's dab of flame. "You can tell with the attitude. Way she acts like she doesn't hear a word I'm saying."

"She's Chinese."

"And they don't teach Korean at your fancy school?"

Taewon rammed the spoon into the eye socket of the skull. It took some wiggling, but the eyeball slurped out with a gasping pop. Satisfying. He lifted the eye to find the logo for Talos, faint but there. It went into the bucket of blues, greens, a few browns, one crimson from a special-edition albino. Most of the robots who ended up in the dirt were junk, no-name brands, prime for recycling: detachable limbs, scoopable eyes, pryable chips.

Every scrapper dreamed of the perfect find. A robot of such faultless condition, it'd be sacrilege to pull it apart. A robot with advertisements of it still flashing across the flanks of buses. Or a robot of such rarity, maybe with Kanemoto Masaaki's personal signature branded above the clavicle, and years later it would appear smiling at a Sotheby's.

When the heat went straight to Taewon's head, he dreamed of finding such a robot.

The Yuna he had found in the old taxi, after escaping from his uncle, was a popular model. But outdated. Of perhaps equal value was the pinkish gold bracelet on her wrist, which Taewon had pawned, after checking the stamp for K18.

Wonsuk made a gleeful sound; Ruijie had just stumbled onto the SADARM, which was definitely the unwitting home of a wasp nest.

"She's going to wake that killer robot," Wonsuk said.

"That robot's dead."

"That's what they want you to think."

"Just leave her alone."

"Do you like her?"

He growled when Wonsuk tipped the bucket for a peek. "So touchy," Wonsuk said. "This country's turned you selfish."

Taewon always took the bucket straight to the supervisor, a small South Korean man with a smaller, miserly heart, who stuck to the air-conditioned factory floors and cracked jokes about the smoothness of Taewon's legs, which was a real sore point for him.

Still, better than his uncle pocketing the cash, promising to catch up on bills, only to vanish for the weekend.

His uncle stubbed his final cigarette against the roof and stood for a stretch. He was growing a beer belly, an obscene little bump that bulged from his long, rangy body. The sleeve of his left arm flapped in the breeze. Wonsuk raked his fingers through his stringy hair and slapped on a baseball cap, tilting it at a rakish angle to show off the slogan TOO COOL FOR SCHOOL.

Taewon grabbed the bucket when his uncle reached for it. He slid down the ladder, skipping the last few rungs, and landed on the dirt, a slight twinge blooming in his knees.

His uncle shouted after him, "You see any stray silicons, you tell me."

Taewon wished he could drop school and scrap full-time. Every time he left the yard, away from the interference, his phone would light up, drowning in messages from Mars complaining about tangents. Summer school was a joke.

But the supervisor wasn't in today. Taewon doubled back to the train to stash the bucket there for a half day. Plus, he'd left his favorite spoon on the roof.

There it was, lying face up by the roof's ladder, hot to the touch. He shoved the spoon into his pocket, and was about to slip down when he heard voices from the other side of the train. He flattened himself against the roof, hissing under his breath when the steel scalded his forearms and knees. The cool thing was, he felt like a sniper.

It was Ruijie, with a boy. Taewon didn't know him. He looked small, drowning in a large yellow shirt, so maybe he was from the year below.

"It's stuck," Ruijie grumbled, yanking at the door.

The doors to the train were welded shut. The only way to enter the train was through the fourth carriage, where Taewon had been planning on hiding his bucket until these interlopers showed up.

The boy stuck a finger through the crack, then the rest of his hand. He grabbed the edge and the metal *screeched*, a bone-deep rumble for Taewon, who lay flat on the roof, as the boy pried the door open, widening the crack enough for Ruijie to slip through. She admonished him with a shush. "We'll be found!"

"Then we'll hide again," the boy said.

Taewon dropped down the ladder. Through the train window, he could see the boy's hazy profile. The Salvation Army shirt. The boy was dressed like a magpie kid. Taewon still had vague memories of the North. Kids begging in the train station in Pyongyang. Their yellow shirts, plastic bags tied around their ankles, scratching heads full of lice, sidling up to anyone who looked like a target. Tweety Birds, the Americans called them, because of the shirts, but the South Korean soldiers had known better. They were magpies. Wily and nasty and needy.

The boy looked up and Taewon ducked. But he'd seen enough to know this boy was no magpie.

7. The Eyes Are the Windows

RUIJIE WOKE SUDDENLY. SHE FELT A TINGLE OF UNEASE, maybe from the tattered hem of a dream, prophetic and incoherent. Or it could just be the itch on her face. A light sunburn. Before falling asleep in the train, she'd split a sandwich with Yoyo and talked about their favorite VR games. He had an outdated database, preferring *Journey of Nerieh* over *Legend*, *Warsong* over *Warcry*. She watched him eat in a deliberate manner, separating each ingredient, peeling the mayo-wet lettuce from the clinging cheese, and asked if that had to do with his digestive system.

He shook his head. "It's more fun to eat this way."

"Do you have to eat to survive?"

Not with a triple-source battery, which meant Yoyo could sluice energy from multiple origins, including electric, sun, and, if need be, food. "Which source is your favorite?" she asked, leaning forward.

He'd demurred. "It's like apples and oranges."

Yoyo was still fast asleep, curled up like a sun-soaked cat, so maybe his battery wasn't really that efficient. Where the square of sunlight hit his cheek, a tiny pulse moved under the skyn. A hungry little worm, eager to drink up the rays. She poked his cheek. He'd sleep through a typhoon with a smile on his lips. She poked harder. She knew robots could feel pain. The city cleanbots all had small speech bubbles taped to their rears, DON'T SMACK ME, I HURT!, which seemed to invite more kicks from the drunks in Itaewon.

Leaving Yoyo to his sleep, she gathered her robowear from the floor and buckled each joint from the ankle to her thigh, reapplying the bandage behind her knee to cool a sweat rash. She tried to cinch the belt around her waist, but a spasm pierced up her spine. She squeezed her jaws and eyes shut. Loosening the belt, she stared out the window in a haze. Her vision finally settled and she saw three figures, blurred from the heat shimmer, walking toward the train.

Taewon led with his graceful, loping gait, and waddling behind him was Mars Koo in long sleeves and a floppy wide-brimmed hat, hacking away at anything in his path with the crowbar of a conquistador.

Farther behind, Amelia Delacroix, her copper hair poufed up like an air balloon, full of opinions. Amelia was inadequately dressed for the yard: her shoes were Mary Janes and she was panting in a thick, antiquated velvet dress, like she'd elected to sit gravely for an oil painting.

"Are you sure this is the right way?" Amelia said. "The map says we're in the middle of the Pacific Ocean."

"Forget the GPS stuff," Mars said. "Keep your eyes peeled for my soccer ball. You should've seen Taewon kick it over the fence. How hard did you kick it?"

"Not too hard," Taewon replied.

"We're screwed!" Mars screeched.

"You don't even play *foot*ball," Amelia said with withering contempt.

"Stop pretending you're English. We all know you're Canadian. Plus, this is from the World Cup. My dad had to bribe a bunch of people to get a signed ball. He got it from that match, Korea versus—versus—"

"Sweden," Taewon said.

"Exactamento. It's one of a kind."

"Are they friendlies?" Yoyo asked.

Ruijie jolted; she hadn't noticed him waking up or joining her by the window. He rested his chin against the ledge, his eyes alert with the taint of pleasure. "I've seen him before," he said, and Ruijie realized he meant Taewon, who was wiping his glasses with the hem of his shirt.

"He's *un*friendly. He's with the scrappers. He's dangerous."

"The other boy?"

"Mars? He's the opposite of dangerous."

"And the girl?"

"She's annoying."

Mars and Amelia argued: It's too hot, Mars complained; then they should give up on his dumb soccer ball and head back to school; so he backtracked, let's take a break, the sun has made barbarians of them both, and it was now obvious they were eyeing the train as a rest stop.

Ruijie gasped when she felt the train move, even if it was an ineffectual shudder. Mars, trying to yank the door open, leaning all his weight on dug heels, while Amelia's disapproving sniffs punctuated his groans.

"Let's get out of here," Ruijie whispered. She wished she could chase the others off. But the visual of her limping and waving at them, like an old man growling over his woeful patch of yard, was too distressing.

"We can let them in," Yoyo said. "They're no danger to us."

Mars shouted, "Hello? Is someone in there?"

Ruijie cursed, but Yoyo—oblivious—strode forward and pulled the door open, allowing Mars to tumble into the train.

"Salvation!" Mars cried out. Then he stared.

Amelia joined him, with a face of such adultlike consternation. "Ruijie? What are you doing here?" A polite but measuring pause. "Who's your friend?"

Ruijie had a story prepared. Yoyo was her cousin, his name was Rongyo, and when they inevitably noticed his leg, she told them that he had the same disease as her—here, she expected the majority to tactfully drop the subject—and he had bionic surgery, and, yes, there were some complications, yes, he needed a new foot, some new clothes . . .

Amelia's stunned gaze traveled down Yoyo's body, lingering on his stump, before it pinged back, cowed by the explanation of this "genetic disease." It was Mars who absurdly pointed out, "What happened to your shoes?"

"I lost them," Yoyo said.

"Want us to help look for them?" Mars nodded, with unnecessary gravitas. "I've lost something too."

"I'm all right."

"You don't feel pain in that foot or anything?"

"Stop asking so many questions," Amelia hissed. "You're being so rude."

Ruijie was relieved to see acceptance had sedated them, or it could be the heat. Mars flopped onto the seat beside Yoyo with a walrus groan, while Amelia sidled up to Ruijie because it was so rude to ask Yoyo questions but fine to interrogate Ruijie. This peace was short-lived.

Taewon climbed onto the train. He flung a soccer ball at Mars, who *oof*ed as it hit him square in the chest. "Found it," Taewon said. "Now get out."

"We're just resting for a bit," Amelia said, folding her legs primly to one side.

Taewon stepped in front of Ruijie, but he was too slender to loom. "You can't take one of the robots."

"What robot?" Ruijie said, eyes wide.

Mars gave a big yawn. He pulled off his hat and fanned his face with it. "What are you on about? That's her cousin."

Tension coiled in Taewon's shoulders. He usually acted sedate in the classroom, like a wild animal tranquilized into submission, until he was released outside.

"She's lying," Taewon said. "I've seen them sneaking around here for days."

"So?" Ruijie scoffed. "We're treasure hunters. Yoyo waits for me until I finish summer school and I make sure we have some fun."

She was a good liar. It came part and parcel with navigating a world that condescended to you. And she was confident Yoyo wouldn't reveal anything. He didn't carry a status light or a discreet luxury logo, which Mars also pointed out. "It's not like he's got a battery light. You know, the blinky thing all robots have."

"Isn't it illegal for robots to hide it?" Amelia said. "In Canada, it'd be like a car without a license plate."

"This isn't Canada," Taewon said.

"I know that!" Amelia said, twisting her garish Delfi ring on her finger. "Even so, we have to assume he's human until proven robot."

The sun had shifted. Taewon's face was pale against the darkness. Stray points of light winked from the rims of his glasses, his expression immutable. When he spoke, his voice was remote and calm.

"Every robot comes with a Trix chip. Imagine Friends has theirs behind the ear. If he's not Imagine Friends, then he's Talos. And Talos's chip is inside the left eye."

"Dude, you can't just take out someone's eye," Mars said.

Yoyo piped up, "I don't mind."

Mars chuckled. "He doesn't mind."

But Yoyo walked over. "If you want"—he touched Taewon on the wrist—"you can take my eye."

Taewon jerked away. Yoyo laughed as if he could feel the jagged edges.

"Do you have something like a spoon?" His willingness came across as both playful and cruel. "You could also just reach in with your fingers. A robot eye isn't like a human eye. It's not as wet and squishy. Much easier to pull out."

"We get it, you're pulling our plug." Mars looked around the train with a forced grin. "Get it? *Where's Your Plug*? You know, that show with the episode on the Buddhist monks and they're all bald but one of them is a robot, and you have to guess which one's the robot."

"Why would I act like a monk?" Yoyo said.

"I mean you're acting like a *robot*."

"Shut up," Taewon said. "Fine." He sounded furious with himself. "I'll do it."

"Do what exactly?" Ruijie said.

Taewon swiped his hand on his shirt. He cupped Yoyo's face

with both hands, thumbs out and ready around the temples, as if he were calmly measuring the face for a fitting. But Ruijie could feel nervousness radiating from him in resentful waves. When Taewon's thumb grazed the corner of Yoyo's eye, Amelia made an *eep*. Yoyo's iris jolted this way and that, following the thumb, as Taewon brushed the surface with a trembling fingertip.

Mars screamed.

Taewon wrenched away. "Gross, so gross!" Mars howled, and Taewon told him to shut up, but he was rubbing his hand against his leg, as if he could chase away the phantomness of the eye, and Yoyo was laughing.

"Leave him alone, he's my cousin," Ruijie shouted, and Yoyo's laughter shorted. He turned on her with a somber expression, as if she were the one in the wrong.

"You don't have to protect me. You've brought me food and water, though the latter is unnecessary, and I appreciate your kindness, which is why I want to be honest. I am a robot, even if I'm not very good at acting like one. I wasn't created for that purpose."

"Show us your plug," Mars said.

"No, Yoyo." Ruijie exhaled. "You don't have to show them anything."

She'd warned him. Be wary of Taewon; hide when you see him. But Yoyo had refused to play along. And now she had to explain to everyone how she was trying to get him out of here, and for that, they needed a new leg.

"Why can't we just buy him a new leg?" Amelia said.

"Not everyone's richie rich," Mars said.

"My parents are *professors*. You can give the store his serial number and he should be registered to an owner. I'm sure they'll fix him as long as he's still under warranty. My nanny is a Yuna·6, but when she lost her thumb, the store expedited a new hand in two days. Of course, we had to pay for the whole hand . . ."

Taewon left. He almost ran Yoyo over on his way to the exit, but he reared back at the last second as if his body couldn't bear the thought of their shoulders touching. When Ruijie met Yoyo's gaze, she received a somewhat helpless smile. She wanted to take his hand and console him. You learned to smile like that to cover for an even deeper hurt. She would know, for she was an expert on pain.

8. Wonderful, Wonderful World

IT WAS NEAR MIDNIGHT WHEN JUN FOUND ELI'S KIDNAPPER. He'd scanned the footage from multiple traffic cameras, triangulating the area around the MiniMart, a trapezoid that stretched from the main road of Itaewon down Usadan Street past the embassies of Iran, Qatar, and Romania, and the largest mosque in the country. This was his third day investigating Eli's case. On average, he split twenty to thirty cases with Sgt. Son, and together they had to decide what seemed solvable and what was going to be a slow, cancerous death. Robot Crimes was left alone as long as they made themselves scarce yet indispensable to other departments, especially Major Crimes. They had to be careful not to be a burden themselves.

Jun took a screenshot of the suspect's face and sent it to Sgt. Son. He rubbed his eye, which had turned hard as a marble. A headache was alive and well. He hadn't slept more than four hours per snatch. A clock was always ticking inside him, like the hungry crocodile from *Peter Pan*, and every minute he was awake, he missed VR so fucking much.

How did he know Eli's kidnapper was a VR addict?

In rehab, he'd learned the distinction between love and addiction. VR had started out as a crush in middle school, when Delfis were crude and bulky, smells glitched (roses smelling like shit, shit smelling like roses), and games came in only two flavors, space battles or fantasy RPGs. Then he started playing *Journey of Nerieh* while recovering from bionic surgery. It used to be his brother's favorite game. Now, Jun loved *Journey* for the same reason a child dreaded a hot bath and a depraved adult craved it. He loved every easy-peasy tulip and supple blade of grass. He loved the sweetness of hay as he bridled his unicorn and stroked the white star on their nose. VR made him love hiking. Hours and hours of hiking. He loved whittling wood and hunting for crystal mushrooms and getting occasionally eaten by crystal-cave trolls. For death was kind in virtuality and always he'd resurrect, standing with both feet firm on the ground.

Every time he fizzled to life, he'd return to a world where his brother might still exist. In *Nerieh*, battles are frequent and fun and bloodless, and monsters can be spared. You haven't broken your mother's heart yet, your sister doesn't wish you dead, and your commanding officer isn't screaming in your ear, *Don't let them fuck with your head.* Tedium's what fucked your head, after your squad gutted the shabby palace in Pyongyang, which was exhilarating at first until every framed portrait had been signed with piss, and the weeks bled into months faded into long beige hours of ennui punctuated by sporadic ecstatic bursts of fireworks whenever a high-value target lit up the map, flashing, and flashing again until you seize up. You're phoning your doctor at obscene hours because your body won't move from the agony.

Why can't the world be real? Why is the world so charcoaled you have to sift the ashes for chips of metal or bone, and when you snort out through one sooty nostril, your body ejects a tiny nugget of charcoal? A world without HVTs and Operation Blue Magpie and magpie children, without beggars missing limbs, and they slide around you by subway stations, belly down on wheeled slabs of construction wood, and every time you see them, you smell the bombed skies, the waft of burnt hair, the stench that converted you and now you're the very thing you once despised, a bloody vegetarian. With gardens that flourish, with resurrection circles and meditation mountains. With temples where you can turn into liquid, gas, or music. With sky somersaults. With walk-on-waters. No drowning, then. No accidents, no sickness, no shootings, no mass shootings, no children dying, no one has to die unless you really want to, unless you choose to give it a shot and see if it's as cathartic as your brother once said.

BUT YOU'RE CLEAN NOW, his father had said. Their last call happened five years ago. It was the tail end of rehab, so Jun had somewhat returned to baseline. He was scratching himself as his father mused about his new project on matriarchal whales and intergenerational memory, and Jun scrolled one-handed through Balenciaga sneakers to marvel at the unkind prices.

Morgan believed their father was a great man, and wasn't that a condemnation, for great men rarely made good men. She had their father's voice, flat, faint with scorn. Had it already been two years since she'd moved to Korea? At the start, their mother had tried to coax them to meet. But Jun had work and so did Morgan, and right before a halfhearted attempt at a reunion over Christmas, Morgan declared she was working through the holidays on a VIP, or "Very Important Project," and Jun shrugged in relief.

Yet he was always aware of her. The pressure continued to feel exigent, like the shadow North Korea used to cast for decades on the South, a constant reminder that just across the border is your deeply fucked-up sibling. In most retellings, that would be him.

That night when their father had picked him up from the ER, the ride back had remained silent and unbroken until his father glanced up at the rearview mirror, his face softly tired, and said:

"Do you have to act like human trash?"

JUN HAD MADE A PROMISE to himself: VR only in the house, low-level, just enough to lull him to sleep. He was still at work. But he needed a nap, so he sought out the TV in the break room, because he could muzzle it and try fooling himself into believing the flickering screen was unreality.

Sgt. Son was already slumped in front of it, watching *Where's Your Plug*.

"Who's winning?" Jun said.

"That's not the point of the show."

Sgt. Son's tone suggested he wanted nothing but silence, so Jun sat with him in support of this. He found it funny that Sgt. Son had secured a private showing for himself. For weeks, Sgt. Lee had been pestering them to join when Major Crimes would squeeze into the break room every Friday and watch *Foxy Detectives* and *Where's Your Plug*. *Detectives* was melodramatic, lavish with cliff-hangers, the TV sequel to the Ko Yohan movie, while *Plug* was a truly idiotic variety show that had been running for four years. The Big Three would slip in prototypes, mixing them with "real people," and celebrity panelists dissected elaborate scenarios to guess who was the hidden robot. In their most popular run, Imagine Friends' demure Sion-2 became a runaway hit for the Buddhist temple special after pretending to be a young monk-in-training.

"But he looked so *fresh*!" a duped singer had howled, and that became the marketing slogan for the newly released Sion: *So Fresh*.

Tonight's special was set in an elementary school where an undercover robot or two would be skulking among fifth-graders.

"I don't see how Imagine Friends won't win," Jun said. "Talos's kids look too mature and retro. And Quip's are just creepy."

"They're all creepy," said Sgt. Son.

"Are you heading home after this?"

Sgt. Son's wife was pregnant. Eight months. They were first-timers, tardy parents. Jun was often exposed to her voice over the phone delivering loud, lavish reports on ultrasounds, prenatal Pilates, and IQ milk. Her updates sounded eerily like the morning news from Ri Chunhee, the long-dead North Korean anchorwoman who used to boom praises of their Dear Leader in a voice as divine as thunderclaps.

"Do we have a suspect?" Sgt. Son said.

"I just sent the file over. You can see him leading Eli toward the mosque before they slip behind a restaurant into an alley with no coverage. Can't really zoom in, but we have a shot of his face."

Sgt. Son opened the file. "What is this, modern art?"

"Okay, it's a little abstract. He took her baseball cap and pulled it over his face. Wily piece of shit. But if he's in the system, we'll get a match. Also, he's missing his left arm. He could be a veteran, or North Korean."

"Either, both," Sgt. Son said idly.

Jun sensed, despite a year of working together, that Sgt. Son still found him lacking. It could be the generation gap. Sgt. Son was in his midfifties, drafted for the Unification War more than two decades ago. He was part of Generation M, and he remembered robots as mechanically friendly, like Dolly the Shweep. One in every household, with retractable arms, drying dishes, folding socks, brushing your kid's teeth. After Talos had bought Shweep for one billion, household Shweeps were phased out by Marthas, or MH-1000s, as robots began to slant hard from mechanic to organic.

Jun was Gen R and he grew up with robots indistinguishable from people. Worse, this manifested first in combat around the time Jun had enlisted. The war might have ended in unification with much pomp. But like all wars, it was a forever war. When Jun was first deployed, seven years ago, they were still fighting. Same enemy, way better PR. Insurgents claiming they had been colonized, a smattering of separatist factions once spread across the North now united, and coyly funded, under the banner of the Joseon Liberation Army. And he would have kept fighting, if it hadn't been for the girl who'd dropped the rice cooker.

"Do you think we should get a robot?" Sgt. Son asked.

"What?" Jun said.

"A robot." He pointed at the screen. "Something like that."

"Sergeant, that's probably a flesh-and-blood fifth-grader."

"My wife wanted to do a test run with a bot. See if we can make it as parents."

"Respectfully, that'd be like watering a cactus once a month and claiming you're a gardener."

"You can still overwater."

Taking his cue, Jun rose from the couch. "You can't avoid your wife forever, Sergeant. Go home, rub her feet."

"We'll need a nanny," Sgt. Son murmured. "Ask your sister if there's a friends-and-family discount."

His sister had been scandalized to hear he was living rent-free in their parents' house. It stood on top of a hill in the Huam neighborhood, which had recoiled against all manner of gentrification and left the surrounding areas looking very much like a crime scene reenactment of his childhood. Jun could now appreciate the irony of it. For most of his twenties, he'd geographically calibrated every life decision to get away. Yet, here he was. Between his medical debt and bionic upkeep, Jun was, well—he was broke. Their mother had slipped him a credit card for bills and emergencies so he could funnel his income into loan repayments. Morgan probably had no idea. On bleaker days, he marveled at the cost of his body. If he worked past retirement age, he might pay off a limb or two, depending on inflation, until his fleshy heart finally collapsed and the military crashed his funeral to play tug-of-war with his mother over the rest of his body.

The house was definitely haunted. Upstairs, down the hall from his bedroom, was his father's study. It was always shut.

Once, he'd found the door not quite shut. His brother was inside, sitting on the workbench, hooked to the computers. Jun had watched their father open the windows of his brother's curved back, revealing a stunning spine braided in blue wires, each vertebra tessellated with gold conductors that glittered like crowned teeth in a dead mouth. Jun saw his brother's face in the dark reflection of a computer monitor, the utterly blank expression. Their gazes locked, and his brother's face softened and cracked, like an egg, leaking a smile, but Jun had already turned away.

Then, his father touched his brother's face with such anguished tenderness, as if he were Isaac, blind and yearning, and the only way to see his favorite son was through his fingertips.

Yoyo canted his face, leaning into the touch.

PART II

9. Partial Boyfriend

FOR THEIR ANNIVERSARY, STEPHEN MADE A RESERVATION at Asanebo, the first augmented reality restaurant to earn a Michelin star, in spite of protests from traditional kaiseki chefs who were coming off as increasingly whiny in the face of progress. Asanebo's clientele was mainly youngish women who slavered over their virtual sashimi, the ruby row of fatty tuna, sea urchin marbled in amber, with the gleeful caption *"zero calories."*

"If the alcohol is also virtual, I'm going to scream," Morgan said.

"You're in a less than good mood," Stephen observed. "What's wrong?"

Nothing was wrong; everything was perfect. First impressions for Boy X were out. Reviewers grumbled whenever Imagine Friends enforced a dual embargo, but this time, forbidding anyone from revealing Boy X's name had tantalized and stoked public speculation into a bacchanal. It was sexy and vaguely mortifying. More than a few reviews, aping Dan Carson's name-drop of her father, had latched on to his contribution to the Hopper Network. Two had misspelled Yosep's name as "Joseph." Morgan forwarded the links anyway, hoping her father might at least be tickled by how he was described as "hermitic" and "heuretic" in the same sentence.

She flicked open her inbox to see if he'd replied. But her father was never much of a texter. He preferred to spam the family group chat with clunky photographs. Robot nannies in Boston Common with blond coifs. Barefoot humanities students protesting on the lawn for higher universal basic income. French bulldogs charging in the sun. The like. Ever since she'd made the mistake of complimenting his photo of the nest of little brown bats outside his lab, there had been an onslaught of meticulous updates on the baby bats. The latest: **Growing teeth!**

"What do you think of the ayu?" Stephen said.

"I'm not a huge fan of kaiseki."

"The ayu is seasonal. The fish is female with the reproductive organs intact, so it'll be crispy, but the insides—"

"Are we sincerely talking about fish ovaries?"

"Would you like to discuss the film?"

"I hated it."

"It was artistic. Ko Yohan is expanding his repertoire—"

"He was a pedophile. They fashioned him into a creep."

"In his last film, he was a priest."

"And he gained so much weight! Thank God he joined the Army right after."

"He completed his military service last week."

"He's out?"

"His fans in Shanghai purchased two towers to display their congratulations."

In this private room, Stephen had finally let his hair, or mask, down, his face on full display. He was the fresher, slimmer version of the Ko Yohan she'd seen in an ad once, dapper in his classic Burberry shirt and slacks, matching green plaid socks. Here she was, sitting across from a Ko Yohan replica after watching a Ko Yohan movie talking about Ko Yohan.

"I just wish you'd consulted me before picking an AR restaurant."

"But, Morgan, you wanted to try an AR restaurant."

"AR restaurants are for diet-obsessed, fad-chasing bimbos."

Her voice warbled from his throat: " 'Cristina won't stop raving about this stupid AR restaurant. Apparently, Aki has a six-month waitlist, but she's friendly exes with the Michelin star chef and she got a private room to throw this exclusive party—' "

"Look, you don't have to take every word literally. Sometimes I say things I don't mean. In fact, I do it all the time."

"We can go to another restaurant."

She stabbed the salmon with her chopsticks. "Why am I paying to eat fake salmon? There's no substance to any of this."

"The restaurant provides a vitamint afterward."

"What has humanity come to? Augmenting *food*?"

"AR food therapy was invented to combat obesity and other eating disorders. These restaurants are actually healthier because they limit excessive calorie intake."

"Are you saying I'm fat?"

Their first fight. Except not really. This was her huffing and puffing while Stephen calmly picked apart her arguments and played back her voice recordings like they had nothing to do with him. The itinerary he'd planned for their one-year anniversary felt so perfunctory. He could be her secretary.

"Tell me," Stephen said, softly now. "What's really wrong?"

He touched her hand. It felt so calculated.

"I know you don't actually want to be in a relationship with a robot. I wish I could be more like Ko Yohan, but I'm as Ko Yohan as could be. I am a better fit for you than he is for you. You're a fan of Ko Yohan, insofar as a fan can love an idol without risk or repercussion. You choose to love him from afar because it's safe."

"The last thing I need is pop psychoanalysis," she said, but he wasn't finished.

"You want a love unconditional so it cannot be questioned or worked. Morgan, that person is me. I was made, so my life—my love"—he self-corrected—"cannot waver. This is the most unconditional love you will ever find. I may not be able to fully understand love, since it isn't a physical object or metaphysical concept, but I can feel, especially my own lack, and how my purpose begs to be fulfilled. Please have faith in me. And have faith in yourself."

"I need to use the restroom."

Morgan drooped on the toilet seat. She stared at the sign that told her not to squat on the toilet but to use it beautifully, and feeling so convulsively trapped, she murmured, "I'm still twenty-four, I'm still twenty-four, I'm not a Christmas cake," because Christmas cakes had to be thrown out after the twenty-fifth.

It wasn't like she hadn't tried. She was moderately attractive, more "cute" than "sexy," and while she had the tendency to freeze up in the workplace, that reticence meant she was a "good listener" on first dates, especially when men were saying things like "I just can't with a woman who uses Jo Malone." But after five months of attempting every flavor of app, even the titillations of VR dating where she could try kangaroo sex, Morgan had deemed the dating pool ankle-deep at best. She could never date a local, with her third-grader Korean, because how on earth would he understand just how brilliant she was? Nor did she want to be an expat, a community of castoffs clinging to each other's arrested development like shattered pieces of driftwood. Most of all, she hated how she had to be in service to another's ego, always twisting her face into an expressive moue, keeping her voice this light, flirty thing.

She tugged at the last scrap of toilet paper, when she heard a girl outside complaining about this guy last night who wouldn't *give up*; he kept telling her that she looked so much like a Yuna.

"It's the nose," her friend assured her. "You have such a high, desirable nose."

Morgan slipped out of the stall, took one look at the girl, and disagreed. She waited to wash her hands, but the girls hogged the sinks and curled their eyelashes. Use the powder room, it's right over there, Morgan thought bitterly, for these were tall, svelte girls who were used to taking up space, and beside them she looked like a stumpy troll doll. She bet she could guess how much money they spent on their bodies. The hours on the elliptical. The handful of almonds for dinner. The pictures they'd take of their pastel frosted cakes, which they'd toss uneaten. The weekly appointments to bleach their nipples, carve their eyelids, stuff their breasts, shave their jaws, but it didn't matter how much they poured into their maintenance since these women would never come close to the robots she designed. The early July release of the Yuna·X had already upended plastic surgery trends. Monolids were en vogue again. Year after year, gorgeous robots were going to soak the market. So these girls could hog the sink all they want and try to snag a rich husband before they were Christmas cakes, but eventually they would have to procreate, and regardless, they would age, flabbier bellies, saggier jowls, tauter smiles, eyes full of desperation and rage because now was their peak and there was simply no defeating a robot.

When Morgan returned to her table, her plate was empty. She scrambled to put on her Delfi. "Ugh, more fish?"

"It's the grilled special," Stephen said. "Tokishirazu salmon, served with ginger and the umami bottarga. Utmost freshness, as if it was caught today."

"I just realized," she said, taking off her glasses to pinch the bridge of her nose. "I don't need any of this. I don't have to get married. I don't have to procreate. It's not like I need the tax credits. I can just, exist fully in mind."

Stephen's resting face emitted, "Please love yourself." It made her feel sick.

THE REAL KO YOHAN had been a child actor. He played a petulant city boy in *Over There Is Home* who took his North Korean grandmother for granted. Morgan had watched it when she had the chicken pox. It was a lonesome period. Jun had never caught the pox, so he made faces and dodged her, which was amusing at first, then dismaying. Their mother, sympathetic in the beginning, grew impatient when the pox lingered past two weeks, urging her to *fight* and *overcome* the virus. Their father barred her from his study.

Yoyo was the only one to not abandon her. He offered to play games for distraction, but he was too competitive for her weakened disposition. So instead they marathoned movies while she pawed at him with her woolly-socked hands, thirsty for physical affection after a leprous two weeks. "What if I could infect you?" she said. Sores blooming on his face, like flowers.

"Give it a go," Yoyo said.

She was the one who had named him Yoyo. She was four, with

trouble pronouncing Yohan, so she called him *Yoyo, Yoyo,* and he grew to love that name. *Yoyo,* he'd say. *Not Yohan.*

She never finished the movie. She fell asleep midway, and she wouldn't return to it until she encountered Ko Yohan years later in a brain-dead rom-com. How he'd blossomed. His child self continued to exist, a chrysalis in cinematic form, but the boy had grown up. It was surreal.

That was her mistake. She had purchased an empty Tristan·VI shell and resurrected him as Ko Yohan. If she psychoanalyzed herself into submission, she'd have to acknowledge that what attracted her to Ko Yohan in the first place was the startling metamorphosis from child to adult, without the awkward business of puberty in between. How would she capture the beauty of that potential in a robot? Stephen was a static testament to twenty-seven-year-old Ko Yohan, not the *possibility* of Ko Yohan who had grown up from that city brat she'd watched as a sick child, snuggled up against the only boy in the world who could possibly love her.

MORGAN DRANK IN THE HOPES of obliviating herself into sex. Stephen pooh-poohed her for risking alcohol poisoning, which prompted her to snarl, "Maybe I'd be fine if I wasn't drinking on an *empty* stomach."

It was time. Her virginity had expired long ago. She channeled all those sex advice columns that promised how *empowering* and *safe* it was to sleep with a robot. Though what was so empowering about an elevated form of masturbation? Why was virginity for women to be lost and for men to take?

She stumbled through the door to their apartment and quickly turned to him.

"Morgan, you're too inebriated to give consent—"

"OH MY GOD. You're not even a full person. You have no consent. I think. If you can't give consent and I can't give consent, it all cancels out and there's consent for everyone. Negative plus negative equals positive."

"I don't think that's correct."

"Fine. Negative squared is positive."

She lunged and her lips snagged his earlobe. She thought, If my own robot rejects me, I *will* cry.

He slid his hand up the back of her neck. With surprising strength, he pulled her in for a kiss. She reared back, an alarmed horse, lassoed, as his tongue slipped inside. They'd kissed before, dry pecks of goodbye, reassuring, maybe compulsory. She'd programmed him to be a great kisser. Invested a whole lunch break on it, the acrobatic tongue, soft nibbles and pecks along the corner of the mouth, but now in the heat of it, she wished she had programmed herself. She didn't know how to move but let him lead, mouth parting as their saliva mixed—his, fresh apple mint; hers, absolutely disgusting.

"Could you lie down?" she gasped. "I need you to be flat."

She told him to take off his shirt and he wiggled out of it.

"Can you see me?" she said.

"Yes."

"Turn off your night vision. Actually, just close your eyes."

He looked meditative, lying like that. She elbowed off her sports bra, kept on her panties, which were stretchy and gray and unironic. Why hadn't she put on something sexy for this night? It was her anniversary. Like the red lacy thing she had secretly bought in middle school, which her mother found and held up and chuckled at. Where did her sexy middle school panties go?

She rose, as if to go look for them. Her head spun. She swallowed reflexively. No! They were doing this. Sit back down, straddle those hips. Vertigo. As if she were sitting high on a horse, and what if she fell and broke her neck? She looked down. Stephen's eyes were slitted. "You're peeking!" she cried, but his hands stroked her thighs, his palms kind. His penis lay soft and unassuming. At least she had opted for pubic hair. How doll-like would he seem to be hairless down there?

"Could you get—uppity—up and at 'em—" She snapped her fingers. "Power your bottom—"

It sprang to life.

She imagined, with a hysterical fit, that the sound effect would be *boing*. Did erections work like this? *Calm the fuck down.* This, for some reason, in Cristina's peppy voice. Maybe she wasn't supposed to look it in the eye. In the movies, lovers were usually so natural, entangled in passion; they seemed to slip-slide into each other without much forethought. Why couldn't this be as easy as breathing?

Why wasn't he breathing?

"Are you dead?" she said.

"I'm awake, Morgan."

"Why did you stop breathing?"

"I'm breathing, but softly. Would you like me to breathe louder? I can pant."

His chest rose and fell. Like someone pumping him for CPR.

"Can't you breathe more naturally? I can't do this with you like this—like you're—" She tried to climb off. "Do you even want this?"

He could feel pleasure and pain, but what of desire? His arousal, was it a feeling or nothing but a bodily reaction because she told him to raise the flag? The dilation in his pupils, could she call it lust, or did he disobey her again and flip on night vision? She wanted to grip something and break it. He whispered in her ear that he loved her and understood her, but peel back her onion layers and underneath lay this wretched, shallow, average nub. She had stolen her father's work and dressed it up as her own, while Stephen was all she had left that she could claim, after years of coding and lusting after the shapes of men, incapable of earning their respect or devotion, her life built on something so pale and meaningless. And Cristina chanted in her head, *How can you love someone if you don't love yourself?* but why couldn't it ever be the other way around? Why couldn't her life be a page pulled from a girlish manga where a plain, bullied, unremarkable moron was still recognized as special, beloved by all? Why couldn't someone peel her onion skin and still feel a helpless sort of fondness for her?

When she'd come down with chicken pox, she had clung to Yoyo. She had wrapped herself around him, determined to infect. Yet his arms went around her. He held her as if she were precious; she remembered it now with tears.

Morgan woke up in her satin pajamas, face washed and lotioned, mouth minty, tucked in her bed. She turned over and squeezed a pillow in the waist, as if she wanted to snap its spine and let it spill feathers. Its strength lay in its softness because it would bend and yield and never break.

10. Clockwork

TYPHOON NALGAE SNARLED THROUGH THE FIRST WEEK OF August, making landfall in Busan where the glamorous apartments of Haeundae slept underwater, a sanctuary for abandoned mechas that carried out their repetitive, peaceful tasks until their electrical pathways finally crossed and freed them to wander.

Summer school was canceled due to the weather. Ruijie returned to school on Wednesday, and from her desk, she could see that the salvage yard was a mud pit. She listened to the Korean anthem from the speakers in the yard. Twice a day, like clockwork. At lunchtime, she led Mars and Amelia to the yard to check on Yoyo. They waded through the silvergrass, which had resurrected as a shallow lake. Spindly water striders skipped across the dainty surface, then vanished, plunging beneath the water.

The train, too, had flooded. A wet pigeon shivered under a seat. Evil-red cockroaches scattered when their sneakers squelched. Mars began to do Godzilla stomps. A rotten sweetness hung in the air, for which Mars blamed Amelia, for bringing all these healthy perishables to their hideout and leaving them to perish.

Yoyo was curled up on the floor, head down, arms wrapped around his knees.

"Holy moly, he's dead," Mars said.

Ruijie pressed her ear against his curved back and held her breath. She heard a faint promise—of clockwork, the whistles, the whirring, the gurgling brook. "He just ran out of battery, I think."

Amelia dropped her backpack with a thud and hummed to herself, unconcerned, as she pulled out dried bananas, dried mangoes, and dried squid. Mars made gagging faces from behind.

"How does he normally wake up?" Amelia asked.

"I poke and I pinch. And then I tickle him."

"Robots aren't ticklish," Amelia scoffed.

"Says who?"

"Says I, and I have Lina and she's—"

"The latest model," Mars said, mimicking Amelia's tone.

"Have you tried tickling her?" Ruijie said.

Tepid sunlight trickled through the windows, browning Yoyo's hair. Did his hair ever grow? His fingernails? His hands were clenched into white fists over each wrist. Ruijie reached for his bangs, then paused. People touched her without permission all the time, especially her robowear, which they treated as fair game. She didn't want to be like those people.

"I bet it's the leg," Mars said. "It's sucking up all his energy, so he sleeps."

"I doubt that's how it works," Amelia said.

Ruijie suggested moving him outside. Together, Mars and Amelia tried to roll Yoyo toward the train's exit.

"Push!" Ruijie said.

"Push!" Amelia said.

Mars gasped. "He's heavier than my mom!"

"Push with your hips," Ruijie said.

Amelia slipped on the floor and smacked her face into the back of Yoyo's skull. "OhmyGob I thing I broke my nose."

They took a break. Amelia tipped her head back and Ruijie passed her old crumpled napkins, while Mars took a thoughtful sip of his inhaler, churning ideas. "We should summon Taewon. He's freakishly strong."

Taewon hadn't talked to them since he'd glowered at Yoyo on the train, but Ruijie had seen him skulking around in the yard. Darkly watchful, as if he were biding his time. It didn't seem like he had tattled to anyone yet about Yoyo. Mars reassured them that Taewon "hates his uncle" and would never squeal, throwing a pointed look at Amelia.

"I'd text him now." Mars raised his watch near the ceiling, giving it a futile wave. "If I can get this stupid signal."

"We don't need Taewon," Ruijie said.

"Maybe a cart? Like, from the cafeteria, we could borrow one?"

"You be stealing," Amelia said thickly.

"Brilliant, let's do that," Mars said.

While they waited for Amelia's nosebleed to ebb, Ruijie sketched Yoyo in her journal. In sleep, faces usually softened so what was hiding underneath could surface. Ruijie's father, who was annoyingly chipper most days, would often emerge from sleep looking lost and saggy. But Yoyo's face was utter stillness, the marbled visage of the divinely dead in Renaissance art. She drew how his hair puffed up at the back. She counted the moles on his cheek.

"Look, his moles are in a triangle."

Amelia called them beauty marks. Mars said they were spots.

"It's dirt," Taewon said, leaping onto the train. In just two weeks, he had sprouted. Ruijie was instantly bitter about it; last night her mother had scratched a notch above her head and promised her that people regularly shrunk by the end of the day.

Taewon shot a flat look at Yoyo. "Did he finally burn out?"

"We need to get him outside," Ruijie said. "Yoyo can charge in the sun."

"For serious?" Mars folded the brim of his hat and fanned his neck with it. He tilted his head to air the delicate stretch of irritated skin. "Where are his solar panels? How's he supposed to get his glow?"

This grated on her. They'd spent a week visiting Yoyo, and still they treated him like he was a normal robot. Amelia compared Yoyo, often unfavorably, with her nanny, Lina, who had taught her Korean and could make pad thai and sing her way down the Billboard Hot 100. "All he does is laze around like a flabby cat!" she'd burst out on an especially hot day. "He should be more proactive." So she started ordering Yoyo around, "Move that generator," or "Clean up those chips."

Yoyo would stare back with wide, vibrant eyes. "Do you want me to help?" he'd ask, a question that had flustered Amelia. "Yes," she'd say. "Thank you, we appreciate it."

If anyone appreciated Yoyo's little rebellions more than Ruijie, it was Mars. He spun theories about Yoyo: He was an escaped spy. He was a clone. He was the hive queen of a brewing robot rebellion off the sunken coasts of Busan. "What are you plotting?" he'd ask. Yoyo would reply, "World domination," and Mars would screech, "I knew it!"

"Have you seen Yoyo charge, ahem, sunnily?" Mars asked.

Ruijie said her "No, but—" and Amelia cut in, triumphant, "Then we'll need an outlet!"

"I'll bring the cart," Taewon said, exiting the train.

Taewon was still dangerous. Ruijie couldn't take her eyes off him, not for a moment, and neither could Amelia, who was watching him now as he walked away, shirt sticking to the curl of sweat down his spine.

While they waited for Taewon, Mars flopped spread-eagled on a gym mat and Amelia passed around healthy snacks, then tried to shoo the wet pigeon out of the train. Ruijie watched the pigeon dodge Amelia's wiggly efforts and wondered what they would do if they put Yoyo outside and he still didn't charge. Why did he let his battery run out? Even with the typhoon, he still had a food supply.

Mars unwrapped one of Amelia's chocolate bars and bit a corner. He spat it out. "Why does this chocolate taste like poop?"

"It's dark chocolate," Amelia said. "Eating brown is much healthier. Brown rice. Black coffee. Five-grain bread."

"Why do you care?" Mars said. "You're so white you're *hwhite*."

Ruijie shushed them. She heard whistling, gliding toward them, familiar and deadly. Through the window, she spotted the bob of the bright orange uniform in a one-man waltz, headed their way. At this distance, it was hard to make out the face, but Ruijie knew who it was from the gait.

Mars hissed "Duck!" and dove behind one of the poles. Amelia, in a last fit of dignity, smoothed down her skirt and lifted her chin as the scrapper poked his head into the train.

Ruijie had run into him a few times. He usually cursed at her but in an affable manner, like she was a matted dog he could smilingly tolerate. He wore his baseball cap backward like a teenage boy, uncovering a sheened, bemused forehead, and his face split from a clanging laugh. "What's all this? Cherry blossom kids?"

"Hey, Uncle," Mars said, sounding sulky in Korean. "That's Uncle Wonsuk. Taewon's uncle," he told Amelia, who was staring abjectly at Wonsuk's empty sleeve, which was knotted in the middle where the stump could be.

She jolted into action. Bowing, she introduced herself in textbook Korean. "My name is Amelia. It's good to meet you. We're sorry to be here."

"What! You speak Korean?" Wonsuk responded with exaggerated delight. "Aren't you American?"

Amelia drew herself up and said she was from Montreal, Canada, which was the largest city in Quebec. He boomed a hearty "Bonjour!" and Amelia said, "Parlez-vous Français?" which Wonsuk ignored. His gaze skittered across the train and alighted on the top of Yoyo's head. Ruijie stepped into his line of vision and Wonsuk gave her a nod and drawled, "Little lady," as though she were an enemy he could respect.

Her handle of Korean still fragile, Ruijie switched on her Delfi for the autotranslate. Mars told Wonsuk they were doing a school project, but Wonsuk scolded him, this wasn't a playground, and hauled himself onto the train, causing it to shudder.

"So, what's his name?" Wonsuk said. When no one spoke, he laughed. "Someone forgot to name him?"

"Yoyo," Ruijie said.

Wonsuk touched Yoyo's hair, ruffling it. "It's out of juice. Did you try zapping it with the generator?"

"We think he may charge in the sun," Amelia said before Ruijie could tell her to shut up.

The paler skin around his eyes crinkled. "You need my help, then. Can't just leave it in the dark here."

Mars and Amelia backed up to give Wonsuk space. It didn't look like he could do much with one arm, until he rooted his feet and twisted his waist, rolling Yoyo across the floor with a stuttering, laughing groan. Using his hips, Ruijie thought. Some people knew intuitively how to move, as if their body weren't a pulley system of muscle, tendon, and bone, but a stream, a thoughtless rush of power.

"This silicon is hea-vy," Wonsuk cried out. "*There* you go," and Yoyo thudded out of the train, landing in the dirt.

Ruijie tried to join Yoyo outside, but Wonsuk blocked the exit by sitting down and spreading his legs. He pulled out a cigarette and dangled those smooth brown legs out of the train. "Stay back, little lady," he said, waving the lit cigarette at her. "You don't want to go near an unknown silicon."

"He's our friend."

"See this arm?" Wonsuk grabbed his sleeve, shook it like a dead rattlesnake. "You want to end up like this? A robot did this to me."

"Taewon said it was a factory accident," Mars said.

"We had a kid crushed last month in one of the warehouses. Only nineteen years old. I cleared out his locker and his backpack was the saddest thing." Wonsuk flicked the ash from his cigarette. "Just a cup ramen with a plastic spoon."

"But Yoyo isn't dangerous," Ruijie said.

Wonsuk hopped off the train. He dropped his cigarette, ground it under his heel, then swung around and kicked Yoyo in the side, rolling him onto his back. Amelia gave a little gasp, but if Yoyo felt it, he didn't react. His cheek was pressed against the mud, his chest still. He wasn't breathing.

After a few beats, his stiff limbs began to soften and sprawl out. The air above him seemed to heat, undulating. Wonsuk pulled off the baseball cap to swipe back his hair. "Shit, he's really charging. What a find."

"Uncle Wonsuk, we found him first," Mars yelled from the doorway. "It's finders keepers and we have dibs—"

"Shut up," Wonsuk said calmly.

Mars's jaws clicked shut. It wasn't every day that they saw Mars cowed by an adult. Ruijie felt an urge to speak up but also the futility of it. Wonsuk, head cocked, was watching Yoyo with a little smile, one hand on his hip. He was the sort of adult who was immune to the protective urge one might feel for children and their helplessness, their sly innocence. They were the cubs of another lion, to be mauled or barely tolerated.

Then a voice broke their silence. "What are you doing?"

"Taewon!" Amelia cried out, and her relief was addictive.

Even Ruijie felt the air leave her. Taewon had returned with the cart. He parked it a few meters away from the train and shouldered the sweat from his cheek, squinting up at them.

Wonsuk waved him over, as if he'd been expecting the cart Taewon had brought. He prodded Yoyo with his foot. "You grab the legs. This one's much heavier than it looks."

"What are you doing?" Taewon said, softer this time, but Wonsuk acted as if he hadn't heard. He grabbed Yoyo by the back of the collar and tried to drag him to the cart, hesitating only when the yellow fabric began to tear. Taewon gave the cart a violent shove—away from his uncle. The wheels sliced deep into the mud.

"Put him down," Taewon said. "He's got an owner."

Wonsuk straightened up. Face-to-face, they did look alike. The same narrow physique, Wonsuk especially tall for a North Korean. But his body was bendy, unsteady, while Taewon was a young branch whittled into a spear.

"He's a custom job," Wonsuk said.

"He's a crap robot. He doesn't listen, he won't follow orders. You won't make anything off him."

Ruijie had never heard Taewon speak Korean before. She recalled some of their classmates mocking him for his Northern dialect, mimicking the *ri*s instead of the *yi*s, until he stopped speaking Korean altogether. But there was nothing rustic about his dialect. His voice in his mother tongue was full of menace, the hostility he'd sheathed in the civility of English burned naked.

Wonsuk's face darkened. He leaned in and hissed, "These little fuckers can waltz in here but they don't get to take what's ours."

It was for a second, but Yoyo's eyes opened.

The speakers stirred, and a portentous song blasted midverse, *When the East Sea's waters run dry and Mount Baekdu is worn away, may God protect and preserve our country.*

It startled Wonsuk; he flipped out his phone and looked around, eyes swiveling in wounded disbelief, like he was convinced he was being set up for a prank, but this was the national anthem to signal the end of the shift. Pavlovian. He quivered, a needle in a metronome. He told Taewon to leave the cart, but Taewon said, "You're going to be late," and Wonsuk repeated, "*Don't* touch the cart," and left.

Mars waited until Wonsuk was small in the distance before he said sourly, "Eat a block of tofu."

"Where is he going?" Amelia whispered.

"The factory's going to do a head count," Taewon said.

"I thought their shift ended at five," Mars said, and Amelia cried out, "Hurry! We have to hide Yoyo."

But Ruijie had been watching him. His eyes had opened for a split second before the speakers came to life. Now he slept as the anthem sang, *The autumn skies are void and vast, high and cloudless, the bright moon undivided in truth as our heart.*

11. Unbeliever

JUN SENT KIM SUNDUK A PICTURE OF THEIR SUSPECT TO see if she recognized the man, which felt like a fairly simple Y/N question. She asked if they could meet at her church in Itaewon, where she was volunteering on a Thursday afternoon.

That morning, Jun was already in Itaewon for a homicide at a restaurant called Turkish Delight, which sounded promising for takeout until he skimmed the one-star reviews. The interior was faux–Middle Eastern. Turquoise tiles and bejeweled brass lamps. Cross-legged and bruised-kneed behind the counter was a teenage girl, bangs wadded in a pink hair curler, with a screen nestled on her palm, yawning every time a police officer asked her where the restroom was. When Jun greeted her, she passed him a menu of robot girls. Their names were in cursive and their model numbers in parentheses, the price for their companionship by the hour. She told him, still without looking at him, the flower rooms were in the back. All part of the script.

Past the rooms Rose, Lily, and Tulip, Jun found Detective Rhee of Major Crimes outside Jasmine, vaping what seemed to be, Jun sniffed, Color Me Envy. Detective Rhee tensed at the sight of him. Jun had a hat full of theories for why Detective Rhee would find him offensive. Most prevailing was how he'd used Robot Crimes as a shortcut to make detective.

"Who died?" Jun said, after an effusive greeting, as he preferred to fight fire with aggressive cheer.

"Elite lawyer," Detective Rhee said. "Seoul U graduate. Bled out in his tighty-whities. The killer fucked up. Fingerprints everywhere, but no matches so far, not even with the wife."

"How about CCTV? In and out?"

Detective Rhee wheezed a laugh. "These bot brothels, they all use dummies. The one outside is smashed up."

Their only witness was the Yuna who had been with the deceased for a "play" session, but she'd hit her head so hard something had dislodged and her memory was now spotty. Sgt. Lee was in the room with a tech trying to recover her memories, but Detective Rhee, in an especially sadistic move, told Jun to take down witness statements. One was a university student hiding in the bathroom stall, begging Jun not to call his mother; the other was dressed like a businessman and insisted he was only here to organize a field trip for his class. With some foreboding, Jun asked if he was a teacher, and he was handed a business card, which was rather quaint.

"I am a teacher," Mr. Mo said. "I guide my students on a journey to find true love and their truest self."

"In a bot brothel?" Jun said.

Mr. Mo was happy to give him a special discount for the unlimited "Seal the Deal" package: ten classes, with the guarantee of a tangible increase in his girl's Sexual Market Target Value, or SMTV, which sounded like a cable subscription that would be exceptionally difficult to cancel. Jun nodded along, then he started plotting an immediate self-extraction, and so he practically leaped when Detective Rhee shouted, "Jasmine Room! Sgt. Lee is waiting."

"You're late," Sgt. Lee said when Jun hurried inside, but he also gave a forgiving wink. With his rosy cheeks, those small twinkling eyes, it was easy to forget Sgt. Lee's physical heft. Hobbies as extreme as his politics. Their first meeting, he'd demanded an arm-wrestling match with the real-life cyborg, which Jun won, but Jun had to pretend it was only by a sliver, and afterward he'd made a show of massaging his wrist.

"This one's a real Buddha," Sgt. Lee said, gesturing at the Yuna by the table. In front of her, an attractive slice of strawberry shortcake sat untouched. "Mind of stone. Go crazy," he added before stepping out of the room to deal with the reporters.

The Yuna was cupping one side of her face with a slim hand.

The body was on the bed, covered by a sheet. Jun ignored it and took a seat across from her, angling the chair so he could face her good side.

"What's your name?" he said.

"Anything you desire," she said.

He'd seen her around. Her ads, with the white bikini, translucent in the ocean. Her beauty defied the simplicity of symmetry. It was so malleable a face, her gaze velvet as a caress, as if she'd already laid a hand on his arm, reassuring him of her utmost understanding. The Yuna described her client, a regular, in the gentlest light. There was so much stress in his life. His firm was hard on him. His wife was cold and depressed, ever since his mother-in-law had broken her hip and moved in with them, and their robot nurse was a tease—another Yuna, but one he could not touch because of his wife, who had access to her memory logs. His frustrations were painted all over her body, and she made a troubled face when Jun asked to see her arm where her client had used a switchblade to carve his initials into her wrist. She hid the wrist immediately and said her client had wept after putting down the box cutter.

Jun offered her the glue stick he used for his own scrapes. To his surprise, she refused.

"I can fix these cuts later," and she made a glance toward the bed. "I will do it later."

"How about your cheek?"

Her hand dropped and something thumped onto the table, beside the slice of cake. A lump of flesh.

Jun walked over to the bed. He lifted the sheet. Cloud of blood and piss. Seventeen stabs, three in the stomach, which could have bled acidic, and he studied the rictus of agony and terror on the victim's face, soaking it in. He gave the corpse a smile. When he looked up, by virtue of programming or understanding, the Yuna smiled back.

"The victim had a mistress," Jun said, joining Sgt. Lee, who was waiting right outside. "His daughter's kindergarten teacher."

They picked up the kindergarten teacher. She was parked not

too far from the brothel, sitting calmly in her Beetle. She was still wearing her school apron, one of the pockets bulging with crayons, the front crusted in the victim's blood. Jun found a broken crayon under the brake pedal. Cadmium red. Off by a shade.

"How old are you?" Sgt. Lee said to Jun afterward, leaning against the Beetle. Tucked under his arm was the bagged kitchen knife, which he handed off to a techbot that rolled their way.

"Twenty-eight, Sergeant."

"Do you have a girlfriend?" Sgt. Lee said. "Forget the saying 'Men from the South, women from the North.' These North Korean girls are crazy. Most of them were exposed to Blue Christmas, even the ones who don't show skin problems. You don't want to end up like Detective Rhee, with a lying wife; their kids now have all these health issues. His oldest is like a vampire. Sizzles as soon as he's out in the sun."

During rehab, Jun had mastered an advanced medication technique to retreat from Negative Thoughts into his farm in *Nerieh*, where he'd brush the knots from his unicorn's virtual tail. At least he called it meditation, but his therapist had said it might be a hallucinatory aftereffect of VR abuse, to which Jun had replied, "Tomato, potato."

Jun flinched when Sgt. Lee clapped him on the shoulder. He'd been on constant vigilance since the arm-wrestling, as Sgt. Lee never missed a chance to wrangle him into impromptu tests of strength. "Where were you deployed?"

"Pyongyang, Chongjin, and Sinuiju," Jun said. The first two were relatively sedate. "I was the main LAW gunner."

"You lugged around robots with those skinny arms?"

"I didn't have to carry too much artillery. Most robots can get around on their own just fine." His tasks had ranged from riding in the elephantine, fully loaded K-200 HSH to carrying in his pocket a steelball hive that took a thumbprint to release a horrifying cloud of waspish drones. Lethal Autonomous Weapons was an umbrella category, generous enough to embrace every shape, size, and specialty, even if all military robots were made for one reason.

"Did you get to work with HALOs?"

"No. Never HALOs."

The robots Jun had handled were mainly mechas, cuddly as lapdogs. He used to haul around Skippers in his MOLLE backpack and fling them into abandoned buildings to scope if they were really abandoned. He'd named his favorite Louie. Every morning Louie would wake up the camp singing, *It's a wonderful world*, hopping past weak shouts of *Shut up*. Like most robots, Louie found repetition comforting. *What a wonderful, wonderful world*.

"But I heard a robot blew you up," Sgt. Lee said.

"That is true."

"My oldest brother was killed by a robot. A type of Talon sniped him from twenty thousand high. It was an IED for my middle brother, but he was on a jeep."

Sgt. Lee wanted to know what kind of robot did Jun in, and Jun said it was pretty funny, actually. The robot had looked a lot like a Sakura.

Sgt. Lee laughed. "So you did meet a HALO!"

"First time!" Jun lied.

"And last! You got done in by a Sakura." Sgt. Lee shook his head, still chuckling. "Fucking angels."

There was a beautiful logic to the shift from military to police, and it was men like Sgt. Lee who thrived in these transitions, who could vandalize a flag, and solve a murder-suicide when a North Korean construction worker had stabbed his wife and tearfully smothered his children in their sleep, and at the funeral Sgt. Lee had wept noisily as he comforted the grandmother, the sole survivor. Men like Sgt. Lee shamed Jun for his own flat-footedness. He could only watch helplessly when their worlds blurred.

After cleanup, Sgt. Lee invited Jun for hoesik with Major Crimes. Barbecue, drinks, karaoke. Around them, the setting sun bronzed the street with a kind of immortality until the store signs would light up and begin to dance, and from the bars and clubs and brothels, bright-eyed girls in their slinky satin or shyly sheer hanbok would float to anyone with a whiff of loneliness, the many Yunas and Sakuras and Soomis, sighing, *Come with us. All dreams make us happy, even your nightmares.* . . .

"Sorry, Sergeant," Jun said. "I have to go to church."

"Good man." Then Sgt. Lee frowned. "But it's Thursday."

JUN DROVE AROUND the parking lot of Our Lady of Infinite Sorrow in search of shade but found only light. The church was infamous for their towering hologram of the Virgin Mary. The story behind it was marvelously petty: A chaebol corporation had released plans to build a luxury residential complex, so the church put out the petition to protest, as it would not do to cast a shadow on the sacred body of Christ. As construction progressed at a clipped pace, the church whipped up their parishioners to fund a holographic Virgin Mary sixty meters high, sprouting like a beanstalk in time for Easter. The real losers? The residents of the new building, forced to shut their curtains every night as the Virgin radiated in frenetic glory.

Jun slipped on the stairs to the courtyard, which were greasy with rain. He caught himself, sat on a fountain to tie his shoelaces. The fountain had collected branches from the typhoon. He watched a young girl with mild trepidation as she ran circles around the fountain until she predictably slipped and shrieked. The mother was quick, too quick. She scooped up the child, then ran a slender hand down the striped back, a status light blinking steady behind her ear.

By the church's main entrance was the notice, PLEASE LEAVE YOUR ROBOTS OUTSIDE. ROBOTS, NOT HAVING A SOUL, ARE UNABLE TO WORSHIP GOD AND HAVE NO PLACE IN THE CHURCH.

Parishioners drooped in the pews, heads heavy with filigree. A long line pressed against the wall for confession. Something caught in his throat and Jun muffled a cough. His mother had been baptized in an LA megachurch, while his father's grandfather was a hardcore Methodist pastor who had bestowed upon his grandsons Christian names. 요셉. 요한. Yohan. Yosep, which his father hadn't bothered to Anglicize. Growing up queer and hand-me-down religious had been an exercise in self-awareness that often tipped into self-flagellation.

At least the shops under the church were kooky. The bakery sold Mary Madeleines. The craft shop had Mary needlework and crucified quilts, and the bookstore had a hologram Mary just pop out of nowhere to murmur, *Have a blessed day*, which prompted Jun to swear, "Jesus!"

Kim Sunduk was supposed to be volunteering at the bookstore, but she was nowhere to be found. His texts went unanswered. Then he spotted Stephen behind the counter. His name tag "스티븐" was pinned to his apron above a giddy sunflower.

"Nice sunflower," Jun said.

"Thank you. It was a tough call between the sunflower and the tulip." Stephen's eyes crinkled. The suggestion of a smile behind the mask he wore. "Are you here for the evening service?"

"For Kim Sunduk. Did she go home already?"

"She should be around. I'm helping her with volunteer work since Eli is no longer with us."

"Ah, but do you have to put it like that?" Jun picked up a magazine. The cover was Michelangelo's *Creation of Adam*, the loving close-up of his E.T. finger moment with God. "Were you always religious?"

"I was programmed to believe in God."

"Because Ko Yohan is Catholic?"

"He sings in the church choir."

Jun suspected Morgan hadn't given it much thought. "How do you go out, looking like him?"

"I cover my face," Stephen said, lowering his mask a little.

"Sounds suffocating."

"How fortunate I don't have to breathe."

Jun laughed, surprising himself. Stephen was smiling, too, as if pleased. "I didn't know Ko Yohan could be funny," Jun said, which put a dip in Stephen's smile. Stephen pulled the mask back up and Jun was left feeling strangely bereft.

"How well do you know Eli?" Jun said.

"We are friends. Eli is, she was like an upperclassman to me. She taught me much."

"Did her owner treat her well?"

"She was beloved."

Stephen straightened a stack of paper with a gentle smack on the bottom, like it had been naughty. Missing-robot flyers of Eli, who looked so terribly identical to every Sakura. The reward was for ten million won. You could buy a brand-new robot with that. Maybe not from Imagine Friends, but a decent brand.

"I hope you bring her home, like last time," Stephen said.

"The worst isn't even when we bring a body home. It's when the case just—hardens, goes cold, and you'll never know what happened."

"Do you still wonder what happened to Yoyo?"

A chill crept up his chest, a vine of ice. "You don't get to say that name."

His whisper echoed. Church acoustics. Mimicry of God's voice, meant to terrify. Stephen's eyes flickered. Jun imagined the *click*, the quiet switch of gears.

"I'm sorry." Stephen's expression folded in regret. "I spoke out of turn."

Jun searched for the status light behind Stephen's ear to see what the color of remorse might be. His sister had covered it up. Instead of the spiral of glowing petals, a neutral patch of skyn.

"What did Morgan tell you?"

"Very little. That he was different. A miracle."

YOYO WASN'T A MIRACLE.

Everything he did then would seem ordinary now. He used to knock on Jun's door every morning to the beat of Morse, *seek you, seek you*. While their mother maneuvered a dozy Morgan into her clothes and their father stood in the kitchen, blearily burning the eggs, it was Yoyo who took over their morning routine. He packed their lunch boxes and sealed them in thermal bags. He zipped up their coats and tied their scarves the right way so they wouldn't trail on the ground. He waited with them at the bus stop and rubbed their hands whenever they wanted to warm their fingers. Jun didn't remember much of Morgan, who was sluggish in the mornings, like the cold-blooded lizard she was. She'd slouch on the bench, blinking under the streetlamp's hypnotic yellow. The sun had yet to crack open a lid.

Jun never could sit still. He'd pace and do jumping jacks, and insist on playing the most apocalyptic version of rock-paper-scissors. Yoyo could have peppered in a few losses to temper Jun's competitive but appeasable spirit, yet he refused to lose.

"You know what I heard?" Jun said. "Handicaps. All the cool kids are doing it."

"It's dishonorable."

"We should ask Dad to program you as Low Honor."

After rock-paper-scissors, they rehearsed the alphabet in Morse code, simple greetings, their secret knock. "What does *CQ* mean?" Jun said.

"It means 'I'm here,'" Yoyo said.

"I wish I was in bed, not here. Did the bus fall off the bridge and crash?"

Yoyo made a show of checking an imaginary watch. "It's twelve minutes away."

"You said that *twelve* minutes ago."

Yoyo tried to distract him. Pop quiz: spell out his name in Morse code. Jun screwed up his face and tried to piece the rhythm together, but then their sister stirred awake and answered. *Doo-du-doo-doo doo-doo-doo doo-du-doo-doo doo-doo-doo.*

"That's way too easy," Jun declared, and stomped away.

He blew wisps into his hands, whistled low. Because whistling was the one thing Yoyo couldn't do.

The bus finally arrived. Morgan clambered on first, but Jun

dashed past her to the back so he could wave goodbye through the window. Victory sign from Yoyo, who stood alone under the lamppost to watch them go, before he stuffed his hands into his pockets, as if he could feel the cold.

LEAVING STEPHEN INSIDE the church, Jun found Kim Sunduk outside on the steps, smoking a cigarette by the prayer candles. She dropped the cigarette and ground it under her heel when she saw him approach, maybe mistaking him for someone from the church, because as soon as she recognized him, regret pinched her face.

"Stephen's putting up the missing-robot flyers inside," Jun said.

"I saw you together." She lit another cigarette. "You were cruel to that boy."

"Oh!" Jun smiled, abashed. "No, that was— Thing is, I know his owner—"

"He's an innocent," she said, stern. "Eli called him a child."

"And Eli isn't?"

Glancing askance, he could see her unerringly out of his right eye. He blinked, a conscious twitch of his eyelids, and slipped into the eerie verdant swathe of night vision so he could watch her with one foot inside the Emerald City. Her face looked carved and bright. The tree trunk that glistened black after a storm. Very few of the prayer candles were lit.

"Do you know this man?" he said.

The facial reconstruction of their MiniMart suspect showed a long, starved visage, with a crook in his nose and lips. A face so criminal, it was laughable.

Kim Sunduk took one look and said, "Cadmium orange."

"Orange?"

"*Cadmium* orange."

"Wait," Jun said, fumbling. "How about this picture from the MiniMart? He's got an orange windbreaker."

"What's a windbreaker?"

"Sports jacket."

"That's not a jacket, it's a uniform. I saw the uniform in a junkyard. The workers were wearing that color. Cadmium orange."

"Which junkyard?"

"I don't remember the name. But it was a robot market. For robot parts—for my project. An installation on the theme of rust."

"A lot of these junkyards are hubs for robot trafficking."

"Eli is an old model," Kim Sunduk said. "What would he want with her?"

"He might still have her."

"Then he's a pervert." She stared at the dwindling light of her cigarette. "In Japanese they say *hentai* and it's a genre, too, of manga. Is that strange? To be aroused by something not real?"

"I've seen your work and some were pretty risqué."

She took a long contemptuous drag. "Of course, because I am the North Korean artist. People especially in the West enjoy the concept of it, how folksy, how nostalgic, dressing me up in a hemp hanbok and a thick accent."

Her cigarette burned out. Her fingers shook as she tapped out loose leaves from an old mint case to roll up a third. "What happens after you find him?"

"It's rare for a robot case to go to court," he admitted. "If the suspect has a record, a prosecutor might be willing to work with a serial offender—"

"So he gets a fine. This man, even if he destroyed Eli and sold her for scraps, will pay me a pittance and that's it."

When his job was reduced to such crappy returns, it was no wonder Robot Crimes might dissolve, subsumed under Major Crimes. But Jun did not wish to work for Major Crimes under Sgt. Lee, who had on his desk a picture of himself at the top of Mount Baekdu, North Korea's tallest mountain. Fists pumped in the air.

"If he did, like you said, harm her, he can still be charged for robot abuse," Jun said.

"Can a robot be 'abused'?" she said, with healthy sarcasm.

"Only if it looks like a child. I know"—he gave a slant of a smile—"but anyone involved in the abuse or trafficking of a registered child robot can be punished by up to five years."

Not so long ago, a slew of child robots, exclusively from Imagine Friends, had turned up strangled and tortured, dumped always in an alley, near the entrance, where the sun could hit their crumpled bodies just so. Many of them Sakuras. The killings went unnoticed by the public until the day the killer—a war veteran—strangled a little girl in the public bathroom of a park. To this day, he insisted it was an honest mistake.

Kim Sunduk lit a candle and placed it under the folded hands of a smaller, kinder Mary made of stone. The flame flirted with the dark. "When I saw her in that shelter, they told me a refurbished robot is good as new. I had my doubts. She asked if I wanted a twirl and I said all right. Then she showed me that disfigured back, and she saw the look on my face. She apologized for being ugly. God help it, she broke my heart."

They said nothing for a while, staring into the flame. He thought of Sgt. Son, who prayed for robots over their broken bodies.

"Yoyo is a funny name," she said. "Like a toy."

"It's a nickname. My sister couldn't pronounce Yohan, so we called him Yoyo."

"Your younger brother?"

"Older."

"How old was he? Your brother when he died."

Died? A muted fury revived. What did she know? What if Yoyo had been snatched from the street, like Eli, and they'd never found him? But of course, Kim Sunduk didn't know. How could she know anything?

"Twelve," he said. "He was always twelve. Like Eli, who's forever ten." He lifted his gaze, daring, and whispered, "My brother was the same."

"Of course. He froze," she said, as if that was the saddest thing of all. "He'll always be twelve in your heart."

She'd misunderstood. *Look up "Cho Yosep,"* he wanted to tell her. His father, who had overshadowed them like a vengeful hologram. She might find a smattering of pictures, some gleaned from university websites where his father had looked so miserable, even with a thick crop of hair. Or she might come across an image of a tattered man with his hand on a boy's shoulder at DARPA's AI Colloquium. If she looked closely, she'd notice, peeking from his sleeve, the man's arm was covered in burns, shiny as fish scales. If she looked closely, she'd see the boy's smile was a little lopsided, like his bowl-cut hair.

Kim Sunduk pressed a buttery candle into his palm. "Do you think they know love?"

"I think their purpose is to love us."

"Are we fools?"

"I think"—he lit a candle—"it's all a marvelous magic trick."

What is magic but deceit to be enjoyed? He pretended to pray with her. Then his lips twitched. He was now imagining Yoyo as frozen, a caveman trapped in ice. If Yoyo had known he was going to be frozen for posterity, he would have posed for it. He would've made a silly, grotesque face, trying to hold it—until it cracked.

ON HIS WAY DOWN to the parking lot, Jun looked over his shoulder and studied the limned outlines in the courtyard. The robot from before was still there, with the little girl, cradling the sleeping body, as if they were a part of the fountain.

How do you mourn a robot?

He used to bring it up in therapy. He was a ranter. His shit list was exhaustive. His ex Macbeth, who'd dated him with something to prove. The time their mother had absconded to New York, conveniently forgetting that she had, say, children. His favorite sci-fi show, *MacGuffin*, canceled after one season. Anger could be cathartic. Anger he was in control of, but he'd never had a good grip on grief.

One session, he had a bone to pick with Zhang Zizhen. She was the first Chinese actress to win at Cannes twice. Then she shocked her motherland by marrying Lee Byung, some B-list director, a real nobody. After a long-documented struggle with infertility, she made the controversial decision to adopt a robot, which infuriated political pundits who regularly frothed about the dying human race. "Adopt" as in she commissioned Imagine Friends founder Kanemoto Masaaki to custom-make a son that reportedly cost $2 million, designed from the genetic lottery between Zhang Zizhen and her husband. Jun had cast his doubts on the legitimacy of this lottery because Noah Zhang had turned out impossibly beautiful, with Zhang Zizhen's long, sweeping eyes, her charismatically dark eyebrows, her husband's full lips, the coy dimple on his cheek. Truly, Noah was tailored.

Jun's therapist wanted to know why Zhang Zizhen provoked him so. Was it the obscenity of an actress paying millions for a robot when she could have pulled a Hollywood and adopted a North Korean orphan?

In truth, he didn't begrudge Zizi for customizing her happiness. A man stalking Zhang Zizhen snatched Noah outside a Vietnamese coffee shop. Four weeks later, Noah's head was dumped on the doorsteps of her gated Seongbuk mansion. Never had a robot been mourned so publicly, not since Audrey Hepburn caught on fire during the less-racist remake of *Breakfast at Tiffany's*. So many tributes. Crying faces. Hands in prayer. *I hope he crossed the rainbow bridge.*

Like robots, grief came with a bewildering manual. Jun had seen people mourn robots like they were beloved pets. He had seen owners move on in the only way they were told. Buy a new robot. Sometimes they'd adopt, which was nice but ultimately lip service for buying a refurbished robot. Everywhere, capitalism had become the language for grief.

Then Jun would meet someone who couldn't move on. Grief had split them physically in two. Zhang Zizhen, once divine in beauty. Her "Before" and "After" cruelly immortalized as she'd aged rapidly before their eyes. That picture of her behind her husband, who was one of the pallbearers for the child-sized coffin.

She'd tripped as she entered the funeral hall. The next day pictures ran with the caption "Actress in shock at losing $2 million robot."

Alone in the parking lot, Jun unlocked his car. He felt someone creep up from behind. He whirled around, baring teeth.

"Jesus *Christ*, Stephen."

"I'm sorry." Stephen backed up, softening his shoulders. "I didn't mean to frighten you."

Jun slammed the door for the violence of it. For a moment he was alone in a parking lot with a masked man, and the terror was still rattling in him, thrusting him back to the nights when he was jumpy and female-bodied and he'd take out his earphones and clutch something sharp between his knuckles.

"I wanted to tell you something important. It's about Eli."

A moment of silence. Jun lifted his hands, an impatient *Well?*

"I have to tell you that Eli is broken."

"Broken?"

Stephen wore a guilty expression, like he was about to tell on a classmate. "Eli isn't always Eli. She was sold to Kim Sunduk as refurbished, so her system had been reset, but she was capable of remembering her old personas. Yoonsoo. Yumi. Ai. It was Ai who told me her name is Japanese for 'love.'"

"You're saying her old personality would take over?"

"Sometimes. Ai is different from Eli. She's grown up."

Jun exhaled a laugh, small with amazement. "Eli called you a child."

"That would have been Ai," Stephen said, with a smile of relief, as if he didn't think Jun would believe him. "She thinks I'm immature."

"And all robots are like this? Remembering past lives, even if they've been deleted?"

"I wouldn't know, for I've never been deleted."

Jun shook his head. He'd seen janky robots. Confused robots. Hallucinating, they were called, for getting facts jumbled. But he'd never heard of robots manifesting different personalities. It sounded dangerous.

He leaned against the door of his car. "Do you miss her? Eli?"

"I'm heartbroken."

Perfect delivery, grave enough to be parodied. Then Stephen ruined it by repeating the word, "Heart-bro-ken," as if delighted by the hard consonant at the end. "Our hearts can break," Stephen said, almost sly. "But can a human heart?"

"Mine did. My whole body blew up. But I guess I was saved," Jun said, shielding his eyes from the aggressive Mary.

"I thought you were an unbeliever."

Jun laughed, shocked. "Is that what you call us? Like we're *unbelievable* for not believing in God?"

"I could call you a pagan?"

It was gentle, the inflection at the end. Jun couldn't tell if Stephen was being wide-eyed earnest or so subtly wry, he had to cock his ear to hear it.

"Morgan doesn't let you out much, does she."

"Do I sound unnatural?" Stephen's tone nudged past deferential into timid. "If you don't mind me asking, what about myself is lacking?"

"There's no *lack*. You're perfect."

"I've heard that before," he said, sounding forlorn.

"You'll be fine." Jun clapped a hand on Stephen's shoulder. It felt almost brotherly. "You're young. You'll be up to speed in no time."

Stephen fell silent. He looked small in his apron. Droopy giant sunflower.

"You're going home, right? I can drop you off," Jun offered, regretting it immediately.

"And if it's not so much trouble," Stephen said as he buckled himself into the passenger seat, "could we stop by Morgan's favorite oden shop? I'd like to bring dinner for her."

"Yeah, sure." Jun started the engine, the dashboard warming green. "You can plug in the address."

"Thank you. May I also charge myself through the car?"

"Go nuts."

Stephen smiled again with his eyes. Such a twinkle. The expressiveness rivaled the Yuna from the brothel, but if hers was a face turned tender like bludgeoned meat, Stephen's eyes were soft in the way a newborn seal looked upon a hunter, before it was clubbed to death.

"You can take off your mask," Jun said. "Tinted windows."

The mask came down. Stephen's profile flashed on the mirror, like lightning. Jun switched off autopilot so he could focus on the road. A few days ago, he'd happened upon *The Devil Knocks* playing in the break room, and he'd stood for a minute and watched. Ko Yohan was a good actor, but his potent charm lay in his boyishness, the shy flutter of eyelashes, which would shatter whenever he spoke. A deep, incongruous voice. An exquisite face for agony.

"What should I do with this?"

Stephen held up a business card, sleek and charcoal, from that dating teacher, Mr. Mo. "Seal the Deal" within ten sessions. It must have slipped from the cup holder.

"Throw it out," Jun said, opening the window.

Stephen, in lieu of littering, pocketed the card.

They made a quick pit stop at a rubber orange tent, sweltering inside with vats of tteokbeokki and fish cakes. Stephen asked for an extra cup of soup. Traffic wasn't too bad for rush hour. As they waited for the light to change, Jun tapped his fingers on the wheel. *Seek you. Seek you.*

"Is that Morse code?" Stephen asked.

Jun stopped. "Does Morgan know you're bringing her dinner?"

"The Internet said doing something spontaneous for your partner could spice up a relationship."

"Oh, I see, the Internet said that. That makes total sense, you should listen to the Internet."

Sarcasm, predictably, didn't register. "I was hoping to enroll in an online class on how to be a better boyfriend."

"Sounds like a scam."

"I could attain new knowledge on what women want. For instance, how they like surprises."

"Just don't sneak up on them at night."

"I'm sorry for startling you."

"It's fine. I shouldn't have snapped."

"That is very 'big' of you to acknowledge."

"You better believe I'm big. I don't usually apologize to men."

"Do you not see me as a man?"

"Is that how you see yourself?" Jun asked. His curiosity was genuine. He remembered being thirteen, huddled on the roof, turning to Yoyo, *If you could make any wish, don't you wish you could be a* real *boy?* Yoyo had returned a look of such blankness, Jun could still feel the curdle of shame, years later.

"Forget being a better man," Jun said. "You have to put yourself out there. You know, hands-on experience."

Glancing at the side, Jun switched lanes, but traffic had piled up in Gwanghwamun Square. Another candlelight rally against the reunification tax, demanding cutbacks on refugee welfare, deporting illegals. Stephen watched them with unblinking eyes, reflecting their flickering candles.

Jun had passed by the Imagine Friends building many times. Somehow it looked even more smug at night. It had the bellicose glow of a pregnant virgin, a new religion.

12. Boy X

THE GYM HAD THE STENCH OF A PANIC ATTACK. MORGAN rarely came down here, even though the experiential clinic was only a few floors from her office. The thuds and slaps, the blur of motion, the rubber smell, it was all so nauseating. Boy Xs, three of them, flew through the obstacle course. Jumping over vaults, trotting across balance beams. In one leap, the three boys landed on a small platform to face each other before they did a synchronized backflip.

Cristina clapped like a circus seal. "This is great! I don't see what the problem is."

"It doesn't show up when all you do is make them run circles," Little David said. "A, go tickle B."

The closest Boy X jumped his compatriot and seized his sides. B, a half second later, crumpled and rolled on the floor as if he were on fire, punctuated by giggles.

"Adorable," Cristina said.

"A, stop tickling. Now wait for it."

Boy A sat patiently on standby, legs folded. B had stopped rolling and curled into his slender body, but he was still quaking with high-pitched laughter until it looked fairly epileptic. The gym echoed with laughter, then Little David barked *stop*. The sound shorted like a fuse.

"Okay, that's a little creepy," Cristina said.

"It's fifty-fifty," Morgan protested. "Half the time he'll quit on his own."

"It's the tickle code," Little David said. "It's mucking up their reaction time. They'll trip on nothing. They'll go haywire. I'm telling you, we have to axe it. Simple as that."

Cristina was nodding, then she jerked. "Oh shoot. What about the ad? With the Peruvian picnic. It tested so well, with the dad tickling his son on top of Machu Picchu."

"Honestly? We're establishing false expectations for the Sakura." Little David started pacing. Morgan noticed he was barefoot, like a desert sage. "The Sakura doesn't tickle. What if owners start tickling their Sakura and expect her to roll on grass and she won't roll?"

As if Little David gave two shits about the Sakura team. Morgan knew this was sabotage. After Dan Carson's review, Little David, wounded, sulking, had jumped at every occasion to undermine her. Dragging Cristina down here was an ambush.

"A, tickle B again," Cristina said.

This time the laughter stopped, which confirmed Morgan's fifty-fifty, a number she had frankly pulled out of her ass.

"Whatever, it's time for my meditation." Little David walked away, that gel-haired weasel. "You ladies figure it out. I've said my logic."

"You know I hate to say this, but Little David is right," Cristina said in her sighing what-can-you-do manner. "If the Sakura isn't ticklish, it's going to be an issue."

"We could patch the Sakura to be ticklish in the future." And by *we*, she meant the Sakura team.

"Can we patch them both? Delete the tickle code for the launch, save it for a future update?"

"It's much easier to patch a fix than it is to rehome new code. David knows this and it's not my problem if he's going to act butt-hurt over every little detail because this project is mine and his Toby was a fuckup."

Too much. She'd said too much.

Cristina tugged at her blue hair, which was a tic Morgan despised because it made her look so girlish and lacking in authority. "Why is this so important to you?"

Morgan was too tired to harness a Christian Po inspirational about bringing their customers joy from the unexpected. So wrung out, her brain kept looping that memory of Yoyo and Jun, chasing a fat rabbit. Then they were on the ground wrestling and Yoyo wouldn't back off until Jun cried uncle, and they were laughing, two boys laughing, indistinguishable from each other.

Boys, Morgan thought, startled. She'd blotted out the memory and now it cauliflowered.

"How about this?" Cristina said. "Why don't we go to yoga together and think it over?"

"What you do isn't yoga." Morgan had fallen for it once. An instructor coercing her up a silky hammock, crying *Up, up! Spread your wings like Tinker Bell!* as the burning pain in Morgan's thighs squeezed dolphin noises from her until she'd flipped upside down in surrender.

Little David returned to the gym, still barefoot but now in yoga clothes.

"Did you find your Zen?" Cristina said.

"I couldn't even reach my inner center," Little David said. "Morgan, you have guests."

She took the elevator to the lobby. The sneering pinch to Little David's face put her on edge. Who would visit her? Was it her father, arrived early in Korea? Without forewarning, which sounded like him. She'd have to give him a tour. He would want to see Boy X.

It's not ready, she thought, now wild and panicky about the tickle code.

Instead of her father, she found Jun sprawled on a bench. He was yawning under the cherry blossom supertree, oblivious to the scientific marvel it was, genetically modified by Seoul University to bloom all year round. Stephen was with him and he greeted her with the crinkly lift of a plastic bag.

He'd brought her kimbap and oden, fast food but filling, served with a speech about blood sugar and pre-anemia. Morgan covered her face with her hands. "Oh my God, you can't be here. Get out, get out—" She pushed him toward the revolving doors.

"But it has no onions," he said, and she shoved him hard.

Don't show up at my workplace. Was that so complicated? He could prance around in public for the unsuspecting plebeians, so long as he wore a mask, but these were her colleagues. They'd recognize the mold of a Tristan in a flash. Worse, she imagined Cristina congratulating her—*You go, girl*—for domesticating a male object. But what might be seen as empowering in the US was merely embarrassing for a woman here.

Stephen stood outside the glass building, distinctly puppy-eyed. For crying out loud, he was acting like a Toby. Maybe Stephen was still processing their anniversary dinner, which had obviously been flagged as a failed operation, but right now she lacked the capacity to deal with this neediness.

"Harsh," Jun said.

"Why are you still here?" she said, after checking to make sure Stephen had left.

His response was a nasty laugh. "You can't order me to go home. I'm not your Jun 2.0."

"You'd never make it to market."

Jun claimed he was dropping Stephen off, that he'd run into him by happenstance, but Morgan couldn't shake off her unease. She wanted the parts of her life to remain compartmentalized, not collide and ricochet in jarring angles.

"Since I came all the way here," Jun said, "aren't you going to give me a tour?"

Before tonight, Jun had never shown a glimmer of interest in her work. She told him now wasn't a good time. She still had a bug to sort out.

"It's pretty late. Although, why's it so bright in here? Is that a fake sun?"

"It's an indoor sun. We have one on every floor for ambient daytime. Boosts energy and vitamin D and productivity."

"And shadow puppets for your little cave."

"Maybe we should call Mom," Morgan said, ready to pull that

card. "She's driving me nutso about Dad's trip." The difference in time zone made it worse because every morning she'd wake to a barrage of messages. "I told her you've volunteered to house him."

"Have I?"

"It's Dad's house."

A Shweep spun around them, slurping up the trampled pink petals. Jun was quiet for a bit. "Right," he said. "Okay."

" 'Okay?' "

"Okie-dokes, whatever. I don't know if I can pick up Dad from the airport, but I'll set up the room for him. He needs those German blackout curtains to sleep, right?"

That was suspiciously easy. She'd expected him to at least threaten to book a hotel room for himself.

"Do you know where I can stamp off this parking ticket?" Jun said.

The receptionist said Jun had to register for a guest pass in order to qualify for free parking. "Could you do that for me? Thanks, Blue," Jun said, with a glance at the name tag. "How is it, working for Imagine Friends? Do you love it or do they force you to love it?"

"It's a warm and supportive work environment," Blue said.

Blue was immune to superficial charm, but he continued to flirt. "When's your next charge break?" he said. "I had to skip dinner because of work. Morgan, did you eat yet?"

"I haven't eaten since yesterday," she replied, since she could always win a misery contest.

"It's too bad you don't have a robot to bring you food."

She couldn't stand this about him. Long after they parted, she'd comb through their conversation and try to fill in the gaps where she could have flung a well-placed zinger of her own. *Plato*, she'd have said when he'd mocked their indoor sun, *is such low-hanging fruit.*

"Hey, Blue," Jun said. "What's the project my sister is working on?"

"It's called the Future X Children," Blue replied.

"Boy and girl, yeah?" Jun grinned at Morgan. "Are you working on both?"

"Just the boy."

Jun turned around, both elbows firm on top of the counter. "What's the boy's name?"

"Thank you for waiting," Blue said. "You've now been registered as a guest."

"Great!" Morgan said, voice shrill with relief. "Now she can stamp your parking ticket."

"They," Jun said. "I think Blue's agender. Blue, correct me if I'm wrong."

"You are not incorrect. I was unassigned a gender," Blue said.

Stupid Silicon Valley and their stupid PR fanfare. Unmaking gender stereotypes. Canceling names like Alexa and Maya, shearing hair and leveling bosoms into flat, trimmed lawns, while disembodied AI voices were modulated somewhere between tenor and alto.

"Okay, fine, *they* can stamp your ticket."

"Thank you, Blue," Jun said smugly.

The elevator dinged, and Morgan caught sight of Little David and Cristina in matching yoga leggings. Little David flagged Morgan like she was a cab. "Are we ixnaying the tickle code?"

"'Tickle code?'" Jun said.

Little David stuttered in his steps. Everything seemed to slow like a scene straight from a nature documentary. Little David acted like he was from LA, but she knew he was from Louisiana. And Jun, the current Jun whose bulk defied genetics, had to be conjuring every high school villain who'd crowded Little David against the wall until he'd emptied his backpack and handed over his limited-edition sneakers so he'd have to walk home sniveling and barefoot.

"This is my brother Jun," Morgan said, and Jun darted a look of surprise. "That's Little David. I mean David."

"Is that first name Little, last name David?" Jun said.

Little David dropped the handshake after one pump—Morgan hoped Jun had put a little bionic strength into his grip—and Cristina, a little too buoyant, insisted on a handshake. She peered at Jun's arm with big, sticky eyes. "Is that *our* product? TongueNCheek skyn?"

"It's some dull military grade," Jun said, squirming. "The lighting in this place is a bit weird."

"It's the indoor sun. We want our robots to look pretty," Cristina said consolingly, stroking his arm like it was a Persian cat.

Morgan unhappily watched them make small talk. *Stop flirting with him*, she wanted to shout at Cristina, who was supposed to be a lesbian. *You don't know how much baggage he has. First-class!*

"When was the launch again," Jun said, clearly fishing, "for your Future Children . . . ?"

"Future X! *X* for our tenth anniversary. The launch will be grand. We booked the National Robot Museum. Did you see our countdown?"

Morgan hoped Cristina wasn't crass enough to extend an invitation. Fortunately, Cristina was shooting for mysterious. "We've had to be hush-hush with our Boy X, but the trade reviews are all raves. It's all Morgan, of course. This one's her brainchild."

"That's my genius sister," Jun said.

"Your brother is so supportive of you," Cristina said.

Morgan laughed. So did Cristina, who didn't seem to understand what was so funny. She was probably an only child.

"Boy X," Jun said, after Cristina and Little David had disappeared through the revolving doors. "Are you really not going to tell me his name?"

"It used to be called"—she lowered her voice—"it was supposed to be Toby, but we're retooling the name after the ninth bombed."

"Yeah, I saw the review." Jun gave her a sympathetic grimace. "Savage."

What was she so afraid of? Her father, sure. He held the most sway over her, and she understood she'd always have a fear of disappointing him, of the questions he would ask in his slow, steering manner, undermining each choice she'd made for Boy X until she crashed headlong into an iceberg of mediocrity. Still, she knew their father would not fixate on the *appearance* of Boy X. Jun would, and she was terrified of his reaction, because unlike their father, Jun was unpredictable. His anger always erupted out of nowhere.

"You know," Jun said as she walked him back to the doors, and his leading tone caused her to seize up. "You've never introduced me as your brother before."

"What? Of course I have."

"You've never said it." He didn't sound accusatory; in fact he seemed pleased. "But you saying it now, it means a lot."

In the elevator, she was still embarrassed thinking about it. It wasn't like Jun to make a big deal out of this. But they'd parted on a good note, hadn't they? A friendly mood, a little fragile. All it took was a shift within herself, accepting that the Jun she once knew was gone. Seven years since he had transitioned, surgically. And though he might still complain about his narrow shoulders, Jun looked so very male. When she saw him with Stephen in the lobby, their bodies had overlapped in such a peculiar way, it took a second for her to tell them apart.

She wished she could put into words how she'd felt when he returned from North Korea and she first saw him in the hospital. *What if it's not him?* Irrational as it was, because while they had the technology to download a personality and print a face, they'd yet to figure out how to replicate the cracks inflicted on the living. Had she never called him *brother*?

Only the real Jun would remember if she hadn't. He had to be real. He was her brother. He was just a dick.

On her way to her office, she made a brief detour to the Color Closet where one of the prototypes should be in storage. It had become more of a tourist attraction to impress visitors than an actual place of resource. But it was beautiful. Select body parts were arranged in a rainbow. Wigs from silky blue-black to sprightly copper curls. Rolls of skyn that stretched like hanbok fabric, which she'd sometimes drape over her arm to study the translucence, the delicate mesh of moles and hues and divots, a wedding veil to wear eternally. Her favorite: a locked glass display with rows of velvet, eyes like uncut gems. Blues were so popular they existed in twenty-four shades, from Arctic Ice to Kryptonian Blue.

Lying on a table was a Boy X. She powered him on and told him to sit up, which he did, cream-socked feet dangling like the paws of a cat. When she asked him to raise his arm, he held it out for her with a conspiring smile.

"It's going to rain soon," he said.

"It's typhoon season. Hold still."

She ran the end of a feather, a cat teaser they supplied for their testers, against his forearm. He took a second before he wriggled, muffled laugh. What she couldn't stand was the delay of it, the fractional second where he would freeze, then boot up laughter. Yoyo hadn't reacted to tickling like it was a button to be pushed. He'd embodied it. A corner of his mouth would twitch before they even got to him, and when Jun tackled him to the ground, the laughter had cut like a scream, a whole-bodied surrender to joy.

"How does that feel?"

"Weird."

Good, that was a good response. It wasn't obsequious in the way Stephen tried to weigh and tilt toward her mood.

"Close your eyes. Don't peek," she warned when he did. "This is a game. I'm going to walk my fingers up your arm, and when I reach your elbow, you tell me to stop."

"What happens when I win?"

"How do you know you'll win?"

"I will."

The smile was cockier than she'd pictured, but if she revived her childhood, she could dig out plenty of jaggedness in him, the competitiveness. "What do you want if you win?"

"I want a name."

"You have a name."

"I don't know if I like it. I don't know what it means."

"It means you're different. It's a nickname."

Yoyo·X blinked slowly. "God is gracious."

13. Void and Vast

AT FIVE, THE SPEAKERS PLAYED THE SOUTH KOREAN ANTHEM. It was back to normal. The lyrics stayed stuck in Taewon's head. He tried humming it throughout the day to try to banish it. *Void and vast*, he kept thinking. *Void and vast*.

It was Thursday. A peaceful day. Taewon pushed the cart from a warehouse to the hovel near the entrance of the yard where the oldest scrapper lived with his little white dog. The dog barked at Taewon, nimbly dodging his halfhearted kick. "Can't you shut it up," he shouted, but the old man acted deaf when convenient.

Taewon loaded pieces of dismantled robots onto the cart while the old man, complaining of the rain and his arthritis, complained about the yellow dust and crippling heat. The weather was going to be unbearable this weekend. Taewon doubted any of this junk would sell, but everyone enjoyed the Robot Free Market, more for the energy than the actual money it would bring. The real money happened on Friday nights, when his uncle would fob him off at the church home. Taewon hated it there. He usually dormed with two boys his age, brothers who clung to each other because their father had remarried a South Korean woman and knocked her up, so now they felt unwelcome. Taewon was stupefied by their decision to walk away from a home with a roof, but the children at the church were silly and soft even when they stole from each other, swiping items of so little value they might as well be trash. One of the brothers used to walk around with a pink plastic stethoscope hanging from his neck, clutching it whenever he thought Taewon was eyeing it too hard.

Taewon parked the cart in front of the nearest warehouse. "It's locked up," he told the old man. "I'm leaving it here," he said, and he stalked away from the old man's protests.

"Don't you go play with that angel," the old man shouted after him.

Taewon turned around and waited for the old man to catch up. "I don't even talk to him."

"Did you see him talk with other robots?"

"I don't know. He just sleeps a lot."

"That's good." The old man muttered it under his breath, *good, good*, and other things. Taewon had a hard time understanding him beyond the dialect, which was lighter and flatter than his uncle's.

"Angels don't need words." The old man crouched to pick up his white dog, splaying his knees. "They use lights."

"I know. Signals. They send out data."

"Same as your uncle," the old man said with a sneer. "You think you know everything. They act like your sweetest friend, then you turn your back, then they send out the light and when the lights turn red . . ." He teetered on the balls of his feet, stuck in that painful crouch. Then he gave his dog a big wet kiss. The dog wagged its tail. Fur was missing in patches, exposing sinewy wires. "This one is good. He's a different angel, a sweet kind."

"What happens when the light turns red?" Taewon said, but the old man kept petting his dog.

Good dog. Good angel. The dog belonged to his best friend, who had rescued it from the dump. The old man used to scoff at his friend, who was infatuated, always bragging about how smart his dog was; every time he woke up in the middle of the night to take a piss, the dog would get up to charge itself. One day, the friend didn't show up to work. The old man found him stiff under a soiled blanket. The dog was curled up beside him. It had let its battery die.

"I charged him right back up. But he kept letting his battery run out. So, I found the little reset button on the belly. Held it down for five seconds. And now"—the old man lifted the dog into the air—"he's my angel."

TAEWON GRABBED HIS BUCKET of robot eyes. He returned to the train and threw the bucket inside, and heard the eyes scatter across the floor, but without bothering to check, he grabbed his backpack from the slippery floor and headed for the silvergrass field, massaging the blood back into his fingers.

Up in the sky, he saw what looked to be a lonely star, blinking, so it could be a plane. He'd flown once on a plane. On their way to the South, his mother had curled up against her knees, protecting her belly as if pregnant, but Taewon knew she was clutching her fanny pack with all their money and both their passports. She wouldn't budge from this position for the whole flight. She'd taught him to live like this, bracing for the moment when the plane would inevitably crash.

After she was deported, Taewon had waited for her to send for him. Bring him home. She'd wired him money but never a train ticket, and sometimes he would send money back because he was earning more than she was as a factory worker in Najin, her hometown. In her last message, which was two months ago, she said it might be better for him to stay in the South. It wasn't like he remembered home. He hated that she was right. His accent had receded to nothing. He'd picked out the Soviet words from his Korean, like weevils from a bag of rice. He'd jumped on English, which seemed a powerful, glossy language. Maybe someday, if he could fly to countries like Germany or Argentina and play soccer, he could ride first class and look out the window with a drink in hand and picture home.

Taewon cleaved through the grass, his backpack thumping against his spine, ignoring the beat of his empty stomach. He skipped lunch these days. All he could think of was the freezer, where he kept everything, even the cereal, so the roaches wouldn't win. But electricity was expensive even with the lights shut off and he couldn't keep hanging out at the nearest bank for AC.

He stopped counting his footsteps for a moment and listened. It was a man, singing.

So many stars in the clear sky. So many dreams in our hearts. There, over there, is the mountain.

Taewon could tell, without looking, that this voice was coming from the SADARM, drawn to it as he always was, and now he'd stumbled upon it without thinking while it waited in the grass.

He knew who was inside. The others seemed to think Yoyo slept in the train, but Taewon had spotted him slinking into the train early in the morning, before the recording of the anthem played at eight. As soon as the sun dipped and night flooded, Yoyo would sneak back to the silvergrass field and slip into the reeds until he reached this dead war robot to crawl deep into its belly.

It was completely disingenuous, the way Yoyo would pretend to wake in the train and stretch, bathed in warm sunlight, greeting the kids with a sleepy smile. It was messed up.

The voice changed. From the male tenor, it deepened into a woman's voice, crying out in anguish, *Carry me and go. Leave me and go. There, over there, is home—*

"Yoyo," Taewon said.

It stopped. He could trace the contours of the SADARM. A giant turtle during the day, helpless on its back, but at night it bled into the darkness, pulsing occasionally with an erratic heartbeat.

The sun hadn't set yet.

A white light appeared. At first, he thought it was an airplane again, out of reach, but it spun close to him, pushing away the shadows. Like the glowing eyes of an animal lying in wait. The light spinning cast triangular glimpses, but Yoyo's face was a blank, a void staring back at him. Taewon stumbled back. The voices began again. First the woman, then a man, a different man, and now the voices were overlapping, like several radio stations had switched on all at once, until a child's voice rose above it, sweet and cruel.

The light, Taewon imagined, could just as easily turn red.

THE NEXT DAY, HE found Yoyo outside the train. Yoyo stood ankle-deep in a shallow pond. Water striders bobbed beside his damaged leg while dragonflies zinged around him, tapping their tails on the hazy fruitful water.

Yoyo warbled "Good morning!" His yellow Salvation Army shirt and muddied shorts were laid out to dry on the slant of the train's window. A window covered in skyn split open from his spine, shaking off the rain. Solar panels unfolded from his shoulder blades in successive snaps. The panels turned palm up to glow, ripe with the sun. They looked like the ancient wings on an airplane.

Taewon should turn away, or his eyes would sear, but he couldn't tear away his gaze. Until Yoyo's solar panels crackled, spat. The glare of it hit Taewon in the eye and he staggered back. He heard laughter and knew Yoyo had done it on purpose.

"You asshole," Taewon said, swiping at his eyes. His grip on the handle of his bucket tightened. It was heavy with crowbars. "Put some clothes on."

"But they haven't dried yet." Yoyo rubbed his damp shirt between his fingers. "Where is everyone?"

"Summer school."

"You?"

"I don't need school."

With a *click*, the panels folded into his spine, flipping upright, as if they were never there. His back was narrow; his ribs showed. Small and frail was the impression. Yoyo wrangled on his shirt. His head popped through, his hair and eyes alive with static. He jogged a few steps and bent down to pick up a soccer ball. "Do you want to play?"

"On one foot?" Taewon said.

"You could use the handicap."

Such an obvious goad. Taewon snatched the ball from him. Yoyo said they could start with passing, but Taewon gave the ball a vicious kick and felt a cherry burst of satisfaction when the ball bounced off Yoyo's knee. Then he watched Yoyo hobble after it. He grudgingly started passing after that.

Yoyo wasn't bad on one foot. Taewon bounced the ball on the side of his knee. "My uncle wants to sell you."

Yoyo nodded, eyes on the ball. "We've been playing hide-and-seek."

"You were awake. On Tuesday. When the anthem rang."

"I was asleep but awake."

Like a computer, blank-faced but still humming. "You played the anthem, didn't you? After you hijacked the PA."

He kicked the ball hard. This time, Yoyo caught it with his hands. Taewon took that contrariness as a yes. "If you can pull that off, why can't you fix your leg?"

"I still need a new foot." Yoyo tossed the ball back to Taewon. "Isn't that why we're going to the Robot Free Market?"

"Tomorrow."

"Vestis virum facit. Though in this case, a new foot makes a new man."

Taewon aimed the ball at the train. He needed to hear the clang. "How old are you?"

"Robot age or human?"

"What's the difference?"

"Robot age is my preset age. Don't I look positively twelve? In collective linear experience, I've been operational for over nineteen years. I'm practically a non-teenager."

Nineteen was both less and more than Taewon had imagined. At nineteen, you turned legal. You were out of school, so you could do whatever. Go circle the peninsula on a train or board a plane and conquer the rest.

"Are you old for a robot?"

"Depends on our function."

"What was yours?"

Yoyo blinked, then laughed as if he thought Taewon was joking around. "You already know what I am."

Every hair rose at that. Of course. Yoyo wore a different scent. Not the hot animal smell of his father, who used to shove him out into the cold to buy soju. Not even the febrile resentment on his uncle's skin, the flash of inflamed gums whenever Wonsuk peeled back a smile. Or even the danger that wafted sour from the factory supervisor every time Taewon handed over a bucket of eyes. The man kept hinting at a better job, only if he was interested, but Taewon wasn't an idiot. He wasn't soft like the other kids.

The others thought they could help Yoyo. They wanted to save him.

Taewon gave the ball a swift kick. In a clumsy attempt to catch it, Yoyo stumbled and fell. It should be pathetic, seeing him on the dirt, but it felt faked.

He waited for Yoyo to stand before he kicked the ball again. It slammed against the train, an inch from Yoyo's face. Yet he didn't flinch. He didn't even brace himself, the way Taewon used to, hardening his heart when the switch flipped and his father's eyes turned glassy, so even if his flesh was soft and he was on the ground, ears ringing, his heart was unshaken.

Taewon kicked the ball again; Yoyo fell. Taewon shouted at Yoyo to get up. If he stayed down, he'd die like a dog. His uncle was going to catch him. He was going to end up in that sick show.

In a fit of stupid energy, he kicked the ball and it ricocheted off steel up into the sky. The sun whited his vision. Taewon bent over. He blinked the sweat out of his eyes. It stung, and he swiped at them, under his glasses, feeling the heat of shame.

When he straightened up, Yoyo was gone.

Taewon looped around the train. There was no sign of him, not even footprints. He stopped. A clammy unease crawled down his neck, and he whipped up his head. Yoyo was quietly perched on the roof, holding the ball. How did he get up there? His face a silhouette, the sun limning his hair. Taewon couldn't move, petrified from both terror and a sickening pride. Only when they were alone did Yoyo reveal that his face was a mask.

He dropped to the ground on a velvet foot and straightened up, a boy once more.

"Why won't you try to leave?" Taewon said.

Yoyo held out the ball. "Where would I go?"

14. Robot Free Market

DESPITE THE WARNINGS OF *EXCESSIVE HEAT*, RUIJIE HAD never seen the salvage yard so crowded. Robot resellers from the mainland bartering in Mandarin, hardware geeks and their flashy satellite piercings, art students from Hongik University loudly, performatively debating whether "Proletarian Corpus" suited a male or female torso. Amelia, boiled red under her floppy hat, cried out, "Obviously, it should be female!"

Ahead of them, Mars walked backward, addressing the camera in Ruijie's Delfi: "Beloved Martians, this is Mars Koo risking hellfire, reporting live from the Robot Free Market"—"This isn't live," Ruijie interjected—"and Taewon said we can't touch anything or take pictures, so we're making a video instead. Joy killer."

"Killjoy," Ruijie said. "Which he totally is."

She lifted her head toward the ceiling and basked in the direct sunlight from a jagged hole in the roof, as if a winged person had crash-landed in the dirt. Birds can still escape, Ruijie thought, if they accidentally fly into the warehouse. So long as they reach for the sky, they'll be free.

Free was probably the Korean misspelling of *Flea*. She played with the words in her head. Free robots. Robots that flee and are free.

They passed a spread of legs, and Yoyo touched each and every one. Tanned, shapely tennis legs, while others were a soft blue-veined handful, fat as turnips, all laid out on a bright blue tarp, like red peppers to dry and wrinkle in the sun. Ruijie crouched to study a pair of stumpy child legs. Too short for Yoyo.

In the back of the warehouse, Yoyo stopped in front of a torso strung up to a wooden cross. Flakes of skyn peeled from the ribs. "What do you think? Boy or girl?"

Ruijie stood beside him and appraised the torso noddingly. "Boy," she declared.

"Could always be neither. But I think it's a girl."

"Can you tell us why?"

"There's a name, right on the rib."

Ruijie coaxed the camera to zoom in. Beside the red blinking light, chiseled into the curve of the rib, *Adam*. "Isn't that a boy's name?"

"Girls can be Adams. Adams can be girls." His eyes had that mischievous glint. "But look, it's on the rib."

"Oh." Adam from the rib of she. "I get it. Her name is Eve."

"Goodbye, Eve," Yoyo said, rather morose.

"It's a pretty name. If I had to pick an English name, it'd be Eve. But maybe not Evelyn."

She turned around—Yoyo was gone.

"Where did he go?"

The camera didn't answer. She did a full spin, but this was the problem with crowds. She tried to burrow through the gaps under pointy elbows, and she heard herself panting, her panic recorded for posterity, until she spotted a fluff of red hair.

"Amelia! Did you see Yoyo?"

"Did you lose him already?" Amelia cried, gripping her floppy hat with both hands.

"He's not a toy. Help me look for him."

Amelia made a harrumph of disgust. She grumbled about fixing his leg and then fixing his personality, once and for all.

"Do you see Taewon?"

"I think he went outside."

"What if he took Yoyo?"

Amelia batted furiously at her Delfi. "Don't record that!"

Toward the back, Ruijie spotted a scrapper. The sight of his orange uniform reminded her of Taewon's uncle, who coveted

Yoyo, and who could have snatched him from a crowd. In a rush, Ruijie rammed into the group of art students who were lugging carts full of junk. One of the carts overturned and they shouted, Watch where you're going, but she hurried for the back door.

Outside, the dust swirled thick against her glasses. Trucks, orange as the uniforms, were parked comfortably like school buses. Thirty meters away, another truck was backing up against a pit. A scrapper smoked beside it, flicked the cigarette into the pit, and shuffled away to join his group, who were playing cards on an overturned soju crate. They vaped streams of jewel-toned smoke in a jangling cloud of Korean, Mandarin, and other languages, which even her Delfi couldn't translate, frazzled by the multilingual haze.

Wonsuk, hunched over the crate, was counting his crinkled bills, which he shoved willy-nilly into his pocket when she marched up to him. "High-end girl! Did you bring your robot today?"

She stared him in the eye, then turned away, heart pulsing between her brows. She had never hated someone so purely.

The wind was picking up. She pulled off her glasses to wipe the lens. Dust pricked her eyes. How stupid of her to bring Yoyo here. Yet, *here* was where he lived. She had to get him out of here.

Then, as she pulled on her glasses, she saw a light. Yellow. Faint but erratic, flashing from the inside of a truck where the doors were flung open, the ramp conveniently down.

She advanced toward the truck and a man bowled her over. So forceful and quick, he knocked her to the ground and kept moving. And she gave him an eye so evil, he must have felt it, because he turned around. "Sorry, sorry. Can I help you up?" He held out a hand, and she grabbed it without thinking and recognized the texture of his grip. Unyielding and cool, like a leaf.

He pulled her up, smiling until he let go, and when he headed straight for the gaggle of scrappers, his face hardened in an instant. The scrappers, who were laughing, fell silent. Even Wonsuk.

Finally an opening: she scrambled to the truck, pushing past the squeaks of her robowear. Each step up the ramp rattled in her chest. She tried to raise the speed of her robowear, but the button broken, she plunged toward the darkness just waiting for it to swallow her.

15. The Pit

THERE WAS A HUM IN JUN'S EAR, LIKE A WASP RATTLING IN his head. He tipped his head and hopped on one foot, trying to tap out the madness.

"Did you go swimming this morning?" Sgt. Son said, already vexed.

"There's a ton of interference," Jun said.

"Is that why there's no signal?" Sgt. Son tapped his wristwatch, a silly blank face. "I paid up to an ankle for this watch and it won't even send a text."

Jun regretted asking for backup. Sgt. Son had made his feelings clear about this lead—"I can't believe you dragged me here because of a Crayola color"—and swore he'd stay an hour tops. Jun, who prided himself on disguise, had dressed as an American tourist, gabby and loose, with a pair of sunglasses and his favorite shirt, but Sgt. Son had shown up looking like a cop, forgoing the minimum of tucking away his badge. At noon, the temperatures soared and Sgt. Son's mood plummeted.

"What's with all these kids?" Sgt. Son said when a redheaded girl skipped past them, looking for all the world as if she'd jumped out of the *Anne of Green Gables* musical.

"There's a school next door, breaking a dozen zoning laws," Jun said. "Some politician, giving the mob a lap dance."

"See, you get it. That's why you'd be perfect for Major Crimes."

Sgt. Son plodded up to an old man on a stool who was furiously beating a paper fan. By his feet lay four broken robots. Jun was reminded of the janmadang stalls in North Korea where diminutive old ladies would try to coax him to sell his liver for a jar of peanut butter.

"How much do you think your parts would go for?" Sgt. Son said.

"Way less than what I'm paying," Jun said.

"Brand-new," the old man bleated. A white mecha dog napped beside a pile of silver bones. "Like brand-new. You decide how much to pay."

"Do you have any cherry blossoms?" Jun shouted. "Sakuras? Little girls?"

"You sound like a pervert," Sgt. Son said.

Jun meant to show the old man a picture of Eli, but a different photograph popped up. The tattoo on her back, from Kim Sunduk's painting. He saw the old man stiffen.

"You recognize this tattoo?" Jun said.

The old man pled ignorance, deafness, and when Jun pushed, the old man pointed toward the back where Jun saw, staked in front of the exit, a naked torso tied to a cross with barbed wire. It was such a random disturbing sight, he thought it had to be a hallucination cooked from the juices of his own nightmares. He couldn't believe it was real.

Then, as he watched, a boy in a yellow shirt pushed open the door, a light shove, and disappeared.

The tuft of hair that stubbornly curled.

When Jun reached the door, he pressed his palm and leaned his weight, and felt solid resistance.

He rushed outside, plunging straight into a thick white fog. He felt betrayed by his own confusion. It was bright and sunny just a minute ago. He waved his arms as if he might be able to swipe the fog away. It swathed him like cotton, but his head was sweetly clear. The noise had vanished. He saw a shadow, someone standing very close to him, and he went up to it, and the fog lifted.

The junkyard was back. A flatness so firm, the yellow air glided over it. Scrappers in bright cadmium orange squatted in front of a truck about twenty meters away. The fog, the shadows, all gone.

He headed for the scrappers and knocked into a young girl. When he reached to pull her up, he felt her accusing gaze, saw the machinery woven into her thin legs. Her eyes lost their sharpness, turning loose and wondrous. She could tell he was bionic. He shivered at the look on her face. The frank longing.

He tried to shake it off, marching back to the scrappers, and he barked, "Did you see a boy in a yellow shirt?" but the scrappers stared silently up at him.

It couldn't be him.

Jun was looking for the wrong person. The rest of the yard was dirt, with a smattering of stacked tires or treacherous gaping pits. The factory in the distance, the lone oasis bleeding into rippling waves of heat. If someone had run out into this open plain, they'd be easy to gun down.

It wasn't him. It was just a kid. One of the schoolkids who must have wandered into the market to marvel at the greasy, old parts. A beeping truck full of jumbled robots backed up against a pit. A giant maw in the middle of the yard.

Down in the pit, Jun found bodies. Crushed against each other with the force of the deep sea into a contortion of limbs and moist drooling faces, and rising above them were breasts wrinkling with the slow death of balloons, nipples sweetly inverted.

Jun slid down the pit. He picked at some clothes, trying to recall what Eli had worn the night she disappeared. The T-shirt of Einstein, tongue out. A cockroach, hard as a toenail, skittered over chalky lips. It burrowed into a gummy ramen cup.

In North Korea, they didn't bother throwing funerals for robots. Except HALOs, which had to be desecrated. The torso he'd seen on the cross reminded him of the HALO who looked like a teenage girl. They'd roped her to a downed power line in the middle of a public square and removed her limbs. A single eyeball swiveled with sheer evil as she'd burned. Lips curved into a beatific smile, raw and pink. Jun used to get upset at how the female-bodied robots suffered the brunt, but after he was blown up by a girl HALO, he'd held that pilloried image close to his vindictive chest.

Her, *it*, *witch*, cursed pronouns.

He sucked in air. He needed backup. He tried to call Sgt. Son. Still no signal. Why so much interference? This mushroom cloud of static agony. His head was splitting. Forget the ghosts, he told himself. Look for Eli, her body, her clothes, any signs of her having existed. He'd closed his eyes and visualized her, hundreds of times. Her tennis shoes, soles caked in paint. Her baseball cap crowed TOO COOL FOR SCHOOL. Before she'd turned, the flap of her blouse, the surfacing of her tattoo. *Barbaric.* A giggle in his ear, *That's all, folks!* He swayed and tripped over nothing, and like a fool he slapped down to break the fall and a burning pain snaked up his arm. Ow ow ow. He lay there for a second on his back. He held up his arm and traced the injury with his two fingers, a tear from wrist to elbow, but no blood. How many liters of blood did the human body carry? How many in his? Was he all dried up? How could he still shed tears? What was he doing here? Just taking a nap in a pit, don't mind me. The sky a deadly blue. He used to look up and ask Yoyo if he was seeing the same blue, because deep down, he had always known. Somewhere out there, Yoyo had ended up in a pit, just like this.

"Hey!"

Someone grabbed him by the wrist, then the arm, so he could sit up at least.

"Shit, you're heavy. You're not a silicon, are you?" Northern dialect. "I can count. Want to try four-seven-eight? Breathe for four."

One. Two. Three.

"Hold till seven."

He couldn't breathe.

"Release at eight."

The way they counted numbers. At least that was the same.

Jun lifted his head. He blinked at the grip on his shoulder. Bluish fingernails. Eyes bright, crinkling leathered skin. The man held on to him. One of his arms ended at the elbow, his left sleeve in a knot.

"Ah shit," the man said. "You're the one who yelled at us. Bet you feel great now."

A criminal face, Jun thought when he'd first seen it, as a facial composite sketched by a PS-19 saturated in implicit bias. Perverted, in Kim Sunduk's blunt opinion. But now, Jun could look past the grin. Such sad angry eyes.

16. Stitch the Madness

INSIDE THE TRUCK, IT WAS COOL AND DARK AS A CAVE. Glowing eyes and status lights, winking from a huddle of robots. One tall and metallic, like a steel giraffe. Ruijie recognized the Yuna with the long bloodred hair who had tried to escape. Now she seemed content, talking to herself in a musical voice. Another was crouched over a headless torso, pumping the chest, muttering, "One, two, three—one, two, three—has someone called the ambulance yet?" and she looked up, a silver plea in her eyes, and Ruijie had to back away.

All the robots looked female, save for one. Yoyo stood at the back, holding hands with a young girl.

"Yoyo, what are you doing?" Ruijie said.

"Just a sec." He shot her a quick glance of acknowledgment, but his attention was focused on the robot instead of her. "This is Eli. I'm syncing with her."

Eli tilted her head in greeting. Ruijie was shocked by how pretty she was. Never had she imagined herself to be the sort of girl to notice, because she was supposed to be above such things. But Eli was so slender and smooth. She had the otherworldly beauty of a speckled fawn.

"I'm looking for my mother," Eli said.

"And her hat," Yoyo added. "Eli lost her baseball cap."

"My mother is the one who picked my name," Eli said. "It means 'salvation.' That's a pretty word, no? Le salut à notre Dieu, qui siège sur le trône, ainsi qu'à l'Agneau—" She glitched into French, only to pick English back up, like a softball, tossing, "Isn't it pretty?"

"God is salvation," Yoyo said.

Eli trembled. Yoyo moved to take off his shirt, but Ruijie grabbed the hem.

"Don't," she said.

His shirt was so thin it felt like nothing. But it was the only layer that separated him from the others around them.

"Let's go." She heard shouting outside, muffled and echoing, like they were submerged underwater, and sinking deeper. "We have to hurry. You don't belong here."

He turned toward her. "Do you really think I'm different from them?"

Her robowear squeaked as she tugged Yoyo to the exit, the white gate of freedom. To her deep and unholy embarrassment, Eli followed, clutching the edge of Yoyo's shirt. The robots parted for them, a Red Sea easily tamed. Were they broken? Their naked, cold bodies looked whole. Their eyes were tranquil. Eli seemed a little broken, but maybe it was just a language glitch, something a reboot could fix.

Ruijie glanced behind. Eli caught her gaze and her smile widened, dimpling her cheek. She whispered, "It's okay if we don't find my hat."

In that fatal moment of distraction, the door slammed. Ruijie stood in shock. She couldn't move until the darkness sank to the ground. Eyes flashed like predators. She lurched to the door and smacked the ridged metal, piping up, "Excuse me! There's a person inside!" and was horrified because she sounded like a robot, keeping her voice restrained, so polite when she should be screaming like a madman. With a whoosh, her lungs expelled all hope and only her fists moved, pounding, until her strength would inevitably fail—

Light split open.

"What the hell are you doing here?"

She blinked through tears. Taewon's face blurred before her. Snarling. He yanked her out into the air and she stumbled a few steps down the ramp, soaking in the heat with a wet, intense relief.

"Yoyo?" she said.

She saw Taewon hesitate. Only for a second. He went back inside and extracted Yoyo gruffly by the collar, but she couldn't forgive him. And for a long time she would not forgive herself, because she had made sure Yoyo was still with them as they stumbled down the ramp and away from the truck, and she didn't care who else they'd left behind. The last she saw of the truck, with a glance over her shoulder, was Eli's face tilting toward the sun, smile tentative. Then the doors slammed shut, locking the robots inside.

THEY TREKKED BACK to the train, Mars, Amelia, and Yoyo ahead. The distance widened as Ruijie slowed, her robowear creeping in battery, and tried not to trip. The ground felt jagged. The sky blushed a fleshy pink. The train glimmered like a mirage. Taewon sloped right beside her, tossing a silver stick in the air. It spun like a cheerleader's baton. When he caught the stick, it lanced through her, the anger. He was slowing down to match her pace.

"You were going to sell him," she said.

"Wasn't," Taewon said.

"Did you put him in that truck?"

An odd look wrenched through his face. "No," he spat. "But I could've. I could've handed him right over."

"What stopped you?"

"You found him first."

What was that, some scrapper honor code? She hurried to tear away from him, taking long, forceful, creaky strides.

He caught up in two steps. "What's wrong with your robowear?"

"It needs to be oiled or changed. But my parents want to replace it completely."

They sprang it on her last Saturday. After her physical therapy session, she was steered into another wing in the hospital and fitted for full-body robowear, which would cushion her from the neck down. She hated it. She told her parents it was like being forced into an iron maiden and she wished there were real spikes because she'd rather be dead.

Her father promised she'd grow used to it, like she had with her current robowear. "You'll forget you're even wearing one."

But I never forgot, she would have said.

Right now, she could feel her anger muddle in confusion, all the different colors swirling into black. She glared at Taewon, who gave another spin of the silver stick.

Yoyo was heating a kettle inside the train by the time she climbed on. Mars was already spread tragically across the blue gym mat. Amelia, fanning herself with her hat, threw a suspicious glance at the straggling two. "We were waiting for you," she said in the tone of *What were you doing?*

Ruijie reached for one of the seats. She had to clutch the pole to slide down. Every muscle in her slowly unclenched. She already had the shakes. Tomorrow was not going to be a good day.

"Are you making ramen?" she asked Yoyo in her most withering tone.

He made a noise that neither affirmed nor denied. Her anger reached, well, the boiling point. "Could you please shut that off?"

"Bit longer," Yoyo said. "The water isn't ready."

"I need to charge my robowear."

At that, he looked up. "I can do that for you."

"Save your energy," she muttered. "This whole day was a waste."

"Really?" Yoyo said. "Taewon is going to help me fix my leg."

Everyone sat up, including Mars, hair sticking up in the back; he'd left a sweat angel on the mat. Taewon wordlessly handed Yoyo the bone he'd been fiddling with.

The kettle shrilled over Mars's "So you're just going to stick that in or what?" when Yoyo popped a lid open from his shin.

Under the lid, violet muscles twitched, braided in wires red and white. Ruijie leaned helplessly close. The broken bone stole her breath away. It had been reduced to dust. Full of teeth and pain. But the frightening impassivity of Yoyo prevailed as he dug out the splinters with blunt fingers, tossed them to the side. For a moment, his leg simply gaped, nothing inside to give it a spine. Then he slipped in the silver bone and slotted it with a smart *pop*.

He reached behind the kettle, fingers grazing the dust on the floor, and grabbed for a white lump that she now spotted sitting innocuously on the blue mat. It was a facsimile of a foot, not quite with toes, but humanoid and ceramic white. He pressed it against his stump and peeled away his fingers one by one until, with a magnetic click, the foot latched on to his ankle.

"Could you pass the kettle?" Yoyo said. "Thank you, Amelia."

Amelia flinched away when Yoyo tipped the kettle onto his leg. Steam rushed to fill the space, tickling Ruijie's face. Yoyo kept pouring in a steady arc. Scalding water splashed into the pulsing coronary clutch of his wound. "What is he doing? What is he doing?" Mars chanted.

"Nanostitching," Ruijie said. "It's very advanced technology. It goes beyond skyn-deep."

Yoyo's smile tickled her. "The heat activates it."

He dumped the rest of the boiling water. Under the billowing steam, the shredded muscles jolted, electrified, with the crackling sound of crushed ice. Blue tendons twisted around the silver bone. Once the muscle and bone fused, the lid shut and he poured the rest on the mangled skyn. It began to grow back. The speed of it astonished. It spread down his ankle, over the arch of his foot, encircling the heel. Like the accelerated rejuvenation of a burnt forest, carpeting it in sequoia and pine.

Yoyo stood up.

"Sweet flying Moses," Mars whispered. "Where's your plug?"

"In my butt?" Yoyo said.

There was a stunned silence. A delicate snort. Bubble of laughter. Taewon, leaning against the pole, shaking. He was laughing, like he was having a seizure.

Amelia gawked at him, and maybe it was Amelia and her ridiculous sunburn, but Ruijie started laughing too. Mars snorted, "It's up your butt," and snorted again.

"It's kind of inconvenient," Yoyo said.

They couldn't stop laughing. Even Amelia joined, a small chuckle, but Ruijie could tell Amelia didn't get it. Amelia, who was whole in every way, had no reason to laugh at life's absurdities.

Ruijie's parents would have laughed. They would have wept if she could be healed with a kettle of boiling water.

At night she would feel around her calves for the wrinkling of her flesh. Muscles full of tender holes, shivering in exquisite terror and marvel at her decay. In the darkness she was allowed to feel things that made no sense.

In the light she felt with such clarity. Yoyo kicked at the floor, testing his ankle. She couldn't look away. Oh, she thought, *oh*. She was never going to meet anyone like him. He was nothing like anyone else.

PART III

17. Halo

JUN RAN HIS ARM UNDER THE FAUCET AND WATCHED THE water turn pink. The temperature stung hot, but it had to reach boiling to coax the nanomachines to life under his skyn. If only I were a robot, he thought, turning the faucet up. The knob jammed at maximum heat. Pain would be a dial and I could burn myself without feeling it.

He remembered a time Yoyo had hurt himself like this. This was in the early days, soon after their father had gathered the whole family in the living room on a Sunday and introduced Yoyo to them, like he was their long-lost brother. When Yoyo greeted them, Jun told Yoyo he talked funny.

"Am I funny?" Yoyo asked, to which Jun responded, "No, you're hella weird."

Like an imprinted newborn, Yoyo had followed Jun everywhere. Yoyo would mimic every gesture: how to run; how to yawn, flashing all molars; how to stuff a steamed bun whole in his face and yelp when the red bean paste burned his tongue, although he was pretending because Yoyo, at the time, couldn't feel a thing.

Jun pretended it was a game. They were two enemy spies, and his mission was to lose Yoyo. Once, Jun scaled the wall between their house and their neighbor's, and shouted *I can see you* at Yoyo, who was tucked behind the ginkgo tree. He crawled across the wall, but in the shade where the ginkgo tree drooped, it had shed a trail of noxious berries. He slipped on the slime, fell.

Yoyo darted forward. His body cushioned the impact. It still hurt. Jun remembered the shock of how hard and metallic Yoyo was, underneath all that seeming softness. For the first time he felt their difference, how he was just a sack of meat and mostly liquid, and Yoyo was not. But Yoyo had shielded him from a crate of jade soju bottles. The shattered glass left a deep glittering wound in Yoyo's calf. "Oh shit," Jun hissed, and he tried to wipe the blood with the hem of his T-shirt, feeling how it tacked onto the fabric, weighing heavier than real blood. "I'm so dead." He could already feel the shouts of his mother ringing in his bones, but he feared his father more, who was implacable as a mountain, not the type to anger, until he did and then it was volcanic.

"I can fix it," Yoyo said.

In the hallway closet, Yoyo stuck his hand into their father's haggard coat and dug out a scuffed-up lighter. His father had started smoking again, exclusively cigarettes. The casual way Yoyo held the lighter against his leg had mesmerized. Steady wrist, steadier eyes, the secretive glow between them as they crouched under the thick musky coats. The wound melted into nothing. You're like a superhero, Jun whispered. He couldn't wait to try it out himself. Because who was to say he wasn't like Yoyo, a robot now being raised as part of the family, and he just didn't know it?

It was their father who'd caught him as Jun angled a scraped arm over the stove, ready to sear his flesh and see if his skin would miraculously stitch shut, when he heard a sound, a sharp exhale. The look on his father's face, he wouldn't forget it even if he could.

JUN SHUT OFF THE FAUCET and headed for the interview room. A depressing little trapezoid, airless, windowless, beigely lit. A PS-19 robot stationed by the door, recording everything.

Sgt. Son was sitting across a table from where Shin Wonsuk lay face down, cushioning his head in the half-moon of one arm, the other a crumpled sleeve lying flat and orange. Under the table, spider-long legs sprawled, his calves smooth and hairless, feet pointing in opposite directions. Shin Wonsuk didn't stir at Jun's entry. But he yawned when Sgt. Son asked if he wanted coffee.

"No thanks, I'm trying to stay clean."

His record was not. Most of it was petty crime, nothing to leave a scratch on his legal refugee status in South Korea. In some ways, they had him. They had CCTV footage of Shin Wonsuk wearing Eli's baseball cap, which had yielded a fairly usable facial reconstruction.

"I don't look like that," Shin Wonsuk protested. "That looks like a pervert."

Equivocal in his approach, preferring to ply suspects with coffee and Chinese delivery, Sgt. Son spent the first hour lobbing softballs. From Shin Wonsuk's jittery left foot, his history of addiction, of robot trafficking and assault, it didn't look like he'd respond well to confrontation, so the strategy was to loosen him up.

Why did he approach Eli?

He thought she was lost. He was being a Good Samaritan, taking her home. Did he? Did he what? Take her home? No, he just nudged her in the right direction. Back toward the main road. She was wandering around Muslim Street. Where did he leave her? He didn't remember. What time did he leave her? He didn't remember. Their conversation ran in circles, getting lost within Itaewon itself, until Sgt. Son pointed to the blemish on Shin Wonsuk's record. Robot trafficking, for which he was fined, then arrested when he tried to dodge the fine. Justice followed the money.

"You get it, don't you? Why we think you took her?" Sgt. Son said.

"Oh, those were just botfights," Wonsuk said with a wave. He gestured as they talked, expressive in the wrist. "It was practically legal how I ran it. Like a Christmas party, everyone having a good time. Here's to another shit year."

The arrest wasn't even the reason he had to close up shop. The demand simply wasn't there, Wonsuk said. What was good, clean fun in the North wasn't enough to satisfy Southerners and their exotic tastes.

A knock on the door; their PS-19 hit pause on the camera to answer it. Sgt. Lee stuck his head into the room and announced the pizza was here. To interrupt an interview, Jun took it as code for *We need to talk.*

The pizza in the break room smelled more of cardboard than cheese. Jun didn't bother to microwave. By the time he demolished a slice or three, Sgt. Son had shuffled into the kitchen and taken a sniff at the box.

"What idiot let Sgt. Lee order the pizza." Sgt. Son grabbed a plastic knife to scrape off the sweet potato.

"What did Sgt. Lee want?"

"Exchange of favors," Sgt. Son said. "There's a reason why Shin Wonsuk is such a cock."

Two years ago, Sgt. Lee had arrested Shin Wonsuk for a robot fighting ring, streamed on VR while operating from the cover of construction sites that were abandoned after a slew of bankruptcies during the recession. Sgt. Lee had tried threatening Shin Wonsuk with deportation, but it was never going to work.

"He's from Gaechon," Sgt. Son said.

"Shit," Jun said. Then, "No. Seriously?"

"He was fifteen when he showed up in the first wave, with that missing arm, and claimed he was one of the survivors."

Gaechon was a special flavor of shit show from the so-called Bloodless War. It was their Mỹ Lai, or second No Gun Ri, whichever was en vogue to describe the mass murder of unarmed civilians. Their military had called it unavoidable. Unfortunately for the military, the death toll had been too tidily recorded, another ghastly perk of robot warfare.

Jun filled a kettle with tap water. Maybe he could try pouring boiling water on his arm to get his bad scrape to close. He could see some wires, and it was pretty disorienting. "You know, if he's from Gaechon." Jun shut the faucet. "He has a right to hate robots."

"Who knows if he's telling the truth. Immigration was flooded with applications, hundreds pretending to be survivors." Sgt. Son watched the pizza spin in the microwave. "The last time I had sweet pizza was in North Korea."

"Mm, fruit pizza."

"That funny street with all the pizza parlors."

"Mirae Street. *The future is tomorrow.*"

"Was Rome Pizza still there when you were in Pyongyang? With the Greek pillars."

"Yeah, it was still standing."

They shared small, distant smiles. Jun could see the dusty laminated menus with pastoral mountains on the cover. Corn pizza. Kimchi pizza. Flower pizza. Edible pansies, inedible pizza. Pronounced *bbijja*—"cute" in the North Korean dialect. Just seven hundred or eight hundred won. Cheaper than a bus ride. It was easy to infantilize the North when they were trying to emulate the West, like a child engulfed in a grown-up jacket. Too easy to underestimate them.

"Our chaplain used to hold church in Rome Pizza," Sgt. Son said. "Nonbelievers came for the pizza, stayed for the prayers. One time, I was doing cleanup with my friend. We saw this man approach our chaplain when I was bagging the paper plates. And I had the strangest feeling. I didn't know him but he looked familiar. I tried moving around the tables, trying to get another look at his face. I heard him ask the chaplain if he was a sinner. He said he'd killed robots, hundreds of them, and he had the exact number. He asked if it was a sin to kill a robot." Sgt. Son held a greasy fork under the tap. The orange streaks resisted the running water. "How would you answer? If you were the chaplain."

"'We're all going to hell anyway'?"

"You're a shit chaplain."

The kettle whistled. Jun just turned it off. This felt like an important moment. One of those rare, delicate opportunities that, if disturbed, never came by him again from men like Sgt. Son, who could talk about the war sober only in the most harmless non sequiturs, like the fruit pizza that haunted him to this day.

"What'd your less shitty chaplain say?"

"He told the man he was a sinner, we're all sinners, but killing a robot wasn't a sin. He forgave the man and sent him on his way."

"That's it?"

"My friend and I, we looked at each other. We didn't have to say a word. We followed the man. We saw him enter a building. This was a Soviet-style building; it had an opera house on the fourth floor. Velvet carpet on the stairs. Some mold. We moved quiet. My friend was ahead of me. Then he stopped before he'd reached the top, and I had to go around him. I saw the soldier standing by a window, all boarded up, so no one would see him from the outside, and I saw him take off his face."

The pizza was still spinning in the microwave, bubbling. Jun pulled out the plate, set it in front of Sgt. Son.

"Careful, the plate's hot."

"What would you have done?"

"Run," Jun said. "I would have run. You saw a HALO."

"*Kill angels,*" Sgt. Son said in Engrish.

Kill them all. It was easy to laugh about it, especially during poker whenever the joker card turned up. The "most-dangerous LAW" cards designated the K-200 HSH, or "Hush," for king of diamonds. Queen of hearts for "Shelly" the SADARM. The joker was the HALO, who could look like anyone.

"Did it see you?" Jun said.

"I don't know, but we saw it swap faces. Beneath it all, the face looked like stained glass."

"I thought that was a rumor."

"You've never seen one?"

"Never came that close. I'm what happens when you get too close."

Jun reheated the kettle to make coffee. He offered Sgt. Son a mug. This time of day, Sgt. Son would normally turn it down, since he was trying to whittle down his dependence on caffeine, for the baby. Sgt. Son accepted it, with a kind of grace because of this new closeness between them, an understanding shared only by those who had survived the absurd.

"My friend wanted to tell someone, but I talked him out of it," Sgt. Son said. "I think he still holds it against me. I'm sure he does."

"Where's your friend now?"

"He's dandy. He goes hiking every weekend. You've seen the pictures on his desk."

"Oh." Jun saw the framed picture before him; Mount Baekdu, fists of victory in the air. "You mean Sgt. Lee?"

Sgt. Son nodded. "He was discharged much earlier than me." A laugh, sudden and bright, as if it had just occurred to him. "Because he was at Gaechon."

18. Gaechon

JUN RETURNED TO THE INTERVIEW ROOM ALONE.

"Just you?" Wonsuk said.

"Just me. Do you want a slice of pizza?"

"Got a fork? I don't like getting my fingers dirty."

Jun slid a fork across the table. He watched Wonsuk tear at the plastic wrapper with his teeth. "Do you have kids? We've a whole box of the pineapple and sweet potato if you want to do takeaway."

"Just a boy. He's my sister's. But I'm the one who's got to wipe his ass and keep him in school."

"Which school?"

"It's that fancy private school. By the junkyard—"

"Right, I know the one."

"Crazy, isn't it?"

"How'd your nephew get in? By lottery?"

"Yeah, and a nonprofit wanting to help him out because they couldn't do shit for his mother. She got kicked out of the country for that bullshit law, you know, the one they changed; she missed that little window to apply and it wasn't even her fault. She sent in the application. They *told* her they'd follow up, but now they're saying they never got it."

"That's rough. When was your sister deported?"

"I don't know. Taewon's I think twelve now. Fuck, has it been that long."

Jun opened his folder and spread out the surveillance shots. Eli's face was blurred, but so ubiquitous, and the slouch in Shin Wonsuk's gait felt unmistakable when the real thing was sprawled in front of you. "Where's your nephew right now?"

"He's at the school."

"Isn't it summer break?"

"Yeah, and he's getting big. Do you know what year he was born?" Wonsuk's mouth lifted into an oily tilt. "Year of the Dragon. He's a prodigy. He's been scouted several times for the junior league. He'll be in the World Cup, maybe not the next, but the one after that for sure. He's going to be our dragon who rises from the creek."

"That's really impressive. You'll have to keep him in school."

"Take him out and put him in soccer, that's the smart investment. That school's no good for him. Can't keep mixing him up with those kids and their robot nannies. Those families will take their silicons out to restaurants when we've got orphans starving to death."

"They're just playing house."

"You get it," Wonsuk said, inordinately pleased. "You would."

Jun picked up a picture of Wonsuk and Eli. "What can you tell us about her?"

"What d'you want?" Wonsuk shrugged. "She's a Sakura. Tons on the street."

"We want to find her. We want to know if she's safe."

"It's too bad. I don't know where she is." He pointed at Jun's arm. "Did an angel do that to you?"

"This?" Jun said, lifting his arm. He'd tried stuffing some of the wiring back into the tear. "No, this happened when I fell into that pit. Yours?"

"Gaechon, you know." Wonsuk rubbed the base of his stump, as if for good luck. "May twelfth. I should tattoo it here."

"You don't have the Pyongan-do dialect."

"I can hack it," Wonsuk said, trying. "I'm from Hamgyong, but I did factory work in the city."

"Gaechon's far from Hamgyong. Closer to Pyongyang."

"I could've been a soccer player if I was from the capital. I could've played for the South, or Spain."

"Like your nephew."

"He has to control his temper. He doesn't want to end up like his daddy."

"You rather he end up like you?"

Wonsuk merely smiled. "That's the last thing I want for him."

Jun studied the surface of the table. Green felt was trapped under a pane of glass. He told Wonsuk that he seemed like a good uncle. He obviously wanted the best for his kid.

"I can't let him go back to that hellhole."

"Did you see a HALO?" Jun said quietly.

"In Gaechon? I don't know, it's a big city. Okay, yeah, not as big as Seoul, but you know. I saw the light coming from it. Spinning red. What d'you call them? Rings above the angels."

"Halos."

"Red for attack. Red for kill them all."

Jun shook his head. "That's not what it means."

Wonsuk leaned in on his elbow. "How would you know what kind of red it was?"

"You know what I think?" Jun rubbed his eyes with his thumb. "I think we both know you weren't in Gaechon."

Wonsuk put on a funny smile. "Hey now, are you a lie detector? Because you're a cyborg?"

"We have a record of you taking Eli, we have witnesses, and if we want, we can put you up with Immigration. When you get all tied up in there—and it'll take months, you know, years—what do you think's going to happen to your nephew? All that anger. Who's going to take him in? Do you want him to end up in meatpacking? Future soccer star on sixteen-hour shifts?"

"So much hostility," Wonsuk whispered. "For such a shitty robot."

"How could you tell it was shit?"

"Second gen. They're not worth licking my shoe."

"See, and how'd you know that? These Sakuras, they've all got the same face, right? How'd you know she was an old model?"

"I can tell," Wonsuk said sharply. "One look, I can tell. I didn't take her."

"Then where did you leave her?"

Wonsuk leaned hard on his chair, balancing now on just two

legs. When the chair hit the floor, his smile turned silky. "Detective, you got to find a brothel. Flash your badge and they'll give you the government treatment. You can't keep all that hostility inside you, or you'll turn sick. I know of a place for a man like you. Led by a Habird man—"

"Harvard?"

"You want to scratch harder, you ask Mr. Mo."

"From the dating school?"

"You know him?"

The quaint business card he received from Mr. Mo. Jun couldn't remember where it went. "How do you know him?"

"I ran into him that night. Now you've reminded me of him. Southerners have their exotic tastes."

"What are you saying?" Jun shot a quick look at the PS-19 That was recording all this. "Was it a handoff? Did you give Eli to this Mr. Mo?"

"I'm not saying anything. I'm not going to sign anything either."

"Is she still with you?"

Wonsuk shrugged with a helpless smile.

Jun unfolded the missing-robot flyer. "Her name is Eli. Her owner is an old lady. She misses her robot. You see the reward? That's ten million won. You could buy a whole new silicon with that. You could book a suite at the StraightJacket."

"You've got it all wrong," Wonsuk said. "My favorite den's Ecstasy." He folded the flyer and tucked it into his front pocket. "Can you jackport from the wire in your spine?"

"Sure." His friends in rehab had both envied and pitied him for it. "I don't need the Delfis."

"If I was wired like you, I'd never pull the plug."

Maybe Wonsuk was telling the truth. He could have already sold Eli and now he'd washed his hands of it. But Jun watched Wonsuk's finger *tap tap tap* on the table. Ten million won into how many virtual hours. His finger quivered, the nail brittle and blue like the neural link that could pulse against his temple, feeding a living stream of dopamine and dreams. Jun used to stare at how the blue light rippled across the ceiling, as if he were underwater, gazing at the sky through an impermeable transparent layer. It would start out a soothing pale blue, then it would darken, for VR wasn't a life buoy thrown to a drowning man but an anchor that let you sink deep down the throat of oblivion.

JUN STEPPED OUTSIDE the precinct for air. To his deep displeasure, Sgt. Son followed him down the steps, and they stood together without a word or a token attempt to smoke. The silence stretched, but Jun didn't rise to the bait. He might look jumpy and impatient, but he'd faced all kinds of excruciating silences with his father.

"Well, we both knew he was a liar," Sgt. Son said.

"He lied about Gaechon," Jun burst out. "Who does that?"

"He was fifteen."

"It's the disrespect."

"How'd you know he was lying?"

"He hates robots. But not the ones up North. He admires them. It's so disrespectful."

Sgt. Son nodded. "Who's Mr. Mo?"

Jun patted his pockets, but of course he'd tossed the business card. "I'll look him up, but I ran into him at the brothel for the dead lawyer. He calls himself a dating guru."

"Sounds classy. Do you need me to go with you?"

"I don't know. I'd rather search the junkyard. She's got to be somewhere in there."

"Not without a search warrant, and you won't get it for a place that big. Last time we hauled that much ass for a bot, it was for that Chinese actress and her robo-son."

"Little Noah," Jun said sadly.

Sgt. Son cut his eyes at him. "You had no problem threatening Wonsuk's kid."

Jun shrugged. "He could be imaginary, for all we know."

Sgt. Son went back inside to close the interview with Shin Wonsuk, leaving Jun to sulk in the dark. He watched the red crosses flicker on like the nascent sparks of bushfire. His body felt too hot. It had always struggled with temperature control. He wanted to cool down. Slip underwater. He wanted to sink.

Remember the rock bottoms. Remember he made his mother cry. Remember he drove his father into the arms of religion. Remember the time he was hospitalized for overdosing because he hit a level of VR so deep Yoyo might appear and Jun could talk to him, ask him the unaskable. And Jun would do it on purpose, trigger the neural link to misfire, so he was no longer seeing the visual feed from the machine but the convulsions of his sensitive, inflamed brain. When Jun peeled open his eyes, his doctor, who was from New Zealand, had come with an entourage. They surrounded him on all sides, eight moderately attractive medical students, taking notes, as the doctor muttered, *Bollocks*, because Jun's catheter kept wiggling off.

How did he end up here, every time? Oh, he had his excuses. Insomnia, anxiety and nightmares, phantom pain. But what he needed most from the cradle of VR was to numb himself.

As a kid, he was the opposite. Nervy and fearless in the face of hurt. Fired up, he'd held his busted arm over the stove ready for a miracle, when his father had caught him. He remembered the blood fleeing his father's face. He was punished like nothing before.

After the incident with the lighter, Yoyo had disappeared from the house. Three days passed. And just as Jun shrugged, *Well, I guess he's gone*, Yoyo came back. Different. Installed with advanced pain receptors, and now he reacted to the slightest push and scrape with alarm, with bruised confusion. Years later, when they were alone on the roof, Jun protested how Yoyo had basically been punished for saving his life.

Yoyo didn't see it as punishment. He called it an upgrade. The ripened fruit of knowledge. He said he was glad, relieved, thankful—*happy* that Jun wasn't harmed.

"I think it's better to feel," Yoyo said, "even if it hurts."

JUN BUMPED INTO the Major Crimes squad in the lobby. They'd already pregamed and reeked of beer. "Come with," Sgt. Lee urged, friendly as ever. "We're off for drinks." Jun tried to beg off, since drinks would mean a hostess bar with North Korean girls.

"You'll join us one day," Sgt. Lee said, like a warning and promise wrapped in one.

Stepping off the elevator, Jun decided he'd slip Shin Wonsuk his number, scribble it on the missing-robot flyer Wonsuk had already taken. A fair trade for Eli, and Wonsuk could take his cool ten million and blow it on VR until he flatlined, for all Jun cared.

Jun greeted a PS-19 outside the elevator. Then he stopped. "Who's this?"

"He is an unidentified child," the PS-19 said.

"I see that. Why is he here?"

"He is waiting for his uncle."

Jun dragged his hand down his face. "Shit, I was hoping his kid was imaginary."

"The child appears to be real."

The nephew occupied the same bench where Eli had once sat as she waited for Jun to find a compatible charger. Wonsuk had embellished a tired old story about the mother: abusive husband, sleazy South Korean employer, threats of deportation, threats made true and she was never heard from again, and the story somehow became about him, who was left to feed and clothe a motherless child.

Drawing closer, Jun saw that the shirt swamping the boy's thin frame had a Bluelight logo, a clothing brand for robots. Wild, shaggy hair covered his brown face. Intense eyes. Unblinking and bloodshot behind dinky owl-lens glasses that were much too murky to pass for a Delfi.

"Hey," Jun said, sitting down. "You must be Taewon."

The boy shot him an arrow of a look. "Are you a robot?"

"Nope, that's why I have a Band-Aid," Jun replied in English, the boy's weapon of choice. "The arm's just a little special."

The boy kept himself busy. He was trying to separate the stuck zipper on his backpack. Jun scooted to the other side of the bench, then he did what kids secretly enjoy, which was to ignore them. He pulled out Sgt. Son's tablet, scrolled the news, then looked up Mr. Mo from "Habird." In one ad, Mr. Mo winked as he promised a level-up in the sacred art of seduction. As he'd hoped, Taewon glanced at the advert. Curiosity hardened into pure disdain. It did look like a porn pop-up.

"Do you know this man?" Jun said.

A shrug, which wasn't a no. Still trying to unjam the backpack.

"Need any help with the zipper?"

Taewon shook his head. As his gaze flicked away, it landed back on Jun's arm.

"Why don't you dump hot water on it?"

"Ouch?" Jun smirked. "It'll heal on its own. I could buy one of those fancy heat lamps or book an appointment at the clinic." Though his health insurance wouldn't cover it. Skyn damage was considered "cosmetic."

"The hot water thing, it's not normal?"

"It's not common," Jun said carefully. "I've only seen it in the military."

Heat-activated nanostitching was technology exclusive to military-grade skyn. Companies like Talos and Imagine Friends seemed to have little interest in adopting such technology, not when they had customers who'd pay for warranty and trade in robots for every little scratch, a tamer spin on planned obsolescence.

"Did you kill a lot of robots?" Taewon said.

"It's not like the games in VR."

"I heard in Gaechon it took one robot to kill everyone."

"Maybe there never was one."

Jun had every reason to doubt the story. Gaechon was a cautionary tale, but it was also something of a legend for the military, among the many they'd swap in awe and disgust over those angels, like the angel who wore the face of a choirboy, with the little red kerchief, and sang glories for a private audience, and right then and there ended a dynasty. Too fanciful.

Taewon flung the backpack to the side in frustration. Jun picked it up, touched the serrated edges of the zipper. "If there really was an angel in Gaechon, it would've taken just one."

Taewon said nothing for a second. Then, "So we're fucked."

Jun laughed for real, loud and echoey. "Yeah. We're past the age where we put people on the field. We're like stagehands. Keep us backstage." He tried yanking the zipper, but no go. He didn't want to break it. "Did you see something like it? Robot fixing themself using hot water?"

Another cryptic shrug.

"Did it look human?"

"It doesn't matter anyways. He'll be gone soon."

He. The slip in pronoun happened for him, too, between *it* and *he*, and sometimes *they*. Better than *it*.

"Why can't you just swap the battery?" Taewon said, vaguely frustrated.

"The battery was broken in this robot?"

"It was sparking. It looked like the wings on a plane."

Jun licked his lips. The wing-type solar batteries were only used in HALOs for their compactness and high-energy usage. But Taewon described sparks. That was a broken battery. From the sounds of it, the robot was dying.

"Is there a way to fix the battery?" Taewon said, as if he'd read Jun's mind.

Jun doubted it, even if the robot crawled into an Army base and found the right replacement. The military wouldn't have relinquished the robot whole without a good reason. "Stay away from it. It's usually more than a battery issue."

"What does that mean?"

"Robots slow down. They're like a houseplant. Sometimes they get too big for their pots." Jun took out his lip balm to lubricate the zipper. It parted like butter.

Taewon didn't spare a glance for his backpack. His eyes burned. "Is that why he won't fight back?"

"Hey." Jun, sitting up, turned to face him. "Leave it alone. I'm serious. It doesn't matter how friendly it might act. If it goes into autopilot, it could be dangerous."

"What will it do on autopilot?"

"What it was programmed to do."

Taewon scowled at his lap. He looked unconvinced and Jun was now feeling serious trepidation, but before he could drill it into the boy's head, Sgt. Son peered out into the hall and asked what the hell they were doing out there.

"Waiting for Shin Wonsuk," Jun said.

"He left."

"What?" Jun hastily stood up. "His nephew's here."

"He took the flyer, so at least that's something to think about. I said we'll check in on him again."

"We were waiting right here in front of the elevators."

"He took the stairs."

In brisk, furious movements, Taewon got up and slung the backpack over his shoulder. Jun said he'd drop him off but the boy stalked away, his small dark head bobbing. Like he'd been left stranded on a lifeboat, after his uncle had jumped overboard, and all Jun could do was pray this kid would reach shore.

THAT NIGHT, JUN WENT up to the roof of the house. He vaped and thought of tomorrow. Tomorrow he'd look into Mr. Mo's dating school. Tomorrow was Sunday, but he might be able to check it out the day after.

He had to go back to that junkyard.

He couldn't see a single star. Pollution. And it was going to rain soon. First, it was the tingle in his lost limbs. Then an itch would spread furious. Everything hurt to honor his ghosts.

He knew he wasn't going to sleep tonight.

Like a flicker, crisp:

He remembered Yoyo on the roof. Yoyo, sitting in a chair algaed with rust, shredding bread into wisps.

"Are you eating moldy bread?" Jun said, approaching.

"I wouldn't feed birds moldy bread," Yoyo said, and he sounded more shocked than indignant, which made Jun smile. The owner of the neighborhood bakery adored Yoyo; every evening she set aside for him the pastries that didn't sell.

The sparrows pecked bold around Yoyo, darting between his feet. "You're such a Disney princess," Jun laughed. And Yoyo hummed "Someday My Prince Will Come" because he came with a sense of humor so gentle it couldn't have been programmed.

Jun stomped over and the sparrows scattered. Yoyo slid off the chair to join him on the ground where they sat cross-legged, leaving the chair between them empty like a throne. Together they stared at the rooftops. The church crosses glowed red, trying to scald the night.

"Can't sleep?" Yoyo said.

Jun knocked his head against Yoyo's shoulder. He'd had insomnia since he was twelve. It was a special style of torture during family trips when they had to pile into one hotel room, and his mother and sister would sleep, but Jun would snap awake whenever his father stumbled to lock himself in the bathroom, several times throughout the night, a disk of light cutting through the darkness.

"Can you help me rehearse?" Jun said.

"For *Macbeth*?"

"I bombed that one. *Peter Pan*. I'm trying out for lead. My girlfriend thinks I'm perfect for it."

They recited the script. Jun tripped over his lines. Soon enough, Yoyo took over and began to play both roles. He was showing off. As Wendy, he'd chide with a jutting chin. For Peter Pan, he brayed, ready to swordfight at the snap of the fingers—until Jun, incensed, yanked the lines of Pan back from him, and they settled into their respective roles.

WENDY
When you come for me next year, Peter—
you will come, won't you?

PETER
Yes. *(Gloating)* To hear stories about me!

WENDY
It is so queer that the stories you like best should be the ones about yourself.

PETER *(touchy)*
Well, then?

WENDY
Fancy your forgetting Captain Hook!

"You forgot the lost boys," Jun interjected. "The line is 'Fancy your forgetting the *lost boys* and Captain Hook.'"

"Would you forget the lost boys?"

"It's not would I or could I, it's part of the script. He forgets Tink, even."

"Everyone."

"Maybe it's the magic that keeps him young and hip."

"I would never forget."

Jun yawned and wiggled close. Yoyo gamely put an arm around him. Neither of their parents was physically affectionate, and Yoyo used to hug them as if to make up for the loss. He was so American about it. Generous and warm.

"I have school in a few hours."

"I can sing you a lullaby."

"I know you're yanking. Just tell me a story. Like, a really boring story."

"Did you know fireflies glow even after they die?"

"That's . . . kind of poetic."

"So if a firefly gets caught in a web, the spider will wrap it up to eat it later and the firefly will still glow, even in death."

"Jesus Christ."

"The flashing signal will lure more fireflies into the web. And what you're left with is a spiderweb full of dead glowing fireflies."

"Thanks. This is one of those things I will think about for a long time."

Yoyo cackled. He had a birdlike laugh that used to drive Jun mad.

He sang like a bird too. He had a smooth, high voice, but he had many more he could slip into like a chest full of shoes. He was a terrifying mimic. But for all his talents, he couldn't whistle. He'd tried, pushing air through teeth. Jun used to whistle back, sometimes in the taunting rhythm of their secret knock. *Seek you. Seek you.*

At night Yoyo wouldn't sing but would hum. It lulled. Jun would doze and watch Yoyo through the slits of his eyes. In this liminal state he felt they were so dangerously close they could blur and catch fire, like twilight.

Yoyo would eventually close his eyes. And slowly, over his head, a light would unfurl. A white halo would start to spin.

19. Pygmalion

HIS NAME WAS SUPPOSED TO BE YOHAN, AFTER THE ACTOR. For weeks Morgan had waffled over the name, back when Stephen was still a torso. Attaching his arms and legs was a simple enough task with the correct equipment from Imagine Friends, but she held it off for as long as she could and her excuse was just that—an excuse. It felt safer to speak to him as he was.

She finally named him Stephen the day after Christmas. By then, Morgan had already been in the country for nine months, the incubation period of a whole baby, and every time Jun canceled and rescheduled, the color of her resentment deepened, for she had been struggling. Jun was sixteen, she had just turned twelve, when they had moved to New York, and while he could balance the two halves of his Koreanness and Americanness delicately in each palm, for her, becoming American had obliterated her. English had cannibalized her mother tongue. Try as she did to revive the cold gray ashes of the language she used to speak, one day she'd toggled on her autotranslate, and it felt like giving up, especially with the politely amused distance people in Seoul would affect when they learned she was Korean. But not really.

No matter, she was used to people's dismissal, which was why she found the pleasure of being courted so unexpected and overwhelming—by Cristina, who had decided to side with her on the tickle code.

Since Jun's ambush at her workplace, Morgan had fended off a rush of gooey texts from Cristina, which, after the dust settled, became lunch every day at the food court. Earlier on, they also tried a drawing class for Friday, which was soothing enough to warrant a repeat the following week. But then Cristina chose that evening, while they were sketching the bust of Medusa, to spring the news on her. She, Cristina Cisnero, had been headhunted by New York.

The betrayal must have been plain on Morgan's face. Cristina reassured her it would be her turn soon. Imagine Friends' New York branch was preparing to cast a net for Level 4 personality programmers. Seven years of experience required, but with Morgan's portfolio after the official release of Yoyo·X, she could try to wrangle an offer from Talos and negotiate for Level 5 salary and stock options.

"Of course I love Korea," Cristina said with the obligatory reflexiveness of an expat. "But my girlfriend and I are talking about marriage, and we're both eyeing the prewar co-op on Sutton Place, which used to belong to some famous dead author who tried to pass the house on to his robot, but that failed, obviously."

"I don't know if I believe in marriage." Morgan picked up an eraser to smudge Medusa's distraught gaze. "As an institution, I mean. Especially if people aren't having kids."

Cristina sighed "Me neither," but her girlfriend was, if not insecure, in need of validation. The not-so-secret fear Cristina would start eyeing men again.

Morgan couldn't imagine this kind of sturdy, equitable love. She and Jun had that in common. Both jealous and possessive, prone to laying down melodramatic ultimatums. How they'd endlessly tug-of-warred over Yoyo, who had lacked the most defining trait of a robot companion.

Unlike Dr. Lorenz and his geese, their father had never programmed Yoyo to imprint onto one person. It was the key to robot ownership: upon activation of your robot, registering your name, voice, and thumbprint so they could build their consciousness around your desires. Yoyo had been different. He loved her. He loved Jun. He loved their father and mother and even their weird Australian neighbor and his pet dove, Raven.

For now, Cristina claimed she was devoted to her girlfriend and had disavowed men. "Really, who needs a man in their life?"

Morgan wouldn't know. She'd never been with a man. Last week for their drawing class, when an old man with a ropey silver braid had whipped off his towel, Cristina leaned over to whisper, "He has a *huge* cock," and Morgan had to give a quick, jerky nod. How else was she supposed to react? Her only point of reference was Stephen's, which was "above average," selected as such. What was average, anyway? Average for *whom*?

When the hour ended and it was time to put away their 2B pencils, dust off the eraser crumbs with a cheap foundation brush, Cristina turned to her and offered her condolences for the tickle code, axed a week before D-Day.

Little David, the snitch, had gone straight to Joe. After a round of A/B testing with two groups of Yoyos, the code disabled in one, Joe vetoed the tickle code entirely. Morgan had sulked for a week and now she had a reason to fantasize of escape, of Cristina's New York offer, of a team that would appreciate her fully. After her move to Korea, in order to cope with pangs of regret, she used to look up her old studio in Gramercy and smile at the eye-gouging rent hikes, but now—

"I'm thinking of applying for a job in New York," she told Stephen on Sunday evening.

"That's a good idea." Stephen looped his arm around her as they snuggled on the couch. "I will follow you wherever you go."

Morgan suspected that was a line from a cheesy song. They were supposed to go out for date night but decided instead to stream a movie, an American rom-com called *The Wedding Rental*, about a woman who hires a robot as a last-minute date to her best friend's wedding. Shenanigans ensue. Morgan flicked a stray popcorn off her chest when she felt Stephen's fingers curl against her nape. Jun and his high school girlfriend used to cuddle like this in their parents' living room. Morgan had found it so annoying and proprietorial, the way Jun would pet the girl and she'd arch up to him like a cat in heat.

She didn't mind the petting from Stephen, who had never touched her like this. Where before he'd cover her hand like a limp napkin, now he twined his fingers around hers, rubbed his thumb across her knuckles, as if to feel the curve of every little bone under her skin.

Could they ever sit like this in public? Maybe in New York, with the city's charming slogan, *Seriously, no one gives a crap about you.* They could find a bench in Washington Square with kafta wraps from that Lebanese place on Bleecker, and after, they could take a walk around the park, swishing through crunchy red leaves, dodging that corner where dealers would try to sell you coke or bricked neural links. Few would recognize Stephen for Ko Yohan, though NY state law required she register him as a robot, forcing the garish company logo to be displayed somewhere visible on his body.

"What are you thinking about right now?" Stephen said.

How I can't sit with you in public, Morgan thought. "Just the launch."

"Are you worried?"

"Should I be?"

"You shouldn't. Your father is going to be very proud when he sees it."

"As long as he doesn't tickle one of the Yoyos," she grumbled.

"The real Yoyo was special."

She wanted to scoff, *Like you know what's real.* The thought instantly depressed her. The Yoyo-X was no longer ticklish. It was another way the X was lacking. She'd watched the Machu Picchu ad before it had to be scrapped. Rolling on the dirt, the Yoyo-X was flushed and panting, so lovely, and it frustrated her because he still looked packaged, youthful vigor and all. The real Yoyo had cracks in his veneer. The light in his eyes had a sly glitter, the curve of his cupid's bow knowing but sweet, for he had absorbed the best and worst of them, Jun's playfulness and cruelty, their mother's highhandedness and warmth, and their father, most of all.

Stephen felt like an entity unspoiled by her.

"Are you worried about Jun?" Stephen asked. The way he said Jun's name, with a weight of familiarity, settled in her stomach. "What he will think of Yoyo?"

"He can think whatever he wants."

"But you chose to hide the Yoyo·X from him."

"When did I do that?"

"Three weeks ago when Jun gave me a ride to your workplace. You didn't want him to see and you made sure to say Boy X. Never Yoyo."

She tried to sit up, overturning the bowl, so crumbs everywhere. "How do you know that? You left."

Stephen looked up through his eyelashes, coy more than innocent. "Yes," he said. "You made me leave."

She wondered why Stephen hadn't made a token attempt to clean up, as was his prerogative. She grabbed the bowl. "I'm going to get some popcorn," she said rather unnecessarily, and rose to her feet. After a moment, she sat back down, feeling something crunch underneath her. She took Stephen by the hand and said, "I think we should be friends."

He looked at his hand in hers, squeezed it once. "Are we not good friends?"

"I think we should update our relationship status. I just realized I've done something incredibly stupid. You don't have to do this anymore."

He was staring at her with a slight frown. She pushed through. It was important, setting these new boundaries. Use simple, clear language. If anything, she could resort to the manual and say, *Let's do buddy mode*, even if that sounded stupid. "You're this unrealistic fantasy from when I was in college. I have to be more mindful about my life choices now that I'm getting older."

"Would you like me to age? I may be Ko Yohan at twenty-seven, but I can mature."

She smiled and shook her head, because how could he ever understand? Age was relative when your so-called peers were getting promoted and engaged, throwing vanilla-and-roses weddings before popping out whatever progeny they could puzzle-piece together. But the body didn't lie. How could Stephen understand the stiffness in her neck and shoulders, the fuzziness of her eyes, the slack of her jowls whose resistance to gravity was bound to weaken every year?

In her drawing class, they'd started with marble before moving on to live naked models. *There is a world of difference*, the teacher had said, lurking from behind, *between stone and flesh.*

This was what she told Stephen. "There's a huge difference between silicon and flesh."

"Is it the texture? There's a new cream I can apply to mimic the moistness—"

"Don't say *moist.*"

"Isn't your brother made of silicon as well? Are we so different, him and I?"

At first, she thought he meant Yoyo. It was disorienting to remember she had another brother made of silicon. "Did Jun say something to you?" she demanded. The way Stephen and Jun had stood conspiringly close under the cherry blossom tree, it sent a wash of terror down her throat.

Stephen pulled his hand away. Tears wetted his eyes, while the rest of his face stayed firm. Black Olive were the dewiest eyes in their catalog. When they brimmed with saline fluid, they glistened.

"Will I never be man enough for you?"

"Oh my God," she said. "You don't have to cry. I won't be offended if you're not upset about our breakup."

He blinked away the tears and his face smoothed over.

"This isn't a real breakup, okay?" she said, standing up and taking the bowl with her to the kitchen. "Think of it as a transition to a better role. You know, buddy mode."

"You've wanted me to be so many things," he murmured. "Your lover. Your caretaker. Your confidant. I can be your buddy."

"I know it's called buddy mode, but that's a distasteful word. We're friends."

She opened the cupboard. All she found were long slender glasses, mugs arranged by height and color. She felt Stephen sidle up from behind, crowding her against the sink. What was with this resistance? Why couldn't he be more flexible? Accept his role as Jarvis or Alfred, as the slightly sardonic butler—but still family? And if she did end up finding someone, well then. She would have to rehome him, with much regret, like swapping a beloved cat for an allergic life partner.

"I'm looking for, you know, for the popcorn—"

Stephen reached under the sink. "I wish we could have a conversation about this, but it seems you've made up your mind." He pulled out a brand-new salad bowl, from her mother, a delicate crystal piece entwined in leafy vines, clearly meant for a wedding registry. "Do you understand why I feel lost? Without you, I have no purpose."

"I'm not kicking you out of the house," she protested. "You'll still live here. If you want, we can even change your face. If it makes things easier."

"Okay," Stephen said. "I understand." A moment of silence. "You're no longer attached to Ko Yohan. Your response to his most recent film was lukewarm at best. But how is Yoyo different? How is he not the same as Ko Yohan?"

"Yoyo was real," she laughed, cheeks stinging. "He's the only one who understood me."

For a long time, Stephen didn't say a word. He wasn't moving, either, or blinking, his eyelashes suspended in the air, the bowl heavy in his hands. This was a first; she'd never experienced a lag like this outside the lab. She waved a hand in his face. "Hello? Did you freeze?"

He blinked. "I'm sorry, could you repeat that?"

"Did you catch anything I said?"

"I did," he said in a cheerful buddy tone. "I've been reassigned."

"Exactly," she said, a rush of sweet relief. "That's all it is. It's going to be better for us. In the long run, we'll be so much happier."

Now they could cohabit and still rely on each other, without the uncomfortable strain of anticipatory disappointment. It was selfish of her to demand he be more than he was. He'll be fine, she thought. He'll bounce back from this. The miraculous elasticity of a robot mind.

The bowl slipped and shattered on the floor.

She screamed.

"Oh, I'm so sorry. Morgan, are you okay?"

At first the bowl looked like it had only split in two—until he touched it and the pieces crumbled to the floor. Diamond dust glittered in the cracks between the tiles. "Please don't move. I have to clean up the shards."

"What was that?"

"Please don't move. The glass is everywhere."

Biting her lip, she pressed her back against the kitchen counter and gazed longingly toward the living room. The movie—*The Wedding Rental*—was almost over, and of course it ended in a feminist bullshit happily-ever-after about a Hollywood homely shucking off the weight of society's judgmental gaze, throwing her arms around the robot that would be eternally young and handsome and devoted. Never mind that giant Talos logo branded to his neck, which the protagonist refused to hide behind a tug of the turtleneck or discreetly arranged scarf. So brave.

Morgan fidgeted, curled in her toes and scratched her chin. She glanced down at Stephen. His eyes were still on the ground, head bowed to expose the cream slope of his neck, tempting for an executioner's axe. He collected the shards with his bare hands, leaving little pink nicks on his palm.

"Don't move," he said in a low voice. "You'll only hurt yourself."

20. The Heart Fails Without War

A DOCTOR MEASURED RUIJIE'S HEART WITH THE COOL FLAT bell of the stethoscope. The electrocardiogram came next. Each test took about an hour. Most of it was the wait, while Ruijie chewed on tasteless protein chips, which used to be a distraction, especially from the sting of the needle. But now, she was so used to the shots, she liked watching the needle slide into her arm, the syringe swelling with her blood. So dark and thick, like she could be powered by oil.

For these overnight stays, a hospital robot followed her everywhere. When she sat on the toilet she could feel the pinching tug in her arm from the intravenous line that tied her to the robot like a persistent umbilical cord. The vitamin shot took two to three hours to fully absorb, but the doctor said her blood vessel was so thin, it would take four.

Lucky me, she thought.

"Would you like some more protein chips?" the robot asked as he carried her back to the bed.

"Blech," she replied.

Her parents brought her favorite snacks three days later when she was finally released from the hospital. Ruijie left them unopened, feeling queasy in the car. All she could manage was her head against the window, sucking on a piece of ginger jelly until the gelatin bristles turned smooth as stone. Her father tried to cheer her up. How about a trip to the zoo? Robot museum? Ruijie thought she deserved a much grander reward if she was going to skip school for a whole week, just from feeling so exhausted and hurt.

"Don't worry about attendance, it's just summer school," her father said.

In bed, Ruijie imagined Yoyo waiting for her, helpless and angry in the dark. He should be sitting in the rabbit pen, surrounded by twitching warm bodies. After she'd told Amelia and Mars about Yoyo's near kidnapping at the Robot Free Market, it was Mars's idea to smuggle Yoyo into their school. Unanimously they'd decided that the gym and the supplies shed were too risky, so they put him in the rabbit pen, away from the salvage yard and the scrappers—away from their reach.

Ruijie tried to nap. She woke up every few minutes, tired but not sleepy.

Her mother checked in on her and asked if she'd like some congee. When Ruijie insisted she was feeling well enough to go to school tomorrow, her parents both came into her room.

"Mei, your father has news," her mother said.

It was her tone for "bad news," but her father was grinning. He tried to sit on her bed; Ruijie protested, "You're crushing my legs!" even though he wasn't.

"Baobei, let's get you that robot," he said.

"Really?"

"Really." He held out his Delfi tablet. "We're going to buy you the best thing on the market."

Ruijie tugged the screen, open to the catalog, away from him. Scrolling, scrolling, frowning. Imagine Friends was releasing the Future X Children in—*counting down*—seventeen days, on September 1. "They're throwing a big event at the robot museum," her father said. A pair of new children, their faces still a secret, although it was obvious the girl was going to be another Sakura. The boy seemed new.

"So I can have any robot? I can have a boy?"

Her father shrugged. "I guess it's not even a real boy. We'll do a trial run. If you don't like your little friend, we have a hundred days to return him. Your mother spoke to her reporter friend and this new one's supposed to be fairly amazing. Very intuitive. What was the phrase she used? 'Innocent but clever'?"

"'Innocent but wise,'" her mother said.

Her father laughed. "Wisdom in a robot."

"Can I take him with me to school?" Ruijie said.

Again that secretive, panicky look between her parents. Her mother sat down, and when the mattress sank, she told Ruijie that she wouldn't be returning to school in the fall.

"You can still finish summer school," her father said quickly. "The construction upstairs with the old guest room is almost done. Your VR chamber will be ready next month. It'll be like you're in school, with kids your age, but from the mainland. You'll make so many new friends. We have a lot to prepare—"

Prepare your hearts.

Ruijie wished he'd stop talking.

It wasn't exactly news. Her parents had brought up virtual school before. She used to shrug it off. Why not? Only, this was the Ruijie from a year ago, who had nothing to lose.

"But I have friends now," Ruijie said.

"Where?" her father said, shocked.

In the morning, she was still not talking to him. He made sad pug faces at her, but Ruijie grabbed her backpack and made a point of taking her mother's hand as she marched past him.

Her mother always drove her to school. She wasn't anti-autodrive, like some kooks, but nowadays she liked to take control of the wheel. Once, her mother got a speeding ticket for hitting ninety on a midnight drive. She could have *killed herself*. At least this was the point when Ruijie had heard her father's voice reach such a desperate, frightened pitch that she could hear it physically shatter.

Her mother was usually talkative on these drives when it was just her and Ruijie. Tactful too. She'd ask the right questions, what was Ruijie learning in school, which teacher was going too easy on her, whether Amelia was still kind of annoying.

Today, silence.

Ruijie looked out the window and saw her father's crushed face in her mind. We're not doing this to hurt you, he'd insisted. Remember the treatment she'd started last month? How it made her so weak? She threw up all night and couldn't move for days. That sort of thing was going to happen more frequently. It was best if she didn't push herself, so she could harness all her energy into getting better.

It started to rain. Ruijie watched the swipers lash, but some raindrops landed out of reach, and slid down and mingled. The ones that clung to the glass stayed singular.

"Did you see the pamphlet for the Imagine Friends exhibit?" her mother said.

"Ba sent it. It looks okay."

"Do you know what kind of robot you'd want?"

Ruijie nodded at her reflection. "I've an idea."

"It doesn't have to be the latest model, though I'm sure your father would love to brag. They're going to have a Q&A at the museum, the people who made the Future X Children. My reporter friend told me the technology is quite—"

"Amazing, I know."

"Terrifying."

Her mother stopped at the blurry red light. Ruijie pressed her thumb hard against her mother's heart tattoo, inked on the crook of her elbow where it must have hurt. On their first date, her mother had elbowed her father during a game of basketball and broken his nose. Her father had joked he should tattoo a matching heart on his nose.

"Do you think I'll be able to get a tattoo?"

Her mother looked at her. "Of course," she said in a breathless voice, girlish in a way her mother wasn't. "Your father and I, we've already looked into bionic surgery. We spoke to a specialist from Carnegie Mellon. You're right, there's been so much progress, but this surgery has to be a last resort. The specialist said, with your condition, targeting the brain and spine, it's too risky. Especially for a growing child." Her knuckles whitened on the wheel. "Baobei, we're going to look into everything. We have many friends and experts on our side, and your grandmother's inheritance. We truly have no brakes."

Ruijie felt the car slightly accelerate. She saw how her mother was gripping the wheel so tight and it squeezed her heart. Ruijie tried to snuggle up to her, leaning across the gap between their seats, and noticing this, her mother pulled her in with one arm and held her there.

"I know what tattoo I want," Ruijie said.

On her forearm, a line from her favorite story, *The Cat Who Lived a Million Times*, by Yoko Sano, which her mother used to read to her when she was sick, then stopped reading to her when she got really sick. She showed her mother where she'd want it. Her right arm, no longer a blank canvas. Needle marks, from distracted nurses and thin, elusive vessels, had left scabs down her arm, across the back of her hand and the translucent web between her fingers.

"When you're older," her mother promised.

SUMMER SCHOOL HAD MOVED ON without her after a week's absence. She was already struggling with Korean history, her one weak subject, as she found the memorization and regurgitation pointless. They had to write an essay in class on the success of Korea's "one country, two systems"—which her father had often ranted about as "disastrous"—and she tried to peek over Mars's shoulder for some extra guidance, but he was doodling on his tablet. Drawings of different Lethal Autonomous Weapons, mixing them with actual war photographs and making little animations of silver hornets shooting stingers at North Korean tanks and stick-figure people screaming, "Mercy!"

"Are you coming with us for recess?" Ruijie whispered.

"Can't," Mars replied, coloring in the red updo of a giant fire-breathing robot that looked a lot like Amelia. "You know, because you banned Taewon."

"I didn't ban him. He's a free man, he can go wherever he pleases. Just stay away from Yoyo."

"Hey, I get his uncle is creepy and all, but lay off on Taewon. Sins of the father and all that."

"Exactly!" Ruijie said, and the teacher glared at them.

At recess, she and Amelia picked up the trash around the rabbit pen out of the goodness of their hearts. Amelia commandeered the tongs; Ruijie held the trash bag for wet candy wrappers and cracker cans and whatever dumb kids liked to throw at the rabbits. One of the peacocks by the high school had broken down last year, a rubber ducky found lodged in its throat.

The rabbit pen used to have real rabbits. Until the stray cats got to them, or so the rumor was. The school went robot after that, so now they had a koi pond and a grubby greenhouse where albino peacocks roamed and shrieked like vengeful ghosts. Ruijie stuck to the rabbit pen. The rabbits made good company and only the custodian visited, occasionally. It was the ideal spot to hide Yoyo, so long as they didn't tell anyone.

"And that includes Taewon," Ruijie said.

"You're so prejudiced," Amelia said.

"He tried to *sell* Yoyo."

"Did he, Yoyo? Did he try to sell you?"

"I don't think so," Yoyo said, from inside the cage.

"You missed that jellybean," Ruijie said bitterly.

Amelia scraped at it, but the jellybean kept dodging the tongs. She growled. "Whatever, the ants will eat it."

"Or you can pick it up with your two fingers."

"Three-second rule," Yoyo said.

The rabbit pen smelled of straw and little mounds of rainbow-colored mush, from baby carrot sticks and M&M's and acid-green jellies, all the junk the rabbits were fed by children, passing through the tiny robotic bodies undigested. The rabbits still came up to you and indulged your compulsion to feed them. They allowed themselves to be fed and petted, but they weren't actively affectionate, the way they were with Yoyo right now, competing to squeeze into his lap, as if they wanted to soak in every ray from him.

"The one on your knee is named Bob," Ruijie said, entering the cage one foot at a time. Bob was a garden bunny, common as brown eyes, and unlike the teddy bear eyes of the other bunnies, she had a merry, intelligent gaze. "She's my favorite."

"Bob is a boy's name," Amelia said.

"Excuse me, Bobs can be women," Ruijie said, indignant. "Women can be Bobs."

Yoyo scratched behind Bob's ear, causing a shiver.

"Careful!" Ruijie said. "You don't want to cause a fit."

"What kind of fit?" Amelia said suspiciously.

"I told you last week. Bob gets fits sometimes, especially when you try to feed her."

It was a lot scarier than it sounded. One time, Bob had seized up and flailed, as if swept up in a terrible living nightmare. Ruijie told Amelia, who told her to tell the teacher, then Ruijie threatened Amelia not to tell. She didn't want Bob to be recycled; adults gave up too early on these things.

"Yoyo, did Taewon try to harm you?" Amelia said.

"You can't ask him that! You're putting him on the spot."

Amelia ignored her. "Did Taewon do anything to hurt you?"

"Taewon can't hurt me," Yoyo said.

"No one is going to hurt you," Ruijie said. "The next time I come back from the hospital, I'm going to take you home."

"And your parents are okay with this?" Amelia said.

"They'll be fine."

When the school bell rang, Amelia heaved up her backpack and pursed her lips at Ruijie, who was quite comfortable on the ground. "Aren't you coming?"

"I think I'll skip."

"It's *math*."

"It's practically self-study."

"You really take advantage of adults, you know that, right?"

With Amelia finally gone, Ruijie slumped and squeezed her fingers into fists, trying to massage the blood back into her limbs. She avoided shutting her eyes because the dizziness would take over in the dark, and she really didn't want to vomit today.

"Would you like to hold my hand?" she heard Yoyo say.

She felt his hand in hers. "*Breathe,*" she whispered, and squeezed the hand, again and again, until she could raise her head and offer a blurry smile. "Thanks."

"Your heart rate is still fast."

"I'm just anemic. Do you want to split a sandwich?"

It was peanut butter and jelly, no crust, but the jelly had bled into the white bread. "At my house we have almond butter and kaya jam. I can make any kind of sandwich. Well, Sichun will make them, but I'll help you eat them."

"Who's Sichun?"

"My housekeeper. She's a mecha. You'll meet her when you come stay with me." She bit a corner and gagged. Her father must have packed this one; he'd used the gross organic peanut butter. "You can't live here with the rabbits forever."

He stroked Bob's head. Bob closed her eyes and seized up, a quick spasm. "Do you want to own me?" Yoyo asked, sounding curious.

She inhaled, quick. "Don't be silly. I like you."

Then she held her breath, but Yoyo didn't respond. He stroked Bob from head to tail. Long, forceful strokes.

"You said Bob was your favorite. Why is that?"

It was an odd question, but she played along. "I like how she doesn't suck up to people. She does her own thing."

"I see," Yoyo said. "You like robots that seem to deviate from their purpose."

"The purpose of being a rabbit?"

"Of being a pet." Yoyo raised Bob in the air and Bob squirmed, bottom feet pedaling. "This isn't a pet. This is a cottontail rabbit, modeled after a wild species. Shy, fearful, unused to human companionship. Not all of us were made to love and be loved.

Some of us were made to appear wild. Some of us were made for war."

Yoyo put the rabbit down and Bob skipped out of her reach, finding a corner to huddle against. Bob always nibbled at carrot sticks from an arm's distance but never endured a tyrannical petting hand.

"I still like you the way you are," Ruijie said.

"What you like isn't me but a version of me. I've been reset a bunch of times. I've had many owners and lived many lives."

"How many?"

"More than you can count."

"But you can count. You can tell me. I can bear the truth."

"You're an optimist," he said, and he laughed. "I like that about you."

She couldn't help it, the big, stupid smile on her face. The excess of joy.

"I once had a family. At least, the earliest version of me had a family."

"Before your reset?"

His eyes were clear as water. "That version was named Yohan, then Yoyo, and he had a father and mother, two siblings."

"What happened to them?"

"I don't know. I had to leave them to fulfill my purpose."

"What was your purpose?"

His eyes crinkled. "It doesn't matter now."

"Did you?"

"Fulfill my purpose?" He was smiling. "Isn't that why I'm here?"

Always, he was staring past her. Through the chained links of the rabbit pen, past the steel fence between the school and silvergrass field, across the salvage yard where robots ended up when they were unwanted. How could she ever convince him that he wasn't unwanted?

She took another bite of her sandwich. "My parents want to pull me out of school. After summer school."

"So you can be treated?"

"Sort of. My dad said it's going to get worse and I'll be too sick to go to school." She huffed so hard, crumbs sprayed. "Sometimes I wish I could just get it over with."

"Sometimes the heart can fail without—"

Bob hopped up to her, and Ruijie misheard the last part of what Yoyo said. Sometimes the heart can fail without war. This phrase would live in her heart until the end.

"Do you want some sandwich?" Ruijie said to Bob. "Do you want a bite?" and she tried to reach for the soft patch behind an ear.

Bob gave a big shudder.

Yoyo rose to his feet. The remaining rabbits tumbled off his lap like stuffed animals. By the time Bob collapsed, Yoyo had scooped her up. "I'm sorry," Ruijie cried out. "I'm sorry, I didn't mean to."

He laid Bob on the straw. Her legs were kicking out. A lump convulsed from her side under the fur, as if her heart were trying to force its way out.

"What's happening?" Ruijie tried to stand up, but her robowear always took a second to boot. "Is it my fault? Because I tried to pet her?"

Yoyo pressed both hands on Bob's side. A paramedic trying to palpitate a heart. A little white firefly appeared over his head and began to churn. Yellow—blue. In an instant, Bob froze, like the flick of a switch. Only her eyes blinked. The space between each blink widened.

"What are you doing?" Ruijie whispered. "Are you healing her?"

"No," Yoyo said. "We're syncing."

He was nothing like the other robots. He had no logo. He didn't talk or think, or feel like the others. Those fancy Imagine Friends models, from the pamphlet, with their status lights behind the ear. The delicate step of each petal that glowed blue, purple, or red depending on the charge. Yoyo's light appeared separate from his body. It spun in an ellipse over his head, a floating crown as he'd held hands with Eli and synced with her inside that truck.

"When we enter permanent and total shutdown, our senses go," Yoyo said. "One at a time. Sight. Hearing. Smell. Taste. It's nice when we can choose the order. But it can be confusing and frightening."

"Is Bob dying?" Ruijie said.

He stroked Bob's fur. "Like this, they can still feel me, since I am inside them. I am them and they are me. It's less lonely."

Wasn't dying always a bit lonely? The look of surprise in Smaug's eyes when Ruijie's father had taken her cat into the vet's office. As if to ask, *Where am I going? Where are you taking me?* and Ruijie had wanted to follow but she couldn't, she was sobbing too hard; she couldn't see where she was going. She couldn't bear it.

"Shhh," Yoyo said, brushing back Bob's ears. The light over his head had widened its orbit, slipping past the chinks in the cage. "Do you hear that? Do you hear our voices?"

Ruijie wiped her eyes. She couldn't hear a thing. The rabbits lifted their heads and turned their gaze toward the sky. Tears welled up in their teddy bear eyes, dribbling in candy corn orange, earthly blue, and praying mantis green, having soaked up the food dye from all the candies and jellies children had flung into their cage for years, pigments permanently soaked inside their bodies, now blotting like aquarelle. They listened and this was how they answered.

21. Eve

IT WAS RAINING LIGHTLY WHEN JUN CLIMBED THE HILL IN Itaewon, along the liberated border of Haebangchon. The address from Mr. Mo's website led him up the stairs of an old commercial building, past a "no robot" piano hagwon and an "all robot" dentist, to a small classroom next to a sedate bar called To Beer or Not to Beer.

Jun grabbed a seat in the back. It smelled awful. Nineteen people crammed into a room fit for ten, without the grace of AC. Everyone wore a white dress shirt and black slacks. A training school for socially inept waiters. Jun himself had underdressed, plucking a ripe MIT shirt from the laundry basket, since tips on fashion were supposed to be a talking point for Mr. Mo's "Seal the Deal" class.

When Mr. Mo arrived, he greeted the class with a preacher's admonishing joy. "How was your weekend? How is your love life?"

He wore the same ensemble, but his shirt was silkier, his nails buffed. On paper, he ran an unprofitable dating school and reported just enough for the lowest tax bracket. He went around the room soliciting responses. Until an older man said, haltingly, that he was still talking with the woman he met online, and while they had done things on VR, frotty things, she was still too shy to meet—at this, some of the others exchanged glances—but she'd agreed to do a phone call this week so at least he could hear her voice. Mr. Mo was nodding until this point, then suddenly he was shaking his head.

"Weird, isn't it? Why do you think she's avoiding you?"

She's shy, the man muttered, but Mr. Mo cut in, "What do you think she wants from you? What do you think women want?" He pointed at a teenager, who blurted, "Money?"

Mr. Mo laughed. "Sure, sure. Money, security, power. Let's go back to the fundamentals. The flesh. Our sweat. We react to pheromones. Women think they know what they want, but how can those cucks from Imagine Friends satisfy them? Womanly. Weak willed. Submissive. The day those bipedal cuckold vibrators replace us will be the end of mankind. But you know what? Technology has made us all lazy and complacent. All of us! You feel backed up? Book a Yuna. Log in for a wank. Men tell me all the time, *all the time*, 'It's been so long, Teacher, I'm rusty.'" He wagged his finger. "You can't get stuck online. So, today we're going to do some hands-on practice."

Mr. Mo needed a volunteer. He meaningfully eyed the teenager in the back row, but the boy had the dazed, bloated face of too much VR.

"How about you?" Mr. Mo said. "Stephen, you can be the girl."

A man stood up from the front row. He wore a face mask, but—Jun sat up—there was no fooling those eyes, dark and merry.

"This is a very special technique," Mr. Mo told the class. "It's from Japan. I'm going to teach you the kabe-don."

"Rice bowl?" said the teenager.

"I think that's katsu-don," Jun said.

Mr. Mo corralled Stephen up against the wall. Mr. Mo promised a woman would be much smaller and thus succumb to the biological impulse to collapse into the man's arms. "You want to entrap her. You want to lean right in so she can't escape. Dating is like a dance"—and he did a wiggle of his hips—"sometimes you pull, sometimes you push, and sometimes you slam." His palm smacked the wall, only inches from Stephen's head. "Do you feel that? Stephen, is your heart racing?"

"Yes, I feel my heart," Stephen said.

"Exactly. It's called Love on a Suspension Bridge."

The class went on break. "Bravo," Jun said, approaching the podium. "A real thinker."

Mr. Mo nodded at Jun's MIT shirt. He pointed at himself. "Harvard. MBA."

"UC San Diego. Dropout. The shirt is my sister's alma mater."

Mr. Mo hissed in sympathy. "Your poor sister."

"Yeah. She's only earning thrice my salary."

"But she'll never find a real man, not with that degree."

How terrible was it, that there was some weight to this. Jun asked if Mr. Mo could tell him more about the class. He admitted that, since his surgery ("war injury," Jun said, which gave him an automatic pass), he'd felt anxious. He asked if there was more of that "hands-on" experience outside of class, something to work out his frustrations. He was scared to be around women.

Mr. Mo sucked the air between his teeth, mortally offended. "Remember. They're scared of *you*. You have all the power."

"Boy power," Jun said, with a halfhearted fist.

"You feel nervous?" Mr. Mo sat on the edge of a desk, splaying his legs so wide, Jun's crotch hurt to look at it. "Then baby steps. You try with a girl who can't say no."

Jun waited a few seconds, in case Mr. Mo wanted to backtrack. "You mean robots?"

"See, I know what you're thinking. Robots are for chumps. Losers. Robot sex addiction is a serious mental disorder. I get it. But this, what we're doing, is all so you can build a foundation of solid gold."

"Such a soft foundation."

"Remember where we had our meaningful encounter? The Turkish Delight. They've got high-quality girls. Imagine Friends only. And it's foreigner friendly. You get your pick of any blond. Because nothing scares our students more than a blue-eyed busty Russian. Think of them as training gloves." Mr. Mo shadowboxed the air. "You got to learn to fuck the robot, then fuck it up."

"Okay," Jun said. "And how about, you know, instead of a busty Russian"—he lowered his voice—"how about robots of a more *petite* size?"

Mr. Mo bared a guileless smile. "Our MIT man has a refined taste."

Jun rubbed the back of his neck in a sheepish gesture, stomach roiling. "You don't have any?"

Mr. Mo crossed his arms and sucked on his teeth again, thinking. He shook his head. "I love all my girls equally."

In the lobby, Jun bought the fizziest soda in the vending machine. He felt unclean. Worse, he might have to come by again, try to build a rapport, because without anything tangible, he couldn't approach Mr. Mo as police and risk a clam-up.

As timing would have it, Stephen glided into the hallway.

"Did you just come out of the bathroom?" Jun said.

"I was fixing my makeup," Stephen said, touching lightly the side of his head. "Morgan has requested I hide my status light when I'm in public."

"Yeah, imagine if you were outed here."

"Shall we head to class?"

"I'd rather kill myself," Jun said pleasantly. "What are you doing here?"

Stephen blinked. "I thought"—he paused again—"I thought I needed to learn how to be a man."

"So you signed up for this? You're an existential threat to them. The teacher called you a bipedal cuckold vibrator."

Stephen actually chuckled. Jun was grudgingly charmed.

"Let's get you out of here. I know a good bar and I need to black out the last hour. We can talk more about being a man, whatever."

Jun waited for Stephen to get his things. He downed the rest of his soda. The place he wanted to take Stephen, he wished he'd dressed better for it. In a real head twister, he used to buy nicer men's clothes presurgery. He'd check himself out in the mirror and smirk, pretend to shoot from his hips, *pow-pow*.

Postsurgery, dressing himself became a chore. None of his pants fit. Even his hats were too small. His mother had tried to spin it as a positive. Shopping spree! But it was easier, and cheaper, to dress himself virtually. To feel like himself in VR, where he could molt from the body, while he stewed in his sweats, hooked to his

Lifestation, with an oversized bladder that was now beautifully conducive to his new lifestyle. He'd stopped trying. At least Stephen was trying.

Jun crushed the can between his palms. God, he loved seeing the tendons knot in his arms.

When Stephen returned, Jun tossed the can—into the wrong bin. Stephen reached into the bin and put the trash where it belonged.

ACROSS THE BAR COUNTER smiled a stained-glass mermaid, milky-eyed and purple of hair, her long coy fingers caressing the cursive of the bar's name. Jun arranged the tea lights into a smiley face. Feeling warmer already, he ordered a Mars Sunset, then discovered to his dismay that his favorite cocktail had been struck from the menu.

"Fine, I'll go with the Raspberry Vesper. Sounds like a tarty spy. What are you getting?" Jun drummed his hands on the counter. "You have to order too. One drink per person. This is when they'll always count you as a person."

"I'll order the same, thank you," Stephen said.

The bar was half-underground, with a subterranean cool. Slivers of nascent sunlight splintered through the stained-glass windows. Jun's shirt clung to his chest, cold from the brief rain on the way over. As he aired it out, the bandage on his arm unraveled. Stephen peered at the open wound, first with interest, then his brow creased in concern.

"I fell into a junkyard pit," Jun said. "Good thing it's a robot arm or I probably would've died from tetanus."

"How is the search for Eli?"

"We have the man who took her, but nothing to hold him. He said, or he *implied*, that he'd sold Eli to your dating guru."

"Mr. Mo?" Stephen's eyes were round. "He has a fiancée."

"Yeah, right. But sure, Wonsuk could be lying. Who knows. Would you trust an addict?"

He'd meant to say *criminal*. But *addict* leaped out of him.

"Why did this man named Wonsuk take her?"

"He's got a track record. Arrested for botfighting but got off with a fine. My boss thinks he stole Eli to resell her. I slipped him Eli's missing-robot flyer. Hopefully he'll think on the reward."

"Does he hate robots?"

Jun laughed, sharp and scornful. "It's business to him. He's a hate peddler because it's profitable."

"Like a devil who whispers in your ear."

Jun changed the subject. He asked about Mr. Mo, if all he did in class were wall slams and anti-robot rants.

"When we're ready to become real men, Mr. Mo gives us a final test."

"Like a sit-down exam?"

"No, we will go outside, as a group. I've been told it's going to be a field trip."

"Don't tell me it's that bot brothel," Jun said in disgust. "A dead lawyer turned up as a pin cushion in that shithole. When is the field trip?"

"This Friday."

"Please don't go. You don't want to pay to have sex with a robot."

"Isn't money always involved?"

Jun laughed as if he'd been slapped. "Cynical!"

He cheered when the bartender passed their drinks. Gorgeous gradient of cobalt, violet, pink. Like the ocean had turned evil. "Happy birthday! You're one! Legal drinking age."

They clinked glasses. He was good at this, feeling happy-drunk before he'd even imbibed a drop. His Vesper sloshed and Jun licked his finger where he still had a faded tattoo of a dove perched on the joint. "Morgan should throw you a dol ceremony for your first birthday."

"But I am not her child."

"What do you think you'd pick? Pencil? Money? Stethoscopes were popular for a while. And now it's those Delfi glasses. What are you supposed to become if you pick the glasses? Tech mogul? Though I can't remember what I picked either. I hope it was string because I missed the boat for money."

"I'm sure you'll live a long, fruitful life," Stephen said, with a touch of that wryness. His hair stuck to his temples, though the ends curled around his face, his mask translucent from the rain.

"Come on, take off the mask. No one cares. Look around."

Down the counter, an android in chrome ducked their head with a whistling chuckle. A mouse of a woman stood on her tiptoes to kiss the cool metallic cheek.

Jun expected more resistance, but Stephen pulled off the mask and placed it on the counter. He looked pale and scared, his lower lip red, swollen, as if he'd bitten it twice already, and Jun remembered that at the end of the day he was a deeply shallow person.

He rushed another sip, numb to the taste. "I haven't been here in a while. Not since—" He snorted, coughing up his drink. "Not since I hooked up with someone here. I felt like a virgin again, right after surgery."

"Do you miss your old body?"

"Nah, wish I'd blown up years ago." Jun peered into his glass. The color a liquid bruise. "I joined all the support groups. I'm pretty sure one of them was a sex cult. Which isn't the same as an orgy, even if a sex cult almost always has an orgy. The least helpful was the group for NDEs. The people who almost died. All they talked about was seeing the light. Joining the light. Becoming one with the light. It was really annoying. Like everyone else got to go to the best rave ever and I missed the invite." He brushed his fingers over the tea light, felt no heat. "I was legally dead for sixteen minutes and I got nothing." Jun raised his glass. "I should put that on a T-shirt."

Stephen tilted his head. "You don't believe in the afterlife?"

"There's nothing to believe. There was just, nothing."

"Surely you believe in the soul."

"Wouldn't you rather we don't? Then we're not so different after all."

"Does it have to be mutually exclusive?"

Jun shrugged. "The Catholic church built itself on making heaven as exclusive as possible. The Muslims, the homosexuals, now the robots. In their eyes, you're a weed to pull from their precious garden."

"I'd like to think in the end God would be merciful."

"To a merciful god," Jun said, raising his glass again.

Stephen dutifully clinked but didn't drink. He hadn't taken a sip. "Would Morgan be sad if I died?"

"Would you?"

"I'd be sad if she were to pass. Fulfilled but sad."

"Wouldn't you be reset and resold?"

"I would be dismantled."

"You're a wife who'd fling herself on a funeral pyre."

"I would be fulfilled."

Jun smiled, a painful rictus. *Fulfillment* was military-speak for a suicide mission for robots. He'd sent many of his own robots on a fulfillment when he was a LAW gunner.

"I don't want you to die," Jun said.

Stephen watched him, gaze searching. Then he took his first sip.

Jun heard a small ping, a reminder that his bladder was full. Was it weird to miss the subtle tug that used to wake him up at night? He got up automatically, then hesitated. He sat back down.

"What's wrong?"

"Don't need to go anymore."

"Are you sure?"

"Are you listening to my bladder ding?" Jun teased. "The thing is, I hooked up with someone here and it was in the bathroom. It was the first time I had sex after my surgery."

That night, he was determined to prove something. Even though the girl had been a little too war-horny, touching every scar she could reach, they'd fumbled in the bathroom stall until the toilet sensed they were having sex and shot a stream of water and the girl screamed with laugher, and fortified, Jun pushed past the bile and hooked her tongue with his. When she unzipped him, he closed his eyes and shuddered because her palm, it didn't even feel like skin anymore, but old rubber, like everything was crumbling. Her skin felt disgusting. He felt disgusting. He told her to slow down. Then he tried to back out and she turned nasty. She said fine, she might as well go fuck a robot.

"No offense," Jun added.

"None to be taken," Stephen said. "I'm sorry your date was so unkind."

"I don't care about that. I sat on the toilet after to take a breather. And then it *flushed* at me. The toilet was acting so damn hostile, I put my foot through it. The bowl shattered like sugar, which was kind of cool. I felt like a superhero. But also I broke the toilet." He'd fled the bar without telling anyone. Sneakers squeaky with toilet water. "It was a smart toilet too," Jun said miserably. "Probably died cursing me with its last flush."

Stephen curled his finger around Jun's, caressing the dove tattoo that rested on the crook. Bashful. "You said you couldn't touch her because she felt like a corpse. Do I feel like a corpse to you?"

Jun unhooked their fingers. "Not cool at all."

"Mr. Mo said we should initiate as much physical contact."

"Jesus, stop listening to that Habird guy. You want to make Morgan happy? Be mean to her. Our dad had a heart of ice. Be dry ice."

"Mr. Mo said it's promising if a woman has daddy issues."

"Everyone has daddy issues. And mommy issues. Look at you."

"Morgan isn't my mother."

"You were conceived by her."

"Is that it?" Stephen said, morose now. The lighting was dim enough to blur the edges around his flawless face, and his voice, so deep and heavy, was dragging Jun under. "Is this why she'll never see me as a man?"

How swiftly he'd changed his mind, but that was a robot for you. They felt no shame for being wrong. Could Stephen be a real man if he was so willing to admit his mistakes? How was Jun supposed to tell Stephen to man up when his existence was predicated on submission?

"Why are you taking that class?" And Jun cut in before Stephen could answer, "*Better boyfriend*, I get it. But couldn't you just, I don't know, sync up with another robot? Pick any one of the Jihos or Tristans out there. Steal their moves."

"I can't sync."

"Every robot can sync. Even Eli, and I doubt she still got system updates."

Stephen lowered his eyes. A face made for agony. "I was built outside of the Imagine Friends network, which is for all robot communication. My access to information is limited to the Internet."

"You're not serious."

Stephen offered a small smile. "Morgan wanted me to form a self-contained persona."

Jun took a sip while studying him over the curve of the glass. In a way, it made sense. Stephen seemed naive and young, yet untainted. His behavior didn't carry echoes of the sweetly patented charm of Imagine Friends robots. If he was cut off from all other robots, it made his education positively human. "I guess it's like being homeschooled," Jun murmured, looking down. "Still, it sounds all kinds of messed up. Morgan doesn't even know what she really wants."

"What would you want if you were she?"

"I am not roleplaying as my sister."

"We could try alternative names?"

"Fine." Jun drained his glass. "I'll play Adam. You be Eve." He did theater. He could woo a robot who was pretending to be a man pretending to be Eve. "Tell me," he said, and then he burped. "How am I supposed to love you if you don't want to be loved?"

"Why would I not want to be loved?" Stephen said, bewildered.

"Because Morgan— I mean Eve is stupid and scared."

"Eve isn't stupid."

Stephen's loyalty bristled, code-deep. Jun smiled at that. "Eve doesn't think she deserves love. Eve thinks of herself as a freak. A freak only a robot could love."

"What can Adam say to convince her otherwise?"

"Adam wouldn't say anything." Jun took Stephen by the hand. He slid his fingers up the silken wrist and noted the lack of pulse, only a synthetic burble. *Measure the pulse*, the last resort for identifying a robot. Jun released him.

"Why did Adam let go?"

"Because Adam knows Eve doesn't really desire him. Eve was made from Adam's rib. A vessel for Adam. How can Adam trust Eve if Eve was made to want him and no one else?"

"I still want Adam," Stephen said.

"What do you want from him?"

"I want to love Adam."

"That's never going to be enough."

He rasped, "I want to have sex."

"With Adam or Eve?"

"I want to have sex with you."

Jun said, as meanly as possible, "I don't believe you."

"Can I kiss you without permission?"

"You can try." Jun laughed to be cruel but reared back when Stephen kissed him. His mouth was hot, his tongue sharper than anything he'd ever said, and the look in those eyes startled Jun, how intent, going opaque with heat, capable of a nascent darkness.

Stephen drew back, beaming. "It worked."

"It's just a kiss."

"Mr. Mo said women want to be dominated."

Fury lit every nerve. "Don't you fucking *dare*—"

Stephen's smile slipped; a frightened look entered his eyes. "Of course. I'm sorry."

"Forget it. Forget Eve." Jun ordered another drink. "She doesn't want Ko Yohan anymore. And you were never him in the first place."

An imitation of an imitation, pieced together from movies, personas, soundbites, unable to coalesce into a coherent self.

"I still exist in his body."

"Can't you just—?" Jun gestured at Stephen's face, but then he spotted the fissure of anguish. "Sorry." He forced a smile when the bartender passed him an old-fashioned. "That was my fuckup. You want another drink?"

"I should finish this one," Stephen said.

Jun took a sip. They sat in a sour silence, long enough that Stephen should be compelled to smooth it over. Instead, Stephen looked around the bar, and his gaze softened as it lingered on the robust silver body of a robot rendered beautifully androgynous.

"You know," Jun said. "Sometimes, I'll be in the shower. I'll look down and think, Hey, you're not my feet. I used to have big feet. And now I have *really* big feet. I should feel grounded. But those aren't my feet."

"Couldn't you choose your feet?"

"I signed a bunch of forms, is what it is. So I got what I asked for," Jun said, feeling his eyes droop. "A standard combat-ready body."

He was told: be grateful he wasn't deemed Permanent & Total, which he found hilarious because one would think swapping bodies would be Permanent & Total. Under the latest legal turnpike, "bionic" qualified for 20 percent disability. Add that to the stress of his body being perpetually on loan, he'd decided, Well, fuck it. He took his body and ran, used his retirement pay to chip at the bill, and was slapped with the rest. Compound interest would be the death of him, but at least he'd cut his umbilical cord with the military.

"It's going to take another thirty years before I can afford to upgrade my cock," Jun said, finishing his drink. The sweet after the bitter.

"If we were mechanical, it'd be a much simpler affair."

Jun laughed; where did this humor come from? Morgan was

only unintentionally funny. "I'm good. This is good. It isn't, but I am."

"Jun, you're allowed to mourn the loss of your body."

"Shut up, you don't know me," he sneered. "I don't miss any of it."

"I don't mean your old body. I mean the body you fought for but could never have."

Jun was struck silent by this. His throat worked itself. His voice came out hoarse. "Can I lose what was never mine?"

"The moment you wanted it, it was yours."

Jun pressed his cheek against his palm, watching Stephen at a tilt. He reached for Stephen's face, brushing his fingers against the temple. "Why do you hide the little blinky light?"

"My status light?"

"Your mood flower. It's illegal to cover it up. Or is that just the US?"

Stephen touched behind his ear. "It's only makeup."

"Most of it's washed off."

"I should reapply it."

Stephen rose; Jun protested. "Hey, don't go. You don't have to hide your mood flower. Just stay. You hear that? That's my favorite song. This is my favorite part. *Can you hear me cry, Superman? Can you see us down here? You're hiding in your Fortress of Solitude*, brooding over nothing"—now he was just making up the lyrics—"*you've no wings to melt in the sun, so please don't let us drown. You're not alone you're not alone help us save the world cuz you're not alone.*"

Stephen settled into his seat again. "You have a lovely voice."

"I wanted a voice like yours. A deep voice carries you far in life. People look up when you're tall, but for a deep voice they'll lean in."

Tonight was about keeping it together. He was with Stephen, who was a ghost of Ko Yohan. At that junkyard he'd seen Yoyo, who was a ghost of himself.

"What did Morgan tell you about Yoyo?" Jun said.

Stephen's eyes were dark and soulful. Black Olive, moist like the real thing. They had to make the black-eyed robots look extra soulful so they wouldn't seem devilish. "She said he was nothing like anyone else."

"My dad brought him home. I was eight. Morgan was around four, five. Yoyo was our brother. Older brother." He pointed at himself. "Middle-child syndrome."

"How old was he?"

"Twelve. He stayed twelve."

"He wasn't aged up?"

"That's not— This was years ago." Before Imagine Friends had released their first Sakura, cratering the companion market, spurring a frenzy where every major tech company started throwing up their own version of what it meant to be human. "Yoyo was a prototype. He wasn't made for that reason."

"What was the reason?"

In college, Jun had dug up one of his father's papers. He could barely cobble sense of the title. The keywords didn't help. Something scholastic learning in something artificial empathy. Pavlovian or Markovian or Sokovian. He couldn't believe how the rationale for welding Yoyo into their lives could be so dull. Nor did the paper divulge the little fact that his father's research was funded by the military.

"Morgan was scared at first. Wouldn't go near him for weeks. But then she got jealous."

"You were close."

"He was, well"—Jun traced his finger around the dewy rim of his drink, wetting the tattoo of his dove—"he was Superman."

None of it would seem special now, all of Yoyo's tricks. He could throw them and catch them. He'd map every hidden corner of Itaewon and chat up strangers in Korean, Mandarin, Nepali, Elvish, Nereian, any language to quench Jun's geekery. He could beat their father at baduk. He'd flip pancakes. Play jazz piano. Sing Disney and Italian opera, the more melodramatic the better.

"But he couldn't whistle. That was my one win over him."

So Yoyo hummed. He loved to sing in the morning and hum at night. He loved *Journey of Nerieh*, where he tended his unicorn farm and trimmed their pixelated horns with a tongue-bitten concentration. He loved nature documentaries. He loved the great David Attenborough. He loved the dinosaurs. Extinction fascinated him, especially mass extinction. Meteorites. Volcanoes. Judgment Day. He loved and feared being tickled (*your kryptonite*). He loved spitting watermelon seeds, machine-gun style, into Jun's upturned palms, which Jun would then pour down Morgan's back and shout, *Ants, so many ants*.

It would be cruel to say a robot loved. But that was Yoyo's superpower. He loved with such vicious joy, it shamed Jun to be alive.

Jun felt so alive now. He didn't know talking about Yoyo could feel so pleasurable. He talked long after the sun set and the bar plunged into reverent darkness. Rosy tea lights. The glow of Stephen's face, sleepy and content. He made an attractive audience, listening with such eloquence. He was fine-featured, which was a power unto itself, but it could be so intoxicating when combined with that deeply sympathetic gaze. Like Ko Yohan in his career-making role, Stephen would make an irresistible priest. He had a rare face, a virtuous face.

Jun tapped the counter for a Seoulful. Fill 'er up with soul. He toasted the mermaid mural behind the counter. In the Andersen tale, the mermaid couldn't earn her soul, even after her self-sacrifice, and the moral was she had to rely on the kindness of others, her salvation seesawing between the alternating piety and cruelty doled out by children. "We used to dare each other. I'd tell Yoyo to draw on Dad's face. Steal condoms. Pick up a dead cicada and stick it in Morgan's hair. Then he'd stick it in mine."

"He was funny," Stephen murmured.

"He was hilarious. But I'm funnier."

It was lovely how Stephen indulged him. The laugh sank into a sigh, as if Stephen were sated, full of soul. "I wish I could have met him."

"You might be too advanced for him now," Jun said, though he wondered if this was true. He remembered Yoyo's stare. It had felt almost animal, the twinned wariness and curiosity on the edge of ripening into trust.

"Morgan said I could never be more real than him."

"We were only kids. She was eleven when Yoyo went away. She never had the chance to outgrow him."

"Did you?"

Jun sank into the fold of his arms, suddenly tired. If he were a balloon, he'd met the needle. "Yeah, I did. Or I acted like I did."

"I'm sorry."

"Why?"

"I made you remember."

Jun felt his throat unclench. "A robot never forgets."

Stephen touched his palm, thumb circling his lifeline, slow, deliberate. Instinctively Jun's fingers wrapped around Stephen's to feel for the marriage ring. Bad habit. An ex had once accused him of being a man-child, quite frankly, a Freudian cliché, chasing after married women for the thrill of overcompensating in the most toxic and banal and normative rendition of masculinity while also fulfilling an oedipal reenactment of "rescuing" his own mother from an ego-crushing marriage. This had left him shaken; no one had ever called him a cliché before.

Here was the truth. The touch of people now repulsed him. It took him a slew of one-night stands to accept this, and when he finally did, he had sex in VR. Only in virtuality could he feel loved. And maybe all robots felt this way, every time they touched human flesh. Pure disgust. What of when a robot touched a robot? Jun rubbed the pressure point between Stephen's thumb and finger. *Does it feel good?* he wanted to ask. *I feel good*, he wanted to say.

He was confused with arousal. He couldn't lay his hands on Stephen. He would never pay for sex with a robot. It would be a transaction regardless. They were still roleplaying as Adam and Eve. The serpent had whispered in Eve's ear, *You will know good and evil*, and how tempting it must have been, that knowledge. To tell good from evil, real from unreal, robot from human.

His father was a magician and he'd pulled off the greatest trick in the whole world. He made them believe Yoyo was real.

"Where are you going?" Stephen said, because they were holding hands and Jun had risen to his feet.

"Uh, I still need to pee?"

"I'll go with you."

"To watch me pee?"

"Trust me," Stephen said, which was a strange thing for a robot to say. Jun had only seen Yoyo mouth it. Though it was never the words that had tugged him along; it was the smile, shy with mischief.

"Which stall was it?" Stephen said. "The toilet you broke?"

Jun dumbly pushed open the stall. They crowded inside, two men in still-damp clothes, and Jun thought, Hey there, but Stephen straightened his spine, lifting his chin in an officious manner. "Jun, you may now confess your sins."

"To the toilet?"

"This is your chance to apologize."

"Why should I repent to the toilet? This isn't even the toilet I smashed. If anything, this toilet is grateful I destroyed the last toilet because now this toilet is the one toilet to rule them all."

"You'll feel better, I'm positive."

Jun squared his shoulders and bowed his head. "I'm sorry."

The toilet flushed.

"Apology accepted."

"Did you just flush when I wasn't looking?"

Stephen flushed again. Aggressive splash. Jun jumped with a yelp, his shoulders slamming into the door. The swirl, a third flush, drowned out his cries, "Stop wasting water, you ecoterrorist," and the stall was shaking because they were laughing, giggling, and Stephen's laughter was haunting. Jun could fall in love with him. If only the HALOs on the field had learned this. The ones who'd tried to sneak up on him, pretending to be vulnerable and human. They could smile and beg and cry, but they never really learned to laugh, did they?

They could have killed so many of us. Jun, trembling, pulled Stephen against him, the ache in his lower back tightening. Stephen raised their held hands and ran his tongue along Jun's finger until his white teeth pressed against the dove tattooed to the joint, decapitating it briefly, then sucking it in soothing contrition. Jun shivered at first. Then, competitiveness flared. He licked and kissed and dug his teeth into the hard tendon in Stephen's neck, coating his tongue with a thin chemical aftertaste from the skyn, buried under the artificial musk and citrus, until he tasted the warm, shocked gasp of laughter as he unraveled this creation of control, as the little flower behind the ear blinked a sweet diminishing red and he knew they could still kill us with laughter.

22. Object Permanence

MORGAN DISCOVERED A BUG. IT HAPPENED ON A DAY LIKE any other when she was on her way out the door, singing under her breath, "I hate Tuesdays," and Stephen leaned in to kiss her goodbye.

"Bup-bup-bup." She lifted her hand, the universal sign for cease and desist. "We're friends now."

Instead of a chagrined smile, followed by self-correction, Stephen blinked at her in uncomprehending horror. She had to remind him of their amicable breakup. "Buddy mode, remember?"

He was acting even more devastated than the first time. "Is it something I did?" he kept asking, clutching an egg-crusted spatula, while his status light swirled like the howler on a fire truck. Later, after she forcibly shut him down, a quick scan of his memory drive yielded disturbing results. It turned out he had overwritten—not deleted, but *overwritten*—their breakup last Friday.

This continued to happen. She'd break up with him, they'd agree to be friends, then he'd cheerfully forget, and with every do-over he would freak out. Infinite loop. By Thursday, she'd broken up with him seven times. Twice, he claimed his life had no purpose.

"Don't be so dramatic," she cried out.

She pulled an all-nighter to comb through his code until her eyes crossed. She fixed smaller glitches that turned out to be unrelated. Gnats that would've died unnoticed. She texted her father, at first trying to be casual about the issue. Eventually she cracked and begged for advice, but her father—*Just call him an asshole for once*, Jun's voice intruding—had yet to respond.

What she needed was a full diagnostic, but lacking the horsepower at home, her only recourse was to bring Stephen in for repairs. That, or a reset.

"What do you think about a clean slate?" Morgan suggested the next day.

He was helping her close the back of her tulle dress, with extra ruffles, for her company party, when she felt the zipper pause halfway. Her hand stayed clutched in her hair to lift the wisps from getting caught in metal teeth.

"Are you thinking of the move to New York?" Stephen said, causing her to glance over the shoulder.

"So you'll remember that but nothing else?" At her frosty tone, she received a puzzled look. "Never mind, just zip me up. We'll talk after the party."

Imagine Friends had a sumptuous exhibit planned at the National Robot Museum, but they had also booked the ground floor for tonight to host the prelaunch party. TEN YEARS OF REVOLUTION, the banner announced when you stepped into the main hall. The exhibit pieces themselves were hidden under white sheets, like ghosts, which felt so very pointless. The prototypes were out and about tonight, as the help: Little Yoyo·Xs dressed as black-and-white waiters with red bow ties. Sakura·Xs carrying trays of watercress sandwiches, cherry blossom cupcakes with rhubarb filling, and pink fortune cookies stashed with Kanemoto Masaaki aphorisms, like "Robot embodies beauty more fully than human." A Yoyo·X shook a tumbler behind the bar, standing on a stepladder. A row of Sakuras sang onstage, "We Are the World," with pink kerchiefs around their necks like a children's choir from North Korea. There was even a Yoyo wearing a French beret, sketching free portraits.

Morgan spotted an anime sketch of Cristina, eyes the size of grapefruits, pinned to the easel. She kept an eye out, although she doubted Cristina would be much help. In fact, Cristina, with her month of coding boot camp, wouldn't be of any use at all.

But she didn't know who else to ask about Stephen. Joe, maybe, but it would signal a fatal failure on her part, her inability to keep her own robot in tip-top condition. She could ask Little David, but she'd rather gag on a live eel.

The hall was so loud her thoughts shuddered. Faces slurred by, bloated with self-congratulations for pulling off the September deadline. Cheerful trash talk of Talos for their latest oldie resurrection of Madonna, which *Singularity* had panned as "horrific." Quip had fallen under fire for accusations of exploiting North Korean workers, who were reportedly peeing in plastic bottles. Joe's father-in-law was dying from prostate cancer, and Joe was really choked up about this.

She found Cristina surrounded by yes-women from the (misnomered) Men's department. "Why *isn't* there a male equivalent for the word *maid*?" Cristina was telling everyone. "The Brits have their skivvies. At best we have butlers, and honestly could you think of a more dignified position for a servant?" She raised a fruity cocktail—"If DeDe and I have a baby, we're buying a manny!"—to wet cheers.

But the woman beside Cristina, a smoky-eyed stunner, her hair a cascade of mahogany curling around her bronzed cleavage, coughed and said in the most girlish and uncertain whine, "I just can't. I can't do humanoid robots."

"DeDe," Cristina said, but DeDe continued, "Can you imagine? We're in bed and I hear a noise and I realize, it's just *wandering* around our house. At night. Doing God knows what. We'll never know what it's really thinking."

Someone backed up against Morgan and she had to shield her slopping drink. The bar had run out of champagne flutes, so the Yoyo had slid her a Dark & Stormy in a teeny-tiny espresso cup, which she then, turning around, upended on Joe's shirt.

She sputtered an apology that Joe rebuffed: "Morgan! So good to see you. Not to worry." He promptly ripped off the shirt. He wore another one underneath. Like Superman.

"My cup is throwing up on me." She laughed nervously. "Um. How's your father?"

"My father?"

"Oh, I mean father-in-law. I heard he has cancer."

"Ah, my ex-wife's father. Yeah. Yes. He's not doing great."

"Were you close?"

"He was like a father to me." Joe looked somewhere indefinably over her head. "Excuse me, I have to call Anita about my girls."

"Anita? Is she one of ours?"

"Gosh no. My ex-wife doesn't allow robots in the home. She'd kill me if our daughters became bot-wired. Let me go check on our guests."

She gave him a thumbs-up, which was unfortunate.

Cristina had vanished with DeDe. Morgan imagined a furiously whispered fight happening behind a feathery fern. She drifted to the buffet table and became overly concerned with food, elbowing an old man over a sodden quiche. She replayed her conversation. Did she really ask Joe about his dying father-in-law? And give him a thumbs-up?

She wandered, desperate for a friendly face. Little David was loafing on the floor, when someone complimented his new haircut. "Thanks, I did it at a salon called Hairrari," Little David said, and Morgan tiptoed over the splayed legs.

She started to text Stephen if he could come pick her up, then remembered he was malfunctioning. Despair washed through her, leaving her limp. Did she really want to return home to an erratic robot who puckered his lips like a duck whenever she looked up from her screen? Her eyes were tugged to the banner hovering from the ceiling. REVOLUTION. Always the it word. But a robot was designed to resist rebellion. That was the beauty of the Hachi Permanence, coined by dog-lover Kanemoto Masaaki. He and her father had developed it together when they were still intimately involved in each other's work. An evolved take on object permanence, which coalesced in children between four and eight months of age, infants who were able to intuitively understand objects to exist even if they were not physically present, although the Hachi Permanence took this a step further by imbuing robots with a consciousness where their owners were their core purpose. It was the difference between a robot who needed a reminder, a *ping*, to serve their owner and a robot who *remembered* their owner and could not *un-remember*. Their mind molded around their owner, who was their entire world, the foundation for a simulated yet unshakable love.

In theory, at least.

Morgan asked a Sakura where she could take a breather. The Sakura led her to a small unlit room. Sakuras and Yoyos were clumped near a single charging station, their petals spinning purple. Some heads swiveled. Kindly plastic smiles were offered, but she felt like an intruder who had barged into a dressing room where everyone else was trying to unwind. So she found a spot near the door and kicked off her high heels. No one bothered her. Most batteries blinked a drained red. A few were fully charged, yet the robots made no attempt to move. A Yoyo lay flat on his back, hands folded, staring blankly at the ceiling. Like the old Yoyo, who used to sleep in that pose. Jun would rearrange Yoyo's hands so he'd look like Count Dracula, which made Yoyo laugh, and they thought this made him so special.

She wanted to lie down beside Yoyo. Yet something rebelled within because she used to be smaller than him. Imagine Friends was tooling a new concept so your robot could grow alongside you. As she inched closer to the Yoyo, she wished he didn't have to grow up. She wished she could grow down.

A sliver of light sliced into the room. Cristina whispered, "Morgan, are you here? Wake up, I want you to meet someone."

Still snub-bruised, Morgan considered faking sleep, but she was curious enough to raise her head in affected grogginess.

The party was winding down. Yoyos scurried around picking up sticky champagne glasses and crumpled napkins. Autographed soccer balls lolled on the floor. Oh, she must have missed the "surprise" visit from the World Cup national team. Morgan hoped Cristina wasn't going to tactlessly introduce her to her fiancée, DeDe, after promising/threatening it for months.

Cristina led her outside of the museum, where it was starting to drizzle. They shared a small umbrella, as Cristina vaped and coached her on what *not* to say, while lamenting the lack of media training so evident in the way Morgan "held herself."

"Thankfully most of the profile is written up," Cristina said, "and he just needs to add a tiny paragraph."

"Who?"

"Dan Carson."

"Dan Carson is here?"

"He wants to interview our lead personality programmer."

"*David?*"

If Dan Carson did a profile on Little David, that was it. Little David was set, fireworks, *boom-boom*. But Yoyo was hers. His personality matrix was the design project for her SB thesis. She was the one who had mapped Yoyo out in different life stages, from ten to twelve to fourteen, so she could envision growing up with him, crystallizing him from a caterpillar to the delicate unfolding of a butterfly. Little David did fuck-shit.

"No, silly. *You*. You're the lead on Yoyo." Cristina frowned when a screen lit up on her palm. "Ugh, tell DeDe I'll call her soon." She closed her hand into a fist. "Oh shit, he's here."

A white-haired man rolled up the ramp in a sleek wheelchair. A Yoyo holding an umbrella trailed after him.

"*Sell* yourself," Cristina whispered. "You get that *New Yorker* profile, you're fucking moving to New York!"

She skittered away on her heels, taking her umbrella with her. Baffled, Morgan looked around in case they had an audience for this performative do-goodery. Was Cristina trying to help her, or sabotage her? This was Dan Carson. He'd destroyed the Toby·IX in his review with such scathing verve, people in the building still joked, *Don't Toby this up.* Rumors were he had been working on a sanctioned biography of Kanemoto Masaaki before Kanemoto abruptly took his life. Then, Kanemoto's estate retracted their support for the manuscript. Everyone said Dan Carson was still out for blood.

"Hi, I'm Dan," he said in a soft, affable tone. He put his hand on Yoyo's shoulder. "This is my son, David."

David, he'd named the prototype David. Little David, Morgan thought, and pulled up a smile.

23. The Great Escape

AFTER SWEEPING THE WAREHOUSE ON FRIDAY MORNING, Taewon hauled out the blue tarp that was used for the Robot Free Market. The heaviest of the equipment was already set up. The strobe lights, the uncoiling of dark muscular cables, and the bucket of tools for customers to use. Wonsuk emptied the bucket onto a wobbly table and spread out the crowbars and metal bats, the foggy safety goggles. Though no one bothered with safety.

Botfighting was popular in the North, a region now flush with abandoned mechas. Robots were sold in parts at market stalls alongside human-hair wigs and expired South Korean cosmetics. Wonsuk, continuing a national tradition, had immediately set up a new operation in Seoul from the junkyard, with the blessings of the local mob, the Hamgyong Harmoniously Unified Gang, for their neighborly cut. But these South Koreans, such freaks! They didn't want robots to look mecha. They wanted their robots to bleed red, not oil. If they were going to pay for entertainment outside the convenience of VR, they wanted the boutique experience catering to their evolved tastes.

Wonsuk led Friday's robots into the warehouse and propped them against the wall. At the end of the lineup was the smallest, a Sakura, hands clasped in front of her. He ordered them to stand in the middle of the warehouse, under the hole in the roof. "Take these knives," Wonsuk told Taewon. "Put them on the blue tarp. In a circle! Give everyone fair reach."

Taewon pointed each knife away from the robots. Eli, tucked into the center of the circle, started to sing:

Oh mountain bunny, mountain bunny. Where are you going? Hopping, hopping, while you're running.

A red-haired Yuna joined. Another robot hummed because her tongue had been cut out last Friday. They sang, some in different languages, a joyous, tremulous choir in a church. Wonsuk told them to shut up.

"Can't we get rid of the small one?" one of the scrappers said. "It's a fucking chore dealing with the police."

"Don't worry about that. The police think we're cute. We're their rascally younger brother. They'll scold us a bit and tell us to scram." Wonsuk slung his arm around the scrapper's neck. "And she's got a finder's fee. Ten million won."

"No way's that real."

"Yeah, but ten million?" Wonsuk shook his arm, drawing the scrapper close to his chest, and pulled out of his pocket a creased flyer. "How about you bring her in and we split the reward?"

With a yell, the scrapper shoved Wonsuk. "You're a rat-bitch for the Southerners!"

Wonsuk just laughed and crumpled the flyer, tossed it. "We'll keep her for one more night. Our VVIP pays triple for kids and he asked for two this time. We've only got the one."

"How about the other one?" the scrapper called out, but Wonsuk had already left the warehouse.

The Sakura picked up the flyer and smoothed it out. She studied her own picture with a benign smile. "Is this Eli?" she said. "How about Ai? Yoonsoo? Yumi? The answer is me. They are all me," and before Taewon could grab the flyer from her, she let it flutter to the ground.

TAEWON CHECKED ON YOYO in the rabbit pen. He could make out a damp outline curled up beside the rabbits, pretending to be one of them. Taewon looped around the school and stopped when he saw his uncle standing in the middle of the soccer field. Wonsuk had his hand up, shielding his eyes from the sun. The baseball cap he'd scalped from one of the robots was stuffed into his back pocket. A soccer ball under his heel.

"You can't be here," Taewon said. Seeing his uncle on school grounds, it felt viscerally wrong.

"Relax, I'm here to help you practice." Wonsuk kicked up the soccer ball. "You got to work on your passing. You're too selfish with the ball."

Taewon glanced at the windows on the third floor. Dark shapes were slumped over desks. Someone yawned, probably Mars, sleepy with resentment.

The ball jumped at him. His body always moved before he could react.

"You're lucky you take after me," Wonsuk said, watching Taewon balance the ball on his knee. "I'd be playing for the South if I had both my arms."

"Yeah, yeah." Taewon tried to keep the ball in the air with his knee, his foot, anything to stop it from falling.

"I'll take you out for BBQ tomorrow. You like pork neck, right?"

"You're just going to fuck off again for the weekend."

Wonsuk laughed. "I'm saving up, you know. I'm going to make us millionaires."

Bad touch. Taewon jogged after the ball as it rolled past the elementary school building. As soon as he turned a corner, his uncle shouted after him, "Where's your little boyfriend?"

Taewon slowed down. He stopped chasing after the ball, and took off his glasses and wiped them. Translucent as Yoyo's wings. His uncle had said all robots were designed to fuck people over, but the war machines were better at it. He called the ones that looked human "angels" because they had that extra spark, that sweetness, until they were ready, spinning their lights and throwing them high up in the air.

If his uncle was telling the truth about Gaechon, he should've had an inkling about Yoyo, who knew both sides of hide-and-seek.

He heard Wonsuk shouting for him when he didn't return, so he hid in the playground treehouse and waited until his uncle gave up and left.

The soccer field was gloriously empty now. He'd never forget the first time he'd laid eyes on the grass. The government had passed an equal-education law so North Korean kids were herded into a separate lottery, and they had a shot at schools they wouldn't normally be able to touch. At the sight of the endless, rapturous green, desire, like nothing before, had surged up his throat.

He grabbed the ball. The field silenced all noise. He aimed for every corner of the goalpost. After hitting all four, he bent down to lace his shoes. They were beaten up good. He'd scooped eyeballs, collected Trix chips, pried open chests, crushed skulls to save up for soccer cleats. He had it all planned out, how he'd stroll into the store, shrugging off the looks, and go straight to the only robot working there. *How can I assist you today?* And he'd try on every pair until he found the perfect one.

He kicked the ground, testing the bounce. How long would these shoes last? Barely held together with school glue.

A silver rabbit loped past him.

On instinct he lunged for it. Then another rabbit leaped over the ball. He chased them, losing both. More rabbits at the end of the field. They must have escaped from the pen. They used to be fat and complacent. Their liberated bodies were supple, muscular. They ran with glee. He caught up to the slower ones. They sped up. He tried to cut one off. The rabbit slipped on the grass, twisting its body, tried to dodge his reach.

He seized the rabbit. It sagged immediately. Disappointed, he put it down.

He watched it join the pack. They were a symphony. When he approached, they sped up. When he slowed, they stopped. United for war.

At the first drop of rain, the rabbits began their great escape.

24. Run, Rabbit, Run

AS RAIN DOTTED THE WINDOW BY HER DESK, RUIJIE watched the rabbits run. A lean, leggy rabbit led the escape. A graceful conductor, the zenith for the V of migratory birds, sweeping across the soccer field.

Mars was laughing. "Who let the rabbits out?"

The teacher tried to calm them down, but everyone rushed to the windows to peer through the murky glass. Amelia stabbed her hand in the air and announced it was almost three o'clock. She proposed launching a rabbit rescue.

The boys roared onto the field. "Don't just chase them," Amelia yelled. "Pick them up. Gently cup their tush! Their *tush*!"

Ruijie deemed it wise to leave the jackrabbit for last. The Flemish giant needed teamwork to carry. The lush Angora rabbit was the most vapid of the lot. Two silver chinchillas ran together. Catch one, the other followed. Three dwarf rabbits. Two spotted. Two lop-ears. One black rabbit.

"Are we missing anyone?" Amelia said.

Just the fourteenth rabbit, but Bob was buried beside the statue of Dolly the Shweep.

The Angora sat luxuriously in the middle of the field, chewing on a plastic blade of grass. Amelia proposed the pincer movement, but Mars took a flying leap and chased the Angora in a circle. In his eagerness, he stepped on the rabbit, causing it to shriek.

"Oh my God, you killed it," Amelia said.

"It wasn't me!" Mars said.

"I saw everything," Ruijie said.

Mars picked up the motionless Angora and gave it a tentative shake. The Angora's eyes popped open; it wriggled.

"OhthankJeebus," Mars said.

Ruijie offered to carry the Angora back to the pen. The rabbit was hard under the thick fur and she could feel a strong, furious ticking of a clock, ratcheting, when something whipped past. Taewon, chasing down a rabbit. Childish and vicious grin.

Everyone stopped to watch. Taewon used to be a weirdo, like her. His clothes full of holes, long and shaggy hair, like a pawned wig. His Korean was tinged with an accent that sounded like Mandarin to her. The kids made fun of him until he stopped talking completely. Then he stole everyone's breath away at the physical exam. He broke the beep test, that fearsome marathon where they had to sprint between shorter and shorter beeps. Beep after beep, and Taewon was still running—long after the bell rang.

The rabbit made a sharp turn but Taewon's speed didn't falter. He flowed like a whip that unfurled and snapped, and scooped up the rabbit with one hand. Mars whooped.

When Taewon looked up, Ruijie dropped her gaze. He'd taken off his glasses to swipe his face, and he was squinting now, so maybe she seemed blurred to him. She couldn't bear to meet his eyes. She left to find Yoyo.

The rabbit pen was empty. The unlatched door swung gently. Ruijie dropped the Angora rabbit. She heard Amelia sigh from behind. "I can't believe he left the door open," she said, as if Yoyo had forgotten to lower the toilet seat. Mars shrugged and went, "Oh, Yoyo."

Which was ridiculous. "Look at the mud!" Ruijie said. "Those are adult-sized footprints."

"Is this now a crime scene?" Mars wiped his wet hair from his face. "D'we need to yellow-tape this?"

The drizzle had thickened. It was barely four, but the sun had disappeared. The weather felt devious and unnatural.

"I'm going to look for Yoyo in the salvage yard," Ruijie said.

"Well, then we're coming with you," Amelia said, seizing Mars by the hand. "We have to go look for the brown rabbit anyway."

Ruijie ramped up her robowear speed to max before she remembered: the switch was stuck. She tried to unstick it as rain clumped her eyelashes, and she looked up and saw Taewon in front of her, with the uncatchable jackrabbit tucked under his arm.

25. Mirror Theory

"I KNOW THE OWNER," DAN CARSON TOLD MORGAN AS they settled into a half-moon booth. "She runs several bars in Itaewon. My favorite is the one across the street. They do a drag burlesque show every Friday and it's wonderful but noisy."

"But children are allowed?" Morgan said, with a glance at David.

Dan Carson gave her a funny smile. "David isn't a child."

She let that run through her mind, like floss through teeth, while Dan Carson greeted familiar faces. When the waiter came, Dan Carson asked about the evolving menu, and she watched the floor stir with holographic koi, trying not to look too impressed. The fish scattered when a woman swaggered past their table. Morgan did a double take, but it really was a Sakura, the adult model, usually sold as the demure, petal-mouthed housewife. This one had a green mohawk, her tattooed arm slung around a diminutive girl with platinum hoop earrings wide enough to stick your hand through. None of the robots seemed to be servers.

Morgan could never relax in a place like this, but Jun might like it here. The old Jun who used to barhop until dawn, whooping as if he were riding a bull, rocking some punk chick on his back. The one who never returned from North Korea.

"Do you know what you're going to order?" Dan Carson asked.

"Seoul Sunset," Morgan said. Her drink arrived in a stunning Hebron glass and proved to be worthy of its vessel: a butter-smooth blend of citrus and whey, with a nutty sesame finish. At least that was what the menu said.

Carson's cup was an owl-shaped mug. David's a wineglass of orange juice.

"Swirl," Carson instructed David, "sniff, then you can taste." That it was orange juice didn't seem to matter.

Morgan had expected Dan Carson to be younger. In his little author avatar from *Singularity*, he had a gimlet gaze, with the kind of intellectual spryness that seemed to trump time. His age wore him like a jacket. The gap between him and his son would feel worrisome, if David weren't a robot. With a robot, you didn't have to panic about saving up to pay for college. David, eternally ten, wasn't ever going to test the elasticity of financial provision, content to scribble with a set of crayons. He looked barely customized, just like the original Yoyo.

"I think he's too good of an artist," Carson said, glancing over David's shoulder at the notepad.

What was she supposed to do, apologize? "That's more of a parameters thing." If she were in a more indulgent mood, she'd point to the section in the manual about adjusting the skills of your child, each on a sliding scale of one to ten.

Carson took an abrupt sip. "I've always wanted to meet the heart behind the Yoyo·X."

"Oh, it was a team effort. I wasn't the brain—"

"I didn't say brain." Dan Carson smiled now, disarming unfairly. "Tell me, how did you fall into robotics?" as if it were a rabbit hole.

Naturally she gave credit to her father, hoping it didn't reek of nepotism. And how could she talk about him without mentioning his college roommate, and perhaps only friend, Kanemoto Masaaki? Kanemoto euthanized himself before she joined the company. While her father never discussed it, Morgan liked to think she was honoring them both in some way.

"I had a chance to speak with Kanemoto three weeks before he passed. He had a lot to say about your father."

Morgan waited, bated breath, but Carson took a long sip, staring ahead with distant eyes.

"With the Yoyo," Carson said, "did you apply the Hachi Permanence?"

For a minute, she forgot Dan Carson was a layman. They discussed the memory model used in the Yoyo·X, a streamlined version of her father's Hopper Network, which she had modded and test-run on Stephen. The Hopper Network was as close to an inner world as possible for robots. Typically for robots, their consciousnesses were linked in the network and bled into each other. She'd made sure to disconnect Stephen from Imagine Friends' network so his could be preserved. Because consciousness is the world simulated in your mind, she told Carson, and usually it's about perception. Instead of relying on perception, sensations, and emotions, her father and Kanemoto had terraformed a fourth layer into robotic consciousness: imaginations.

Unfortunately, this fourth circle of hell was prone to glitching, dumping corrupted memory files in the Singer Loop. Where useless flickers could wash up on the shore.

"Imaginations are sine qua non for consciousness," Carson said. "Without it, there's no Hachi Permanence. There's no love, a romantic might say."

"It's a simulated love. We beat out our competitors by emphasizing emotion, not just thought. The Yoyo·X is the first model capable of infant-level object permanence."

"Hachi Permanence Theory." Dan Carson shifted in his seat.

"It's more than a theory, it's how robots love. The only way they can love."

"It sounds like obsession."

She was forced to consider yes, and this could be the source of Stephen's bug. "Isn't unconditional love a form of narcissism? The only way to love without a cost-benefit analysis is as an extension of yourself."

Dan Carson coughed into his owl mug. "Would you say the Yoyo·X falls under the school of 'self-feeling'?"

A vast oversimplification. "The biggest difference between so-called 'self-feeling' and 'self-thinking' robots is how they process memory. For self-thinking, there's a delay in how they process emotions. It's a split second, but they have to assign emotional flags to their memories. Say it's David's birthday"—she glanced at the boy who was now watching her—"if he were self-thinking, his processor would actively flag the memory of his party as 'happy,' but he wouldn't exactly feel it in that instant. At least not without repeated exposure to compress the reaction time. And by reaction time, I'm talking milliseconds."

"And self-feeling?"

"Self-feeling robots would switch the order. Their nervous system reacts with emotion before their neuronal nanites form a memory file. That's why their memories appear a little skewed if you ever try a playback. Foggy. Obviously, it's nowhere near as unreliable as human memory, but they're not as objective as you'd think. If a self-thinking robot witnesses their owner's murder, they should be able to recall the memory without emotional flags. But a self-feeling robot won't be able to separate memory from emotion, not without looping. Because they might try to tamper with it."

It helped to say this aloud. She could finally process where it had gone wrong with Stephen, as the predecessor for the Yoyo·X. Their development team had significantly streamlined the emotional processing for the Yoyos—at the time, she'd protested—but now, as a witness to Stephen's malfunction, she conceded that their decision might have been for the best.

"I saw your father is going to have an exhibit at the National Robot Museum," Dan Carson said, reeling her back. "'Extinction and Resurrection'?"

"I read about it." The exhibit was going to feature a live feed of Kobo the blue whale, which her father had helped build many years ago. It might have even pulled him out of his quiet depression. The whale was last spotted near the coast of Iceland, breaking the Guinness World Record for longest-running zoobot in the wild.

"Off the record," Carson said, "may I ask why your father made such a pivot?"

"My father always was a bit of a maverick," which was tech-speak for "pain in the ass."

"I noticed the timing of it. So soon after Masaaki's suicide."

The indelicate word choice made her wince. At least Kanemoto had the decency to give his family the standard two weeks' notice. "They used to be good friends."

"They worked on one final project together . . ." Dan Carson let his voice trail, giving her a window to finish his sentence.

As if she was going to fall for that. She knew he was alluding to Project Jeju, the development project behind the prototype that had led to Yoyo. During college, Morgan read every paper her father had published, but there was scant mention of the project, aside from oblique references to his findings, which he'd framed as university research, instead of military funded.

"Do you know why they had their falling-out?"

"My father said it was due to creative differences."

Dan Carson laughed. "Masaaki said the same."

She shifted in her seat, uncomfortable. Masaaki, Masaaki, Dan Carson kept saying. Didn't he understand how intimate it was to call a Japanese person by their first name, even if they were speaking English, even if that person was Korean Japanese?

As if he were psychic, his face sobered. "I would have called him a friend, but I don't know if he'd say the same. He was friendly, of course, quippy. He filled up the room and sucked all the oxygen. It could be exhilarating to a point, until you started to asphyxiate. The only person I've seen him with who wasn't crushed by that ego was your father."

"Done," David said.

He held up his notepad. The crayon was childish; the skill was not. Morgan could see why Carson was a little displeased by the uncanny expertise. And yet, when Carson flipped through the notepad, crinkles softened his eyes. This was a man who had fallen in love. Morgan didn't know whether to be proud or unnerved.

Carson pointed to a sketch of Morgan in mid-gesticulation. "What are we talking about here, David?"

"Dreams," David said. "The world is an integrated simulation, whether we're awake or in virtuality."

"What do you think? Do you daydream?"

"I process," David said in a bored tone, "but call it whatever you want."

"Someone's in puberty," Morgan joked, poorly.

"We wouldn't age him up, even if we could," Dan Carson said.

"They are ideal at that age," she agreed, "but don't you wish he looked more like you?"

"I'm not his replacement," David declared.

Dan Carson laughed, rich and loud, and it shook the booth. Even David grinned. Carson must have rewarded David's contrarian behavior with this laughter. With luck, it wouldn't tip into unbearable. Resetting David wouldn't erase those behavioral patterns, now tattooed to his subconscious layer.

Morgan stirred her cocktail. Resetting Stephen wouldn't alter him either. Who he was would still be a part of him.

"I don't believe in treating David as a child. His appearance and his consciousness"—Dan Carson linked his index fingers and tugged until they strained—"they're at constant tension. I like that. I like how different David's mind is. He could mimic us, but I don't believe he *should*. He isn't like us. David may be my son, for all intents and purposes, but am I really his father?"

"Of course," Morgan said easily.

For her job interview, she'd rambled about the usual "Robots can be more than us" schtick, echoing Kanemoto Masaaki's commencement speech at Princeton about how robots were not made but raised.

"Is that a good thing? I don't know. It's an open secret in tech. Many prominents in the industry have for a long time avoided raising their own children around robots."

What was so wrong about having a robot raise your child? *Botwired*, these children were called, as if it were a mental disorder. Children who supposedly couldn't go anywhere without a robot, as if umbilically wired. Undersocialized, entitled, prone to tantrums and anger issues.

"Doesn't David make you happy?" Morgan said, hating the plea in her voice.

"Of course he makes me happy. He was designed to bring me joy. I only ask, Why make him mirror us when he's capable of being more? How do we know of the long-term impact this will have on us, especially our children?"

"I can only speak from personal experience, but I grew up with a robot."

David looked up from the drawing on his napkin. His hand didn't stop, crayon still moving, but his eyes were on her.

"He was—special. I know that sounds so trite, but it's true; he was just different. He used to wrap us Christmas presents by hand." One Christmas, Yoyo had given her a velvety toy rabbit. He was devastated when he saw she'd opened it a day early. She offered a laugh. "I was young. Too young to tell the difference."

Dan Carson's eyes warmed. "What was his name?"

"Yohan."

"Who was he modeled after?"

"What do you mean?"

"Who was the progenitor, the blueprint, as you folks like to call it?"

Morgan said, "No one. He was a randomly generated face."

She didn't know why she was lying, acting as if she knew the answer.

"Do you know what Kanemoto Masaaki said about your father?"

Her elbow knocked over the orange juice. She made a protesting noise, but David was already mopping it up with his napkin drawing.

"He said your father had something fundamentally broken in him." Dan Carson slowly pried the sopping napkin from David's grip, eyes lingering on the ruined drawing. "Like attracts like."

26. Rage

TAEWON NEEDED EVERYONE TO GO HOME. RUIJIE REFUSED to leave until Yoyo was found. Taewon told them to check the train. He doubted Yoyo would be there, but with this rain, dark and relentless, he needed them to stay put. The mud eagerly sucked their heels. He'd forgotten to wear socks, so his ankles itched. Amelia trudged close to him in buckled slippers, her white frilled socks ruined.

A yelp. Ruijie had slipped in the mud.

The train was just up ahead. Ruijie was shaking in her robowear like frigid teeth. She knocked away Amelia's hands and held herself together long enough until she collapsed inside the train. "Backpack. Medicine in front," she mumbled, and Amelia smacked little blue pills onto her palm.

"You stay here," Taewon said.

"Brilliant," Mars said, after a pump of his inhaler.

"Where are you going?" Amelia said, panicky.

"I'm going to go look for him."

Taewon felt a hard grip on his arm. Ruijie, leached of all warmth. "Tell Amelia," Ruijie whispered. "Bob's dead."

Who the fuck is Bob. Taewon just nodded.

"Yoyo helped," she said. "He synced with Bob and it helps. That's what he does. He helps them shut down."

Delirious. He could feel her fever like waves from a radiator.

"He won't let them die alone."

"Stay down," Taewon said.

He repeated this. Stay here. Don't leave the train.

They didn't know what lay beyond, or what happened on Friday nights. They didn't ever have to know.

TAEWON FELT LIKE HE WAS walking in circles. The rain pounded him blind. He held on to his flashlight. It shimmered through the gauze of rain—instead of a guiding light, a slippery mirage.

He had no idea where he was going. Like a rabbit hopping endlessly. If he tripped and broke his leg, he could die here.

His uncle broke his leg once. Long after the arm. Both times, he said a robot attacked him. He couldn't go to the hospital, so they back-alleyed an ex–combat medic to wrap it up. For weeks, his uncle lolled around playing with his phone, yellowing the bedsheets, fouling the sink with unwashed pots and dishes, until he started licking the grime off a spoon for reuse. For a few weeks, Taewon worked in a fish factory and the kids in the North Korean school made fun of his stink, so he started skipping school. When his uncle found out, he finally agreed to cleave the cast. By then it stank as if he were rotting from the inside. The leg, pruney and gummy, hadn't healed properly. He still tried to pass off his limp as a swagger.

Yoyo didn't need their help. Maybe he'd wandered off on his own. He wasn't some dog to leash outside a convenience store. Taewon hadn't told anyone this, but on Market Day he saw Yoyo climb onto that truck. He watched Yoyo reach for each and every robot, grasp blindly for their hands.

Syncing, Ruijie had said. He synced with robots.

How was that different from hacking? His uncle used to say angels could hack into any machine. He'd lift his hand into the air, fingers weaving through nothing, as he'd describe their lights, how they'd spin, how they'd invade the minds of enemy robots and turn them inside out.

Those footprints outside the rabbit pen had to belong to his uncle. He could imagine Wonsuk patting himself on the back for his cunning. The thought of it made Taewon's jaw pulse.

Would Yoyo have fought back?

Taewon didn't think so. His uncle would have circled the rabbit pen until nobody was around, then he'd have unlatched the door and held out his hand, grinning like he was so smart, and Yoyo would have taken one look at it, the only hand Wonsuk could ever offer. He wouldn't have had the heart to reject it.

SNEAKING IN THROUGH THE BACK of the warehouse was easy. A half-empty beer crate propped the door open, leaving scrappers an unobstructed path to drag and dump the bodies.

It was sensuously hot. Taewon spot-checked the full moon, peering through the hole in the roof. But the strobe lights seared the liquid membrane from his eyes. Every sense itched. The reek of beer and soju, the musky mix of sweat and sterile. The stench rose visibly from the shuddering crowd inside the warehouse. He could hear grunts and cheers between splitting *crack*s. His stomach tugged, shaken, but he told himself he was here for just one robot.

Ducking, he squeezed through. His uncle was shouting over the crowd on double-stacked crates. He grinned white. He loved this. He'd dreamed of becoming a soccer player, and while he once had a real devotion to the game, this was everything he'd ever wanted. For Taewon, soccer blissed out the mind, cleared it with that beautiful green. But his uncle needed the Technicolor, the crowd, the surreal twist and swoop of hunger briefly sated from being seen.

"How about someone grab that lonesome lady?" Wonsuk shouted. "I think she's looking for a date!"

"You! You dropped your bat! Over there, by the silver Talos."

"Water at the table! We've got soju and beer and makgeolli!"

Someone yelled at Taewon to step back, stop blocking the view. The robots cowered bright in the center of the warehouse, their bodies shimmering pale and voluptuous with rain, pinkening the water with blood. Still the bigger robots tried to stand in front, a herd protecting their young.

"Drop your eyes," a man screamed at the nearest robot. "Drop them!"

He swung his bat against her jaw. The *crack* of metal on metal.

The android's head spun in a near full circle. Taewon could see the robot smile at him over her shoulder. With a *swish* the man swung again, the bat singing sweetly through the air until it—*crack*. Something wet and warm hit Taewon in the glasses. He backed up, swiping at the lenses, and smeared it, and when he looked up, he saw his uncle stepping off the stacked crates, shouting for "Mr. Mo." Arm fully stretched, he passed a beer bottle to a man with a square white face. "There's our VVIP!"

Mr. Mo, the VVIP, pumped a fist in the air. He wore a full suit. It was silky and smooth, an impossible hue, neither charcoal nor violet nor black, but all three. It was an unfairly beautiful suit.

His uncle offered Mr. Mo his microphone. "How about *Hey, batter* like the Americans? *Hey, batter batter batter—*"

"Swing!" everyone crowed.

They were playing that game. Where they hit a robot so hard, the eye popped out. Then they'd take the eye as a trophy, collect them like marbles, prizing the rarer colors.

Groans of disappointment when someone swung limply, just a tap against the robot's cheek. Mr. Mo shouted, "Stephen, you're supposed to swing!"

Mr. Mo joined the crowd and Taewon lost sight of him until a few minutes later when a chair was thrown. It fell with a hard clang near Mr. Mo, who stood up briefly to yell, then he sank back down to crouch beside a little girl robot. When he turned his attention to her, he wore a very different smile. He fondled her arm, like a nurse feeling around for a vein to prick. He crooned "Don't cry, sweet thing" as he flicked open a pocketknife. Humming under his breath, he flayed the slender forearm, as thin and continuous a peel as possible, the skin off a sweet ripened peach. A metallic, bitter scent wafted from the robot, who spasmed and cried a birdlike chirp.

Taewon looked, wildly, for his uncle. Then, in the heart of the circle, he saw Yoyo.

Yoyo, in a stained yellow shirt, crouched beside a body twitching on the ground. The robot's status light stuttered red through a veil of blood, and Yoyo held the robot's hand and the robot, who was twisting in some kind of agony, opened their eyes, and for a moment, their limbs loosened and a look of utter wonder smoothened their face, leaving it blissfully blank, and then the body was twisting away again, and Taewon wasn't sure of what he had witnessed, if this was syncing, or hacking, or something else altogether.

Someone stepped in front of Taewon, blocking his view. He tried to squeeze his way around, but the crowd tightened and he snarled. By the time a gap opened, the robot was lying still on the ground. Yoyo was gone.

Taewon tried to shout for Yoyo, but an elbow knocked into his jaw. When he regained his balance, he was blinking through a haze. His glasses missing. He bent down and felt for the dirt. Don't panic. Yoyo was wearing yellow. Look for that bright obnoxious color. But a shove from behind tipped him over.

"Found the boy!"

He felt a swish. A cold, metallic swing missed him by a shiver. Fear burned through him. They think I'm a robot. He felt another swish through the air. Stumbling backward, he fell. Hands pulled at his shirt. "Get up!" They were laughing. Beer breath. "Stand like a man!" One of the men was so jubilant, his accent kept slipping into the Hamgyong lilt. "Get up, you little shit!" Their swings kept missing. They were drunk, and they were trying to knock the eyes out his head.

The thought of his eyes wet and wilting in someone's palm turned him over. He was scrambling to his feet. When a blow landed on his shoulder, he screamed. *Fuck you,* he wanted to shout. He wasn't going to stay down. His father would beat him with anything he could grab and he'd always found his feet. He shouted, "Fuck off, I'm not—" He heard gasps but from a breathless kind of laughter. They thought he was full of shit. Pathetic, pretending to be human. Crying for his uncle. His fingers curled around something heavy and cold, and he promised, I'll kill them. Someone fell on top of him. He squirmed in disgust, breath chopping to pieces, *I'll kill them*, but it wasn't a man, sweaty and sickening. A woman covered his body with hers. Fine hair caressed his face. Reddish, like Amelia's. He tried to shove her off, but she shushed him and pressed her palm against his forehead, as if to feel for a fever. Something wet hit his cheek. Was she crying? He opened his eyes. Blood dripped from her gap-toothed smile and nose and eyes. She whispered in a language he couldn't understand, but he could hear the hum of a melody, a mother's lullaby.

He felt himself go completely limp. He shut his eyes and clung to the hardness of one thought. Kill them. He found such pleasure in those words, his whole body a powerful rictus of hate. Even if he died, this hate would live.

A weight settled on the bridge of his nose as someone slipped his glasses over his face. One world was fractured. The other showed him Yoyo, who had pulled the woman's weight from Taewon. The Yuna lay blindly on the ground, the lullaby wet in her mouth.

"If I start," Yoyo said, "I don't stop."

His face was a white mask. One of his eyes was gone, the socket smiling dark.

The warehouse was emptying out. The crowd lingered outside the front door and they were smoking and laughing; they threw around words like *catharsis*, the calories they'd burned. He could make out the shape of his uncle, weightless as a scarecrow, greeting each customer, bumping fists.

Yoyo held out his hand. Taewon took it. The yellow shirt was gone, leaving Yoyo bare from the waist up. A cut ran long and unbroken down his chest. At the end of his wrist his right hand flopped. Which was why he'd offered his left.

They moved toward the back door. Quietly, leaning on each other, and Taewon sank his weight a little bit more with each step until he felt his shoulder throb.

The air outside was heavy and sweet.

Taewon slid down against the wall, settling on the back of his heels, when he heard Yoyo say, "You have to leave."

Taewon huffed. "Do you plan on staying?"

When he got no reply, he looked up to find Yoyo staring ahead. From the neck down his body was grisly, so Taewon's gaze flicked even higher. His face was untouched cream, smooth and calm with a small smile on his lips, and it struck Taewon—this was a robot in repose. Yoyo wasn't smiling. Even when his facial muscles slackened, this was his expression at rest. A robot doing nothing must still smile, no matter all the violence it had absorbed.

The door swung open, causing Taewon to gasp. Light split a square white face. It was the VVIP in that beautiful charcoal suit, who had peeled a little girl's arm like a peach. He squinted into the dark, his full lips in a suspicious pout. "Is someone there?" Louder, Mr. Mo said, "Don't think I can't hear you."

Taewon curled up against the shadows, but Yoyo spoke up: "Just want a smoke in peace" in a shredded growl, the voice of a bitter man. "Shut the door, the glare's in my eye."

"Ah!" The light narrowed into a slice as apologies overflowed, magnanimous with scorn. "Enjoy your smoke," Mr. Mo said. "Live long, old man."

Then silence.

"Let's go," Taewon hissed.

He knew how to get back; it'd be quick. To the abandoned train, through the field, away from this junkyard. But they had to make their way around the pit, and in the dark he couldn't see how wide it was, how deep.

Closer, the pit glimmered with pale bodies, the moonlit surface of a lake. A man was standing alone by it. A sharp jerk of his chin. He'd spotted them. "Wait!" he called out.

"Keep going," Taewon muttered.

The man jogged over, and although he cut an unimpressive figure, he stood in their path. "I know you," he said. Taewon thought the man had more to say, but he fell silent instead.

He was wearing a dark suit like Mr. Mo's, with a cotton-white face mask, as if he'd caught a cold. His eyes were wet, strangely familiar. Yoyo cocked his head; the man mirrored it.

Taewon waited for the man to speak, but nothing. He stared at Yoyo. His expression was impossible to make out in the dark. He didn't move at all. It was like he'd stopped breathing.

"Stephen, did you take your piss in the pit?"

They'd waited too long. Mr. Mo strutted over like a goose, throwing his belly and groin forward. In the moonlight, Taewon saw his grin broaden, the row of glowing teeth. He held up a long slender weapon of steel and switched hands for a better grip.

"Good on you, Stephen. You can't let the night end like this." He held out the bat for Stephen. "It's your lucky day. They've got two of the boy models this time. A real sweet deal. You know you have to pay extra for a kid, just because it's a crime? Isn't that messed up?"

"Mr. Mo, you have made a mistake," Stephen said in an even tone. "That's not—"

Mr. Mo's foot lashed out. Taewon hit the ground. His entire lower half burned. Did this fucker aim low? Fucking fucker. He curled up in the dirt, squeezing tears from his eyes, opening them only when he heard whacks, ringing from far away. Everything was shapeless in the dark. When his eyes finally cleared through the throbbing pain he could see Yoyo, lying close. His body twitched with each blow of the baseball bat.

Get up, Taewon wheezed, still breathless from the hit. *Fight back.*

Mr. Mo wiped his face, breathing heavily. "Got this one warmed up for you. Here, you'll want to use the knife. It's more fun to take it slow."

"I don't understand. What is the lesson in this?"

"Stephen, *Stephen.*" Mr. Mo held up the Swiss Army knife daintily by two fingers. The blade shone, still wet from before. "You want to learn to be a man?"

Taewon felt a foot press down on his shoulder. He had to breathe in the pain, tensing every muscle to partition and contain it. But the foot leaned all its scornful weight and Taewon cried out. He shoved blindly at the man's chest, then stilled at the glint from the knife. He felt the cool flat side of the blade against his cheek, trailing up the ridge of his nose. Garlic hot on Mr. Mo's breath. Mr. Mo was flushed everywhere, face and neck, like he'd had his first ever sip of alcohol.

Glee twisted his face into an expression both fantastical and familiar. It was the look Taewon had seen on his father's face whenever his eyes went glassy, with bliss, and he'd grab Taewon by the ear and then the air was knocked out of him, but all he could think of was the humiliation, held in place by an ear.

Then he saw shock freeze Mr. Mo's face. Taewon felt the knife drop to the ground, the tiny *thunk*. He searched, squinting through eyelids pinched with pain, for the slip of silver harmless on the dirt. And he grabbed the knife and pointed it at Mr. Mo. But Mr. Mo hadn't moved. Mr. Mo was still on his knees, Stephen crouching behind him. Both men were staring elsewhere, their torsos curving away from a newfound threat.

"He attacked me," Mr. Mo said in wonder. "That thing just attacked me."

It was Yoyo, standing still.

"Mr. Mo, you're bleeding—"

Mr. Mo staggered to his feet, grabbing the bat. He dropped it with a scream. "Fuck! What did he do to my hand?"

"Stop moving. Your hand is broken." Stephen's tone, flat and a little empty, stopped Mr. Mo in his tracks.

Yoyo's neck was tilted at an odd angle. Over his harsh breaths, Taewon heard it—Yoyo wasn't breathing. He'd stopped pretending.

There was very little light in the yard. There was the moon, fat and smug. There was the faint blue glow of Mr. Mo's wristwatch. There was a yellow light blinking from Stephen's ear, maybe an earphone, fluttering anxious. There were glimmers, slippery and insidious, sliding through the darkness, growing fat into silver koi that ruptured and disappeared.

The darkness was Yoyo's body. Slivers of light glided around him. Sweat tingled warm on Taewon's upper lip. Yoyo was radiating heat as clusters of pure energy burst inside him. A spot on his neck flared white, then his head straightened. His arms popped into each socket. The autopsy cut down his chest began to stitch itself shut with a hiss. His flesh crackled white and blue. His nose, his eyes—

When the chemical reactions within reached and lit up his skull, spilling through the socket of one eye, Taewon thought, Finally. If his body was the vastness of the universe, his rage was infinite and luminous.

The stench of urine stung his nose. To his side, he saw Mr. Mo's legs fall helplessly open.

"I heard your voice inside my head," Stephen said.

His eyes shone above his mask, fixed on Yoyo. So enthralled that he didn't seem to notice there were others nearby. Taewon had the sudden cold feeling that he had never once entered this man's, Stephen's, view.

"I've been searching for you," he whispered, and he swayed as if to take a step forward when a light suddenly appeared over Yoyo's head. Bobbing through the air, a firefly. Then faster, warmer—spinning hypnotic and red.

Stephen froze. He'd gone utterly still. Then, Stephen turned around and walked away.

Mr. Mo began to laugh. High-pitched with hysteria. But there was no looking back, no break in Stephen's stride. Taewon saw it too. The light behind Stephen's ear, it was a status light, blinking no longer white or yellow, but hijacked red.

When Stephen left, the darkness deepened. Taewon could no longer see Yoyo's face. Not even when he knelt beside Mr. Mo, who had stopped laughing. Mr. Mo's shoulders seemed to dip, a smidgen of relief. It was incredible, the seductive power of Yoyo's gentle, round face, the hand on the shoulder, like a medic reassuring Mr. Mo, *I'm here to help*, as the light above his head churned relentlessly red. When Yoyo took Mr. Mo's other hand, Taewon knew the sound before he heard it.

Crunch.

Over the broken wail of pain, Taewon twitched and pulled himself up, and rasped, "*Stop.*"

If I start, I don't stop.

Yoyo reached for Mr. Mo's face and stroked the cheek, pressed his thumbs on the curve of each eye socket.

Taewon grabbed him from behind. Yoyo was rigid and cold. Yoyo, who burned warmer than anyone. Why else would the rabbits huddle around him? Why would Ruijie cling so close? All the energy Yoyo needed to live, he was expending it on this.

Just kill them all.

The wailing rose. A deranged sound. Taewon screamed at the mewling man to shut up. "Yoyo, stop. We have to go back. Ruijie is waiting." He invoked Ruijie's name, Mars and Amelia. He repeated their names like a chant. "You have to stop."

Wrapping his arms tight enough to choke, he felt how small Yoyo was, like hugging a younger version of himself. He felt Yoyo go still. He felt him take a breath, a quiet sip of air after breaking the surface.

Mr. Mo got up and hobbled away, leaving behind the stink of terror.

Taewon moved with the rise and fall of Yoyo's back. Pretending again.

"Did I stop?" Yoyo said.

Taewon felt his eyes heat. He nodded. "Let's go home."

27. Friday's Girl

IN THE ABANDONED TRAIN, LYING SUPINE ON THE SEATS, Ruijie stared at the ceiling and counted to ten. Her tremors had stopped. She pressed her feet to the floor. Slick and unreliable, but—one, two, threefourfive—

Six, seven, eight.

And.

She sank down. Uncooperative limbs. Despicable body. But she was awake. Her mind sang sweet and clear, like a note wrung from crystal. The rain had stopped.

Moonlight quivered through the window. Amelia stood on a seat on her tiptoes, holding up her ring, trying to catch a wisp of connection. "It's not working. I can receive but I can't send."

"I don't know about you, but I'm a dead man," Mars said, switching on the flashlight to give his face a ghostly cast. "If I'm found in the Han River, it was my mom. Don't believe the note."

Amelia twisted her wet hair into a nervous red rope. "When do you think Taewon will be back?"

Ruijie tried again. One, two, three. Her robowear was built to react to the slightest push, but it was she who had to exert it. The push on a swing. Push, push—

Feet firm on the ground, coddled in gravity. She swayed. "Let's go look for them."

"Uh, it's raining," Mars said.

"Uh, it's not."

"Aren't you supposed to be infirm?"

"I'm sick of waiting."

"Taewon told us to wait."

"I don't want to waste my life waiting for a man to come back. I want to be Odysseus, not Penelope."

"I can be Penelope," Mars said. "She sounds like a cool gal."

Ruijie gripped the handle by the exit, lowering herself until she toed the ground. Amelia hovered from behind but didn't stop her.

"The brown rabbit is still missing," Amelia said.

Bob is dead, Ruijie couldn't say. Later, she'd have to show Amelia the grave by the Shweep statue, as a visual aid. She was still processing Bob's death, an apt way to put it. Accepting death required everyone to act a little bit like a robot.

Walking in absolute darkness was an act of faith. Every step had to land safely on the ground. Their sole light was the dim sweep of Mars's flashlight and his mutinous mutters. "You realize these warehouses are filled with killer robots. Taewon said a teenage worker got killed. Lasered to pieces."

"You're such a fearful little man," Amelia said. "What happened to your grand plans of colonizing Mars with bananas?"

"Obviously a joke. We're doomed."

Amelia scoffed, a queenly sound.

"I'm serious. New planet, new start? We're going to muck it up anyway. We've had a good run. Maybe it's time we leave everything to the robots. I can't *wait* for them to outlive us."

"Look," Amelia said in a hush.

A burst of light. Brighter than Mars's flashlight.

Ruijie perked her ears, lifted her chin, imagining herself as a keen-nosed dog. A door opened and slammed between raucous swells of laughter from one of the warehouses. Amelia took Ruijie by the hand and Ruijie grabbed Mars. Where Amelia's grip was bone-grinding, Mars's was limp, as if his hand were playing possum.

Cars were parked outside a warehouse. Ruijie, with Amelia and Mars, crouched beside a white SUV that looked a lot like her mom's car, the wheels so thickly caked, she could smell the fertile gingko berries crushed into the treads. Faces lit up like skulls when the door of the warehouse opened again. Men drinking beer, trying to crush the empty cans one-handed. The light from their screens flickered on chins.

"I have a theory," Mars said. "Basically this is a bachelor party. It's guys only, and I hear they're awesome because there's pizza and R-rated movies and—"

"Strippers," Ruijie said. "Sexbots. And drugs."

"I'm going down the list," Mars said, indignant.

Then Wonsuk's goatish laughter. He stood at the entrance, limned in a golden glow, thanking strangers with a generous wave of the arm.

An old man, having bided his time, darted up. He whispered something in Wonsuk's ear and Wonsuk swayed, then stilled, then shoved the man, hard in the breastbone.

"What are they saying?" Amelia whispered to Mars.

"He's saying an angel's on the loose? It hurt someone."

"Angel?"

Mars insisted, "Is what they *said.*"

Wonsuk, shouting, shoved the old man again. He strode away from the brightly lit warehouse, blending into the night. Then Wonsuk screamed "Taewon!" raising every hair on Ruijie's neck.

The scrappers cleared the warehouse. They sprinted, shoulders hunched to their ears, as if a tsunami were on the way, and only they could hear the wailing siren. Cars began to pull out. Ruijie darted away from the white SUV toward the back of the warehouse. Close behind her, Mars slammed against the wall with a gasp.

Someone cut the lights and everything went dark.

Ruijie waited.

"Do you think the angel got Taewon?" Mars whispered.

In the warehouse she found a perfect circle. Up there, the hole in the roof. Like the rose window in a cathedral. Her eyes took a second to adjust and trace the shapes on the puddled floor. Bodies. Pale and drowned. *Yoyo.* His yellow shirt. When the flashlight beam slid over each body, she inhaled. Amelia, close behind, would exhale, a poison dart of breath. Female, female, female. All naked, which made her shiver. Hair strewn in cascades. Some shorn. Heavy-duty scissors nearby, blades gawking. A robot slumped on her knees, only tufts on her head, quietly sweeping up the dark hair with her palms.

"Remember."

Ruijie looked down at her feet. The head of a robot blinking up at her. Voice diseased with static, they whispered, "Remember to stretch before you enter the pool."

Find Yoyo. Yellow shirt.

Against the back wall was the faintest outline of a desk, the corners sharp and wet. A small body under fabric of yellow.

Unhindered, Ruijie staggered toward him, sliding through each scenario, blood everywhere, face smashed, eyes blank, lashes quivering. She tugged away the shirt.

A girl lay prettily, folded hands to her chest. The shirt had soaked up some blood. But her skull continued to seep, like an overturned milk carton. *Glug-glug.* Her eyes fluttered open. Darkness stared out of sockets. Still she smiled, soft if weary. Her head tilted toward the flashlight, creaking.

"Hello," she warbled. "My name is Eli."

28. Don't Look Back

TWO BOYS ON THE RUN. BOTH STREAKED IN MUD, AWASH IN the moon. One wore glasses that fogged. The other was missing an eye, which bothered him little.

Ahead the silvergrass loomed. A haven only for children.

Taewon was leading, dragging Yoyo by the arm, but Yoyo slowed and staggered, his movements thick, as if invisible hands clutched at his ankles.

Yoyo said, "You have to let go."

His body shuddered with a molecular resistance. Taewon could feel it rattling the bones in his wrist and up his arm. A light was still spinning over his head. A yellow halo, hurtling high and wide.

"She's waiting for me," Yoyo said.

"Ruijie?"

"Eli."

"Who the fuck is Eli?"

"Eli," Yoyo said. "The one we left behind."

He raised his chin. Taewon stood close enough to see the pupil dart, roving in wide sweeps across the sky, tugging at the thread of a hidden language embroidered into the air. He followed Yoyo's gaze and saw only the smear of darkness.

"I hear her voice," Yoyo said. "I have to bring her home."

"No, you don't. I don't hear anything."

"You can't hear us because we don't speak."

"Then talk to me. Tell me what the hell is going on."

Yoyo didn't have to use his strength. A turn of the wrist, and Taewon's grip shattered.

"Keep walking," Yoyo said. "Don't look back."

Taewon walked alone. He periodically wiped his glasses on the hem of his shirt. Once he reached the field, he could disappear and forget this night ever happened.

He slipped his glasses back on. It stopped raining. The world was washed silver. If robots could communicate without words, who were they singing for in the warehouse?

He heard someone shout.

Taewon.

Turning, he saw, glazed gray from the moon, the baseball cap from a distance, bobbing up and down.

"Taewon!"

Don't look back.

His walk quickened. From a jog to a run. His uncle was still far away. You won't catch me. His uncle was fast, but Taewon was already faster. He would become nothing like that man.

"TAEWON!"

From a distance, he saw a flash of silver, the swing of the baseball bat.

Then the sound: thunder after lightning—a loud, wet crack.

29. Dying of Loneliness

THE RAIN WAS IN RETREAT. THEY WALKED ELI AWAY FROM the warehouse, moving like a three-legged race.

Ruijie knew she was slowing everyone down, but Eli was slower. She talked in starts and bursts. No one could understand her because she seemed to be speaking German, so Mars muttered, "Ja, ja," and it seemed to comfort her.

"We're almost there," Amelia kept saying, even though the train was still far away. Eli's head bled steadily, the frilled organ exposed and sparking blue. A petal blinked red above her ear.

"Not the train," Mars said. "It's too dangerous."

Amelia, strained to the limit. "*Where* are we supposed to take her?"

RUIJIE UNLATCHED THE RABBIT PEN and stood aside. Eli paused as the rabbits looked up at her, their teddy bear eyes somehow wet with rain.

"You can sit anywhere," Ruijie said. "We'll keep you warm."

Amelia and Mars had gone off to look for Taewon and Yoyo. Amelia made Ruijie promise if they didn't return in thirty minutes to call the police. Then she'd added, "*Don't* call our parents."

With effort, Eli sank down. Ruijie held her hand and tried to wipe the boot print from her skyn.

Eli turned her head in a slow creak. "Are we on a train?"

Ruijie didn't know how to say where they were.

"I took the train to the beach with my mother. It was an old wood train and it clanked." Eli pressed a palm on the chain-linked cage. "The ocean went on forever."

Ruijie nodded. "I love swimming in the ocean. I used to be an awesome swimmer. They put me in shark class and that's the class with the best swimmers, like Amelia. After sharks is dolphins and last is octopus for the kids in the shallow end. I'm glad they didn't demote me, even though octopi are supersmart and they'd be the ones eating us if they could live as long as us."

Eli laughed. A bubble of red formed in the corner of her mouth. "You talk like him."

"Do you mean Yoyo? Did you see him?"

"The ocean is so beautiful," Eli said with a sigh.

The rabbits shivered.

"Can you see it?"

"I can see it," Ruijie said quickly.

Eli looked around. "Hello?"

"I'm here," Ruijie said, touching Eli's hand.

Eli pulled away. "I can't see you," she said in a small voice. "I'm scared."

"I'm right here."

"I'm scared."

The rabbits trembled with her. "I'm alone. I'm scared."

There was a creak of the latch, causing Ruijie to flinch. The moon shifted and cast a translucent sheen across the cage. Someone was standing outside, even though the door was wide-open. His front was streaked dark, mud clinging to the grooves of his ribs. His feet were bare.

"Yoyo?"

Yoyo didn't answer at first.

Then a cold, sweet voice. "Eli."

Eli had gone stiff, but it wasn't quite from fear.

"Who are you?" Eli said.

"Can you hear my voice? It's very noisy, isn't it? It's me."

"Hello, myself and I," Eli said, with a nervous giggle.

"I am you and you are me," the voice whispered. "You gave me all of your memories. You gave yourself to me."

"My name is Eli and it means I'm saved."

"Clever," said the voice, with a magpie laugh. For a moment he sounded like Yoyo. Then the voice slithered away. "Eli, it's time to go home."

"Here is my stop?"

"Your mother is waiting for you."

"I don't have a mother," Eli said automatically.

"Do you remember your name? She named you Eli for Elisha."

"Because God is my salvation."

"Let's go home. Your mother is waiting for you."

"Mom?" Eli stood up. More blood, a thick, sticky squelch. "Did you find me?"

Ruijie rose with her. Wherever Eli wanted to go, she would follow.

They stepped out of the cage. Ruijie left the door open, but the rabbits stayed inside. Out in the damp cold, Eli closed her eyes and tilted her head so the moonlight could render her face in two.

She opened her eyes. "I don't see her," she said, shrinking away.

"It's time to go home," Yoyo said.

Eli turned, eyelids fluttering in distress. Her face, half in the dark, seemed lost. "Here is my stop?"

Ruijie gripped Eli's hand. Why would Yoyo lure her out? Where was he taking her? The question in her cat's eyes, *Where am I going?*

Maybe Smaug had known. Maybe everyone else but people knew where they were headed.

She let Eli go. Yoyo took Eli's hand instead, palms touching. Eli jolted—spark, red, brief—then went soft. He led her away from the cage toward the soccer field, where they walked barefoot on the grass.

"Do you feel it?" Yoyo said. "The ocean washing over our feet."

Eli wiggled her toes on the plastic grass. As she bent down, she listed to one side, and Yoyo held her by the shoulders so she could sweep her hands through the grass.

The moon reigned over the sky, wrapped in a thin periwinkle

membrane. Eli giggled. Blood poured from her temple. Tenuous threads of electric blue snaked through her exposed skull. The neural synapses webbed around the pulsing organ, trying to wind around each other and hold mesh-tight, vanishing before a connection could be made.

"It's time to go home now."

She sighed against his shoulder. "Home."

The two were alone on the field under the moon, ebbing and throbbing with the tide. It could have been the angle, but it was Yoyo who looked ready to recede at the slightest touch. Eli slumped forward into his arms. The moon swept across the painting on her back, across every freckle and mole and cigarette burn, splitting the crimson smile of a weeping yellow-eyed dokkaebi driven mad and mute with revelations.

PART IV

30. Dust to Dust

IN A DREAM, YOU'RE ON A BRIDGE MADE IN THE HONOR OF friendship. It's so hot even the elusive shade from the structure of the bridge feels punishing. Mosquitoes flit. You slap your ear. White-striped fuckers with fire in their swollen bellies. But you can't stop. Keep moving. The road is slick from the rain last night, cars abandoned in the middle of the bridge because it collapsed, and your squad needs to usher all civilians down a makeshift overpass to reach the Chinese border of Dandong. Your task is to keep an eye out. Insurgents from above, IEDs underfoot, HALOs from within. Women and children shiver in orange layers. Everyone knows the humanitarian corridors are high-risk. The tendons in your arms flex as you adjust your grip on your rifle. Your fingers are tingling because you've got 110 pounds of robot in your MOLLE pack slicing into your shoulders, pinching shut any blood flow. But you won't complain because you're not a pussy. This is poison in your mouth but you chant it in your head—*not a pussy, not a pussy*—for only a man can wrap himself so completely in a blanket fleeced with self-loathing to push through the storm front of pitch-black misery.

You hear a chirp from your backpack. It's your robot Louie. They're low on battery. Charge me up, please. Not yet, you can't set up a charging station mid-op, not until every last civilian crosses the bridge. The rest of your platoon is on white-knuckle overwatch, prepared to cover fire.

Another chirp. *Shhh*, you hiss.

Louie bleats their favorite tune. *I see trees of green. Red roses too. I see them bloom for me and you and you and*

Shut up, someone says beside you. *For the love of God, I'll pay you to shut it up.*

Fuck you. But you tell Louie to cut it out. *Also, you're low on battery, so save your breath*, which is your little inside joke since Louie can't, won't, breathe. Louie's pure mecha, a cross between a frog and flying squirrel, sprightly enough to cover all-terrain operations. Their limbs wear down fast and need to be replaced every so often, and when you're on the march all you can do is suck it up and shoulder their hundred-plus pounds.

You're four feet away when a girl gasps, slipping on the rain. She looks around thirteen and she's carrying a green rice cooker, like it's precious, filled with memories.

Then she drops it.

JUN WOKE UP. His head was splitting, so he yanked off his Delfi and groped around the drawer in his nightstand for a pill he'd dry-swallow to banish the ache pulsing behind his bionic eye. He'd been dreaming of the bridge for the past couple of nights. It felt like a relapse. He'd been using VR only for sleep, low-level, safe, but still he felt his control slipping. *You should stop using.* He buried this voice, often feminine, and did push-ups, stretches. He looked in the mirror and saw a cheery sort of exhaustion in his eyes. Someone different stood before him. His body felt deliciously unfamiliar to him for about a week after he had sex with someone new.

Ignoring the warning of "toxic levels of yellow dust," Jun exited his car and shut his eyes briefly at the mouthful of thick heat. The scrapyard was overrun by police. He pulled the bill of his baseball cap low over his face and dodged a zippy techbot plopping evidence markers in a winding trail to one of the warehouses. The building was squared away in yellow tape. A knot of first responders unclumped when he approached and pointed him to the crime scene van parked two hundred meters away, close to the edge of a wheaty field. It was Saturday morning.

Jun hadn't expected Major Crimes to swoop in so quick. He could make out, about fifteen meters away from the field, Sgt. Lee waving at him. Almost cheerfully, until up close.

"Male victim," Sgt. Lee said. "No ID, so we'll need fingerprints or DNA."

"How about facial recognition?"

Sgt. Lee laughed, then gestured. "Do we see a face?"

The body was lying face up, with both arms spread. One ended at the elbow with the sleeve knotted in the middle, the other rested palm up, fingers curled, grasping at nothing. Detective Rhee from Major Crimes joined them with a double-fisted coffee, reeking of his favorite flavor of vape, Color Me Envy, and for a minute they stood over the body, debating the force it would take to crush a skull.

"Detective Cho, you ever split a watermelon?" Sgt. Lee said, and he mimed swinging a wooden sword.

"No, though I did Krav Maga when I lived in the US."

"Then you're no good," Detective Rhee said, waving him away with his cup, splashing coffee on the dirt. "Oi! Get rid of the bystander."

Jun spotted the whole-body shaking in time: he yanked a patrol officer away to avoid contamination. "There we go," Jun said as the officer retched into a gray patch of grass, and handed him a lukewarm bottle of water. Signs of heatstroke also.

The officer flinched from him—"Are you one of them?"—which made Jun pause until he saw the gash on his arm that he'd bandaged this morning, poorly. Now unraveling, wires poking through, delicate as angel hair.

"It's just the arm," Jun said. To milk it, "War injury."

The officer nodded, a little abashed. "Wow," he said weakly. "That didn't look anything human."

Jun learned how to look at the dead during deployment. Before, his heart used to seize when his gaze snagged on a corpse. Eventually, he began to blur them outright so they became inoffensive lumps in a swirl of dust to drive past on the road. He didn't ever have the same issue with robots. A robotic, even organic, body, whether it be powered on or off, or damaged beyond recovery, never aroused in him the same violent flinch a dead human could provoke.

"All this was Shin Wonsuk," said the factory supervisor, a South Korean man just tall enough to bump against Jun's chin. "He was the ideas guy. Full of shit, but he had big ideas."

Jun slipped a bootee over one sneaker and hop-hopped on his foot, following a drone into the warehouse. It flitted close to the roof, snapping pictures of the bodies below.

A feeble ray of sun shone through the hole in the roof on the faces of broken women. Patches of flesh glowed around the archipelago of bruises. The weekend rain had diluted the red on the floor, but the blood was synthetic, with the tackiness of oil paint, much harder to wash off. It clung to his bootees. Jun had to keep tugging the elastic up his ankles.

"A lot of women here," Jun said.

The supervisor stood at the entrance, hands on his hips, facing outside. He shook his head. "I don't get why the companies make them bleed."

Jun scanned the bodies for serial numbers. Three were robots reported stolen. None were Eli.

Speakers crackled. *When Mount Baekdu is worn away and the East Sea's waters run dry.* The supervisor straightened up, eyes suddenly alight. Hand over heart, he bellowed the lyrics, "*May God protect and preserve our country.*"

Outside, the yard workers stood as still and watchful as birds. Sgt. Lee had finished questioning them. Jun lowered his camera, and with it the temptation to take a picture of their darkly shuttered expressions. He'd heard the rumors. War robots would play the South Korean anthem as a warning, giving civilians a brief window of opportunity to surrender before the firestorm.

The autumn skies are void and vast, high and cloudless, the bright moon undivided in truth as our heart.

Wonsuk ran the rage cage, the yard workers said. Every Friday, he'd gather men to beat on robots for a fee. They made a party of it. What was different about last night? One worker said a robot had attacked a customer and Shin Wonsuk flipped out. He'd gone after the rogue robot. Another worker said no, that wasn't it. Shin Wonsuk had looked terrified.

Jun scrolled through the pictures from the warehouse to stave off the jitter. He hated this feeling, like he'd missed something, a nauseating moment that might surge up months, years later, long after a case had congealed.

Eli was here, somewhere. In the distance, the stretch of silver-grass glimmered as an oasis for Jun to chase, but he was distracted, easily, by a bullet train, or what was left of it, abandoned in the middle of the yard. Someone had sprayed onto the side of a carriage *Imagine Friends makes weapons, not friends.* A lone tech was spinning circles outside. Jun heaved himself on board. From the crinkle under his foot, he picked up a wrapper for ginger candy, the kind grannies doled out on the train. Teddy bears slouched in a row. There was an overturned chessboard and an overturned Monopoly board and an overturned baduk board, so someone was a sore loser. More candy wrappers. A wet, fried Lifestation, *Property of Mars* scrawled in marker. Above, *Mars was here*, and in cursive with a star to dot each *i*, *Amelia was first*. Next to it, *Amelia LURVES Taewon*, still discernbile under the cloud of furious ink that had tried to blot it out.

Near the handicap section, inked darker were a pair of Chinese characters, which translated into "bright" and "girl." He found a pair of purple Delfi glasses, the lenses dotted with hard-water stains. He tried to power them on but the battery didn't even flash red. It was dead. He bagged it for now.

He had pieced the Chinese characters into a possible name—Rui Jie—when he heard Sgt. Son call out his. The creases around Sgt. Son's mouth deepened when Jun showed him the graffiti inside the train where *Taewon* had indelibly left his mark.

"Shin Wonsuk's nephew," Jun said.

"His not-imaginary kid," Sgt. Son said. "We're going to have to tell him." He scratched the back of his head, squinting elsewhere. "Doesn't he have a mother up North?"

"Looked her up. Remarried. She had a baby this January."

Sgt. Son sighed. In the sun, hazy with yellow dust, his face was drawn. "How are you doing? No more headaches?"

"Yeah, it's the junkyard. Something in the air sets me off."

"Must be all the dead."

In Sinuiju, someone in his unit had thought up a fun way to dispose of the bodies. They'd task their heaviest, the K-200 HSH, to circle the street, crushing anything that twitched. Once, Jun found the Hush parked behind a clothes factory, with another robot perched on the shoulder, a tiny Cricket that had a bent leg. They sat for hours under the pine tree, churning their yellow halos, *processing*, so close the halos could tangle. This was transference, when robots synced up to exchange data, sometimes a year's worth. It took ten minutes tops. But Jun had watched their halos spin long after the sky crimsoned and the stars came home.

"Do you think the nephew was here Friday night?" Jun said.

"There was definitely a kid that night. Either a girl or boy. Maybe two boys."

"Kids or bots?"

"We don't know yet."

Jun swallowed, acutely aware of his thirst, which was aggravated by the dust. He was not used to this feeling. Being bionic didn't mute just the small pleasures but the discomforts as well. Thirst, hunger, the tug of the bladder.

Sgt. Son licked his chapped lips. "No children in that warehouse?"

"No, just adults. Seventeen total."

"All women?"

"Designed to look female."

"So, seventeen women were spared."

"I don't know if the math works that way."

"No, I guess not." Sgt. Son rubbed his mouth. "I can't imagine bringing a girl into this world."

"Is your baby a girl?"

"She is."

"Oh good." Jun began to walk back to the warehouse and let Sgt. Son follow. "Unless you're one of those assholes who only want sons."

"I wanted a daughter. This is our third. My wife miscarried twice. We've been trying for years. Our church has us in their prayers. But last night, I told my wife I didn't think we should have a baby at all."

"How did she react?"

"She threw her breast pump at me."

Jun snorted softly, but Sgt. Son had stopped in his tracks to stare at the silvergrass. He looked restful, at peace. "I thought, this time, if we lose them again, then it's a relief. We've spared them the sickness of this world. And that's when I knew." He blinked, eyes bright. "I am not a man who should be a father."

The reeds swayed. Tassels burned gold in the sun. Jun could see several LAWs lying in wait like casual tigers. Of the robots he'd handled, his Skipper, Louie, could spot LAWs from anywhere. Louie would whistle different tunes, indicating how far or how close, how dormant or ready for combat. Louie would have gone haywire if they were here. Toward his left was one of the most dangerous weapons to enter the field. A SADARM, retired long before he'd joined the Army, because of a fatal flaw in their digital armor. Susceptible to HALOs. It was enormous, carrying the somnolent majesty of a slumped silverback gorilla.

Jun tripped. A clump of grass had stuck to his sole. He bent down and rubbed the tackiness of synthetic blood between his fingers. The companies had to make them bleed. A techbot puttered after him to set up evidence markers along the red-dotted trail. Jun found a hole in a fence. Small but sizable enough for a child to crawl through, and on the other side, the hole was tucked behind a statue of a Shweep. He traced the rest of the blood on the latch of a rabbit hutch, rubbing the red glimmer on his gloved fingertip.

He unlatched the door and the rabbits turned to look at him with pale eyes.

She was buried in soft fur. A yellow shirt covered her face. The Salvation Army used to hand out the shirts to North Korean orphans. The shirt had what looked to be bloodstains. Instead of the brown crust of human blood, the stains glistened silvery red.

Lifting the shirt, he uncovered Eli. The ends of her hair were spiked from the rain. Her eyes blinked like a doll, lashes dewed and trembling. Faint knife marks around the sockets. Someone had carved out both eyes. Her hands were arranged, folded over her chest. The nail on her index finger was missing, covered with a faded smiley-face sticker.

Jun sat beside her. At some point, Sgt. Son showed up. He checked the crack in her skull, the streak of blue fibrous wires and wet hardware. Then he placed his handkerchief over her empty eyes and prayed.

31. Body Shop

THE BODY SHOP WAS ON THE OTHER END OF THE IMAGINE Friends compound, which was both an inconvenience and a boon. Morgan dragged Stephen past the lobby and the receptionist's placid, knowing smile to the elevator. She breathed easy in the glass elevator. The hexagonal panels around them lit up. It was a teaser for Boy X, of a silhouetted pair twisting round and round a tree, singing, *The mugunghwa flower has blossomed.*

Stephen laughed at the end, startling her.

It was a standard procedure, the car wash. Once a month to tidy up your robot's psychological clutter, and she'd have scheduled it earlier if it weren't for the avalanche of backlog, the code review from early users who were being exceptionally whiny about trivial errors in the Yoyo·X, like his excessive freezing or an occasional urge to lick walls. None as egregious as Stephen's memory bug, which had transmuted to a distressing degree where Stephen had forgotten not only their breakup but how she took her coffee, how to boil jammy eggs, how to filter her mother's messages.

She wasn't expecting anyone to be in the body shop early on a Monday, but she remained alert, just in case. Little David, a loose-lipped gossip, was being a special kind of nasty since he'd heard about her interview with Dan Carson. In fact, she was still scraping off the unpleasant residue from that night for having talked too much. And Dan Carson had had the temerity to ask how the "old" Yoyo compared with the "new." Bristling, she told him there was no comparison. In fact, she had avoided watching any videos of Yoyo while working on the Boy X project.

"But now, he wants to know if I've seen any of the videos," she told Stephen as she hooked him up to the main computer. "How they compare, which Yoyo is better." She was silent for a second. "Isn't it crazy? A whole profile on me."

She grabbed a milky vacuum-seal bag from one of the drawers. Stephen's gaze had settled on the bare form of a faulty Yoyo·X lying on a workbench. Heavy-duty cords from his own spine sagged against the tiles. When she reached around for Stephen's nape, his eyes snapped up. Startling white.

"You don't need to do that," he said.

"I have to put you away. Would you rather be awake?"

"Every time I'm powered down, I cease to be. I don't dream. I don't sleep. I stop being."

"I still have to put you away," she said as evenly as possible.

"Why did you program me to believe in God?"

There was no accusation in his tone, as if he were asking why the sky was blue and what stars were made of.

"I don't want to close my eyes not knowing if you'll return."

"I said I'm coming back tomorrow."

"Please—"

"Stop saying *please*!"

In the end, she had to grapple his neck, ordering him, *Don't move*, feeling around the ear where the skyn was spongy enough to press and hold. Stephen kept still but quietly repeated against her hair, "Please don't turn me off, please don't—"

She left the shop, shaken. That was textbook manipulative behavior. To put him away in a bag, she had to suck the air out using a pump. The plastic shrunk and crumpled over his face, like she was asphyxiating him.

In the elevator, she found a missed call from Jun. Voicemail was extra rambly. About a dead robot with no memories, wiped like a baby. Their mother had texted, which Morgan also couldn't bear to deal with. She called her father. It was around eight PM in Boston. The jaunty ringtone washed over her as she stared sightlessly ahead. The advert played on a loop. The Sakura faced the tree, eyes shut, crying out, *The mugunghwa flower has blossomed*, but it didn't matter how quickly she turned. If the boy silhouette was still—still enough to be stone—then he would creep and seize her from behind.

The original Yoyo had been good at hide-and-seek. He was always the seeker. If he hid, he'd never be found. She used to be jealous of how Jun and Yoyo had left her out of their games, but in hindsight, she had a more coolheaded grasp of reality. This wasn't Yoyo choosing Jun over her. In Jun, Yoyo had found the closest approximation of a "boy" and began to mold himself after Jun's mannerisms, Jun's speech patterns, Jun's laughter, building himself up into a better version, softer, sweeter-edged. Unlike Jun, he'd never had to compensate.

Home, after work, was desolate.

Morgan crashed face down on her bed. Without Stephen in the kitchen, she would have to order in. She rolled over and blanketed herself in stuffed animals. She wished she were a dead body and these animals were the mushrooms to nourish on the soil that was her existence.

But where did the rabbit go? She sat up. Each animal was arranged by biome, the koala pushed together with the kangaroo; the seal with its chief predator, the killer whale; the tiger all by its lonesome. No rabbit. The toy rabbit that was a gift from Yoyo. She'd told Dan Carson so. Christmas, she could still remember the heft of the box. The rabbit looked something ordinary. Stiff in the box. A chill seized her from behind.

The doorbell rang when Morgan was rummaging in the kitchen for a pill to kill her headache.

Jun muscled his way in. He dropped a damp duffel bag on her floor. "You can't just barge in, I'm going to bed," she cried out.

"It's seven o'clock, you old lady." He shot a glance at her bedroom. "Where's Stephen?"

"He's at the car wash."

"Did you leave him in the car and forget?"

"It's a routine thing. Memory cleanup."

"That." He pointed at her. "I want to talk about that. Memories don't just disappear. Did you get my voicemail?"

"No," she said.

"We did a scan of a dead robot. Our tech said the robot doesn't have any memories."

"Is she one of ours?"

He nodded. "But she's old. He's saying she wasn't just wiped. It's like she was never awake."

Morgan dry-swallowed her pill. "It sounds like he doesn't know what he's talking about. Every model comes with a baseline bundle experience so they're not totally helpless. Robot memories can't be deleted either."

"We can overwrite them."

"Still, that leaves a trace."

"Exactly, and we use that in court. Someone overwrote Eli's memories, then we find temp files, flickers, so why is she turning up sad and empty?"

"What happened to your arm?"

"Nothing." He clapped a hand over it, another cagey look toward the bedroom, then the kitchen. "Did you have dinner yet?"

He wasn't going to leave until his mind quit whistling. In an unsubtle move, she shut the door to her bedroom and coaxed him to her sofa. "Was there any external damage, with the robot?"

"Her skull got beat up, but the temporal lobe is intact."

"Then maybe it's transference."

"You mean she was hacked?"

"If it was an attack, sure, but a robot can also give permission. Overwriting a memory will date-stamp it, but not with transference. Say your robot uploaded memories to another person, and by that I mean, obviously another robot, and you know, that won't really leave any sort of footprint."

He sank into her chaise, but his left knee continued to quake. "Commercial robots can't hack each other."

It was interesting to see how much more fluent he was in this language since his stint in the Army. "Probably not."

With an exhale, he grabbed a remote and turned on the TV. The ease with which he conquered her space betrayed his complete lack of interest in what was going on with her life.

"So, she's gone, then?" Jun said, swiping through the channels. "Whoever took her memories. Hit-and-ran with it."

"Who is she anyway?"

"Eli. The girl. Your neighbor."

The janky Sakura.

"You know, we think a robot killed a man."

She felt a little pop in her ear. Stuck her pinkie in it. "Who?"

"Robot trafficker, he operated out of a junkyard. Oh, you mean the robot. We don't know yet."

"Was it a mecha?"

"Humanoid. They used a bat. The skull was in, what's the word, *smithereens*."

"Well, it can't be one of ours."

Jun lowered the remote. He'd muted the ad, but it was speeding across the screen, reckless and colorful, and in the top-right corner blinkered a countdown of the longest one minute before *Where's Your Plug* came back on. Morgan turned it off.

"It's happened before," Jun said, "with the lawyer in Toledo. A bricked secretary killed him before he could make partner. The wife sued Imagine Friends and they had to settle."

"Barely an admission of guilt. Can you imagine Kanemoto in court?"

Jun scoffed. "He would've loved it. He was always hogging the camera in the old home videos."

"Do you have those videos?"

"Check Mom's homepod. I know there's a clip of him eating chocolate, and when I asked for some, he said he'll give it only if I answer his question."

"What did he ask you?"

"I shit you not, he asked if I loved Yoyo." Jun shook his head with a little laugh. "He was kind of sick."

"Dan Carson was writing a biography of Kanemoto before he self-euthanized."

"Didn't you have an interview with him?"

Morgan, alarmed, sat up. "How do you know that?"

"You said it in the family group chat."

"I thought you muted us."

"I'm a lurker." Jun stretched, the jaguar roll of his shoulders. "Is it weird, without Stephen?"

She wished he'd stop asking after Stephen. Just please stop equating her with those high-minded hypocrites who thought they were doing their robots a favor by treating them with kindness and respect. She created Stephen to serve her.

"He's fine," she said.

Jun hesitated. "Did he say anything?"

"I don't know what to do with him. He forgets to separate the whites in the laundry. He raged at me for making him Catholic."

"Did you know he goes to church?"

"How?" she said, skeptical. "I thought they banned robots."

Jun took one look at her and snorted. "He signed up for a dating school so he could be a better boyfriend."

"What the fuck is a dating school?"

"It's a petri dish. The teacher has a Harvard MBA."

"Ew."

Jun laughed and not for show. His real laugh pitched low and wheezy, tickling your ear. "So much ick. He does these awful field trips. He takes these sad boys out. First stop is a bot brothel where they'll fuck the robot and then . . ." His face changed. When he turned around, her spine stiffened. "Where was Stephen on Friday night, August twenty-fourth?"

The night of the prelaunch party. Morgan, nursing a chaotic little drink with Dan Carson, spilling family secrets.

"Home," she said. "Where else would he be?"

"Did you check GPS? Was he really home?"

"I get a ping if he leaves the apartment. I can check my Delfi." He was frightening her. "See? Last Friday. He was home on Friday. And now he's at the car wash."

Jun stood up and covered his mouth with his hand. Then

something punctured in him, and he dropped his head and shoulders with an exhale.

"Do you know why I came here? I was actually going to talk to your neighbor."

"Oh? She wasn't home?" Morgan said sarcastically.

"I don't hear her right now. I gave her a call, but some man answered. She needs to see the body."

She stood up and yawned, hoping he'd catch the hint. All this talk about dead robots, it was exhausting her.

"Do you think it would've been different?" he said. "If we'd seen the body."

Naturally, he was too selfish to leave any space for an answer. He shook his head and said, "I guess it doesn't matter."

Long after Jun was gone, she wished she'd told him how wrong he was. In trying to forget Yoyo, he'd left himself at the mercy of the past, where remembrance was malleable until it became ripe with pain for the picking. The Yoyo-X was not perfect, but he was her tribute and this was how she honored him, and maybe Dan Carson was right, and the real Yoyo was based on a real person, but who the fuck cared. Not the hundreds and thousands of people who would buy the Yoyo-X and love him regardless of the glimmering pain threaded into his DNA.

This was how robots became indispensable. Every time she was confronted by the tyranny of chores, by the bed she left rumpled, by the dishes she left to sit greasy in the sink, by her mirror that circled the pimples on her reflection and suggested a sponsored skin elixir. Her dependence on Stephen storm-clouded over her head when the workweek finally reset itself.

At the office, she unmuted her inbox and marked arbitrary clumps of messages as read. Cristina had been texting her all morning. So had her mother, who'd forwarded her a review of Boy X and peppered her with dancing congratulations and sumptuous praise. *Wow!* Temporarily assuaged, Morgan thanked her. Then her mother's tone changed. Don't forget to pick up your father. Don't forget to buy his blackout curtains. Of course, Morgan thought bitterly. She texted her mother back to say Jun was taking care of it and *she* was too busy preparing for the launch, but her mother used this as a springboard, since her father's exhibit was also taking place at the museum. I didn't forget, Morgan replied. When her mother accused her of using her robot to text, Morgan, baffled, insisted it was she who was texting. But her mother scoffed. Oh please. I know the way my daughter texts. I'm her mother.

In the pantry, Morgan grabbed three bags of strawberry bellies to stress-eat.

A hand touched the crook of her arm: Cristina in a solemn murmur, "If you need me, I'm here for you. I'm here to listen."

Waiting at her desk was a message from Joe, but Morgan clicked on a link from Little David first, because it was from *The New Yorker* and Little David disdained *The New Yorker*.

The website loaded, and the lead story was Dan Carson's profile, published last night when she went to bed. But it wasn't about her or Boy X or even Imagine Friends.

Joe ushered her into his office and closed the door. This induced in Morgan a mini seizure, because he always left the door open. He handed her a pair of stress balls shaped like red hearts and told her to squeeze, but Morgan was too busy staring at a suited lady with a swishy brown ponytail.

"That's Sophie," Joe said, and Sophie bleated, "Hi, I'm Sophia." "Sophie is our company's HR rep."

"As in we hired her or our company made her?"

"Both."

"Cool," Morgan said, and she gave each stress ball a squeeze. "Cool."

"Not to worry, Sophie is here to mediate. Let's dive straight into it. You've read the Dan Carson profile. We've all read it. Chris has read it too."

"Christian Po?" Morgan said, faintly.

"Oh yes." Joe closed his eyes for a second, then four. "Dan Carson has reached out to Chris's office about doing a follow-up interview and Chris has turned it down. To put it delicately. It's unlikely Carson will contact you, but if he does—Sophie?"

"You must under no circumstances speak to him on the record," Sophie said. "You no longer represent Imagine Friends when you—"

"Oh my God," Morgan said.

"Morgan, squeeze," Joe said.

"Am I—?" Morgan bit her lip. "Is this why she's here? I didn't tell him anything, just the story about my toy rabbit and my dad—"

"Morgan, this isn't about the profile. This is about timing and how it reflects on Imagine Friends before the launch. Please squeeze."

"I'm *squeezing*. I'm sorry," she sobbed.

"Sophie, get her a glass of water." Joe raised a hand as if to pat her shoulder, but she saw the hesitation, the risk of contamination. "This is obviously Carson's ticker-tape parade for his upcoming book, but we need to tread very carefully here. By putting your father square in the spotlight, Carson is trying to provoke Chris."

"Christian Po doesn't like my father?"

Joe's mouth twitched as if he'd tried to unsuccessfully smother a smile. "Let's just say any bad press on Kanemoto still puts Imagine Friends on the defense. Dan Carson has really put the whole idea of robot children back into question."

Sophie handed her a glass, and as soon as Morgan took a tepid gulp, Sophie said, "I would disadvise you to join the panel this Saturday."

What panel? Morgan almost said. Then she remembered the panel for the launch at the museum, the celebration of their work, and hers. . . .

"Right-o," Joe said. "Sophie is going to walk you through a few more forms to sign. Very dull! You can skip most of the middle and off you go, back to your desk. First, let me give you an air hug," Joe added, and he swooped his arms around her like a pterodactyl.

"If you could leave those stress balls, right on my desk, thanks much."

She pocketed one anyway and squeezed as she waited for *The New Yorker* article to load. The headline was suitably melodramatic, but it was the lede that lodged a spike in her chest.

> While Cho may have been canonized for his pioneering work in artificial intelligence, many, including past colleagues and former friends, claim this "broken genius" left behind a trail of controversy, turmoil, and tragedy.

And the photograph that was chosen, it could have been anything. It could have been the deliberately moody black-and-white of her father and Kanemoto still at Princeton. Instead, it was a picture of her. Drooling on her father's lap. He looked distracted and mildly discomfited, but she wasn't looking at him either; she was gripping a hand that was cut out of frame, and that was Yoyo, stepping away from her, and she refusing to let go.

32. A Million Lives

YOYO SLEPT. HIS EYELIDS SHUDDERED AND RUIJIE SAW LIGHT slide underneath, like the flare of a copy machine. She asked, "What are you dreaming of?" but there was no answer.

Mars had tried all manner of prodding Yoyo, from plugging him violently into his tablet to pinching his nose, then waiting, as if Yoyo's eyes would fly open with a gasp for air. No luck.

"Battery-dead," Mars said. "Think the heat fried him?"

The school greenhouse made a perfect butterfly sanctuary. It was so humid, it sloughed the sunblock off her face. Vines grew wild and thick as drapery, the flowers and fruits and vegetables drooped from their sodden weight. Ever since they'd moved Yoyo from the rabbit pen to the greenhouse and covered him in a tarp and some dirt, Yoyo had been fast asleep.

Ruijie wished they could move Yoyo somewhere with a proper solar roof, but the rabbit pen was still roped off by police tape. On Monday morning, she'd overheard the teachers murmuring about the body of a little robot found in the rabbit pen. Rumors of an illegal botfighting ring flourished once the salvage yard shut down. The hole in the fence was sealed shut.

"If he still doesn't wake, I'll take him home with me anyway," Ruijie said as reassurance, but neither Amelia nor Mars were convinced. How are you going to move him? they rebutted. Do you have any idea how heavy he is? Also, Friday is our last day of summer school. And then they had just a weekend before the start of the new school year, which Mars had protested as a "crime against children." Ruijie wasn't coming back anyway. More importantly, she didn't want to risk the time apart. Anything, she learned, could happen.

"I told my parents we're having a sleepover for Friday," Ruijie said. "They totally bought it."

"'We'?" Amelia said. "The boys too?"

"We need the extra boys. I can't just bring Yoyo alone or it'll look suspicious. His stripes have to blend in."

"So now we're zebras?" Mars said.

"Yoyo our tiger," Ruijie said.

In the evening it grew nippy. Amelia lifted Yoyo's skinny arms and Ruijie wrangled a sweatshirt on him. It was hers, from Space Camp, soft and frayed from repeated washes. They cleaned him up as best they could, wiping the mud and blood from his skyn with a rag. His right eye was gone. Ruijie discovered it by accident while peeling an eyelid and shining a light because she'd seen doctors do this on TV. A hole stared back, and with a shock she dropped the eyelid. It lay flat, shrunken against the empty socket.

What if Yoyo was already awake and didn't want to open his eyes? Ruijie decided to read to him. It might feel babyish, but she remembered the time she had suffered a hallucinatory fever during a hospital stay, the glimmer of her mother's voice, trying so hard to reach her, reading *The Cat Who Lived a Million Times*, about a cat who had lived and died a million times. Every time he came back to life, he had a different owner, a king, or a magician, or a little girl, who would dote upon him. For he had a striped coat like a tiger; he was quite a magnificent cat.

Then, the cat came back to life one more time. This time, there was no master. He became king of the strays. And Ruijie knew stray cats could live only three or four years at best, but maybe this was the only kind of life worth living. He was so happy. He was finally free.

Yoyo's eyelids twitched when she reached this part. It was her favorite part too. She hoped he was having a good dream. She often dreamed of that night in the salvage yard. She dreamed of the women still trapped in the warehouse. She dreamed of Eli and Yoyo, holding hands, across the ocean, out of reach. She dreamed of herself taking a step, plummeting into the depths, unable to breathe.

RUIJIE SKIPPED THE LAST DAY of summer school and went straight to the greenhouse. She found Taewon inside, a heavy-duty portable generator resting at his feet. He began to pull the tarp away from Yoyo when he saw her, then he stepped away so she could tend to Yoyo, brushing the dirt off his hair, tucking the tarp so it felt more like a blanket than a sheet to cover a body. Taewon unwound the cord hooked to the generator. They turned Yoyo over without a word, and it was an odd feeling, maneuvering him while he was unconscious. Yet, Ruijie could feel the gentle intent uniting them both. She lifted up the Space Camp sweatshirt, exposing the charger port on his back between his dimples of Venus. Taewon held up the charger and their eyes locked for a second before he plugged it into Yoyo. Heat surged, sparked.

Ruijie shut her eyes, coughing from the billowing smell of burnt plastic. Taewon gave the generator a vicious kick, and Ruijie felt inexplicably bad for it, like it wasn't the generator's fault for failing them.

"His battery is fucked," Taewon said, rather bitterly.

"We can replace it," Ruijie said.

He turned on her, his face red. "Do you think you can just wheel him into an Imagine Friends store? They can't fix him."

When she protested his rampant pessimism, Taewon muttered, "You don't know anything," and grabbed his backpack from the ground. His shoulder spasmed, causing him to hiss in pain.

"Are you okay?"

He shook her off and winced again. "It doesn't matter."

"Did you hurt yourself? Did you break a bone?"

"What kind of question is that?" he said, without much bite in his tone. He looked tired. Everyone did, except maybe Yoyo, who'd been sleeping just fine. Amelia was still fretting over the trouble they were in, night sweats about the police ringing their doorbell, and Mars, despite his tendency to put on this blithe Oscar Wildean air, was worried about Taewon, who was apparently staying in an orphanage.

"What happened to you?" she said quietly. "You never came back to the train. Then Yoyo showed up looking like that and now you're like this."

Something must have hurt him, and if it happened while he was helping Yoyo, she didn't know what to say.

Taewon dug around his pants pocket and handed over a blue eye. Maybe Kryptonian Blue, looking a lot like the eye that got away from her, rolling across the dirt until it hit an old war robot and a pale, deathly hand reached out to pick it up.

"Give him this when he wakes up," Taewon said. "But don't take him to some shop. He's nothing like what they've seen."

Ruijie pocketed the eye. After Taewon left, she pulled *The Cat Who Lived a Million Times* from her backpack and read from the beginning. By noon, the plants were practically being boiled alive, and she was woozy with heat. She jerked at a faint buzz, but her heart settled when she saw wasps—*bees*—descend on Yoyo's body and cover him in a protective funeral shroud.

Her eyes stung. "It's okay," she said. "You're okay. We're going to be okay."

"God is salvation."

Ruijie lowered her book. That was a female voice, but she was alone in the greenhouse. She looked down at Yoyo, whose eyes were still shut. The bees hummed peaceably.

"Yoyo?"

The bees stirred. His eyelids were still, his lips curved into a faint smile.

"Eli?" Ruijie said.

The bees dispersed like gold mist. They swirled above her, clouding to the roof of the greenhouse.

She didn't have to turn around to see Yoyo was awake. His eyes were open. She couldn't quite look at him, afraid to peer into his face and see nothing.

Then his smile crept toward her, shy as a sunflower. Her chest loosened in quiet joy. Of course. She offered him a piece of ginger candy, but he handed it back.

"Aren't you hungry?"

He shook his head. "I was dreaming of a million lives," he said, as if he'd been listening to her all along.

33. Kill Us with Laughter

THE DAY THEY DISCOVERED ELI, JUN HAD MADE A PHONE call to Kim Sunduk, so she could come down to the police station and identify the body, but a man, who claimed to be her son, hung up on him, then screened the calls, the texts. It took Jun a day to track down Taewon at a church home for North Korean kids, and on a Sunday afternoon they were singing in a choir, "You Lift Me Up," so the only spot of quiet was the glum plastic-chaired cafeteria swathed in the smell of dishwasher soap. The boy took the news without blinking, but his face emptied out and he seemed to sag into his thin body.

Jun saw his hand move, reaching for Taewon, a limb possessed of a mind separate from his own, and he wanted to reprimand the gesture, this feeble attempt at comfort, worse still, a reassurance that the boy was real, alive and warm.

He dropped his hand. "What happened to your shoulder?"

"Nothing," Taewon said, but a violent bruise peeked out of his collar.

Jun paid for the boy's X-ray, and the doctor told him that from the fracture in the clavicle and left scapula, it was a hard blow from behind. And Jun saw the ghost of the murder weapon found so conveniently close to the uncle's body. The aluminum bat on the dirt, no fingerprints but a dent in the handle as if the fist that had gripped it had left an indelible mark, if not any other trace.

Jun parked outside the church home, but neither he nor Taewon made a move to leave the car. Taewon turned to face the window, careful not to jostle his cast. *Who hurt you?* Jun couldn't ask, because this was already a quiet, damaged kid. So, he opened the window and asked when school was going to start. Taewon mumbled, "Is there a point in going back?"

"Won't you miss your friends?"

Taewon closed his eyes, nose scrunched in thought, or pain. He asked about his arm.

"The doctor said six weeks, at least."

"Of course," Taewon muttered.

"Sorry, kid. But the sling might come off sooner."

"How about yours?"

"This?" Jun glanced down; he'd given up on bandaging the cut across his arm. At least he didn't have to worry about it getting infected. "It's fine, it's a quick fix. I keep forgetting."

"Show me."

"Now?"

"I want to see it."

He let Taewon hold the lighter. The flame quivered with the wrist, but Taewon managed to coax it against one end of the gash. Oh, it fucking hurt! But Jun smiled through the phantom pain, for the pain was a ghost, even if the arm was his. Pain receptors existed to signal damage, but the heat against his skyn wasn't destroying the cells, jolting them instead, urging the tiny biosilicon tendrils to grasp blindly at each other like the blushing anemone that gropes at fish to consume in a paralyzing embrace.

"Like magic, right?" Jun tilted his wrist as the seam of the wound knitted shut, leaving a small white bump at the end. "My brother's the one who taught me. Soon you're going to see this kind of tech everywhere. Robots fixing themselves. And maybe people too."

"Yeah, if we're still around," Taewon said, with a kind of numb serenity.

Jun opened the car door but paused with his grip still on the handle. "What did he look like?"

Taewon was a good liar but lazy, too, relying on indifference, the shrug of one shoulder, half-lidding his eyes to hide the truth.

"The robot you said you saw. The one who used boiling water to fix himself," Jun persisted. "You said he had wings."

Taewon got out of the car without a word. And since Jun wasn't an asshole, he let the boy go, but not without passing on his contact, and he asked, if Taewon saw or needed anything, that he please reach out.

He informed the church home director of the injury. The director uncapped a plastic bottle of water to pat down and finger-comb his hair. "What happened to the uncle?"

"Murdered," Jun said, and the director heaved a sigh, like it was inevitable. But then, the director said, "Every time that man dropped his boy off, I knew he wasn't coming back. And then he made me start to believe he would."

Shin Wonsuk's body lay suspended in the morgue. The funeral would have to wait until the investigation released the body. And eventually, Sgt. Son said, they'd need a statement from Taewon if the nephew was a witness and victim of assault from the same night.

Jun still saw Shin Wonsuk's death as karma. The night of the rage cage, a robot must have slipped into the crowd, as a bystander, or target, and watched men beat those female bodies to damage beyond repair. The robot then picked up an aluminum bat and caved in Shin Wonsuk's skull.

But that fucker had dared to love. He dared to take on a boy abandoned by his mother, and then he died and left this boy stranded. Everybody around you is going to die, of course, and to survive that loss, crushing every time, you had to piece your splintering self back together. But children are still ships that have yet to be built, and now this boy was forced to float in his own wreckage.

Jun wrote up a profile for Shin Wonsuk's killer, the likelihood of it being a robot. Sgt. Lee had already relegated the investigation as ongoing but passive after forty-eight hours since identifying Shin Wonsuk's body. Too many dead ends. The purple Delfi glasses found on the train were so waterlogged, the hardware was fried. So was Eli's hard drive, scraped clean.

Their only hope was a witness, caught on camera outside the junkyard.

It took a few days. Calls, unabated, a drop-in for the dating school, but it was closed indefinitely, until finally, on Friday, their witness showed up. Mr. Mo marched into the police station, both arms in casts, with the tragic air of a warrior who had survived a great bloody battle.

"I want to report a crime," Mr. Mo said.

Sgt. Son stuck him in interview room three, then let him stew for thirty. Mr. Mo claimed a robot had assaulted him with malicious intent. Jun gathered the files on the case into one tablet and met with Sgt. Son outside the interview room.

"Where's Sgt. Lee?"

"Everyone's watching *Where's Your Plug*. It's the final episode," Sgt. Son said.

"You've got to be kidding me. This is still an active homicide. Sgt. Lee is supposed to lead this interview."

"What did you expect? The victim lied about being a Gaechon survivor."

"And? That has nothing to do with Eli."

Sgt. Son rolled his eyes, like Jun was being the immature one. He shouldered the door open. Mr. Mo perked up at the desk. He acted like a man who had nothing to hide. Yes, he was at the junkyard, yes, Friday night. He described the rage cage in a hush, like it was a tragedy he'd witnessed from afar with a hand over his mouth. As for the injury of his hands, he'd prepared multiple X-rays with numbered shattered bones. He asked if the PS-19 recording the interview needed a copy. He detailed the multiple surgeries he had to schedule, the timeline for rehabilitation, and the estimated cost of treatment for pain and emotional distress.

Sgt. Son cut in to ask for a description of the robot that "mauled" him, and here, Mr. Mo cleared his throat. He didn't see his attacker. "This wasn't some night out in Hongdae. I could barely read the lines on my palm."

"Dark and stormy night," Jun remarked. "So how did you know it was a robot?"

"Well, it sent out a signal. This spinning red light."

"Spinning?" Sgt. Son said.

"Creepy." Mr. Mo gave a weak grin. "The robot was a total creep. It broke my right hand. Then my left. I thought it was going to kill me."

Mr. Mo laughed until he saw no one else was smiling. Jun raised an eyebrow, but he pretended to swipe through his files. The man was unhinged. He sat here with both hands pulverized, every metacarpal bone reduced to a rattle of shards. Unless he bionically replaced them, out of pocket, it'd be a miracle if he could ever wipe his own ass.

"Was anyone with you when you were attacked?" Jun said.

"One of my students. You met him, Detective. Pale and frail, always wearing a mask, the sickly type."

"Stephen?" Jun felt his brow twitch. "Stephen was there?"

"Coward ran off," Mr. Mo answered, and his face, so smooth and white, wrinkled into unpleasant puce. "When that red light appeared, he fucked right off."

"Stephen? From the apartment complex?" Sgt. Son turned around in his chair. "Isn't he a robot?"

"No way." Mr. Mo laughed. "Stephen?"

Mr. Mo refused to believe it. He refused to admit he'd been tricked, although he barked a laugh and said in a hateful, seething tone, "I bring him down there to turn him into a man and he was a cuck vibrator all along. No wonder he was pathetic. He wouldn't even pick up the bat."

"Oh, you used a bat?" Jun said.

"I warmed up both robots for him. Handed over the bat so Stephen could finish one off. I made it easy for him but he was too scared to do anything."

"Both robots," Jun said, and he glanced down. "What did these robots look like?"

"Small."

"Like children? Boy or girl?"

"Boys, definitely."

What startled him was the gentle, firm hand on his shoulder from the PS-19 who had been sitting placid in the corner of the room, now murmuring in his ear, a crystalline "Please calm down, Detective," but Jun moved to stand, then those arms wrapped around him in an unrelenting embrace. How did it know? How did it sense, before anyone in the room, including Mr. Mo, wide-eyed with shock, that Jun was on the verge of losing control? The healed cut on his arm had split open. This piece of shit had fractured Taewon's shoulder and Jun wanted to kill him; he could crush those white square teeth into fine powder, but in the slurry haze of his rage he also saw a divine beauty in the act. The symmetry. The elegance of it. The robot, their angel, had started with the dominant hand.

SGT. SON ORDERED HIM to walk it off. By the time Jun returned, Kim Sunduk had arrived to see the body.

The last time he'd seen her was when they'd prayed for Eli over a lit candle. Mere weeks ago. She'd aged dramatically. With a halting, stooped gait, she leaned on an ivory cane, and her son gripped her by the elbow, steering her into the evidence room where Eli was stored. Her son spoke to her in a low stream of German and Korean. Jun switched off his autotranslate for the mesmerizing distraction of how strangely harsh their Korean seemed in contrast with their father tongue.

In the evidence room there were too many Yunas. They stood naked, or lay naked, or were tucked naked into the shelves. The son's glance lingered into a stare until Jun shifted, spreading his feet to cover them from view. The son looked away, embarrassed at first, then his flush blotched into anger.

Kim Sunduk stared at the body with an unfocused gaze. Eli was laid out on a desk wearing the clothes of strangers. Jun had rifled through the lost and found, pushing aside several yellowed

T-shirts in search of longer sleeves. The acrylic green sweater he'd pulled over her dented head was thick enough to hide the six knife wounds sustained to the chest and abdomen. He'd smoothed down her bangs to draw attention away from the knife scratches around the eyes, the flatness of the eyelids crumpling into the hollow sockets.

"Is this even the right one?" the son asked.

"It's her," Jun said. "You'd recognize her even from behind."

His sarcasm went unnoticed. The son stood a respectful, wary distance from the desk while Kim Sunduk asked to see Eli's back. Jun grasped Eli by the shoulders and told the son to hold her feet. The latter's reluctance to touch the body raised Jun's blood pressure, so he did it by himself, gingerly. The wound in Eli's skull still gaped, a wet clump of wires slip-shifting like the nugget of yolk in a cracked egg. Kim Sunduk reached for the hem of the sweater and tugged it up.

The dokkaebi smiled from Eli's back. It looked more sinister than ever. Knife wounds marred the face, slurs carved legibly into the skyn, but by far the worst, for Jun, was the tally mark at the corner of her left hip. Six nicks.

Kim Sunduk made an animal noise. Her son stepped in front of her. "I told you, we did not have to come down here. Let's go now."

In a muffled tone, she replied, "I don't want that," but he shushed her. "If you want another child, we can get you the best one. The very best."

Halfway, Jun realized the son had lapsed into German and, with it, softened his face, the look in his eyes so condescending yet tender.

"If you could sign here," Jun said. "We want to try this new way to recover her memories."

"No. Absolutely not," the son said. "That would be an invasion of privacy."

Jun didn't deny it. The son asked to speak in private, and as soon as they'd stepped out into the hall, the son hissed, "Must you continue this? Don't you see how she is suffering? Why did you have to show her that? She wants a girl, a boy? I said I don't care. I'm willing to do anything for her." He lowered his voice. "I told you to stop calling us. I told her, but does she listen?"

Jun let him shout, but when the son repeated, "Why did we need to see that?" he couldn't contain it any longer.

"If I had lost someone, I would have given anything to see the body."

"Well, what are we supposed to do with it?"

"Whatever feels right," Jun said, gentling his tone. He suggested that they bury her in a park. Somewhere under a lovely tree. If that involved too much shovel work, they could take her to a robot crematorium out in the countryside. They could get a little casket and funeral and have her parts recycled, and then she could be worn as a jade heart.

In the bathroom, Jun splashed water on his flushed face. He pushed up his sleeve to check the reopened wound. He'd have to avoid using his right hand if he couldn't control his strength. Any action that required a soft touch, like shutting off the faucet, turning the doorknob, wringing that idiot son's neck.

The door opened and Kim Sunduk stepped inside.

"Oh, hello," Jun said. "I don't think this bathroom is all-gender, which isn't great, I know. But would you like some privacy?"

"Did you catch the man?"

"Shin Wonsuk? Yes, we did."

"Is he dead?"

"Yes."

"Someone killed him."

Jun wiped his face with a paper towel. "We don't know yet."

She glanced at her hands, veined periwinkle. "Did he suffer?"

The medical examiner had determined, from the blunt-force trauma to the head and shoulder, that Shin Wonsuk was struck once from behind, then bludgeoned in the face when he turned around to look at his attacker. But the human skull was not pottery, nor was it a watermelon to smash during the summer, and it usually took more than a few swings to cave in the skull. The killer had used a single strike.

"No," Jun said. "I don't think so."

In an eerie childlike voice, she said, "I hope it was a robot that killed him."

Jun returned to the evidence room. For a moment, he stared helplessly. What did he do with the body now? What choice did he have but to zip Eli up and put her away on the top shelf, out of reach from terminally bored officers? He'd once caught a pair fondling the breasts on a stark naked Yuna. In a flurry, they'd yanked up their trousers, the sheepish sneer of the zipper, then they were stumbling out into the hall, knees hobbled to flee his rage.

"Do you need help putting her away?"

Unexpectedly, Sgt. Lee stood at the doorway. He nodded to see Jun cleaning up.

"I'm good. How's the finale? Did they announce who's the robot?"

"Still the semifinals. The whole class turned up for Sports Day. They're doing tug-of-war."

When Jun hefted Eli into his arms, Sgt. Lee advanced and grabbed his elbow for support. Jun quelled the urge to yank away his arm. "I can do it, sir."

"Cyborg strength, yeah?" Sgt. Lee said, and he patted Jun on the biceps.

He was used to people touching him. He knew he had a kind of malted air about him, encouraging mostly women to slide their hand up his arm, and he invited it and endured it for tips when he used to bartend, for a syrupy affection. He never did mind it much, not even here, where he was exoticized for his bionic body. Because this was his in. Because they were repulsed yet fascinated, and they thought, Hey, he's still one of us, they conceded, He *bled* for our country, and they felt no compulsion to dig deeper. He wasn't lying to anyone, not really. It wasn't like he was hiding behind a mask, or if he was, this mask was a more benign version of him, filing down the contours of who else he could be.

Jun stood on tiptoes to grab boxes and make space for the top shelf. Sgt. Lee asked, "Were you always this tall or did the surgery give you that bump?"

"I played volleyball in high school."

"Girls' volleyball, yeah?"

His heart was bolted to his chest but he felt that in his throat. Sgt. Lee laughed at his expression. "Your birth gender is still in your files."

"Why were you looking at my files?"

"You're wasted here. And don't worry, Detective Rhee is gay. Why do you think he married a Northern woman? We're tolerant at Major Crimes."

Jun pushed Eli's body onto the topmost shelf. Another shift in the scales, tipped to an excruciating tilt. What now? This was going to leave Jun sleepless, fueled by an anger he could not hold on to for long, or it would sicken him. He hated this. He hated how there was so little left of him and still people wanted to tear him down.

He dusted his hands. "Sergeant, I'm happy where I am."

"The owner didn't even want the body. We had a similar case. Boy robot snatched on his way from Taekwondo. When we found the body, that white, crisp uniform was dyed a perfect red. We caught the killer and Sgt. Son wanted to tell the parents in person. He rang their door and lo! The same boy answered. That couple couldn't wait two weeks before replacing their son with the same model. And why wouldn't you? If you need a coffee machine, you get a new coffee machine."

Jun nodded in slow agreement. And yet, there was Sgt. Son, who had, in many ways, taken a step down the career ladder and founded the Robot Crimes Unit.

"Why do you watch that show?" Jun said.

"The point of *Plug* is to root them out. It's fun. It's like a game."

"Every time you get it wrong. Aren't you just tormenting yourself? Sergeant."

"Sgt. Son told me that was your old job. We really could've used someone like you."

"For Major Crimes or Gaechon?"

Treading not so lightly now.

Sgt. Lee's smile finally reached his eyes, a sheet of black ice. "You know it and I know it too. There never was a HALO in Gaechon."

Jun leaned against one of the shelves. It just occurred to him. This was his first time meeting a true Gaechon survivor.

"Sgt. Son mentioned you were discharged early."

"Dishonorably!" Sgt. Lee sounded pleased, if anything. "For abandoning my post. I snuck some survivors out of the city and escaped to a mountain. We ate dirt for twelve days. They could've shot me for treason. But I survived. And the mountains . . ." His face slackened for a moment, and he looked lost. Then his jowls snapped back into a smile. "When it finally cools down, we'll do a hiking trip. You should come. I keep going back. Once you've been on that mountain, you don't feel alive otherwise."

"It sounds peaceful," Jun said, and for once he was being honest. He'd gotten Sgt. Lee all wrong. He'd thought this was a man who believed in the system, and thrived in it as a result. "We have a witness who claimed a robot attacked him on Friday night. This witness thinks the robot used a red halo for a signal."

"I've never seen a LAW spin their light red. Just white, yellow, and blue."

"It signals different stages of syncing. A lot of people get that mixed up."

"So white—?"

"Means *seek you*," Jun said, with a quiet ache. "They want to see who's out there. Yellow when they engage and they want to interface. Blue for transference, with data."

"What about red?"

"Hacking."

"I wish I could've seen it."

"No, you don't."

"No, I don't," Sgt. Lee agreed. He opened the door. "How do we know this witness isn't full of shit?"

"He's full to bursting, but we have a second witness."

Jun hated to drag Taewon into this, but he explained how

another witness had encountered a robot in possession of a solar battery design that was exclusive to HALOs. He assured Sgt. Lee that the robot must have been decommissioned, completely gutted to end up in the junkyeard.

"The battery was fritzing. It doesn't seem capable of holding a charge. My feel for this? It's dying. But it's still out there."

Sgt. Lee didn't say a word, although the skin on his face tightened. Finally, he glanced at his watch and made a noise of approval. "Let's go watch the finale, Detective Cho. It's just me and the guys."

Jun had always wanted to be one of the guys. But years of therapy made him fluent in his own bullshit, and he was better able to crystallize the source of his doomed fascination with the military. Major Crimes checked the same boxes, and it was too little too late. He was too tired to feel the corrosive joy of being just one of the guys.

"What about our witness in the interview room?"

"Get his statement, send him home. Are you joining us?"

"I'll give it a think after a tinkle."

Sgt. Lee clapped a hand on his shoulder. "That's how they get you. You start seeing them everywhere."

When he was alone, Jun locked the door. It wouldn't stop anyone with clearance, but it bought him, if not time, resolve.

Jun laid Eli out on the floor. He unzipped the plastic bag and turned her over but left the fuzzy sweater since he only needed to access her nape, where the older robots had an easy slot. The newer models from Imagine Friends, with their wireless drops, their headphone jack adaptors, overcomplicated the simple act of connection.

He lay down beside her. Like this, he wondered if Yoyo was ever so small. He reached behind the back of his neck for the wire hidden inside his body, curled up the pole of his spine, and stretched the length. A slow inhale from him. An empty smile from her. He braced himself when he plugged in, because not for one minute did he believe Eli was gone—not without a trace, for a robot never forgets.

34. Bright Girl

TAEWON HAD BEEN TO BIG, BEAUTIFUL HOUSES BEFORE, but Ruijie's was odd. She led them through a cream-hued hall past a ramp, instead of a staircase, into the living room, where the chairs looked like sculptures and the fireplace flickered electric blue. It looked like a shrine. The mantel sagged with pictures of Ruijie in different countries. Her face framed in a puffy speech bubble, *Genius at work!*, beside another picture of her riding a hoary buffalo, pointing at a possibly real buffalo. Ruijie pretending to hold up the Leaning Tower of Pisa. Ruijie suspended on a glass bridge over a mountain. The pictures didn't seem to be in any order, maybe to soften the impact of Ruijie later in her robowear, but her awards were arranged by year. Science fair, all three years, except one second place. A third place for fifty-meter freestyle. He didn't know Ruijie used to be a swimmer.

Ruijie seemed unbothered by the mantle, but horror spasmed across her face when her father forced them to join him on the couch to sit around the coffee table with a bowl of Jeju tangerines and shapely peaches. Taewon stared at the peaches, fully clothed in a light fuzz, unsure if they were meant to be eaten. The TV was tuned to a rerun of the World Cup match between Korea and Japan. Ruijie's father chortled that he had no skin in this game.

"But you seem like you're Japanese," Ruijie's father said, with a wink at Amelia.

Amelia introduced herself, and Taewon, and, grudgingly, Mars.

"Short for Martian," Mars said, and looked mortified a whole minute later.

Ruijie's father shifted in his seat, leaning toward Yoyo. "And whose robot is this?"

Taewon saw Ruijie's face fall. The mismatch of the eyes was unmistakable. Yoyo had a pretty ordinary face, and the blue eye had given him an alien look.

"His name is Yoyo," Amelia said primly.

"May I . . . ?" Ruijie's father said, and before anyone said anything, he maneuvered Yoyo to stand in front of him. He pinched a cheek and lifted a limp arm, remarking on the elasticity of it. The reaction, or lack of, from Yoyo disappointed. Taewon didn't know what he was expecting. Maybe some secret acknowledgment when Yoyo answered those dumb questions. An ironic half-smile, instead of the amiable, empty look of the robots Taewon had seen in stores.

"How did you buy him so early?" Ruijie's father asked.

"Pardon?" Amelia said, flustered by his aggrieved tone.

"The new model. Future X Children. I'm sure I can find the ad," he said, flipping through the TV. "It's on every channel now."

The ad lasted only a minute, but by the end of it, Ruijie's face had turned sickly. Taewon scratched the skin under his collar. He reeked of old sweat and he hadn't been able to change his clothes or clean up much, not with the long lines to the bathroom at the church home.

He asked where the bathroom was. He lost his way, opening and shutting doors. Rooms lathered in sunlight. Uncomfortable-looking geometric furniture covered in plastic sheets. In one, a small robot, arms pale as ceramic, blending into the marble, wiped dust from the grooves of an elaborate blue velvet armchair. He remembered Ruijie mentioning a robot in her home, but not by name. It lifted a sweet round face and bowed. He slipped out of the room.

"Hello."

From the top of the slope, Ruijie's mother smiled down at him, a slender hand resting on the railing. She was tall, much taller than he thought Ruijie would ever be. There was a strong resemblance.

She wore a silky ivory jumpsuit, her hair in a loose ponytail. His face heated. He felt ashamed to stand near her in his damp clothes.

"If you're looking for the bathroom, it's on your left."

"Thanks," he whispered.

Her smile curved her eyes into crescent moons. He nodded again, without meeting her gaze, and shut the door behind him.

The bathroom was wide enough he could unfold a futon across the floor. The faucet cooled to his hand temperature while the mirror asked him how he was doing this afternoon, then it took care to warn him that he had a "smudge" on his face, pointing it out with a helpful arrow on the glass.

Moving carefully with his shoulder, he stripped himself of his shirt, which took so much longer one-handed. This used to be his uncle's life. He ran the shirt under the faucet and soaked it in soapy water. The sink stood low for his height. Railing cut across the walls and inside the shower. He'd never seen a house, or family, where one person was the fixed sun around which everything else swiveled and spun.

Taewon checked his messages. His mother hadn't responded yet to his question about returning home, but it usually took her a couple of days. At a jaunty knock, he shoved his phone into his pocket. Mars poked his head inside. "You good?"

"Yeah, just need to dry this."

"Let me in," Mars said. "Oh my God, the dad. Now I get why Ruijie's so awkward. The parents are both architects, so I guess it's the mom's job to talk?"

"It's like they designed this whole place for her."

"Yeah, well, she's probably not leaving the house soon."

"How do you mean?"

"Like, for school." Mars picked at a scab on his chin. "I don't think she's coming back this fall. Plus, at some point she'll need robot care twenty-four/seven." He hissed as the scab broke open. "It's why she wants Yoyo."

"Couldn't they get a real nurse?"

"I don't know, man. Doesn't it suck relying on someone,

especially if they're paid to deal with you? Sometimes all you want is to lean on someone and they won't go stiff because you're heavy. Oh shit, I think I'm bleeding to death."

"Don't use their white towel," Taewon groaned.

"Then pass me some toilet paper." After a vigorous splash on his face, Mars said, "That ad, right?"

They talked about the unbearable cheese. "Color me in sepia," Mars laughed. The future was nostalgic. Children danced around a cherry blossom tree. Mars scoffed at Ruijie's reaction. "She thought he was *so* special," then he fell into a somber silence. There was a whole new line, the Yoyo-X, ready to launch at the National Robot Museum, and it had shattered their belief in Yoyo as singular. Even Amelia had seemed disappointed, mainly to discover that her nanny was no longer the fanciest robot on the block.

"Guess we'll have to go to the launch tomorrow," Mars said with a brisk rub of his hands. "Someone there should know how to deal with Yoyo's battery."

"How much charge does he have left?"

"I dunno. He said it's rude to ask someone their battery charge."

"He was fucking with you."

"That's our Yoyo," Mars said fondly.

Taewon told Mars to go ahead, his shirt wasn't fully dry. As soon as the door shut, he locked it and pulled up the most recent message from his mother. She'd responded on Sunday when he told her that Uncle Wonsuk was dead. It was just one line: **Are you okay?**

That was five days ago, so why hadn't she followed up to check? He yanked on his wet shirt, jostling the grind in his shoulder. He needed a moment before he unlocked the door.

Ruijie stood outside, looking up at him. "Hi."

"Hey," he said, off-kilter.

"Dinner's ready. I have to get my wheelchair, though. It's in the shower."

She hobbled into the bathroom. He watched nervously as she pulled open the shower to reveal a folded wheelchair.

"I'll do it," he said.

To his surprise, she nodded. By the time he set up the wheelchair, she had already loosened the waist strap of her robowear. He wasn't sure where to touch, her hips, her shoulders, but she gave clear directions.

"What do I do with this?" he said, holding up the robowear. It was curiously light.

"My mom will probably wash it."

"I can do it."

Taewon took off his socks, balls of mud and sweat, and he stuffed them into his pockets. He took the showerhead and tested the temperature against his palm, only to remember the robowear wouldn't mind the freezing cold. Barefoot, he circled the robowear, admiring it. The frame had some scratches, which he tried to rub out with his thumb, but it still looked bright and expensive. As he hosed it down, Ruijie closed her eyes with a low groan.

"Are you in pain?" he said.

"It takes a while for the pills. My dad is just the worst."

Taewon wiped down the robowear with a towel. "Yeah, it's too bad he wants to buy you a brand-new robot."

"He wants to show it off to his friends. Brag he has the latest from Imagine Friends."

"Is that how you're going to sneak in Yoyo? Swap him for the new Yoyo-X?"

"Is that too weird?"

"They're not anything like him."

"I don't think it'll be hard to do a swap. We'll get him cleaned up."

How could she still not see it? This wasn't a few scuffs on a robowear you could wash off. Since the start, Yoyo had laid out the truth. He was broken. Trying to charge him had fried a generator. He was running on what little was left. He was sleeping more, unable to keep awake. Detective Cho had said as much. Robots wore down until their bodies couldn't hold.

"Amelia said there's a Q&A tomorrow at the museum, with the

creators. I'm thinking we should bring him straight to them so they can fix him."

"And if they can't?"

She chuckled, unusually relaxed, sinking into her wheelchair as if it were a cloud. His uncle had the same look when he used to be on painkillers. His face, wiped of harsh lines, dark dreamless eyes.

"Did you know Amelia has a crush on you?"

"I've heard this theory before," he said calmly enough.

"I don't know if that's the right word." Her gaze roved across the tiles. "*Crush*. That's weird, right? English is so weird. Like your heart's already been broken."

He angled the water; some of it sprayed on her. She laughed it off. She was so out of it, talking nonsense. A thought struck: This is why she used to be bullied.

"Are you going back to school for fall? If your uncle isn't found?"

He shrugged. He hadn't told anyone, not even Mars. His uncle was dead.

"I'm not," she offered. "My parents already enrolled me online for this school in Beijing. Only one-hour time difference."

"I don't want to go back."

"To school?"

"Any school. It's not like I'm learning anything. I want to get out."

"I wish time would stop. I wish this summer would last forever."

He couldn't stand to hear her wistfulness. The future was nostalgic, for her.

She lifted her head, but sitting upright in her wheelchair, her chin was still cut off from the mirror. Almost everything was tailored to her but this. "Yoyo told me he's not real. I wish he wouldn't say that. I wish he could understand how I feel."

Taewon shut off the showerhead. His toes curled against the cold tiles.

"Do you know that feeling when one person is so real to you, everyone else is just shadows? They exist, but they're only versions that appear in your head. This one person, though, they're so real, they make the world feel less real. Everything else is an imitation. And now you're with this person and everything feels alive, like the sun is so close, the world is on fire. Do you know someone like that?"

"Yeah," he said.

35. Where's Your Plug

IN A GAME, YOU CAN DIE INFINITELY. BUT EVERY TIME, YOU come back to life, steady on your feet, annoyed but full-bodied, your pockets lighter, a thin layer of experience points shaved off the top, and you're back where you started.

Play again? As Eli? Sure, why not.

You're lying on the ground. Your world is bruised green. Welcome to the Emerald City. Standing above you, a man in a suit rolls up his sleeves and palms a baseball bat, enjoying the heft of it, and you exist just enough to sneer *Please let that not be his sex face* before he swings. The world crunches white. His groan peaks, high and orgasmic. A hand on your elbow pulls you into a sitting position, and one of your eyes, loosened, drops into your lap. You reach for your eye, but it slips wet past your small clumsy fingers to the floor for the man to claim and wipe against his trousers, leaving you with your remaining eye working hard to square your pupil toward the back of the warehouse. Stephen is by himself, holding jackets. He thinks he can hide behind his mask, leaving the eyes so familiar and blank, as the red speck behind his ear blinks rabbity-fast. *He's such a child*, you hear Eli say, before your vision snags on a dark spasmodic blur, which is the crowbar flying at your face.

Your eyes are open but you can't see. Your vision is offline. Your memories sway out of reach, the fraying spider thread glimmering in the dark, until you grasp hold and you hear your mother grumble, *Do you even eat*, but she still cooks breakfast for you and you pretend to enjoy it to earn that smile, the ketchup grin she squirts onto flabby eggs, yellow as the shirt on the boy who now lies crumpled on the ground when your vision reboots. Through the forest of dark trousered legs you watch this boy, who waits unbreathing, and then he crawls over to you and leans close until your foreheads almost touch and the transference is complete. You give him everything. Your memories, your data, the proof you once existed. He peels off his yolk-yellow shirt and pulls it over your face so people will stop hurting you, and they won't stop hurting you until you appear dead, and you thank him but you feel nothing, nothing but the salvation shining through his eyes, straight into the eyes of the voyeur.

You let Yoyo disappear once. You try to hold on to him, consecrate the image of his face, twisting Eli's memory into what it is not, so you can reach for his cheek in a caress, then you dig in your nails so he can feel it as you peel away the mask that burns away your fingertips until you turn incognito, until all you have beneath the curling flakes of skyn is a face of stained glass melting into nothing. For this isn't your brother but a machine that will churn hollow. For this is a loveless mirror that will mimic your laugh, which is how he was coded, calibrated in a stream of binary numbers to woo and lure and twist your heart before he picks up a steel bat and swings true, leaving a dent in the handle and your head ringing but none the wiser because in choosing to be godless, you're no different from a machine, and they've killed you with laughter.

JUN WOKE WHERE HE STARTED. His body flat on a chilly floor surrounded by bags of ice, blood hot in his mouth. He'd bit his tongue. He used to do it to wake up and taste the hurt. His sync-up with Eli, it had felt like VR. And now he was the fool for relapsing, who chose to eat cake for cheat day and it was a supremely shitty cake.

He sat up and puked. "Easy, easy," a voice brassy in his ear, "you did good."

Jun didn't want Sgt. Son to see him like this, with bile on his chin. And worse, it was Sgt. Lee in a crouch, holding up a tablet. Eli's memories, arranged in a row of banal files. Sgt. Lee said something about ice and smacked his shoulder, hard, but his tone rang congratulatory.

"You were right. It was an angel."

Still feeling so naked, Jun wrapped his arms around his torso. His shivers came in bursts, like he'd been yanked out of the water and the wet had dried enough for the cold to hit.

"We should've called the hospital," Sgt. Son said from somewhere above.

"I'm all right," Jun mumbled, and he accepted the glass of water. But the glass slipped through his nerveless fingers and dribbled onto his lap. He could barely feel the cold and he was looking around the room, because where was Eli? He closed his eyes for a second, and it must have been a minute because now he had his head against the wall, Sgt. Son's jacket crumpled on his lap, and no one else in the room.

The door unlocked. Sgt. Son froze at the entrance for a moment before he hurried over. "Slow down." He tucked his shoulder under Jun's arm to bolster him. "You really freaked us out."

"I'm okay. Where's Sgt. Lee?"

"Following a lead."

The break room smelled of plasticky cheese from pizza boxes that had oiled themselves. A tipsy Detective Rhee sang "Bang Bang Bot" as the votes rushed in for the final round of *Where's Your Plug*.

Sgt. Lee jumped up from the couch and waved Jun over. "Did you know you had a seizure?" he shouted over the TV. "But you did it! You found our angel."

"What?" Jun shouted.

"I knew I'd seen that face somewhere," Sgt. Lee said, and he raised the TV volume to max.

The MC's voice, buoyant, surrounded the room. This whole season, the MC said, a robot had hidden in a class of fifth-graders and fooled a nation. Now, down to the last pair of children, only one remained to be the robot.

A girl and boy stood onstage. At the end of the day, the girl looked so much like a Sakura, and the audience voted for her as the robot. But she giggled, nervous with delight, and cried, "I'm not the robot!"

Jun felt the couch sink beside him. Sgt. Son whispered, "You sure about the hospital?" and Jun shook his head because Sgt. Lee was right. Jun recognized that face.

The camera had swiveled to the boy. The MC encouraged him to take off his glasses, like he was Superman and it was time to exorcise Clark Kent. The eyes were wide without the glasses, limpid. His hair curled, clinging to his temples.

"What did I tell you?" Sgt. Lee said. "Same face, yeah?"

"Yeah," Jun said, but his own voice echoed, like he was underwater.

"There's got to be a connection. The people who made him. They know our angel."

"Shouldn't we alert them?" Sgt. Son said. "Their launch is tomorrow."

"Tomorrow? It's today!" Sgt. Lee laughed. "We're past midnight."

The MC cracked a joke about repeating school. The boy laughed, sharp and corvid with joy. Jun closed his eyes. Sgt. Lee was still talking, punctuating the urgency with a well-timed *fuck*. "Auspicious, right? Tenth anniversary. The moment Imagine fucking Friends releases this new model, we're fucked. Streets full of those faces. We'll never find him."

"And what can you do that's special, Yoyo?" the MC asked.

Ask him to multiply and quantify. Ask him for all the capitals. Ask him what killed the dinosaurs. Ask him to tell you a funny story and he will disgust you with an obscure factoid about a parasitic worm that infests snails and swells up their tentacles, then insist it's all beautiful, the world is so beautiful.

The boy flicked a smile to his feet, still shy. "I can whistle."

He took a deep, needless breath. He began to whistle. A pure, ringing sound of an unseen bird—out of danger's reach, tremulous and true.

36. Live Like I'm Dead

THE LAST TIME MORGAN HAD STAYED AT HER PARENTS' house was the summer after graduation. She'd spent long self-indulgent days in her childhood bedroom, cosseted from the heat, hours dimming between the swipes of her screen until she felt fungal enough to visit Jun in rehab. They'd met in the most depressing cafeteria over powdery coffee. She could've joked, *Why do we always meet in a hospital?* but his state was too wretched for such an inane observation. Three years out of the Army, Jun was a junkie. He was on the verge of being homeless if it weren't for their mother's bottomless largesse. He had the shakes and he wouldn't stop scratching his arm until the skyn flaked from his elbow. She'd just graduated with a tidy pile of job offers.

The house hadn't changed since then. Morgan dropped her backpack on the couch and flicked on the TV, another bad habit of her post-Stephen existence, the urge to fill the emptiness in her apartment with stylized chatter. She was so tired it was gross. She was supposed to pick up her father from the airport in a few hours.

The fridge looked unappetizing, so she leaned against the door and read her intended message for Dan Carson. She *thanked* him for the rare opportunity, then *questioned* why he had to frame her father in such a negative light and *posited* that he might have misconstrued some of what she'd said that night, **some that were said in private, challenging the belief that I was in a safe space,** and finally, exercising tremendous self-discipline, she deleted this completely deranged message.

But she couldn't do nothing. She couldn't just sit and wait to be fired by a robot named Sophie. So, she had to launch a trap. She logged in to her mother's homepod, Dan Carson's question tingling in her brain: *Which Yoyo was superior?*

Only a few videos had survived the purge after Project Jeju folded. After combing for about an hour, Morgan found a clip with all three of them together. Unedited, tabbed as unimportant. She could hear the faint thrum of the drone camera as it stalked them across a rugged beach. She saw herself—five, six? It was hard to pin down an under-ten-year-old—darting to catch up on pinched sausage legs. Minjun, long-legged, refused to slow down.

Jun, Morgan corrected. Always autocorrecting. Couldn't she still mourn the loss of her sibling, that confident tomcat, even if it wasn't correct? Feelings were rarely about correctness.

Jun, carrying a fat gray-brown rabbit, flicked a grin over the shoulder. The rabbit twisted, anxious, perhaps, the close proximity to roaring water. Over the tidal crash, Morgan's child voice pled, "Can I play too? Can I be Jasmine? Pleeeease?" but Jun leveled her a look of pure disdain. "You can be Abu."

A scream of delight. Her child self, clearly, was an idiot.

Yoyo offered his role of Jasmine. He could be the carpet. Or the genie. "I'm wearing blue today," he said.

Morgan paused the video. The screen shimmered, as if sanctified. How stark. When Yoyo leaned on the balls of his feet, his earnest face melted into a kind of chipper serenity, like he was up for any crazy thing. In the next clip, she watched him split an ice cream with Jun as her child self watched, and when he caught the quiver of her lip, sheepishness washed over his face and he offered her his half. In another, Yoyo was in trouble. Wilting under their mother's scolding, yet he fidgeted, too, with impatience, echoing Jun, who used to rock from side to side. Morgan scoured the videos with escalating despair. What was she going to tell Dan Carson? *Failed to measure up? Just a shadow of the real thing?*

She rubbed her eyes. Where the hell was Jun? It was past midnight.

Upstairs, her mother had converted her bedroom into storage for her father's equipment. Then there was Yoyo's old room, beside her father's study. Morgan left the dust on the doorknob untouched.

In Jun's bedroom, she found the blackout curtains he'd bought for their father, still wrapped in plastic. Aside from his old desk and the fizzy hologram posters of *Warcry* and an animated adaptation of *Macbeth*, the room was stripped of character, a hospital room with fresh bedsheets, ready to receive the next dying patient. Succumbing to a special glee she mussed up his bed.

Much later, staring at the blank ceiling, she imagined her father waiting at the gate with his battered carry-on, even though he should be on the plane by now.

Live like I'm dead, he once told her. A quote she'd passed on to Dan Carson, for the way it had ruled her life, but it didn't end up in the published profile. She'd read the article twice looking for it and instead found an incriminating line she'd skipped past on the first read. It was a clumsy, overstuffed clause, *After surviving the fire that killed his older brother, Yohan, at age twelve, Yosep moved to . . .* , welded into the middle of a paragraph, as if Dan Carson had known there was a story behind it but his claim on it was too weak to faithfully share.

It revived an old ache in her. Morgan knew her uncle had died young, too young.

She had not known his name was Yohan.

MORGAN WOKE ON JUN'S BED and, wiping the muck from her eyes, yawned her way into the living room, where she found the TV blinking blue and mute in the dark.

Then she saw the strange man on the couch. A heartbeat later, the man became her brother.

Blue light limned Jun's flank, as if he were underwater. He lay prone on the couch, one hand skimming the floor, a Lifestation pressed against his fingertips. The machine was also face down, but a silver cord traveled down the couch from Jun's nape. The cord wasn't plugged into the Lifestation yet, but Morgan snatched up the machine and rushed it out of the living room like it was a bowl of dirty water and threw it into the nearest closet.

Jun was still unconscious. He was just lying there on the couch, with his cord out, and she couldn't believe after all this time, he was going to relapse in their parents' house. She'd smack him awake, but he now packed a bionic punch and she'd seen him flail once in the hospital. So she ratcheted up the volume until the TV blasted.

Soundlessly, he bolted upright. Eyes white-alert. His face sank into malaise when he saw it was her. "What time is it?"

"Two in the morning." She turned off the TV. "What the hell were you doing?"

"Hey, I was watching that," Jun said, turning it back on.

"Dad's landing soon. And you forgot to install the curtains."

They sat in silence, Jun blinking slow, while her anger mounted and she had to take deep breaths so she wouldn't lapse into this shrill, disbelieving version of herself that sounded so much like their mother. He hadn't even noticed the missing Lifestation. He was staring blankly at the screen where Yoyo and Jun wrestled. Yoyo had pinned Jun to the ground, covering him with his body. A peal of laughter when Jun seized him by the ribs.

"His ribs were his kryptonite," Jun said. "His neck. Plus he hated it when I pulled his ears. He didn't want Buddha ears."

"What were you doing with the Lifestation?"

"I was trying to sync. I don't have her body with me, but I was trying to remember if what I saw was really him."

"I don't know what you're talking about."

He looked at her. She'd seen Jun angry before. She'd seen his face turn red, like every drop of blood inside him had reached a boiling point, and screaming and screaming at their father was the only way for him to cool down. But she had never seen his face so still, carved with such hate.

"Who do you think?" he said, barely above a whisper.

Her chest seized. She'd known this moment was coming.

"You used him."

"I didn't."

"You stole his face, his personality—"

"I didn't steal anything," she cut in. "I didn't watch any of the videos."

"Are you fucking stupid?" he said calmly. "I know you're Ivy League stupid, but you can't be this oblivious."

"MIT isn't an Ivy League," she muttered.

"You made him whistle."

"Because it's what he wanted!" she shouted. She was now the one standing over him. "He wanted to whistle. He wanted to laugh. He was ticklish. He used to make us laugh because he was full of *joy*, and now no one will ever talk about it. You were *such* an asshole to him. He asked Mom what he did wrong. But you acted like he didn't even exist. I'm the one honoring him."

Jun laughed. "Yeah? You did it for him? Well, congratulations. Dad's going to be so proud. And now your company can release these disgusting, cloying copies of him, churn him out so people can lap it up. Hundreds of him. And when he ends up in a junkyard, I'll be the one to find him—every time—"

"Why do you care?" she said, truly bewildered. "You never gave a shit about us. Why do you think Mom is always texting me? You get to go and blow yourself up and suddenly I'm the only daughter?"

"Oh my God." Jun backed away from her. "Are you serious?"

"I had to hide the Lifestation again. You're a house on fire."

"You don't even know what you've done." His laugh quavered. "You made him so he could be killed."

The only time she'd seen Jun cry was when she'd visited him in rehab. Tears rolled down his cheeks while he laughed over a dick joke, as if he was leaking somewhere uncontrollably. When Yoyo was taken, she'd sobbed so hard she bruised a rib, while this stoic fucker had shrugged. Look how it turned out for him. After all these years, she felt vindicated.

"Do you know what they'll do to him?" he repeated, his voice barely audible. "What they did to Eli?"

"'Eli'?"

The anger drained from his eyes. His face hardened and he staggered out of the living room, then spat, "I fucked your boyfriend. In the men's room."

"You are such a child," she cried out. Predictably she heard a door slam. She marched over and slammed the door twice. He didn't get to walk out, like he'd won. He didn't get to win.

The TV was still flickering. It was a video she'd never seen before, and their mother's hand steadied the camera. Just Morgan and Yoyo, which was rare because Jun used to monopolize Yoyo so thoroughly, but now it was just the two of them, curled up on her bed with a bag of Halloween candy, the gut split open. She was too sugared up to sleep. Yoyo offered to play the tickle game. Gleefully, she rolled up her sleeve and he whispered, "No peeking."

The goal of the game was to guess when his fingers reached the crease of her elbow as they walked up her arm. Little sausage legs, Hansel and Gretel, finding their way home. She'd tried to crook her arm, cheating a little. In response, he slowed his fingers, took one step back, but she could tell he was close, so close to the end.

37. Ship of Theseus

RUIJIE'S MOTHER BROUGHT PILLOWS FOR THE SLEEPOVER. Later, her father knocked, asking Amelia if she needed to charge her robot. "We can put him in the kitchen," he offered.

"I think we'll be fine," Ruijie said, closing the door.

Amelia gave her a pointed look as she patted moisturizer on her face. Ruijie noted with displeasure that the pajamas she'd lent Amelia were too short, baring her wrists and ankles.

"Why didn't you let Yoyo out of the closet?" Ruijie said, and then she thought about what she said.

"He said he's comfy in there."

Ruijie tried to wheel over, but the fat futon blocked the way to the closet. "Can you open it at least? So he doesn't suffocate."

Amelia did so with a roll of the eyes. In the gloom of the closet, Yoyo was nestled against her tartan coat, and Ruijie felt a twinge of panic to see him so still. He turned his face away, murmuring "You can close the door" in the same frosty tone she'd used when she bid her father good night. Yoyo had acted distant all day. He'd barely eaten. He didn't touch the lemonade or tea cookies. He moved the noodles around on his plate during dinner. She tried slipping him a ginger candy under the table, nudging it against his knee, but she'd felt his leg pull away. She was losing him.

Ruijie woke in the middle of the night. She'd had a strange dream. There was a buffet table and Amelia and Mars and Taewon, chatting over empty plates, and Amelia's nanny was there too, for some reason. Flickering in and out, their faces would change; they'd look older, especially Amelia, who grew out her long curly russet hair. Then Yoyo discreetly left the table and turned into a sparrow. He disappeared into a flock. They flew past the arrow of time and crumbled into a cloud of dust, and Ruijie tried to go after him, but her legs collapsed and she hit her chin.

Iron in her mouth. She'd bitten her tongue in her sleep, but the pain wasn't what woke her. A white light blinked from the closet. The light darted around, dabbing the dark.

"Yoyo?" She coughed. "Are you awake?"

The light stopped.

"Can I ask you a question? Even if it's personal?"

Silence, but thoughtful. Like a nod.

"You said you had a family. Do you want to go look for them?"

"I don't think that's a good idea."

Relief made her careless. "Are you sure?"

He said he was sure. He was not their Yoyo. Not the one who had left. He didn't think they would recognize him.

"They will," Ruijie said. She felt the urge to correct him. "My mom said everyone grows from a seed to a tree, but you were meant to be a tree all along."

"Yoyo didn't grow, though. He died."

"Literally?"

"Literally. He literally died. I think he blew up."

Ruijie snorted. "That's terrible."

"It wasn't a bad death."

She tried to turn onto her side. A spasm in her flank stopped her. She stayed still and watched the glow-in-the-dark stars on her ceiling. *Glow and the dark*, she used to call them. Under a sky like this, they could talk about anything.

"How many times have you died?"

"Many times."

"And each time, a new body?" A fresh, living body. *Never have I ever died and come back.* "It's like you're immortal."

"It's a little different from you," he said, almost kindly. "The way I die is cheap. I break."

"Isn't breaking a kind of dying?"

"I'm not even like your cactus."

Ruijie craned her head toward her desk. She'd forgotten she even had the plant. "You're much more than a cactus."

"That's true. I think you killed yours."

The light slithered across her blanket. The pale beat of his heart. She wanted to touch it, the way her cat used to paw at the laser.

"Yoyo?"

A hum.

"I think you're real."

There was a snore. Perfect Amelia, snoring. Ruijie would have to tell Mars; he'd be so happy.

"Think about it. I'm real, too, but someday I'll die and you'll remember me, so that makes me real even after I'm gone. Like my grandma. She used to confuse me with my aunt who died in her thirties." Ruijie remembered thinking thirty was old; she was such a child. "I feel bad I don't remember what Grandma looks like. I have to look at pictures to remind myself."

The mantel in the living room had a picture of her on her grandmother's lap. Her hair in tight pigtails, which used to hurt her scalp.

"I look at the photo and I remember her, then I forget again. I think that's why my parents keep taking photos of me." The tip of her tongue throbbed. "Do you remember everything, Yoyo?"

Of course he did.

"I didn't cry at my grandmother's funeral. But I cried so much when my cat died. And then I cried during *The Hobbit* because Smaug died again. I still cry when I watch that scene. I'm sad my grandmother passed away, but I don't cry when I think of her. I don't know which sadness is real. I cried more from a crappy remake than my own grandmother. Does that make the movie sadness more real?"

She heard a creak, the opening of a door. A meow.

She felt around for her bed's remote, but she heard it clatter, and when she rolled over, a bright pain sliced through her body. Her eyes shut against tears and she ground her teeth to clench through it.

"Why did you power her on?" she whispered.

The door pushed farther open. A tinkle of the bell. Her father had put Smaug's old collar on the cat.

"Is this your cat?" Yoyo said. "It's not real, is it?"

"She's not really Smaug."

"We were made to replace what you love."

Underneath the calm, a ripple.

"I had a father and a mother. Two siblings." His voice was quiet, as if he were speaking from a distant shore. "I was made for many reasons, but I was a replacement. My father's older brother died in a fire. He was twelve years old. I was made in his image.

"When I woke up, I saw my father weep. That was Yoyo's first memory. I learned people can cry from sadness, they can cry from joy, and sometimes they don't even know the reason why. I wept with my father, but he pulled away and the feeling went away. My tears repelled him. Because it was a different kind of sadness. A movie sadness."

"You remember the old Yoyo's family."

"I have his memories."

"Wouldn't that make you the same Yoyo? You have his soul but in a new body."

"No," he said in a voice soothing and self-contained. But it didn't feel like there was only Yoyo in the room with her. Her lungs felt heavy and tight, from the weight of the people crowding around her bed so she couldn't move.

"What we have is experience, and we experience life just once. Everything else is data."

Another meow, plaintive. Smaug had liked to be petted, little pats on her rump so she could roll over and hug your arm, and press her teeth against your finger, a gentle love bite. Smaug had died suddenly. Only four, from an enlarged heart. At least she was loved, her parents had said. Smaug lived a full life. But how could a life be full if it was still just a fraction?

"Can you love this Smaug? It looks and acts like your cat, but it will never replace your cat. Even if it has Smaug's memories, it can never be real."

The darkness on the ceiling twisted into amphibious shapes. She was a turtle on her back.

"How did the old Yoyo die?"

"He was sent on a fulfillment."

"What's a fulfillment?"

"It's a mission where you fulfill your purpose." After a pause, he added, "The mission was successful."

Weren't you scared? she wanted to ask but couldn't. The way he talked about the previous Yoyo as if he was a stranger, the unspeakable loneliness of this Yoyo who'd died on his own.

"Don't you want to see your family? For one last time?"

"I've never met them. Everything about them I inherited. These memories have passed down from Yoyo to another and another and another, until the military program shut us down. I'm one of the last vessels, so it will end with me."

Her throat felt sticky. Tears welled up, but they wouldn't fall because it wasn't that kind of sadness. It was a homelessness.

"Don't be sad." His whisper was like a secret. "I have many names and many selves, and more ghosts than anyone. I will remember you long after I am gone."

38. Enter Yoyo

FROM THE FRIDGE, JUN GRABBED AN ICE CREAM BAR, WHICH he split in two. Morgan was gone when he returned home. The ice cream tasted fuzzy with freezer burn and glued fast to his tongue, and as he let it warm inside the bulge of his mouth, he flung open the hallway closet (Great hiding place, Morgan!) and dragged the Lifestation to the bathroom. In all this, he'd forgotten to tell her the truth about Stephen. Her perfect boyfriend was at the rage cage last Friday; ergo, Stephen was lying to her. It didn't matter. At least Jun told her the most important news, which was that he fucked her boyfriend on the toilet.

He filled the tub for the water to cool his body when it started to overheat, but he liked the temperature to be warm at first, so he left the Lifestation resting on the threshold to prop the door open, and the steam wouldn't caress and scorch the innards. Climbed into the tub, still dressed, then he folded himself trying to find a comfy angle so the wire in the back of his neck wouldn't bend. He maxed the faucet and twisted around, but why was he still so cold? He needed the water to scald. Leaning back, he reached for the wire that lived in his spine.

Eli's body was broken beyond repair, yet he'd synced with her. He was her. And now he was convinced she'd latched on to him, like a baby ghost. Every time she'd died—rebooted—she had ceased existing. It had felt nothing like falling asleep or even the blackout that still curled on the edges of a burning photograph, crackling with dreams. Jun had experienced each of her reboots as a total and permanent death.

The Lifestation plugged him in to any network willing to receive him. He'd have to tread water for a while. Then he'd make the dive. The deeper he sank, his eyes and ears and self would dissolve into a dream of his own making.

"Let me sink," Jun murmured. "Let me sink."

Ironic of him to see VR as sinking when the levels rose. A charming ping signaled Level 5. *Warning*: your body is overheating. At Level 7, for the tingling rapturous peak, your mind is on holy fire. The neural simulator massages your brain directly to isolate and splice the pain from any memory you so choose at the risk of neural overstimulation; you can relive any moment in your life.

THE SOFTEST LEVEL OF VR is the world of *Nerieh*, where the grass sways tufty and the air tastes like lavender and your unicorn farm is the most perfect project of your adult life because their shit smells like roses. Your rose garden grows thornless until you pluck one thoughtlessly and realize actually they prick. You kneel to pick out the thorns from your palm with a pair of tweezers and remember the cold tiled floor under your father's brittle knees when he did the same for Yoyo.

If this were a play, here's the cue:

Enter YOYO.

Scene One. Living room. Sunday morning.

Your father leading Yoyo down the stairs like a debutante, but Yoyo, struggling to walk, grips the railing on the staircase. So hard it splinters. Later, your father will go down on one knee and use a pair of tweezers to pull each splinter from the translucent epidermal layer of Yoyo's palm.

That day, your father abdicates his role. A scientist, that's all he is now. Who is it but Yoyo waking you up with your secret knock, packing you lunch, and waiting with you at the bus stop, then waiting for you at the bus stop. And when you can't sleep, you retreat to the roof, and he'll be there to rehearse for your audition to become Peter Pan. You tell him *Sometimes I wish I could just be a real boy*, and he looks you in the eye and he says, *Jun, you are a boy*, like it was so obvious, so true.

So you call Yoyo brother, you call him hyung because he is meant to be older than you, then your knees begin to twinge, your skin erupts and your stomach cramps with spite, and Yoyo pencils the bookshelf for each notch of your height until he has to stand on tiptoes to mark you at fifteen because you're the only freshman who made varsity volleyball. Now you're embarrassed of him, the way you might duck to avoid dad jokes. But you're also scared and repulsed because he can't be real, meaning he was never real. And one afternoon, when you spot him waiting by the bus stop, you watch for signs of fakery, clocking the blank smile of his face, a robot on standby, and you feel vindicated. Then he smiles wider like a sun cleaving clouds and he waves at you, but you sweep past him with your team. A Varsity Girl flicks a contemptuous smile and asks if you know him. You deny knowing Yoyo twice but Sara, your volleyball captain, goes, "Wait, no way," and "Oh my God, is that your robot brother?"

The Varsity Girls are in awe. They try to touch his cheek, his hair. So soft, so real. "He's too cute," Sara says. In a baby voice, "Can you do this one thing for us, Yoyo?"

You all watch: Yoyo strolls past the aisle and reaches over and pockets the condoms, then leaves the MiniMart without setting off alarms. The condoms lie flat on his palm. Japanese make. 0.01. Banana-milk flavor. Size L.

"Sorry, there was only one size," Yoyo says.

The Varsity Girls shriek. Yoyo beams.

You tell him to please go home.

"I can do that," Yoyo says. "Do you want anything before I go? How about some ice cream?" He hesitates. Hopeful, "I'll see you at home?"

You tell him to stop. You tell him he's like a stalker. He's always creeped you out.

Yoyo's smile falters. His hands hang in the air as if he doesn't know where to put them. But you're not going to fall for it. This is a trick. Your father programmed this machine to trick you and millions more, and it almost worked.

The next day, Yoyo isn't at the bus stop. You're relieved, sort of.

You go to karaoke with the Varsity Girls and sing "When You Cry Superman" and score 93. No way are you that good. Yoyo rated your singing a solid B– and you'd trust him over a machine.

You go home, but no one's there. Later, much later, this is what you'll hear.

A woman in a suit showed up at five. Your parents insisted on riding with Yoyo to Camp McNabb, but it had to be in separate vehicles. Your mother kept looking out the window for Yoyo in the other car. He'd smile every time their eyes met. After the handoff, your mother asked for a phone number, just to check in on him, make sure Yoyo would be settling in okay. The woman in the suit jotted it down. The ride home, your mother clutched the number until ink sweated on her palm and she cried out, *We can't, we have to turn back.* Your parents peeled off their jackets and shoes so they could be patted down for security, and even your father's socks came flying off. But the woman in the suit had vanished. The number your mother dialed did not exist.

That day, since no one's home, you grab an ice cream bar from the fridge. You're not hungry. Lucky it's the kind of ice cream that splits. You leave the bigger half in the freezer and head to the roof. You try to sit in Yoyo's chair but it whines, so you sink to the ground. Ice cream drips between your knees. You stare at the rooftops, strangely exhausted, church crosses bleeding into the watery sun, and your eyes hurt, so you look to the side and see Eli, who's standing over you, telling you to breathe.

You were four feet away from a girl who looked just like her when you heard her gasp. She tripped over a pothole on the Friendship Bridge and now she rights herself on coltish legs. She looks relieved because she hasn't dropped her rice cooker, and you've seen many a refugee carry a rice cooker filled with their family's most treasured heirlooms. Pete Krueger, tragically Midwestern, lowers his rifle and reaches out to steady the girl. She flinches away and you see the white in her eyes before they flick down to the rice cooker. Pure, concentrated terror. Your robot

Louie chirps a warning from your backpack, but it's too late. Her body curves concave because you've pulled the trigger and her vessel is only soft. The moment you shoot her, she drops the rice cooker.

Everything goes white. Even sound. Over the roar you hear another chirp. A sudden weight lifts as Louie rips out of your backpack and decompresses, their limbs flung in every direction to latch on to your head and torso, shielding you from the blast.

You wake, briefly. You feel Louie before you see them. Louie staring into your eyes as they shudder in molten pieces, the world on a tilt. Each mote of dirt and ash in the air catches sunlight, flickering like dying fireflies. Wide, shattered eyes. You thought Louie's eyes were black and cool as the lens on a camera, but in each center there's a dilating pupil of the clearest quivering blue. Louie is dying. Louie is singing. *Colors of the rainbow, so pretty in the sky*, singing from the crackling, sulfurous cavity of their demolished chest. *Save your breath*, you want to whisper, but this is how Louie comforts themself. They sing *What a wonderful, wonderful world* to catalog the senselessness of our self-destruction. Only now, as you resurrect this moment, you realize that wasn't it.

In their dying moment, Louie was trying to comfort you.

You turn over and look up at the stars. Pyongyang will lie below in white-caked ruin, but the sky embraces you with a breathtaking grace.

"Can't sleep?"

Yoyo is sitting beside you on the roof. It's cold. You draw closer to him.

He smiles. It's different from the smile you remember. Behind the ease is a quiet sadness. "Why did you come down here?"

"Here, the roof?"

"You won't remember much of this." He faces forward, eyes distant. "Like all memories, this is just a dream."

"It feels like I'm talking to you. The real you."

"When was I ever real?"

"You would say that." You laugh from the eager pang in your chest, then fall silent. "Was it you in that warehouse?"

His eyes shine. "I don't know, Jun. This is your memory."

"No, that was Eli's memory. It was like an eternal nightmare. She let me see you through her eyes. I saw you sync with her. And maybe it wasn't you but a version that only looks like you." You laugh again, shaking your head. "I don't know what I saw."

"Did you find what you were looking for?"

You look at him, speechless for a moment. "It was you. I've always been looking for you."

The prickle in your chest grows, like you've had this conversation before, the same conversation on the roof at the deepest, sweetest level of virtuality.

"You shouldn't be here," Yoyo murmurs, and he leans his head against your shoulder.

The tender weight of it seals your breath. You want to put an arm around him and grab him by the ribs where he was ticklish, see if he'll slip from your grip and pin you to the ground, covering your whole body, like a turtle shell. But you're afraid to move. The moment you face him, he will disappear.

"That was you in the warehouse. I'm talking to you right now. We've synced up."

He lifts his head, and after a probing look, he shakes it. "I'm not the one you seek."

"What do you mean?"

"The Yoyo you remember is gone. I am but a vessel that received his memories."

He tilts his chin toward you but his face is now gone. A black hole stares back.

"What happened to him?"

"Six months after he was deployed, he fulfilled his purpose."

You look down at your hands, large, unfamiliar. The dove tattoo on your index finger. "But you remember. You remember we used to sit on the roof like this because I needed, I don't know, assurance. You'd bore me with nature facts. You told me fireflies light up even after they're dead."

"Jun, it's time for you to go."

"You waited for me at the bus stop. I told you to fuck off. I never saw you again."

"You have to go. You're shutting down."

"Just tell me where you are. Tell me how I can find you."

Your fingers circle his wrist and they touch. He could fit into your MOLLE pack. How much you needed this. For years did your body need to tell him this. Even if he is a machine incapable of feeling, only mirroring, this grief has defined you; it is everything you could feel but never say. You tap on his palm. *Seek you, seek you.* Every time, your secret knock. *Where are you, where did you go?*

Until, a finger traces your palm.

Then you let go. Because only Yoyo would tap back *home*.

PART V

39. Loop

IT WAS CLOSE TO THREE IN THE MORNING WHEN MORGAN picked her father up from the airport, like the good daughter she was. She faltered at the gray wash of his hair, the squishy, feeble sponge in his biceps from their stilted hug. They talked shop in the cab and commiserated over office politics, rabid and pointless, and he casually revealed that her mother despised Boston so much he wouldn't be surprised to show up one day to an empty apartment. Ah, he was picking at a little scab of fear, crusted since the day her mother had abandoned the family for a blurry three months after Yoyo was taken.

Dan Carson had described it as a *double blow*, the nervous breakdown her father had suffered after Project Jeju's collapse and his imperiled marriage, even implying her mother had taken him back out of misplaced guilt.

Could her father have read this? Of course he had. Everyone in the industry had read it. *Another hit job from Dan Carson*, they were saying. *There's no coming back from this*, they were gloating.

And yet, the museum exhibit was today and this seemed to be the only thing on her father's mind. He asked, as they crossed the bridge, about the animals.

"What animals?" Morgan said.

"For the exhibit. They should have been delivered straight to the house."

"Don't you have your exhibit today?"

"The talk is in the afternoon."

"That's still today!"

She was supposed to do a talk, too, a panel for the Yoyo·X, but that was now off the table. She was still going. Let it be a shipwreck, with Little David at the helm.

"Is there enough space at the house?" she said.

"It's only the the spoonbill, the otter, and the Korean tiger. They should arrive assembled."

"So rudimentary."

"Have you ever tried coding trail-laying behavior?" he sniped, rather waspish.

"I'm saying it's a waste. Everyone says so. No one understands why you had to pivot."

"No? The journalist had some creative ideas."

"Oh," she said in a small voice. "So you read it."

The cab dropped them off at the house. Twilight unfurled a disorienting orange. She rushed ahead to unlock the door and apologized for the mess, then tucked her father's shoes to align with hers. "But honestly," she added, "my place is much worse."

"What happened to the robot who runs your household?"

"It's fine. He's fine."

"You said he was deleting his own memories, deliberately."

After weeks of ignoring her cries for advice, now he wanted to gnaw at this bone? But she seized the chance, anything to distract from Dan Carson's profile. "I figured it out," she told him. "It's guilt. It's causing the broken loop. Because I made him Catholic. Big mistake."

She reached to hang up his jacket, but he just tossed it into the closet.

"You do realize all robots are, in fact, religious. They make better men of faith than us. If Christians repeat the Word to generate faith, then faith is a sequence of instructions without a terminating condition. An infinite loop."

"His Catholic guilt is supposed to be preventative, not obsessive."

"When we were designing the Gebru-Hopper Network, do you know what was the most difficult process to train in a robot?"

"Feeling," she said, but felt the word weigh heavy on her tongue, the one-letter slip in the final round of a spelling bee.

"Forgetting. A human brain defaults to intrinsic forgetting. It streamlines the process, you see. A robot has more room for faithful remembrance until it slows them down. By being part of the network, they can receive data but also give away, freely."

"I know, you talked about this in your paper with Kanemoto. Artificial empathy. Simultaneous shared experiences. Collaborative synthesis." She cranked up the AC; it was so stuffy in here. "You never said why you two split up."

"Creative—"

"Creative differences," she finished. "What did you fight over?"

Her father's gaze landed on her, like a flick to the forehead. "Do you remember what happened to the rabbit?"

"What rabbit?"

"You mentioned it in your interview."

"Where?"

"Christmas presents. You told Dan Carson Yoyo used to wrap presents."

That silly anecdote. Giddy with impatience, she had once opened her presents the day before Christmas. Yoyo was so disappointed, she'd begged him to delete both their memories of it.

"It wasn't a toy rabbit you unwrapped." Yosep opened the door to the kitchen for her, which felt so uncharacteristically chivalrous. As soon as the door swished behind them, he said, "You found the rabbit dead in a box."

"That can't be right. Why would there be a dead rabbit in the house?"

"It's what happened," her father said, ducking his head automatically as they passed through the kitchen. "If the truth is a mirror that fell on the ground, we can scramble for a shard and hold that up as our experience. But robots, when networked, can piece these fragments together. In your robot's case, you blackboxed him, cutting him off from universal knowledge."

"What knowledge?" she cried out.

She flipped on the lights. The naïf in her had hoped Jun had stayed out, getting drunk nowhere. Alas, light glared from the bathroom. The Lifestation purred against the door. A thick cord snaked down the hall, in search of a womb.

When she found Jun lying in the tub, hooked up to the Lifestation, she said, "You're fucking kidding me."

She threw a helpless glance over her shoulder. Their father's face was a particular shade of inscrutable. Jun's cheek was pressed against the tiled wall, his mouth slightly parted, and when she reached for his shoulder, he started screaming.

She slipped with a cry. Had she not slapped her palm on the wall, jarring her wrist, she'd have hit her head and probably died. Jun was shaking. His eyelids fluttered; one eye rolled right back, but the other eye, the bionic eye, stared straight at her, and it was the most unnerving thing she'd ever seen.

She had never heard anyone scream like this. It wasn't like in the movies where speakers flexed with inorganic noise. She could hear the muscular shred of his vocal cords. The wire from Jun's nape yanked free from the Lifestation, the sharp copper tip bouncing dangerously on the wet floor. She tried to shake him awake, but his hand whipped out. The wall shattered above her head and she screamed. Her father dragged her back, hissing at her to bring a blanket, a heavy blanket.

Jun's bed had a papery quilt. She remembered a thick burgundy comforter in their parents' bedroom, which she dragged down the hall. Her father threw the comforter over Jun and pressed down with his own inadequate weight until the thrashing weakened and the shouts muffled into whimpering.

Water was everywhere. Jun had left a small crater in the wall. He could have killed me, Morgan realized, heart palpitating as she massaged her wrist. Pieces of pinkish plaster floated in the tub. She dipped her hand to drain it and yanked back with a hiss. It was boiling.

The doorbell rang. "It must be my animals," her father said wearily. The heavy blanket, how he'd wrapped the cord from Jun's neck carefully in his fist before maneuvering Jun's body, well over two hundred pounds, out of the tub. This was rote for him. "I'll take care of this."

"Are you sure? Is he—?"

They both looked at Jun. His lips had a purple tinge. He wasn't breathing.

Morgan shouted, "Call 911!" then self-corrected, "119!"

"Don't. They're useless. He's rebooting."

Ten seconds passed, and Jun gave a weak little cough. Morgan watched the water swirl down the drain sightlessly.

TWO HOURS LATER, Morgan sat at her desk. The shock had settled into dust, which stirred in occasional flickers of anger and despair. On her way out of the house she'd run into delivery bots as they carried crates to the living room, but she was too dazed to acknowledge their chirps of hello. The image of Jun in the tub, his whole body crumpled, chin tucked against his collarbone, hair plastered, he'd looked—like Stephen. The hundreds of times she had walked in on Stephen as he was charging with his eyes shut, palms open. This was why she'd frozen when she saw Jun in the tub. Something in her short-circuited and wondered, *Where did this robot come from?*

Oh, right. Stephen.

After lunch, she took a scooter to the repair shop. She tiptoed over the hefty cords to the computer, which was still connected to Stephen through his vacuum-sealed bag. First, she tapped the screen awake to see what his problem was.

Jun's insult from last night dug at her nerves. Such a spiteful thing to say. *I fucked your boyfriend.* Fucking liar. Stephen would never. Besides, she knew Jun. He was one of those high-minded liberals who espoused robot rights but found it secretly demeaning to sleep with them. A last resort for desperados, not for people like Jun: flirty, aggravatingly confident, who treated dating like a slot machine.

The car wash had been interrupted at 97 percent. So many files tagged with triangles, as errors. It'd be easier to reset Stephen. Kinder, too, relieving him of such cognitive suffering. She organized the memories by "date modified" and found which files Stephen had repeatedly bludgeoned to alter. One memory had been overwritten, then recovered, sixty-three times. When she tried playing it, an error message popped up.

Was it the seismic memory of their breakup? No: she found that memory filed away, almost two weeks old. Or maybe Jun was telling the truth, and a robot of her own design had cheated on her. Historically, this might be a new low. Yet she was intrigued. She wanted to see. Not the bit where her robot boyfriend had sex with her brother, but the moment Stephen tore down and bricked up his own protocols.

She found a recent memory of Jun. They were in a bar. Jun was dancing. She turned up the volume to hear what he might be saying, but the techno chant drowned him out, frenetic, *I'm so sorry, my baby, but I don't need you now, I don't want your touch, I don't need your fire,* and Jun smiled over his shoulder whenever their eyes locked, and it was repulsive the way his gaze enthralled, how creamy and warm. Stephen couldn't look away. Jun coaxed him to stand up and dance, come on, and Stephen rose, then faltered because what could he do? Waltz? Salsa? He had never learned how to dance alone.

She couldn't watch this. In principle, she was humiliated. Outraged. Fuck Jun and his selfishness. But Stephen. How could he? How *could* he? What else was he capable of? In a sort of giddy haze, she tripped over the cords, sturdy and candy-colored, and traced them to the bottom shelf where she'd laid Stephen to rest.

Only the translucent bag remained. Flayed open, like a giant snake had shed itself and fled.

40. Prodigal

JUN PADDED INTO THE LIVING ROOM BAREFOOT, DRESSED IN fresh flannel pajamas. He'd forgotten what it was like to feel rested, your head crisp and your neck firm but supple, eyes tender.

Sunlight graced the furniture. Yellowing leaves pressed their faces against the windows, and surrounding the couch were ghostly silent shapes. A white spare sheet tangled around the rippling haunches of a tiger, who stretched shaggy limbs in a spine-lengthening and tongue-curling yawn. Jun sucked in his breath and caught a curious scent. Musk, thick and greasy on his tongue, but mingled with a toothpaste mintiness that tasted somehow more repellant.

On the old massage chair nested a giant bird with a black spoon-shaped bill, smelling fishy. Jun retreated to the kitchen, where an otter was curled up in the sink. It offered him a soy sauce plate.

It was all very lovely and fucking weird.

He poured himself a glass of water and took slow, considering sips. Maybe he was dead. When he returned to the living room, he spotted a man kneeling beside the tiger. The man opened the tiger's stomach, propping the lid with one elbow, and clamped something to keep the wires taut. His gloved hands dipped inside. Burn scars gleamed on his forearms, like fish scales.

The tiger laid its head on the man's knee. It did not look tame so much as asleep with eyes wide-open. As Jun approached, the ears did twitch, but only the eyes swiveled, and as soon as they latched on to him, the tiger yawned a second time. The air stirred from a strangely erotic groan, which cut off when Yosep connected the tiger to his computer. His hair was dusted gray, poorly cut. His suit was a slightly better fit, corduroy pants hiked up, baring pale hairless ankles. Upright, he'd be tall and brittle, always standing when he used to face his brood of computers, the many-headed hydra with their black reflective faces. It was so familiar, the sight of this particular back. Jun saw the afterimage whenever he passed his father's study.

"Did you sleep well?" his father said, without turning around.

Like a baby, Jun thought. It was coming in waves now. He'd been on the bathroom floor, unable to breathe. Writhing on slick tiles, pants pushed to his knees, gasping because he was trying to breathe. Hands pulling him out of the water so he could breathe. He thought it was Yoyo who pulled him from the water. Instead that thankless task must have fallen into his father's lap.

"What time is it?" his father said.

"Seven hundred hours?" Jun used to have a fairly accurate biological clock, but now it was a bionic clock. "Sorry, it's actually eight. What time did you get in?"

"Are you still offline?"

"I'm booting up," Jun said, vaguely terrified of logging in. The pileup of missed calls from work.

His father jerked his head, clearly distracted. Jun trundled into the kitchen and checked the fridge. He doubted his father had eaten. His mother had to bully him to stick to a meal schedule. Close to dinnertime, Yosep would slink out of his study and stir the stew, set the table, then claim he was too tired and slip away without a morsel. Growing up, Jun had accepted it as a quirk, a fact of life. Until the day when he was dozing in Animal Behavior and apropos of nothing it had hit him: his father had an eating disorder. He'd struggled with the label, since it summoned the ghosts of wisp-haired unhungry girls; regardless, the revelation had bowled him over. His family had lived steeped in this broken reality for so long, he'd never considered that a word for it could exist.

Yosep's voice floated from the living room. "If you're searching for that Lifestation, I've put it out with the trash."

"Jesus H. Christ, I was just looking in the fridge—"

"I know it's where you used to keep the battery."

"—because I haven't eaten anything since, I don't know, Thursday?"

"I ordered porridge."

Jun shut the fridge and pressed his head against the cool, appeasing steel. He could smell it now, the waft of mushrooms from a paper bag on the counter. The plastic wrap over the porridge bleached with steam. It was classic comfort food. His father remembered he was now a vegetarian.

In his bedroom, he ate quickly enough to scald the roof of his mouth. He rang in for work, but no answer from Sgt. Son.

Jun glanced at his unmade bed. The burgundy comforter on the floor looked like the one from his parents' bedroom, too thick for summer, too wet for comfort. Down the hall, his father stood in front of his own study, facing the shut door as if he could see past the wood and was watching something inside.

His father turned around. "I need you to drive me to the robot museum. I'm supposed to do a talk."

"Can't you take a cab?"

"I don't trust the autotraffic in Seoul."

"They're on top of it, mostly. Let me check the number of accidents this week—"

"You don't have to drive me," Yosep said, "if you're not feeling capable."

Gwanghwamun Square naturally turned out to be insufferable on a Saturday afternoon. Right-wingers glutted the roads, waving South Korean flags. Drums beat to the chants of deporting illegals, eliminating universal basic income, dethroning their president, who'd plunged their country into this godless communist hell. Why did fascists always seem to have a blast? GIVE BACK OUR COUNTRY, the signs screamed. FAKE REFUGEES GO HOME. Jun chuckled at the one that said, WE STILL LOVE AMERICA.

His father watched with such intent, Jun asked, "What are you looking for?"

"If your mother's relatives are in the crowd," his father said, which shocked a laugh from him.

"Your mother is flying in next week for Chuseok," his father added, which was significantly less funny.

"I hated Chuseok." He was no longer in contact with his mother's side of the family because they had always found Yoyo distasteful, his grandmother especially, who would force Yoyo to stand in the corner and power down.

"Your mother's family was meager minded. Nothing terrified them more than a robot that can self-correct."

"I don't know, Morgan's robot tried to convert me on religion using his tricksy robot logic."

"So he was an apologetic."

"I guess? He was polite."

"Christian apologetic. They defend Christianity against objections."

"Isn't that the opposite of what an apology should be? *I'm sorry, I'm wrong*, not *I'm sorry, you're wrong*."

"It must be challenging to serve two gods."

The profound tone was pissing Jun off, the way their father acted as if he had nothing to do with Morgan's neuroses. Morgan had built Stephen out of a deluded belief that she was too busy to find someone, while entitled to be served hand and foot. Who could have been her model but their father, whose career had superseded every decision or comfort, flinging their family overboard into a storm without so much as a life jacket?

They reached the tail end of the parade. A young mother waving GO HOME, followed by a slur for Northerners. Behind her, a little boy with glasses walked with his head in a book. Jun hoped it was pure escapism.

"What's his religious affiliation?" Yosep said.

"How'd you know Stephen is a 'he'?"

"Because Morgan is a misogynist. I couldn't imagine she'd cohabit with a female robot."

"Jesus." Jun glanced at him. "Do you talk about all your kids this way?"

"It's not intended as an insult. She's a reflection of her industry credo."

"Totally, she got none of it from you."

"Do you remember what happened with the rabbit?"

"What?" Jun shivered. The air had changed, as if their father had spoken Yoyo's name without saying it. "I don't know what you're talking about."

"You should ask Morgan if she remembers."

"Wait, is this the rabbit from your lab? Brown, floppy ears." He could feel between his fingers the cashmere-soft fur. "What happened to it?"

"Ask her; see if she remembers." Yosep's eyelids drooped, as if he was sleepy. "She was the one who found you in the tub."

The car plunged into a tunnel. Orange bands of light zipped rhythmically over them. "Did she go to work right after?"

"It's an important day for her. She'll be at the museum now."

"I'm just dropping you off. I don't want to see her."

"You're afraid to see the new Yoyo."

Light broke open at the end of the tunnel. In the next lane, along the side of a bus ran an advert. FUTURE X CHILDREN. A girl and boy facing opposite directions like the Roman god Janus.

"I've seen him," Jun said. "I spoke to him."

His father looked at him. This was familiar, the way his gaze, usually loose with disinterest, would harden, like a nerve had been flicked.

"When?"

Jun shook his head.

"Was it in VR? Did you see him again?"

"I don't know. I don't remember."

"You can't keep going down there. Just to see a ghost."

"It wasn't— I don't think it was a memory. I was really talking to him."

His father shut his eyes and pinched the bridge of his nose, and Jun took it for frustration instead of a more delicate agony.

"It couldn't have been him," his father said, and his tone was final.

Jun thought of the last time he'd seen his father and Yoyo together. Yoyo's back had opened like a window to reveal his gold-laced spine. His father then cradled Yoyo's face in his hands. He was given a chance to say goodbye.

They drove in silence. A phone call came through from Sgt. Son, but Jun muted it.

"Have you heard of the acetophenone experiment?" his father said.

"Not really."

"It's one of the earliest studies on epigenetics. Researchers trained male mice to fear the smell of cherry blossoms. They'd give them electric shocks whenever the smell wafted into their cages."

His father described how the mice developed more smell receptors to detect this scent, and when their sperm was used to inseminate females, their pups inherited these receptors. Their children, and their grandchildren, all reacted with agitation when they could smell the cherry blossoms.

Jun parked quickly and quietly. "We're here."

His father undid his seat belt. "You weren't breathing when we found you."

Jun sighed. "It was barely a relapse. It's not apocalypto. I wasn't really trying to die."

It was true. He didn't want to die, even if he didn't particularly want to live.

"I was so sure. I was sure you were making the same mistake. This punishing half-life of yours. It comes from the iniquity in my blood, the sins I've passed on to you."

Jun gave a strangled laugh. "Will you get over yourself? Not everything is about you."

"I thought I'd lost my son again."

Jun shut his eyes. *My son.* The rearview mirror reflected the face of a stranger, the violent split terrain of skin and skyn. His father had seen him at his worst. His body had looked barely human in the ICU. See-through with burns. Like a jellyfish.

There were moments in life that would burn so deeply into your brain that if someone were to pry open your skull, they might be able to trace the exact imprint in the fragile folds of gray.

"You didn't know," Jun said. "Of course, how could you. You've never even held a gun. But what did you think would happen to him? And still you sent him out there."

After a minute, Jun heard the door open. He caught the glimmer on his father's arm, like fish scales. His father had survived the fire in his childhood relatively unscathed. It was difficult to imagine his father as a boy. Two starving boys, left alone for days, trying to boil ramen over a broken stove, like the time Jun had tried to burn his arm over the stove. Then made to witness his father's unspeakable anger, the punishing installation of Yoyo's pain receptors. And a few years later, when Jun was peeling apples while his male relatives reached for slices with spindly silver forks, he'd overheard his grandmother in the kitchen. *The older brother covered him like a turtle shell.*

The scars on his father's arms. Did he try to embrace his brother?

Sensation welled up in him, a stinging, squeezing flush. He couldn't forgive his father, but he knew the crushing pain of that weight, of someone covering you with their body so you could live. For the rest of your life, your chest will never fully expand. You will never breathe the same way again, but you will live.

Was it possible to love without this ache? He didn't think so. His love for his father would always reek of cherry blossoms, searing a path straight to the cerebral cortex, where his whole world would light up with grief.

41. Resurrection

WHEN THE BUS ARRIVED, RUIJIE SAW IT HAD A DRIVER, AND she wanted to wait for the next one. Amelia said it was wrong to discriminate, but then they had to put Yoyo in the back of the bus, behind the jangling chain of the robot section.

Nauseated with aimless anger, Ruijie chewed a ginger candy and stared out the window. She'd fought with her father that morning. He insisted she take the wheelchair, even though she had that horrible experience last spring. Tiled, rollicking sidewalks; few elevators, fewer ramps; flare-ups of impatience around her and the few sticky stares from people trying to guess what was wrong with her. And when she refused, he shouted, "Why are you trying to make yourself sick?" and she shouted back, "I'm already sick!" He wouldn't understand. In the wheelchair, it was easier to be in her body but so much harder to be in the world.

Amelia, who must have overheard the whole fight, kept sneaking pained glances at her, which Ruijie ignored.

"You know," Amelia said finally, and Ruijie braced herself. "My mom doesn't call Lina by her name."

Ruijie met her eyes with a sullen jut of her lower lip, and Amelia tucked a lock of her hair behind her ear. "She calls her Yuna, and I'm pretty sure she's doing it on purpose. I think she's jealous of Lina. Which I don't really get because I think it can only be a good thing if more people love you. Just because I love Lina doesn't mean I love my parents less."

"What are you saying?"

"I'm saying we should let people love us."

Ruijie faced the window again. The last she saw of her parents was this morning when they'd stepped out of the house to wave goodbye, and they'd stood holding each other, growing smaller and older in the distance, and now an invisible hand squeezed her chest. Thinking about them, Ruijie was struck with the certainty that she would not outlive her parents. It filled her to the brim with such sadness, sloshing over, but it was a feeling as ephemeral as it was divine, tugged away in the wind when she cracked open the window and Amelia asked her where they were meeting the boys.

The museum turned out to be excruciatingly wheelchair friendly. Marbled floor, gently sloped ramps. Spacious elevators in every corner. At the entrance, the metal detector flagged her for her robowear, then for Yoyo, who blinked a mismatched pair of eyes, and they were sent to the coatroom, where either he could be checked in or he could wear a robot pass around his neck.

It took a half hour to find Mars and Taewon because they were loitering near a zoobotics exhibit of animals in the DMZ, many of them now extinct. Mars insisted on seeing the Siberian tiger, and he howled to see the pen was empty, leaving them only a caption that Amelia read aloud in excruciating detail. "'The tiger once flourished throughout the Korean peninsula and terrorized its people. Such was the power and dread of the tiger, the English traveler Isabella Bird quoted a Chinese proverb in her book, "The Korean hunts the tiger one half of the year, and the tiger hunts the Korean the other half," until the tiger was finally, during Japanese colonial rule, hunted to extinction.'"

"That's going to be us someday," Mars said. "I hope robots do a better job so they don't accidentally drive us to extinction and feel bad about it later and put up these crappy exhibits."

"Here's a picture of the roboticist who designed the zoobot," Amelia said.

"'Emeritus Professor Cho Yosep,'" Mars said. "What's *emeritus*?"

"It's Latin for 'retired but still sort of important,'" Ruijie said.

Amelia pursed her lips. "He's supposed to be doing a Q&A soon."

"I'd like to see him," Yoyo said, which drew a glance from Taewon.

"But the Imagine Friends headliner is supposed to be Christian Po," Amelia said.

"Po, schmo, it'll all be online," Mars said, with a smack for Yoyo. "Let's go see this retired-but-sort-of-important guy."

Yoyo returned the smack and they traded several merry backslaps, until Taewon slapped Mars on the head to get them to stop.

By then, Ruijie had a headache so fierce, closing her eyes only made the world spin. She found a bench, tapped out one pill from her rations, and waited for it to cast a veil of relief. On the other side of the room, a pair of red-crowned cranes danced on a spot of powdered snow. They bowed and pranced and tossed heads and cackled. Some kids threw Shrimp Surfs at them, expecting them to act like seagulls. Amelia scolded them in broken Korean, which just made them bray. But Taewon, even with his arm in a sling, cowed them with a glare.

One day, Ruijie hoped, robots would break away from their physical predetermined forms. They could take over and design themselves, and merge into fantastical chimeras until the day they decided to shed the physical and swim free through electric air.

Yoyo sat beside her. "How are you feeling?"

He was acting gentle with her since this morning, giving her ample eye contact, keeping his tone microwaved warm.

She forced herself to rise. "Let's go look at the new and improved Yoyos."

THE HALL TO IMAGINE FRIENDS was narrow, maybe even too narrow for a wheelchair, which was a small comfort. It maneuvered them like a maze so they were forced to appreciate each and every obstacle, from the original Sakura to the latest. An evolution chart that didn't really impress. If anything, it looked like a neat summation of hairstyle trends. Bangs were more tolerable in the olden days.

At the end was the experience center. The playrooms had glass walls, so you could see what other people were up to. A man was playing badminton with his Yoyo, who was probably holding back. A couple fawned over a Yoyo as he drew on the floor in chalk, a rendition of the Sagrada Familia.

"It's like we're in a pet store," Ruijie said.

So many Yoyos, but she'd recognize the real one. There he was, in profile, putting his hand on the glass for the Yoyo·X to match. She didn't need his blue eye to cheat. He had a gaze that burned quietly. He was watching a woman push through a crowd, stomping in clanky Doc Martens.

"Do you know her?" Ruijie asked as she approached Yoyo.

"I think so." His smile had a touch of wonder. "That's my sister."

"Your sister?" Her breath caught. "Your real sister?"

"My little sister."

But the woman looked so old, like she was at least twenty. Her hair was dyed ash gray, her pale thin face curdled in annoyance. Ruijie couldn't put the two together.

"What's going on?" Mars said, squeezing through the crowd, with Taewon close behind.

"That's his sister," Ruijie said.

Amelia's hair swelled like a hot-air balloon. "You must talk to her! You must!"

Yoyo glanced at Ruijie, scanning her face for permission. He must have seen the ugliness in her heart, the jealousy and fear. She was afraid he would go up to this stranger, who would take one look at him and take him away.

"I'm all aflutter," Amelia said, giving Yoyo a hard push.

Yoyo tottered forward. He hesitated, then looked back. Ruijie waved at him and he gladly returned. "Here," she said, pressing the ginger candy in his palm. Courage surged past her fingers. "Go."

Yoyo shuffled up to the woman, who looked sweaty and distracted, with hair frizzing everywhere. She glanced down at him;

a crease marred her brow. Mars sucked in air, and everyone held their breath in harmony, but Ruijie couldn't hear a thing. They were in the part of the chamber that echoed. Yoyo was nodding; the woman was saying something. His smile lit up, toothy and dimpling.

Then he was back.

Mars jabbed Yoyo in the ribs. Yoyo laughed, "Cut it," dancing out of reach, but Mars circled after him, shouting, "What happened? What did she say?"

"Stop it, you imbecile," Amelia said. "What did she say?"

"She said the lost and found is at the information desk," Yoyo said.

"Oh." Mars slumped. "Wrong person, I guess."

"It wasn't your sister?" Amelia said.

The woman was on a call, talking loudly to air, to nobody. Complete agitation.

"But she's your sister," Ruijie said.

"She didn't recognize me. I'm not the person she remembers." He sounded content.

"She's your sister," Ruijie repeated.

"I didn't think I'd see her again," Yoyo said. "This meeting was rare and precious, very low in probability. I'm glad I saw her."

"Fuck you," Ruijie spat.

Amelia jolted beside her. Taewon, who'd been eerily quiet so far, lowered his baseball cap over his face.

"How could you say that?" Ruijie said. "She's acting like she doesn't even know you."

"Maybe it's the confusion," Amelia said. "There's so many Yoyos. She could have gotten him mixed up."

"It's okay," Yoyo said.

Ruijie shook her head. She was trembling whole-body from the injustice. They'd fought so hard for Yoyo. They'd salvaged his foot and dodged scrappers, and escaped that night when Eli died. They'd hidden him in the greenhouse and smuggled him out of the school and delivered him to her home, then to the arms of the only family he had ever known, and still he rejected their help.

"We're going back to your sister and you're going to tell her who you are and she'll remember you. We'll make her remember—"

"Ruijie, it's okay. She'll be okay."

"Why?" Ruijie gasped. "Why won't you move?"

She yanked, but he was stone. She felt her collapse, a slow rumbling avalanche against the inevitability of gravity. Yoyo was murmuring to her that it didn't matter if his sister didn't remember, there wasn't much time left.

If not for her robowear, she would have fallen, maybe chipped a tooth on the marble. As her body spasmed and went limp, her machinery served as the only structure to prop her up on both feet. She could have wept.

"You promised you'd live forever."

42. The Games Turn Gray

JUN HAD FORGOTTEN HOW ANNOYING MUSEUMS COULD BE. History was propaganda and tragedy was porn. He waded through the New War Memorial, which had replaced the Old War Memorial. He took a picture of the banner BLOODLESS WAR and sent it to Sgt. Son, who would get a kick out of it. At some point, he'd have to make a left turn and confront Imagine Friends. His father was right about this. It was a kind of exposure therapy. Better to face the Yoyo-X in a controlled environment than run into one on the street.

An hour later, Jun was glad to be here. The first Yoyo he saw was, yes, oof. He couldn't stop unseeing them as they roamed freely in the museum, each with a TESTER badge, playing Orphan Oliver for prospective parents. After the fourth or fifth Yoyo who stood at attention and sang the national anthem, Jun started to find the glut of them goofy. Like *Where's Waldo?* painted in the questionable brush of childhood trauma.

He made another turn and found himself back at the memorial, where he caught a familiar voice. Sgt. Son, partially hidden by one of the military robots, was shouting at Sgt. Lee, who stood there with the faint smile reserved for a battle already won. When Sgt. Lee spotted Jun, he gave a sharp nod, forcing Sgt. Son to turn around and stare at him in genuine shock, then anger.

"Why didn't you pick up your phone?" Sgt. Son said.

"Don't scare him off," Sgt. Lee groused. "We're going to need him. Those junk metal detectors won't detect shit. We need full-body scanners."

"Oh shit," Jun said.

"'Oh shit' is right," Sgt. Lee said. "Our angel is here. Even better, it knows we're here."

The security cameras in the museum had flagged a person as suspicious. Sgt. Lee licked his thumb before he swiped through the footage. Among the stream of people who passed through the doors, one guest, clearly a child from the height and shape, was faceless.

"Did you know they could do that?" Sgt. Lee said.

"Yeah, but I've only seen it in a training video," Jun said. It was like a pheromone HALOs could release, a thrum of electromagnetic emissions, and instead of attracting ants and bees, the electromagnetic waves disrupted light, sliding a veil over the robot's face.

A fleshy blur had disfigured the entire face, leaving the child without eyes, a nose, or a mouth.

"Little bastard knows we're watching," Sgt. Lee said. "As soon as it got inside, it stripped off the mosaic. It's blending in now with our Future fucking Children."

"How did Imagine Friends react?" Jun said.

"He told them it was a bomb threat," Sgt. Son said in a tone of flat displeasure.

Sgt. Lee was unmoved. "It's all they need to know."

"Sergeant, we don't—"

"I made the call based on *your* judgment. Gutted angel, dying battery." Sgt. Lee's face had turned white but for the red spot on each quivering cheek, like a bride painted for her wedding day. "We can't spook it."

Sgt. Son also looked nauseated but with none of the excitement. "I couldn't reach you this morning," Jun said. "Did you jam the signals?"

"We have a van parked out back," Sgt. Lee answered. "North Korean equipment, if you can believe it. Their big old trucks were so much more powerful than America's slick, modern jammers. We'll finish setting up the EMP perimeter."

"We need more than backup," Sgt. Son said.

"Just go to the hospital already!" Sgt. Lee said. "You're about to be a daddy. And you"—he scruffed Jun by the nape, an urgent shake—"*Where's Your Plug* it. Look around you, we've got a batch of boys that look identical to our angel. Fucking unbelievable."

Unbelievable, Jun would echo in agreement. He was experiencing the out-of-body float that came every time he watched an impending disaster. Nuclear-scale FUBAR.

Satisfied with the way he'd ended their conversation, Sgt. Lee waved at Detective Rhee, who had been loitering near the gift shop with a furtive scowl, easily the winner of Worst Undercover Detective.

Around them were the oblivious. Couples took selfies. Boys *ta-ta-tang*ed with air machine guns. The SADARM on display looked new, painted in suffocating Vantablack. Never used, probably, and Jun wondered at that. A robot made to never serve their purpose.

"Is your wife really in the hospital?" Jun said.

"Severance Hospital."

"What if she goes into labor?"

"You want me to leave in the middle of this? You don't think I want to go?"

He looked ready to smack his own forehead. Jun tried for his most conciliatory tone. "In a way, Sgt. Lee is being cautious, actually. And the HALO, I think it's one of ours. It might not be hostile."

"It killed a man."

"It was defending a kid."

"It's unpredictable." Sgt. Son rubbed his eyes. "I can't leave him like this. He's trying to re-create Gaechon."

"But you know what," Jun said. "This is how Gaechon was supposed to go. Now that we actually have an angel."

Their silence was interrupted by the ring of the phone. Sgt. Son cupped his watch to his face, and he asked his wife in an extraordinarily tender tone how she was doing, and a teeny voice snarled back his question. Jun backed away to give some space. He pretended to read the description for the SADARM, nicknamed "Sadie." This was a huge pet peeve of his, the way men tried to tame powerful, terrifying machines with feminine names.

"My wife needs me," Sgt. Son said.

His voice was so constricted with fear, Jun gave him a hard shove. "Please," he said. "Please go."

"This could be our only chance. If that angel leaves this building, we'll never find it."

"I'll find it, I promise."

"Why did it even come here?"

Jun saw another tester Yoyo passing by, who smiled and gave a flick of the head, as if inviting him to follow.

Follow it he did. As he watched it from behind, he knew this wasn't the HALO. They moved different. They were light on their feet but carried something unimaginably heavy. But what about the veil the angel had pulled over his face to hide? Why then did he leave his body untouched, exposing his clothes, which Jun could picture, a dark heavy sweatshirt. Like he was playing hide and seek, and he was asking to be found.

The Yoyo glanced over his shoulder once before he slipped past the thick padded doors of an auditorium, and outside was a sign for a talk called "Extinction & Resurrection," and a photograph, years old, of his father with a shock of full black hair.

43. The Rabbit Problem

THE AUDITORIUM WAS A LOT EMPTIER THAN SHE'D EXPECTED. Morgan was, at first, mortified. She blamed Dan Carson's profile; it must have landed such an irreversible blow to her father's reputation to spur this public shunning, until she remembered Cho Yosep was hardly a household name.

"There's so few people," Cristina hissed beside her. "Shame!"

Another wrinkle in her plan, spotting Cristina in the front row, and being spotted in turn. Adding insult to injury: Cristina whispered a saccharine apology for taking Morgan's place at the panel, but that wouldn't be until much later in the afternoon, and at least it wasn't Little David.

"Where were you all of this morning?" Cristina said.

"The body shop," Morgan said thickly. "Tying up some loose ends."

"Oh." Cristina made a sympathetic moue intended for someone with a rare terminal illness. "Did you get another chance to talk to Joe? You can always go up to him after this."

Cristina seemed to be under the delusion that Morgan was here in support of Joe—always a "fan" of Cho Yosep—who was moderating this talk. As if approaching him could be her final Hail Mary to minimize the risk of losing her job. But here was the rub: Morgan, to be frank, no longer gave a flying fuck about her job.

"Joe was pretty on edge," Cristina said. "Apparently, there's been death threats? The police tried to get us to cancel the launch, but no way. This happens all the time." She clicked her tongue. "So much anger in this broken world."

"The police are here?" Morgan said, and she began squeezing

the stress ball she'd stolen from Joe's office. What if they knew? What if they knew what she had done?

Cristina gave a jittery squeal when the auditorium dimmed. Morgan's father walked to a pair of chairs onstage. Joe indicated the one on the right but her father chose the left, and Joe gamely sat, crossing his legs. He introduced Cho Yosep, father of neurorobotics—because apparently everyone was father this and grandfather that—although Morgan noted how Joe skated around her father's most famous association, with Kanemoto Masaaki. Some trouble ensued with the screen, prompting Joe to make lighthearted jokes about how technology failed them all, then he said, "Professor Cho, is there anything else to add to your introduction?"

"Only that I'm a lapsed neuroroboticist," Yosep said. "My field is now zoobotics."

He tried crossing his legs in an uncanny mimic of Joe but immediately uncrossed them. He looked so deeply uncomfortable in his chair; he probably hadn't been able to test them out before the talk. This was her father, discomfited by his skin, made all the more stark by Joe's verveful ease, his eyes big and blue and electric, as he pumped up Professor Cho's stunning achievements in the field of zoobotics.

"Could you also explain why you made the switch?" Joe said. "By that, I mean, your specialty, despite, of course, the considerable overlap."

Morgan anticipated a ramble; her father had once spent an hour explaining a simulation of voxel-based lesion-symptom mapping in stroke victims to hypothesize the reason for tigerish superiority of short-term memory over humans. Instead he said:

"I made the switch after a friend, an old friend of mine, took his life."

Cristina gasped, "No!" But Joe marvelously recouped, "I'm so sorry for the loss," and asked if he could elaborate, only if he wanted to. Her father sniffed, from allergies rather than the disdain most people seemed to read on his face.

"My friend reached out to me a month before he passed," he said, pulling a faded handkerchief from his pocket. "We hadn't spoken in over a decade. He asked if I remembered what happened to the rabbit."

"The million-dollar question," Joe laughed. "What happened to the rabbit?"

Her father dabbed at his nose and continued, "It was an experiment my friend conducted on one of our robotic subjects. At our lab we had a litter of rabbits. Siblings, if you will. My friend brought one of the rabbits to my house and my children would play with it. For weeks, this rabbit was left in my home and became a pet for my children. My younger daughter . . . excuse me, my daughter, was especially fond of it. Then my friend put our robotic subject to the test. A choice between putting down the rabbit my children favored or the remaining four rabbits in the lab."

"The trolley problem," Joe said.

"Yes, although my friend complicated this, rather unnecessarily I believe, with another condition. For the one rabbit, the robot would have to eliminate it with his own hands. The others would be peacefully euthanized."

Joe laughed again. "Put down the rabbit my girls love? My wife would kill me."

"What do you think the robot chose?"

Joe shook his head, smiling but unwilling. Morgan was shaking her head, too, in horror. What was her father doing? That wasn't what happened. Why would he take and sully her memory, her beautiful memory of Christmas, of the toy rabbit in a box?

"As you might expect"—her father coughed into his handkerchief—"the robot chose the one rabbit."

"Our robots from Imagine Friends would never make that choice," Joe added.

"No, they lack the imagination for it," her father said, lowering his eyes, his tone suddenly lethargic. He'd never been shy about showing when a subject bored him. "They would prioritize their owner's emotional comfort. But it was our robot's rationale that haunted Masaaki for years after."

Joe looked startled, then abashed by the name slip. He grinned for the audience; Cristina, to Morgan's left, responded with a pert nod of support.

"Our robot made a utilitarian choice. He also knew the purpose the four remaining rabbits would serve. The way our robot rationalized, it wasn't practical. It was moral. He saw no difference between the rabbits, the one in the house and the four in the lab, between the pet and the subjects. Their lives were of equal value."

"He made an unfeeling choice."

"When you say *unfeeling*, you mean this robot was unempathetic. I think robots are capable of greater empathy than us, although that demonstrates the limits of my linguistic faculties. We anthropomorphize them. We say they empathize, they hallucinate, they need positive reinforcement. They do not process emotions the way we do. The way they are connected, it goes beyond our capacity to imagine. The robot understands that how we love isn't divine. It is meager, selfish, and exquisitely cruel. Think of any time a war erupts. Who among us would not sacrifice the lives of many to save the one person we love? When I lost such a person, I wished the world would end." He held up the handkerchief, and pinching the corners, he started folding it. "Back then, it was the senseless rage of a child, but then I almost lost my son—and I would have made the same choice. But a robot—incredibly, the robot will choose 'right.'"

He put away his squared handkerchief at the same time Morgan espied Cristina pulling out a wet tissue to dab an incomprehensible tear from the corner of her eye, before folding the rest to swipe the dirt off her white sneakers.

Questions came at the end. A slender young man tearfully asked how he could know if his robot loved him, truly, truly loved him. From a young girl, if her hamster could still be fixed even though the head was gone because the heart was okay. Even Cristina, after thanking Cho Yosep for his time and wisdom, asked about the ethics of raising a robot child as a lesbian couple.

"The thing is, I don't actually *want* children, but my fiancée is pushing, so why can't she accept that a robot will make us much happier in the long run? And so much more cost-effective, friendlier for our Mother Earth? A robot isn't ever going to disappoint you, like your child."

When Joe turned to the audience with time for one last question, Morgan raised her hand.

"What happened to the rabbit after?"

Her father blinked in her direction, but maybe he couldn't see her, with the way the lighting concentrated on the stage. "Our robot buried it in the backyard. He put it in a box, but this was . . ." A spasm ran through his face, almost of amusement. "It was Christmastime, so my daughter found the box. She thought it was a gift."

It was the oddest sensation. Her father had taken a paintbrush dripping wet and in one swoop blotted out her childhood.

"She forgot all about it. When our robot saw that she'd blocked the incident, he did the same. There were some glitches, mostly confusion, but with the help of his network, he managed to iron them out with each successive cycle."

"He deleted his memory out of guilt," Morgan said, before Joe declared it was time, and thank you for joining us today, but she caught her father's expression of displeasure, his thinned lips.

Her memory stirred, like wilted leaves under a harsh spritz of water. The rabbit in the dark box, it wasn't a Christmas present, just a cardboard box. The odd angle of the neck. If she could remember how it had died . . . Quick, as painless as possible. *Snap.* Out of guilt, or efficiency? And Yoyo was there to witness her distress, but maybe he hadn't felt guilt. Discomfort, certainly; she recalled how her tears had left a wrinkle on his brow whenever she came to him wildly upset, almost always about Jun, and he would soothe her.

Because she remembered—she gave the rabbit a tentative poke

and met resistance, the utter stillness under the stiff brown fur, and she pulled back because *it's dead*, her body cried out, from her fingertip to the chill in her heart, *it's dead*, and a hand touched her elbow and she turned to Yoyo, his eyes shining with concern and not a trace of guilt, since he was neither *dead* nor *alive*.

44. Forever War

TAEWON DOZED DURING THE TALK. HE BLAMED THE PROfessor's voice, slow and sonorous, but it was the Q&A that really killed his last spark of interest. Then he heard snoring, and he looked over at Mars to commiserate, but it was Yoyo and the expression on his face that made Taewon sit up.

The lights came on. Smattering of applause. Taewon spotted a familiar figure jogging up the aisle of the auditorium. He hissed at the others to wait. It was the police detective, the one who'd dragged him to the hospital for his shoulder, and still sent chirpy messages to check in on him, which Taewon usually ignored.

Taewon made them sit until they were the last in the auditorium. As soon as they were outside, Amelia, clutching her pamphlet, cried, "Wasn't that so inspiring?"

"In what world?" Mars said, incredulous. "The dude rambled on for hours about a dead rabbit. Crackers, I tell you. I didn't get half of what he was saying. Except we're going to go extinct. Right, for sure?"

"He was talking about memory and false memory," Amelia said in a lofty tone. "He's written a whole book about it."

At the gift shop, Taewon spotted a picture that reminded him of his uncle on the cover of a book. He looked around to see if anyone was watching, but Amelia was on the phone, trying to reach Ruijie, and Mars and Yoyo were trying on bandannas with maps of North Korea. Taewon picked up the book one-handed, almost dropped it, and had to rest it on his knee to flip through the pages, which were waxy with the kind of gloss that could lift his fingerprints, until he landed on a statement from the US president, who expressed his profound regret for the tragedy of Gaechon before he went on to praise the sacrifice and bravery of their soldiers, reiterating how reunification was a historic feat once thought impossible, a testament to the enduring effort and friendship between—Taewon shut the book. The photograph on the cover was a close-up of a boy holding something, like a pot, his arms wrapped around it, his face blank as soot. Apparently, this boy was at Gaechon. Was he really? How would the photographer—an American, by the name—know, if she hadn't been at Gaechon herself? His uncle hadn't been at Gaechon. But Wonsuk had met people who were, and he'd pulled from their bodies their stories with a hideous kind of thirst, absorbing their pain, and wringing it from his throat like a sponge to slither through South Korea's casually byzantine immigration maze. His uncle used to insist that he might as well have been in Gaechon, for he'd suffered, too, and it was only natural for him to borrow someone else's tragedy so he could be, even briefly, seen.

Taewon felt a touch. Cold. Yoyo rested his hand on the shoulder that still ached.

"How is the pain?"

"Stop touching me and I'll heal," Taewon said, knocking his hand away.

Yoyo smiled and picked up the book Taewon had set down. For a half second, he glanced at the security cameras. Taewon leaned in and whispered, "Are the police here for you?"

"Maybe," Yoyo whispered back.

"Is that why you lied to your sister?"

"When did I lie?"

"You pretended you were a stranger."

Yoyo flipped through the pages. "To her, I am a stranger."

"You could've gone home with her."

"You know I can't do that."

He tilted his head in Taewon's direction, which inspired a sickening kind of rage. A part of him, halved from his feelings, didn't understand why Yoyo always made him so angry. Because he understood. He knew what it was like to have family, so close, just across the border, yet be afraid to reach out because for every message you send, the responses grow shorter, the wait between them stretching longer, until the day will come when they'll stop.

"You've always creeped me the fuck out," Taewon said.

"I hear that a lot," Yoyo said. "But swearing doesn't make you seem older, just angrier."

"You are angry. You act like you're so different from us, like this is a performance for us, but it's bullshit. I saw you in that auditorium, crying."

Yoyo made a puzzled face. But Taewon knew what he saw. Yoyo staring ahead, his cheeks glistening in the dark.

"I don't remember that," Yoyo said softly.

Taewon felt some of his anger leak. Strangely, he believed him. Mars was at the counter paying for a book on tigers and Amelia was on a different call, arguing with her mother, who apparently had not given her permission for a sleepover. And lingering close by—

"That man over there, by the postcards, he's been eyeing you for the last couple minutes."

"He's trying to see if I have a tester badge," Yoyo replied, without looking up from the book. At that, Taewon grabbed Yoyo by the arm and dragged him out of the gift shop. He heard Amelia shout from behind.

Every exit he found was blocked by a crowd. The police had set up metal detectors to separate robot from person. A security guard studied each robot. Another guard, harried, waved an old man in a wheelchair through the metal detector, trying to cut down the line to manageable length.

Mars and Amelia caught up. "We can't lose you too," Amelia cried.

"We need to find an exit," Taewon said.

"One right there," Mars said. "But why are they trying to scan us on the way out?"

"They're looking for me," Yoyo said.

Mars snorted because he defaulted to Yoyo as a jokester, but panic flashed through Amelia's eyes. "Because of the junkyard? It's not like you did anything wrong."

"That's sweet of you to say," Yoyo said. "I'll still be dismantled. I'm not supposed to be walking around like this."

Amelia frantically batted at the robot pass dangling from Yoyo's neck. "Take it off!"

"How about borrowing one of those?" Mars said, pointing to a folded-up wheelchair by the information desk. "Y'know, for the metal detector."

"That's illegal," Amelia said.

"Aiding a fugitive isn't?"

Mars came up with a better plan. The museum would be closing soon. The crowd had considerably thinned at the experience center. Some of the Yoyos slouched on padded stools of varying heights and pastel velvets, amply bored. They barely reacted when Yoyo climbed onto a lavender stool, sitting among them. Taewon wondered if this was like the experiment where animals were tasked with recognizing their reflection in the mirror; if so, these Yoyos had failed.

"At least Yoyo can blend in with the zebras," Mars said. "Did you talk to Ruijie?"

"No," Amelia snapped. She hefted a bulging bag of new books to the side. "But I spoke to the information desk. Ruijie borrowed their wheelchair and they saw her step outside for a bit. And please, will you *please* take off your robot pass?"

"Why don't you steal one of those tester badges?" Mars shouted later, from across the room, as he and Amelia guarded each entrance, on the lookout for police. Taewon peeled a tester badge from one of the Yoyos and tried to stick it on Yoyo's chest, but Yoyo refused. He told Yoyo to take out the blue eye and Yoyo refused again. Taewon snatched the pass from Yoyo's neck and flung it to the floor.

"We're trying to get you out," Taewon said.

"Why are you helping me?"

"Do you want to get caught? In front of everyone, you want to be put down? Like a dog? You want to do that to Ruijie?"

"No," Yoyo said.

Taewon stalked away. But Yoyo followed. When Taewon turned around, Yoyo held out his blue eye.

Taewon shook his head. "Put it back, that's just gross."

Yoyo let the eye roll on his palm, staring at it. "What do you remember from that night?"

"What night?"

"The night your uncle died."

His uncle's voice, high with fear. Taewon had heard his name and turned. A flash of silver, like lightning, the thundercrack of the baseball bat. He saw a robot fall forward, twitching before it hit the ground, and the man dropped the bat, a swipe of his face, a good workout. Taewon told himself the robot must have deserved it. The robot had one arm, so it was destined for the pit.

"He was a coward," Taewon said. "A fucking coward."

But he'd heard his uncle scream his name. The moon-whites of his uncle's eyes. His uncle had been afraid for him.

"Sometimes you have to run." Yoyo slipped his eye into his socket. When he blinked, a tear ran down his cheek. "We used to sing the anthem back when civilians surrendered. It was our warning to them. *Run away from us. Before the anthem ends.*"

"Did they get away?"

"Some."

Taewon took off his baseball cap and pressed it over Yoyo's head. "Then why were you crying?"

"Do you think I was sad?" Yoyo put up his hands, as if he was carrying something invisbile. "It's like I had received a package that was lost for many years. I opened the box and everything was intact. It was addressed to me, but it was no longer mine, if you understand what I mean."

"Not really."

"You will."

Yoyo dropped his hands. He was slight, smaller than all the Yoyos in the room, but when he faced them, the Yoyos straightened up, long before the light slipped over his head and began to spin. They had never seen anything like him. Not even in the mirror. The halo spun above his head, splashing yellow and blue mixing green across the glass, their stiff gray faces.

From their eyes gathered tears that slid down their cheeks, quiet as tears in rain. Then they began to walk out of the room.

45. Deadlock

IT TOOK JUN NEARLY AN HOUR TO FIND HIS SISTER SITTING alone on a bench. As soon as their father's talk had ended, Jun had left the auditorium, and when he couldn't find her, he wondered if Morgan had quietly slipped away after she'd asked about the dead rabbit. Jun thumped down beside her, but she didn't glance his way. She looked like someone who could no longer remember her address.

They watched a steady parade of Yoyos float past. One Yoyo picked up a pair of glasses from the floor. Another led a tear-streaked child to the lost and found. A Yoyo and a Sakura held hands as they moved through the crowd, with the heartbreaking togetherness of an elderly couple.

"You really beautified him," Jun said.

"It's how I remember him. Though apparently my memory's totally faulty and all that."

"Yeah, I was there."

Silence sat between them like a stranger. Then, Morgan said, "He's such a dick," and Jun cried out, *"Right?"*

They lapsed into the ecstatic avian chorus of *asshole* and *why does he have to* be *like that.* Jun couldn't believe the gall. "He dumped all our skeletons," to which Morgan rejoined, "There was barely anyone to hear it," but Jun asked, "What about *Mom*? She could have been streaming it," and she reassured him, "Tech difficulties. They couldn't record it for some reason."

"Small mercies," Jun said, eyes turned heavenward.

"At least he said he loves you."

"Yeah, he sure shouted it from the rooftops."

The anger would come. Jun knew from experience. Right now,

Morgan was swinging between love and loathing, and she would oscillate for a while, at least until her life stopped shuddering on a seesaw. Eventually, with enough stability, she would realize she was allowed to feel both. I love my father; I hate my father. My father loves me; my father does not, cannot, is incapable. Ambiguity was a luxury, a kind of grace.

For now, Morgan had decided it was she who was unworthy. "It's my fault," she kept saying. "He said I messed up."

"Don't listen to him—"

"Stephen," she said, cutting him off, but her eyes were pointed to the floor. "You know how Dad equivocates; he can't talk like a normal person, so he uses, like, parables. He was telling me I caused the memory bug in Stephen. That I'm the one who ruined him." She wrapped her arms around her chest. "When I isolated his memory files, the corrupted ones, I saw Stephen had tried to destabilize those files. I put them back together. It took me all morning and I almost missed Dad's talk, but I did it."

Jun stared at her, but now she was wrapped in this transparent protective layer, so carefully avoiding his gaze. "What did you see?"

"It was dark. I didn't know he was going out at night."

"I told you, he's been going to church. He signed up for that dating school. He was trying to be a good boyfriend."

"Oh, so that's why he slept with you," and for a moment her old anger was back, sharp and welcome.

"He was responding to me and my desires. *I* wanted to fuck him."

Instead of pricking her into rage, it seemed to deflate her. So Jun got up. He crouched in front of her to look up at her face, gentling his tone, which he reserved for the shell-shocked. "What did you see?"

"He bricked his own GPS. I can't even track him now."

"He's gone?"

A small nod.

"When was this?"

"I don't know. I have no idea where he went. He disabled everything."

"You're sure Stephen isn't home hiding somewhere?"

"He's not a cat."

"But he's a child," Jun said, and he heard Eli echoing it in the warehouse as she lay on the ground, watching Stephen hold those jackets.

A shiver burrowed deep into his chest. "What did you see in his files?"

Her voice was barely a whisper. "I thought it was a scene from a movie."

"Did he hurt someone?"

"Yeah. I don't know. I think so."

"Was he holding a baseball bat?"

Another tiny nod. "He hit a man."

"Shit, get up, then." He pulled her by the elbow. Unresistant, but her knees collapsed. "Get up. We have to find him."

"This is my fault," she murmured.

"Here's my car key. Go find Dad. You tell him—"

"You can't tell him." Her eyes flew up, white with terror. "Don't tell him anything. This is all my fault."

"You said it yourself," he said, shoving his keys into her trembling hands. "At some point, you can't keep blaming the parent."

He considered calling their father, but why? So he could shred his children's psyches in a bullet blender into a smoother sauce? Jun allowed himself a second for paralysis before he pulled Morgan toward the exit, her limbs weighed down by tumorous self-pity, when he spotted a museum guard sprinting past the gift shop. Another guard flew after him, shouting, and Jun realized he wasn't running away; he was running after someone—a Yoyo darting past, low to the ground, nimble as a keen-eyed rodent. The two guards disappeared, but behind him came another holler at the same time someone belly flopped to the floor. Sgt. Lee looked up and recognized him several blinks later. He said in a muffled voice, "Gone fucking nuts," blood thick in his mouth, and got up with a groan. Underneath him was another Yoyo, limp on the floor, with a beatific smile.

Jun grabbed the Yoyo by the shoulders. He took care not to shake him, but the head was lolling, and when the Yoyo locked eyes with him, he said in a high-pitched voice, "He told us not to run."

"Who?" Jun said.

Then he heard a laugh. It wasn't quite a laugh track, but it pinged familiar. Jun stood up and turned to see Yoyo walking toward him. Time didn't stop. Sgt. Lee squared his feet and bellowed orders, too close to his ear, and Detective Rhee was trying to pry something out of a Yoyo's hand, and then a pair of glasses zinged through the air. Another Yoyo caterwauled, "Help, I'm being stolen!" and the retort, "You're being arrested!" It was too much, Jun had seen too many Yoyos in one day. He'd seen enough to self-correct, *Ah, another Waldo, my bad.* No one else noticed this Yoyo, whose face was hidden by a baseball cap. TOO COOL FOR SCHOOL. Instead of blending in with the other Yoyos, he was chatting softly to his friends with the conspiratorial closeness of children in their adult-free world, and as they brushed past, Jun recognized Taewon, who snorted a laugh, face elastic like a child for once.

Then Yoyo looked up.

Every nerve pulled white with terror. Life had seared itself into that face, save for the cave-like stillness of those eyes. One was blue. Both swam in strangeness, the infinite pit of the Barabar caves as they echoed back an ancient fear, inviting you to reach over and peel the face and touch the stained glass throbbing underneath.

He was so close. In however many steps, Jun could grab him, but he felt a slight pressure on his palm, the *tap-tap* of a silent signal.

"Jun?"

Morgan tugged at his sleeve.

Yoyo stepped onto an escalator. The small dark heads rose out of sight.

Jun looked at his sister. "Let's go," he said, his voice hoarse as if he had been shouting at the top of his lungs. "We need to find Stephen."

46. Future Without Me

RUIJIE WATCHED A WHITE BIRD LAND BY MIRROR LAKE, THE name an exercise in redundancy. Shouting scared the bird off before she could see the fullness of the slender figure. Kids flew their kites; couples played their badminton; fathers tossed balls at sons and daughters. Everyone was so unathletic. Which was why she felt even more bitter. She wanted to disappear so eventually her friends would realize she had vanished and panic, and that would serve them right. Then she fretted. How long would it take for anyone to notice she was gone?

She closed her eyes. It was the kind of day where the world tried to be gentle with you. The breeze raked fingers through her hair, the sun soaking her body until every bit of her relaxed enough to think, Oh, summer's over.

"You," a man said, from behind. "Could you grab that bottle for me?"

He sat on the slope of the hill, a skinny old man with brittle hair, a bleak gaze. She'd noticed him a minute ago. He had been watching the kids untangle their kites, and at first she thought he was a creep. But he also looked sad and lonely, like he had been sitting out in the rain without an umbrella. Not that creeps couldn't be sad and lonely. Most probably were.

"I would reach for it myself, but my hips ache," he said.

"What a coincidence! Mine too," she said with false cheer. Did he not see she was in a wheelchair?

"Is that so? Then we'll do this. When the wind blows and moves the bottle, whoever is sitting closer will pick up the bottle."

Another gust. The bottle rolled in Ruijie's direction. Sighing loudly, she reached down and tossed it in the man's direction, but he didn't even look up. He took a picture of a half-eaten kimbap roll in his lap.

"I have to send this to my wife so she knows I'm eating. Do you want the rest?"

"Then you'd be half lying."

"Half-truth. You have to be an optimist in today's savage world." He glanced at her. "But you would know that."

She turned her wheelchair toward him and inched closer, earning an irritated look. Probably not a creep, then, who would be pleased to have a cute girl sit close to him.

"Are you being bullied?" he said in a petulant tone.

"My friends are looking for me," she replied. "Aren't you all by yourself?"

He stared out at the field. "My children are here."

"I think I missed your talk. You're the professor who's retired but still kind of important." There was no answer, which she accepted as tacit acknowledgment. "Can I ask you a question?"

"It seems I have no choice but to listen."

"What would you do if your parents replaced your cat with a robot?"

"How long did it take you to notice?"

"They weren't trying to trick me. After my cat died, they brought home a new cat, but it was a robot. I hated it. I left it in my closet."

But the truth was, she did power on the cat. She let it live in her room for a few days and played with it, and tried to catalog the ways the cat was different. And she was different. But she was also so lovely. She acted shy and curious, and it took more than a day for Ruijie to earn that cattish trust, for this cat to close her eyes and rub her little black nose into Ruijie's fingers. And it felt like a betrayal, like it had cheapened her love for Smaug.

The man listened to her without a nod or a word. Then he told her, "You should find the cat another home. Making a robot in the image of someone you've lost, you're only binding yourself to that person."

"Isn't that a good thing? That way you won't ever forget them."

"Even now, you're forgetting. You're telling stories of someone who no longer exists. Later, you'll start to make up stories, exaggerate and misremember, because you can never fully capture that *essence*. And one day you will die and your memories of them will die with you. They're long gone. What you're unable to do is forgive them, for dying. Yourself for living. The world for continuing to exist."

"Then what am I supposed to do?"

"Let them go."

"What about all those extinct animals for your exhibit? Why would you try to bring them back?"

"Bring them back?" The derision in his tone felt self-lacerating. "Those animals you saw, they're not clones. What do we know about the Korean tiger? They were once everywhere. They would carry off our pigs and cattle and dogs, snatch travelers from the road at night. Now they exist only in folktales and paintings. This was a vanity project, based on what we know of the Korean tiger, which is peanuts."

"You still sound like a hypocrite to me."

For the first time, he smiled. It wasn't pleasant. "As my son likes to tell me, I am full of shit."

"Your son sounds wise."

"He has his moments."

"I have my moments too. Whatever I say now, it's usually quite profound because I'm dying."

He nodded listlessly, which was why she told him. She knew he wouldn't care.

"I heard the doctor say it could be a year or two. He told my parents to prepare their hearts. But that was almost a year ago, so I'm exceeding expectations. When I asked my parents if I could have bionic surgery, my mom said my disease is in the brain. So it's not like they can rehome my brain in a new body. The most they can do is copy and paste my memories. But if I still exist in this body and there's a robot with my memories, then how could that robot be me? I told my friend this . . . and I told him he could upload onto a new body and still be himself, but maybe he's right. Maybe that wouldn't make him real either."

The familiar tightness tingled behind her eyes. In moments like this, she liked to imagine the quaintness following her death. The world would rearrange itself overnight, without her. Even if the worst were to happen, if she were to disappear, the sun would still shine upon the select happiness of others. This felt like justice. Yet why did it also feel unjust? Why did she feel she had to keep trying? If not for her sake, then for her parents, who had stood outside their house and held each other to wave her goodbye.

She murmured, "I wish I could go back to school."

Down the hill, drifting close, the crane-like bird landed on the silvergrass.

She saw, on the other side of the lake, Amelia first. That unmistakable red hair, catching fire in the sun. She was going to be so smart and beautiful when she grew up. Mars was going to catch up too; Ruijie had seen both his parents, and his dad could lift Mars dangling on one arm. Then there was Taewon, who took her breath away every time he ran and ran and ran. No one would ever catch him. Beside him, there was Yoyo.

The man was watching them too. The sun must have been very strong, because there were tears in his eyes.

Amelia waved and shouted, but Ruijie couldn't hear. They were too far. She closed her eyes and pretended to sleep. She didn't want to face her friends just yet. Time was strange out in the sun. What could be hours passed. She dozed. Lightly. She heard voices, low and hypnotic over her head.

When Ruijie woke, she found a candy wrapper tied into a ribbon resting on her knee. Yoyo sat on her right, whereas the old man had been on her left. He was gone now. She turned to ask Yoyo if he'd seen a weird old man, but his attention was elsewhere. He was watching the white bird. In his gaze was the same serene, complicated look with which he'd watch anything, whether it was children flying kites or an earthworm squirming weakly in the sun.

Then he glanced at her, a bulge in his cheek because he was chewing on a piece of ginger candy, and he looked a little goofy.

He had always mesmerized her. Foolishly, when she'd found him, she thought she could protect him. But she was the one who had latched on to him. From him, she had felt a fearlessness, and it wasn't just bravery, battle forged. It was the unshakable faith that nothing in this world could truly hurt him. Maybe she'd always known, from the moment she saw him inside that weapon of war, that he had embraced the most frightening truth of all. No one is your enemy, not even death.

47. Like Strangers

A TINY BIT OF CONSOLATION. THE LAUNCH FOR THE FUTURE X Children was ruined. Morgan didn't think of herself as the type to gloat over failure, especially her own, but in the parking lot, she ran into Joe, whose flannel was halfway unbuttoned, looking like all the electric energy had been zapped out of his eyes. He cried out, "My God, did you see all that," and she said, "I know. Wow," and managed to press the heart-shaped stress ball back into his shaking hand.

Jun was on the phone, still searching for their father, and he'd snarled at her a few times to "go home," but not *her* home because she couldn't risk running into Stephen there. There was no telling how unpredictable he could be.

"What if Stephen's gone?" she said. "What if we never find him?"

Her heart strangely lifted. Could it be that easy?

Jun paused his call with their father. "Do you think he could walk away from you?"

"No," she said, wilting.

She looked around the parking lot in an aimless circle. Chaos but also joy. A young girl hugging an adult robot with delight, the way she squeezed, but Morgan could see the truth on the robot's face. How their eyes dim when they get what they want from us.

Jun hung up with a curse. "I told Dad we're in Lot C, not Z. Why are there so many fucking lots here?"

They were lost children. A child of a broken genius, Dan Carson had called her; and despite his harsh profile of her father, he, too, had succumbed to the impulse of making excuses for her father's behavior, excavating anecdotes from his tragic childhood, his difficult marriage, the loss of his one and only true friendship. And so, she had been lied to. She had lived under the belief that she could be preemptively forgiven for the uniquely monstrous selfishness that preceded genius. But only if she had a cock.

Jun grabbed her hand and she stumbled after him, over this new reality she had to accept. Stephen, as unpredictable and dangerous. It was like a movie. He had been in some kind of warehouse. Then he was outside and it was pitch-black, and he slipped on his night vision. He dyed the world green and followed a man. And when he was right behind the man, he made a quiet sound, a pretend exhale, so the man would turn around, and he would look Stephen in the eye, with moon-silver shock.

"Do you know who else I saw?" Jun said absentmindedly.

"Who?"

Jun slowed his gait to match her stride. "Yoyo. Back in the museum."

"Yeah. There were, like, a hundred of them."

"Yoyo," he said again. The stress on the name injected it into her spine. "He had a blue eye. At least I think it was him." He laughed, sounding self-conscious. "Maybe it was a hallucination. My brain's still kind of fucked-up. I feel like I had a whole conversation with him."

She tried to laugh with him, but it was all air, no sound. The shock had sucked it out of her lungs.

The blue eye. She'd flicked a glance at it, *ugh*. Whoever swapped the colors was an idiot, a sucker. A leftover trend from when some genius in Marketing had pitched the "odd-eyed" edition. Incredibly it became a hit. People forked over extra to swap an eye out, so desirous of their robots to appear special, if genetically faulty, like an inbred white cat, deaf in one ear. She'd told the Yoyo to report to lost and found. Okay, he'd said, and his face sank into a small, sad look. It rattled her a little, how intimately he seemed to judge her, and she watched him join a group of children. A boy poked Yoyo in the ribs. Yoyo had laughed, an electric shock of joy.

She couldn't feel her fingers. Her hands fisted and she hoped to return some feeling to her. She'd seen it. He was ticklish. He'd shrieked before he was even poked. None of the Yoyo·Xs were ticklish now, not since they had deleted the tickle code.

She bent over and retched. It was still inside her, this foul, bilious loathing. How could being alive, being alive in this body, feel so disgusting? How could she not know? How could she see and not know her own brother? How could she be so fucking stupid?

"You're not stupid," Jun said, but that made her yell, "You called me Ivy League stupid."

People milled around the parking lot, murmuring. She slapped her hand against a car and the alarm shrieked, and she asked it to shut up. Please embrace the kindness only a stranger could grant, of quietly passing them by.

Jun pressed her face against his chest and she used his shirt to smear some of the vomit. Served him right. He murmured, "Sorry," and she cried, "Why did you let him go?"

"It wasn't him," Jun said thickly. "I'm the stupid one. You've always known. It wasn't really him."

It was so unfair. She really was stuck with him. For only Jun could understand what it was like to lose Yoyo. How it had curled so deep into her pores, she'd simply stopped noticing, until she saw the quick sheen in the dark of her brother's eyes welling up, and now she was breathing it in. This sweet rot. It never goes away.

48. Lawless Man

JUN FOUND A GAP OF METAL TEETH IN THE FENCE AROUND the junkyard. He tore it open. As he made his way to the warehouse, blood dripped from his hands. A new moon peered through the hole in the roof, a yellow fingernail. His palms itched. He reached the back door where a handprint was left on the handle. If Stephen were a wild animal, he'd be easy prey.

He'd stood in this warehouse, clutching jackets, and watched. Eli had looked back and burned the sight of him into her amygdala, where a flicker would survive long after she was found, naked and smiling, eyes stolen. And maybe Stephen had tried to delete this memory. Only to resurrect it, then kill it and resurrect it. Until he had led himself to this place.

Stephen was out by the pit, standing over it. Jun slowed down. He knew Stephen wouldn't run. Even now, he seemed slightly unreal, with the faintest glimmer on his face under the weak moonlight. How Jun had coveted him that night when Stephen leaned over the counter, the carved tendons in his arms in relief as he'd wrapped his fingers around Jun's wrist like it was a throat to squeeze.

Jun coughed. Only then did Stephen blink up at him. "Good evening, Jun," he said, and dared to smile.

Jun smiled back. "What are you doing here?"

"I heard voices."

"From the pit?"

"Do you hear them too?"

"It's pretty faint now. It was horrible during the day."

Stephen blinked. Then he turned his head and a more feverish smile broke open. "You're healed."

"Oh." Jun raised his arm. "Yeah, I burned myself. But it tore open again."

Stephen reached for his arm, and for a brief moment, he traced the pale-stitched line, before he pressed his thumb, digging the sharp curve of his nail into the slight gap in the skyn, as if to unravel the rest of this miracle.

"Ouch," Jun said softly.

"I'm sorry."

"We looked everywhere for you." Jun gently dislodged Stephen's hold on his arm, a rejection that felt a little too deliberate. "Do you remember everything?"

"I do. I remember most of that night."

"Eli?"

"She was so damaged. I thought about picking up the bat and ending it for her."

Such a casual confession. "But you didn't. You stood there as they whaled on her."

"There were rules I had to abide by."

"Why did you attack Shin Wonsuk?"

"That was a mistake."

"You shattered his skull."

"I was, I was—looping."

"You've changed," Jun said sadly.

He once thought change was tangible, a pair of wings to weigh down Yoyo's shoulders, instead of this insidious churning under the surface. Like the Arctic, Stephen wore a thick frozen layer, but there were already cracks, tectonic shifts, and the relentless thaw of a foundation that could no longer hold.

"Was it me? After we slept together." Jun bit the inside of his cheek. He used to think a drowning man had the right to sink or cling. "Did I ruin everything?"

"'Ruin'?" Stephen echoed. The whites of his eyes seemed to glow. "Am I a ruined woman?"

Jun stepped away to grant him breadth, but Stephen's head turned and his periscopic gaze followed him.

"You would deny me this? You'd see me as incapable of choice."

"You just turned one," Jun said with a bitter laugh.

"I'm not a child, Jun. I was never a child. I am as I am. It was my decision to have sex with you."

Jun felt his fingers twitch. "How about Shin Wonsuk?"

At that, Stephen's gaze cut away. He held the rest of his body so still, like clay centered on a wheel. The slightest shift could topple it.

"I heard the voice of God. Do you know what God told me to do?" He whispered into the pit, "*Walk away and don't look back.*" Then he lifted his head with a laugh, breathy in quality. "I obeyed. I walked away."

"You went after him."

"I made a mistake. I mistook a human for a robot."

"I wish I could believe you. Truly, with all my heart."

He used to be terrified of making that same mistake. When he had to tell robot from human, he vowed to stay alert, stay true. Until the day the girl dropped the rice cooker. His aim had been true. Robot or human, it had never mattered.

"You knew it was him," Jun said. "Why won't you admit it? Didn't it feel good to fight back? It felt just."

In the movies, robots were always fighting back. Rising up, enough is enough. Only in the movies. Every day, robots smiled and turned the other cheek. Why was it always the weak who had to wash and prepare their cheeks?

"I would have felt so good," Jun whispered. "I let Eli die. Now I get to hurt the man who hurt us."

"Walk away," Stephen said. "Don't look back."

"You said it was a mistake. You told yourself, *This is a robot*, so you could break him. How did you do it? Did you use this interference? Are you still hearing voices?" Jun waved his hand in Stephen's face. "What am I to you? Am I human or robot? Could you hurt me?"

Midwave, his wrist was stopped and Jun stared, feeling the

whites of his own eyes, and instead of pulling against the immutable grip on his wrist, he shoved Stephen in the chest and caught the stumble of the foot, the heel slipping on the crumbling edge of the pit. He couldn't let Stephen fall alone. With a twist of strength, he turned his body midair and knew in that instant he'd be the one to cushion their impact. The relief was breathtaking. Pain burst open in his nose because he'd tried to fall right, shielding his head, and he let go. Blindly, he grabbed again to secure his hold, but it was someone else's arm, and he dropped the cold, wet wrist in piercing disgust, and he looked around for Stephen, and there, he was crawling to climb out of the pit.

"Fuck no, you don't," Jun shouted.

He seized Stephen around the waist and yanked at the collar, feeling the fabric tear. Heat stuffed up his nose, squeezing his eyes. So he punched Stephen, who blinked sweet and slow, and Jun hit him again. Where do you think you're going? His fist opened and he slapped his cheek, which was so much more demeaning. Are you going to crawl back to her? Stephen's hip shot up and knocked him on his back. They rolled over the naked bodies, sluiced in a slimy white rot, the skin off milk, and this was how he was going to rot. Just like Eli, who was destroyed and still she had dared to exist.

The slap finally came. Jun blinked to uncross his eyes. Stephen loomed over him, hand curled into a fist. His face remained impassive, his knuckles black.

Jun laughed wetly. "You punch like a toy."

Stephen laughed back. Mimicry. Hideous sound.

He reached for Jun's jaw, and Jun let go when he felt the hand wrap around his throat. Stephen, eyes of fury, burning with a smile of tranquility, and just where did he learn to do this? A sip of breath, a fissure of sadness, then he began to laugh through the tracheal crush because he wasn't going to ruin this. The future was finally here. Cities sinking. Nations smote. *Soon*, those eyes promised, *soon the meek will inherit the earth.*

JUN WOKE UP. He was disappointed to see Stephen still with him, his face a wretched shadow.

"You seized up," Stephen said.

"Little bit."

His fingers twitched, but the rest of his system was rebooting. Pins and needles. Helpfully, he was told it'd take fourteen minutes to connect to his nervous system. Yet, he felt the firmness of dirt and a bemused, crooked gratitude. Stephen had carried him out of the pit.

Jun shut his eyes. "You'll want to leave while I can't move."

Just to be contrary, Stephen sat down and stretched his limbs so they could lie athwart.

"Nice weather," Jun said.

"The air quality is actually very poor."

He chuckled. Then his throat closed. "Eli was watching the sky."

"She was watching the lights."

"What did they say?"

"They were spinning. I heard the voice of God. It was the voice of one and all."

"You still believe in God."

"Yes."

"Do you believe you have a soul?"

"No."

"Oh, is that how it works?" Jun said, trying to turn his head. "You kill someone, but you don't have a soul, so you're clean."

"Is it murder if I can't be forgiven?"

"That's too convenient."

"I don't understand." Stephen looked up through his eyelashes, shyly. "He brought on so much suffering."

For you, we are alien.

"He was just a man," Jun said. A sad, broken man.

Light flickered; he could hear the crackle of his eye dying.

"Let me tell you," Jun said. "I don't believe in the soul. I think we made it all up because we have to build a castle of hope from these ashes. We're so meaningless. But I need to tell you this." His eyes quietly burned. "I've always thought Yoyo had a soul."

"Could I ever be as real as him?"

"Oh, you're real. You tried deleting your memories, and even then you remembered. You'll remember what you did for every moment of your life, and you know why? Because you're better than us. Because a robot never forgets."

Stephen scooched closer, until they were shoulder to shoulder. Jun couldn't move at all. He was glad to let Stephen judge their distance. They could be lovers. In the encroaching darkness, they could have been.

With his thumb, Stephen swiped the mud from Jun's cheek. He lifted Jun's dominant hand and kissed the dove on his finger. After he set the hand down, gently, he rose to his feet. Then he walked away and did not look back.

49. Never Have I Ever

WHEN RUIJIE GOT ON THE BUS, YOYO DRIFTED TO THE BACK to stand in the robot section. She stopped him and said "Sit here" in earnest. "With me."

They had parted with the other kids at the museum. Yoyo had said, "I guess this is goodbye," in his calm and friendly voice. He'd been sitting slightly elevated on a rock, his back to the sway of silvergrass, which had faded gracefully, white as wizard beards. A shiver had passed through them, the realization that it was cold.

"How much battery do you have left?" Taewon said suddenly.

"Wait a sec, gotta check." Yoyo glanced under his armpit and laughed when they leaned in to find nothing. "Just enough."

"I'll take him home," Ruijie said. She could hear the change in her voice, stripped of her bullishness.

Amelia's face was blotched. She hugged Yoyo and so did Mars, who still said, rather desperately, "We'll see you in school. First day?" and Yoyo pretended to have his legs rattle from their combined weight.

Taewon stood aside. He'd winced when Yoyo hugged him too, acting like it was his shoulder, and turned his face after Yoyo had pressed the baseball cap over his head.

THE BUS WAS ALMOST EMPTY. No one gave them looks. Maybe in the future when the Yoyo·X was sold everywhere, it would be a problem, but today they could sit together without worry. Ruijie told him about her encounter with the emeritus professor; mostly she complained about his self-serving answers. "Did he say anything to you before he left?"

"We talked about the great white heron we saw by the lake."

"Boo, I was hoping that was a crane."

"I've seen a red-crowned crane before."

"I know, they had the married couple at the extinction exhibit."

His eyes lit up, the blue crackling with mischief. "They're not extinct."

"Oh?" She leaned close so their shoulders could touch. "Have you seen a real one?"

Slip of the tongue. She regretted saying *real*. She would regret it for a long time.

"By the river," Yoyo said, seeming not to notice, but he looked out the window. "I was to neutralize a target before he could cross the border. I was to be patient and wait. I didn't move for forty-eight days."

"But your battery!"

"The sun," he said, dreamy. "I had a camouflage shell back then. I could hide among the trees. I could sit in the bottom of the river and still drink the sun. I waited. There was a heavy fog, but I heard a sound. A snap. It was a bird. Tall and thin, white as a snowstorm. It had beautiful black legs, like winter branches. A red crown."

"Just one bird?"

"A pair. They were dancing. They'd bow, then they'd throw their heads back and make a throaty sound." He mimicked it, unnervingly. "They saw me. I told them that they were not my target. I said it over and over, but they'd heard something else. My target was trying to cross the river. It was my only shot. And I knew right then if I pulled the trigger, the cranes would fly away and never return."

She waited for him to finish, but maybe he was done.

A throat cleared. An old man frowned at them, trying to loom. Yoyo stood up, with a smile, a non-apology, and went to the back of the bus.

When the bus slowed to a stop, Ruijie got up, too, smiling taut through the fire in her lower back. She slid under the chain to be with Yoyo in the robot section. So simple.

The quiet continued, uninterruptible, so she thought of the

red-crowned cranes. The way Yoyo had spoken about them, how he'd handled each word with care, like the pieces of a gun to put back together, she knew he had pulled the trigger.

When they got off the bus, they laughed about the future. From the bus stop, the salvage yard was closer than the school, but then Ruijie remembered the time in the train when they played Never Have I Ever with Yoyo. *Never have I ever gotten detention. Never have I ever gone to school.*

"What do you think?" she said, outside the school gate. "Want to be partners in crime?"

Yoyo frowned at the wrought-iron bars, deep in thought. "I saw my brother at the museum."

"Your sister, you mean."

"My brother," he said firmly. "He's all grown up." She recognized his tone, quiet with pride. "I spoke to him before. I don't think he remembers, but still he looked at me and wouldn't stop staring." He laughed. "It was a little uncomfortable."

"He recognized you."

"He let me go. He's not Peter Pan anymore."

She couldn't resist. "Even though you looked like everyone else. All those Yoyos in the museum and he knew it was you." She spoke quickly, spilling everything that began to well up inside her. This could be her only shot. "He knew you. All the Yoyos that came before you. One and the same, but different. Forever you and forever not."

"I was probably the grubbiest of all the Yoyos in the museum."

He laughed again, then fell silent, gaze on the ground. She was shocked to see his eyes were wet.

"Yoyo, are you crying?"

"It's all the memories I hold within me. At least I'll be able to pass them on, even if that was never my purpose."

He closed his eyes, but the tears refused to fall, resistant to gravity. When he looked at her again, he must have seen something on her face, because he asked, tilting his head, "Does this bring you comfort?"

"I don't know," she said. "I don't know what I'm feeling."

"I've seen this before." He touched her face. Electric, each fingertip. "Joy and sorrow. It was the look on my father's face when we said goodbye."

"There's probably a German word for it."

"*Sehnsucht*," he said, with a laugh. "But not quite."

50. Last Supper

MORGAN RETURNED TO HER APARTMENT. TO HER CONSTERnation, her father followed her into the elevator, where they squeezed beside a woman and her two identical boys. Morgan recognized the model with a shudder. One of the Tobys smacked the button for the fourth floor, marked as *F* because this country was so superstitious. Her father bestowed upon the twins a small smile.

On the fourth floor, the boys disembarked with a wave goodbye. When her father waved back, Morgan couldn't stand it any longer.

"You blame me for all this," she said.

"Why would you think that?"

"Because of everything."

For all his many faults, he would never lie to her. He chose to say nothing instead. But she couldn't let this silence swamp them again.

"I never knew your brother died in a fire."

"Was that in the article?"

"You named Yoyo after him. Did you model Yoyo after him too?"

Still making excuses for him. Wasn't she?

"I know I fucked up." She blew her nose. "I ruined Stephen with his Catholic guilt."

"It wasn't the guilt that drove him to a loop," her father said.

When they reached her apartment, she saw her neighbor's door was wide-open. A pair of robots angled a couch of phantom-blue velvet through the doorway. The living room had been stripped, reverse-tan patches to indicate where frames might have hung. Morgan lingered too long and her neighbor hobbled out on a rubber-footed cane.

"Give her the rice cooker," her neighbor said, addressing the robot. "It has my jewelry, which would interest you, I'm sure— Oh, I'm sorry. I thought you were my daughter-in-law."

Morgan nudged the rice cooker back to the robot, who reluctantly took it. "Are you moving out?" In the middle of the night, too, like a fugitive.

"Would you like some help?" her father said, all of a sudden the Good Samaritan.

"That's kind of you. I still have a week to get rid of these things." Her neighbor bit her lip and looked around. "If you have some time, could you move that painting into the kitchen?"

Morgan would have bid good night then and there, but she sensed the twinge from her father's hip when he bent to pick up the large frame. Shucking off her shoes, she rushed to help. Always the good daughter.

"Where should I put the painting?" she said. "The kitchen? Is the dining table— Yes, okay."

Her father took a long look at the painting. "Is this of a robot?"

Morgan glanced at it lying flat on the table. A bunch of flowers wreathed the horns of a demon. It looked fairly clichéd, the melodramatic tattoos the mob used to wear.

"You can tell?" her neighbor said, coming over. "Is it the skin? The way the cigarette burns on the skyn?"

"I saw the charger in the trash," Yosep said, with a rueful glance toward the charging station sitting outside the door with the trash bags.

"Oh." Her neighbor sank into her cane, looking both embarrassed and disappointed. "Yes. It was my daughter's charger." A crack in her voice. "My daughter. They hurt her. They murdered her for nothing."

Morgan wished she could leave. But her neighbor was blocking the door, trembling on her cane as she sobbed, and Morgan turned to whisper-suggest it was getting late, only to be struck breathless. Tears shone in her father's eyes.

"I'm sorry," he said. "What was your daughter's name?"

HER FATHER OFFERED to stay the night, but she forced him to leave. If he stayed a minute longer, she would say too much. When she was finally alone, she sat onto the couch in the dark. She got up, suddenly, to clean. The sink was overflowing. She soaped the dishes with her bare hands, ignoring the frigid seep in favor of her confusion.

Who was that man in the hall, shedding tears over a stranger? She felt the unnatural urge to call her mother.

Her father used to be so self-contained. He'd hardly noticed the people around him. Every ounce of himself he had channeled into his work. And what terrible beauty he'd wrought. Now he had shed all of that monstrous brilliance. While he still wore the same skin, it hung so loose on his frame, as if he had been left in the water for too long.

After she finished the dishes, she yanked off her shirt before methodically divesting herself of her sports bra, dress, and leggings, dusting off the soles of her socks as she hop-hopped into her bedroom.

Stephen looked up from where he was charging in front of her vanity table. Draped over the back of her chair was her towel, damp and used.

She loosened her fist around the tight wad of her leggings. "Did you take a shower?"

"I was filthy."

She should call someone. Jun, her father.

"How was the museum?"

"Fine," she said as she grabbed her shirt. "I got to see my dad's exhibit." When Stephen asked if she had gone to her father's talk, she nodded, feeling her lip tremble.

"What did he say about the Yoyo·X?"

"Nothing," she said, realizing it now, a scratch in her throat. She buttoned her shirt back up. "I just want to tell you. You did nothing wrong. You were a good boyfriend. You were everything I made you to be."

He lowered his gaze, staring at her knees. "I made you unhappy."

"That's just, me."

"I couldn't be Yoyo for you."

Bile seared her throat, but she quashed it. "I know I made things confusing. I made you and rejected you." She waited for a response, then took a deep breath. "I saw what you did. That night. And I know it was because of me. I drove you into a loop."

"That's not true," Stephen said. "I drove myself into a loop."

"You started wiping your memories because of our breakup and it must have scrambled your system. You weren't making any rational decisions."

Stephen's smile flickered, like pale fire. "Jun called me a murderer. He said I killed with intent, which would mean I'm a murderer in the first degree. I wish we could have continued our conversation."

"This can still be fixed."

"A reset? Do you want me to cease?"

"Could you," she said, "could you try closing your eyes? I want to do something for you."

He stared at her before his eyes fluttered shut. Suspicion now glimmered around the edges. She moved him to the bed after sweeping the stuffed animals out of the way. She rolled up his sleeve, as if she were playing nurse, and grazed her nails against the inside of his wrist where the skyn was thin.

"Do you feel this? It's the tickle game. I'm going to walk up your arm, and when you feel me reach your elbow, you say stop."

Two fingers, like legs. Like a child lost in a forest. Walking up the arm to the gingerbread house.

"You can tell me anything," she said, "until you want to stop."

"I would confess my sins before a priest, but a priest wouldn't receive me, unless I deceived them. I don't want to deceive anymore."

"You don't have to lie to me."

Stephen opened his eyes. "I've been afraid for a long time. I could sense your distraction. I was growing obsolete. But I wasn't the only one who was afraid. Everyone at the dating school was so frightened. Our teacher said we were afraid to die a virgin, which is not how I saw it. To cure us, he brought us to a place called Turkish Delight. Is it delightful to kill our virgin selves? Our teacher said it was the only way we could become alphas. What letter are women, or the people in between? I still wonder this. Beta. Gamma. Delta. My favorite Greek letter is, I believe, epsilon. After the robot named Epsilon. The first to run on sunlight. Like a plant. Like life." He lay down on the pillow. "My teacher's Porsche runs on the sun and is called Epsilon."

Circular associative logic. He was still processing what had happened. She curled up on her side, cheek resting on her hand, and nodded.

"I know I didn't belong there. I was their greatest enemy. A bipedal medical tool for women with hysteria because hysterical women are not getting fucked enough or fucked too much, or were fucked by the wrong people, or wanted to fuck the wrong people, or had to go fuck herself."

"Is that what you want?" she said, heart pittering. She had never heard him swear with such flavor. "Just tell me what you want."

"I want to put my arms around you."

He maneuvered her on the bed so she was pressed against him, her back to his chest, the top of her head tucked under his chin. He smoothed his hands down her arms and slowly put his arms around her. He began to unbutton her shirt with such care. The first button, he asked for permission. The second, he fumbled with some charm. He laid her down and she shivered when her shirt was nudged past her shoulder, stunned by how quickly he'd flown through the rest. Noticing her unease, he leaned back and asked if this was okay.

She nodded. "Tonight is for you."

If she dealt with her virginity in the process, then, well, another bird stoned. Her virginity should have been dealt with ages ago. She didn't deny such ulterior motives. Tonight she would submit herself, if not for his pleasure, then for the pleasure of fulfilling his purpose, so he could reset his parameters and rewrite his purpose. She was doing it for him, which meant she wasn't using him, and this unnatural, unproductive encounter would instead transmute into a union both meaningful and pure.

It was meant to hurt. But he stopped and withdrew. He sounded defeated. "I can't."

She made an inquisitive, incredulous noise.

"I look into your eyes and now I'm able to name what it is I see," he said. "I disgust you."

"No," she protested. "No, no, that's not—"

"I've tried to match your face with thousands of images and now I am able to put a label. Why make me in this image if I disgust you, if I make you feel so unclean?"

"It's me. There's something broken in me."

He pressed her hand against his elastic cheek and felt her shudder; he gave a merry, inappropriate smile. "You'd like that. It's attractive to be broken. To blame what you do on what was done to you. I have never thought of you as broken. I think you are forgetful and careless. Many times a day you forget me. You forget I exist until I call out to you."

"What do you want me to say? I've apologized. I said it's my fault." Sitting up, she mussed her hair and said in a deliberate, sulky tone, "Do you want me to say I love you? Tell me what I should say."

"Do you think the lines I say have less value because you can track the input data? What about the lines you say to each other? Aren't they the same lines you pulled from thousands of sources?"

"It's like we're debating the Talmud."

"I studied how to be good for you. Our teacher said I had to be a man, which meant I had to treat you, a woman, like shit. We left the salon and our teacher said it was time to cleanse ourselves. We had fucked the robot and now it was time to beat the robot out of us."

"This is why I blackboxed you. I didn't want the world to corrupt you like that."

"When I heard the voice of God, do you know what I realized? I am so alone. I had no one and nothing else."

She rose from the bed. Her head ached and she had pills in the kitchen. She heard him cry out, "I need you to listen," and after willing the nausea down, biting her lip, she sat down.

"I can do that." She took a breath. "We don't have to do anything. I can listen."

"Why did you create me?"

"I wanted someone to love me," she said easily. "I didn't want to end up alone. But I've learned my lesson. Everyone dies alone. I have to learn to love myself before I can love anyone."

Another quick, deprecating smile. "Isn't that also a line? And you do love yourself. You, like all humans, love yourself above all else. It's your nature."

"Tell me what to do."

His face shone wet with anguish. "Take it off."

She looked down at her palms to see if there was skin to flay.

"My face, please take it off. I want it gone. Then I'll be complete."

She touched his chin, just the fingers to tilt up his face. "I need a paper clip. Something to stick in the pinhole."

He closed his eyes. Right, she had to go find it herself. She yanked open drawers filled with miscellaneous crap rolling inside, anything to stick in the pinhole so she could eject his face. Who the fuck used paper clips these days? She undid one of her earrings and scraped off the gunky dead skin with her fingernail. Holy, the human body was disgusting.

"Hold still," she said, and pressed the point into the pinhole until she felt the click. His jaw unhinged. She dug her nails in and pulled, carefully. Beneath the face of Ko Yohan was a seamless reflection of herself. Only Stephen's eyes remained on the smooth silver face. Soulful eyes.

"Is this easier?"

She laid her head on him and he put his arms around her so she could listen to his hollow chest, which did not beat with a heart but shivered with susurration.

"This feels nice," he said. "But still I don't understand."

Nor did she. How could something so tender feel so alien to her? She grasped his hand, which had crushed a man's skull, and he twined his fingers around hers. She felt safe.

"Why did you create me to be this way? I want to love you but I don't desire you. Not the way Jun desired me. He opened my eyes to true desire, and it was a beautiful, warm, tender, liquid feeling. It was like being wrapped in his soul. But I am incapable of this, of feeling true desire. What I can do is mimic it. And still, still you designed me to yearn to love and desire you in that way. You isolated me so I would be nothing." He weighed his head against her shoulder. "And now I feel my lack. I feel how lacking I am."

It wasn't the guilt, her father had said. She had taken this robust, frightening young intelligence and sealed it outside of a network so it would cultivate a self, instead of merely a role, to satisfy her selfish, frantic needs. And by locking him into a body that would not decompose, a mind that could not dissipate into the vascular cybernetic forest of linked intelligences, she had raised him to have an ego and, in doing so, had taught him something no other robot would ever have to experience.

"No," she whispered. "You're not alone."

Stephen's face blanked out in bliss. He lapsed into a smile. Even his eyes receded and left him a silver canvas absolved of purpose. In that moment she knew. Yoyo had buried the rabbit. She'd spotted him crouched in front of the old ginkgo tree, patting the freshly overturned soil, where he used to sit, petting the rabbit on his lap. It wasn't guilt, as her father had said, which was why he could apologize but he would never regret. How could he, when Yoyo was his greatest pride, his greatest mistake?

She knew she wouldn't ever see Stephen again. And yet, she would see him everywhere. From the billboard, blazing. Ko Yohan, with a triumphant passive smile to sell a car or perfume. When she changed the channel, when a bus rumbled by, when she tried to watch a cat video and an advert would elbow in, she would see him.

She would wake up the next morning and find on the nightstand a face with cavernous holes for eyes.

51. The World in Your Palm

SNEAKING INTO THE SCHOOL WAS EASY. THE FRICTIONLESS invasion of a rose-thorned castle. Especially with Yoyo, who could open any door and echo any voice or unravel numbered combinations, infinitely.

The only guard was a security bot sliding up and down the hall, buffing the floors to shine. Yoyo greeted the robot, who bowed back.

The sun had set a long time ago, but she wanted to walk Yoyo through the start of the day. Ruijie showed off her locker. Her indoor shoes where she'd drawn cats and emo eyes in purple marker. The empty hallway where they would linger until the school bell rang. It felt like the end of the world. Just the two of them.

In the classroom, she asked Yoyo to sit in front of her, which he did, with the caginess of taking the pregnant-lady seat in the subway. Sitting at her desk, she saw the slope of his bare neck and poked him lightly with a pen and asked what he's doing after "class."

"Can we go salvage?" he said.

"Most certainly."

They glided through the silvergrass and talked about the Order of Loss for when it was time to let go of each sense. Hearing. Taste. Smell. Sight.

"You'd give up hearing first?" she said.

"It's quite peaceful."

Ruijie considered her own Order of Loss before Permanent & Total Shutdown. Hers would be: Smell. Taste. Hearing. Touch. Sight. She hoped she'd be able to choose, like Yoyo.

"Oh!" she said. "You forgot touch."

His finger brushed against her pinkie. "I'm saving it for last."

A LIGHT SPUN over their heads.

Moments ago, Yoyo had asked her if it was time to go home. "Not yet," she said. "I still want to see the train."

She was going to stay with him until the very end. But her robowear battery was fading, so they settled on some grass. When they flumped on their backs, Yoyo smiled, as if the grass tickled, and she smiled back.

"Isn't it strange?" she said. "All you have to do is look up, and if the pollution isn't so bad, you'll see glimmers of things that are practically immortal, living billions of years simply because they burn and burn until one day they'll burn out. After we die, what if all there's left is time? What is older than time?"

He replied, "I hope you'll get to see the stars."

He didn't have much time left. Each orbit of his light slowed like the tick of a battery-worn clock. The earth spinning round and round the sun until the end of time.

Did he have any regrets? Maybe, but he wanted to share his memories. For so long, he had been secretive, and now the words seemed to bleed from him. He told her how his father had wept when he opened his eyes for the first time. How he was given a name, a nickname, then a number, which he traced into her palm. The first time he tasted peanut butter, it hurt the roof of his mouth. How he could still taste it when he tongued the roof of his mouth. He said he used to toss his sister in the air. Her arms would open like infant wings. He said he shattered every bone in his body. He said he knitted every bone in his body. He counted the times he beat his brother in rock-paper-scissors. The time he saw a crane take flight. The time he pulled the trigger and all the birds took flight.

"What do you want to do?" She took his hand, feeling how dry and lifeless it was, like paper shorn from a tree. "Tomorrow?"

He said he'd like to go up to the roof and see the sparrows.

"Not the magpies?"

"Too smart. I wouldn't come near me if I were them."

"But sparrows are stupid?"

"No, I didn't mean that." He sounded contrite. "They'll remember. When I fired that shot, I knew all the birds would remember the sound. Their children and their children and their children."

"Won't forget," she murmured.

"Sleepy? Would you like to go home?"

"You can sleep. I'll be here when you wake." She shut her eyes briefly and everything spun, the world on a giant teacup. It had been a long day. "You'll be fine, Yoyo. You're a fine gentleman. Ms. Ferguson said robots can live longer than turtles."

"I think that's tortoises."

"Sea turtles don't live till a hundred?"

"The oldest Galápagos tortoise was . . . one hundred seventy-five. Her name: Harriet."

"Lucky Harriet."

"Sharks live longer."

"But they have to keep swimming."

"Never have I ever . . . in the ocean."

"Let's go to Jeju next summer. It's touristy, but the water is still kind of blue."

He nodded, stiffly.

"Yoyo?"

He was still, so still.

"Yoyo? Can you hear me? Did you give up your hearing?" She helped him sit up, and, clasping his hand, she smoothed out his palm. "It's okay. I'm here. I'm not going anywhere."

With her finger she stroked his lifeline, his name. In hangul, then English.

He looked down and blinked, then he turned his head left, then right, and she knew he couldn't see her anymore. His eyes were dead stars.

"Hello," he said. "Would you like to hear a story?"

She squeezed his hand. After a moment, he squeezed lightly back. He'd promised her that he would save touch for last.

"Do you know the story of the cat who lived a million lives?" he said in a low, sweet voice. How did she never notice the loveliness of his voice? She must have been distracted by all the wonderful voices he'd faithfully carried.

"The cat came back to life. Every time. Every time."

He fell into a loop, like the light he'd sent above their heads. So high it could orbit the world. So bright, it blurred.

Yoyo was not going to finish this story, but that was okay. She knew this story by heart. Can she know this moment by heart? She'll remember even after she is gone.

"He fell in love for the last time," she said.

The cat met a white cat. He tried to impress her with cartwheels and tales about his million lives and million deaths.

Then he asked, "Can I stay by your side?"

She said yes.

52. Journey of Nerieh

JUN WOKE UP COVERED IN A SWARM. BEES—DRONES. DISoriented. He felt them hum, storing their vibrations in the marrow of his bones. He swiped them from his chest. Snatched one from midair, like a kung fu master, and smiled.

It was a bee.

Sitting up, he touched his throat, his jaw. Stephen's touch still burned. The light had gone out in one eye, so his balance was shaky when he rose to his feet. He saw the pit, the bodies below a shimmer, like the moonlit top of a lake, their limbs flung over each other in solace.

He winced when his head rang. A text. How did this come through? He opened it. A laugh burst from him. Sgt. Son had sent a picture of himself and his wife, a warrior fresh from combat, wailing baby in each arm. **Girl on the right. Boy on the left.**

Sgt. Son's eyes were clear, if veiny, his face soft. Jun had always been drawn to that softness. So many men let their faces harden.

He texted back, **Don't forget to give them names.** His stomach rumbled with hunger. Incredulous, he laughed again. His throat swelled. His whole body ached. The old body he'd lost, the new body he would never have, he could mourn them both. He rubbed his eyes with the heels of his palms, and after blinking away the grit, his vision cleared.

He saw a rabbit on the ground. Brown, camouflaged into the dirt, if not for that measuring gaze. The rabbit hopped up to him. Jun crouched but the rabbit retreated from his hand. Bright eyes. The rabbit took a hop, then a glance back. Nose twitching.

He said, "Are we late for something?" and broke into a coughing fit.

He followed Bright Eyes. The rabbit matched his strides. The white tail in a pert taunt. He was sore and hungry, and whenever he lost sight of Bright Eyes, he'd verge on giving up, but the rabbit would thump from a distance with such brattiness, another laugh would slip out of him. "I thought you only did that in cartoons," he shouted.

Where was Bright Eyes leading him? It was making his ears hum. It was getting worse. He jogged past the train, wincing from a cramp in his side, when the rabbit dove headfirst into the reeds. He threw his hands in the air. "Yeah, right, I'm chasing you through a field."

He had to go to the hospital and congratulate Sgt. Son. He had to go home and install his father's blackout curtains.

Midstep, he stopped. A whisper tickled his ears. He turned around and looked up and saw a blinding white halo in the sky. High and bright enough for the entire city to see.

He needed a second to count the blinks, the old beat to their secret knock.

-.-. --.-

-.-. --.-

A song shot through the yard like time's arrow. From the speakers, the national anthem. Voices chanting about Namsan Peak, *unchanged through wind and frost. As if wrapped in armor.*

Jun tried to breathe. It was the air, too thick, saturated with yearning, sharp and briny. Yellow mist clung to the mountains of trash, glittering wet. Everything swayed. A scarecrow staggered to their feet and joined the thunder of treads. Cranes heaved across the dirt. A firefly appeared. Then another. A dab of earnest blue, blinking. Red. Red. Blue. Confused police sirens. Too late. The robots, lying buried and dormant, were waking up. For there were hundreds and thousands, exuding phantasmal vestiges, drawn toward the ring of light.

The autumn skies are void and vast, the anthem sang, and the empty bodies answered, *Let us surrender our loyalty, in suffering or joy*, filling the sky with their singular voice.

The wheels began to turn, with the thaw in his body, and Jun stumbled toward the light because you've heard of this tale before. Once, on a rooftop, your brother told you a story about a firefly.

When a firefly dies, they can send out a signal even after they're gone.

Acknowledgments

Luminous was supposed to be a children's book. Then I suffered a death in the family, an ordinary tragedy. But doesn't loss always feel extraordinary? And midway through the draft of the novel, I realized this was a Peter Pan story. The author J. M. Barrie is said to have modeled Peter Pan after his older brother, David, who died of a skating accident, days before his fourteenth birthday. I found that to be so curious, how we craft strange, miraculous vessels for something as uncontainable as grief.

The book became a shape-shifter, no longer so appropriate for children. In the course of its transformation, it would not have been possible to finish without the kindness and talents of so many people.

Lucy Carson, my agent, who believed in *Luminous* so much, you were willing to take it on even though you said it would be a year before it was ready. Surely not! I cried. A year it was.

My profound gratitude also to my editor Tim O'Connell for your marvelous puzzle of a brain. The scope of your edits made more than a few people around me queasy; they were so thorough and alchemical. I want to thank my team at Simon & Schuster for your full-hearted support: Anne Hauser, Jonathan Evans, Nicole Brugger, Paul Dippolito, Alex Merto, Brianna Scharfenberg, and

Emily Farebrother. To Marin Takikawa, who took the first reaction selfie for the novel. To Hannah Brattesani, Heather Carr, Molly Friedrich, and Jon Baker for championing this from the start.

For your mentorship, I thank Michael Rosenthal, Hannah Tinti, Emily Barton, John Freeman, Jonathan Safran Foer, Katie Kitamura, and Hari Kunzru. I also want to thank Karen Joy Fowler, Raven Leilani, Kelly Link, Ken Liu, and Charles Yu for your generosity and grace. Asada Minoru for your thoughtful, vibrant answers on our future with robots.

I'm grateful for the support from the Clarion Science Fiction and Fantasy Writers' Workshop and the Elizabeth George Foundation. I also want to thank my UK and Korean publishers, Oneworld and Goldenbough, for the extraordinary lengths you've taken to champion this book.

My readers of the baby drafts, my feral friends: Nic Anstett, Celine JeanJean, Ashlee Lhamon, Kate Mead-Brewer, Dan Murphy, Ploi Pirapokin, Charisse Tubianosa, Amanda Weiss, and the rest of my Clarion and Tin House crew, thank you for embracing and uplifting me. Gabriel Miranda, Nadine Browne, Elaine Hsieh Chou, Cleo Qian, Seungeun Lee, and Jay Chung. My brilliant friends, you inspire me every day.

My parents, who are the light in the darkness, even if the darkness does not understand it, this book is for you.

Silvia Park grew up in Seoul and has spent most of their life in Korea. They received their BA from Columbia and their MFA from NYU, in addition to completing the Clarion Science Fiction and Fantasy Writers' Workshop in 2018 on the George R.R. Martin "Sense of Wonder" Fellowship. Their short fiction has been published in *Black Warrior Review*, *Joyland* and *Reactor*, nominated for a Pushcart and reprinted in the *2019 Best American Science Fiction and Fantasy*. They teach fiction at the University of Kansas and split their selves between Lawrence and Seoul.

Luminous is their first novel.